Happy B'day Heeru

God bless you xx
Manisha
23-4

RAISE
LANTERNS HIGH

Also By Lakshmi Persaud

For the Love of My Name
Sastra
Butterfly in the Wind

RAISE THE
LANTERNS HIGH

Lakshmi Persaud

BLACKAMBER BOOKS

Published in 2004 by
BlackAmber Books
3 Queen Square
London WC1N 3AU

1 3 5 7 9 10 8 6 4 2

A full CIP record for this book is available from the British Library.

ISBN 1–901969–20–7

Typeset in 12.5/13.5 pt Garamond Three
by RefineCatch Limited, Bungay, Suffolk
Printed and bound in Finland by WS Bookwell

Acknowledgements

I am indebted to Sakuntala Narasimhan for her invaluable book *Sati, A Study of Widow Burning in India* and for its passages from the *Puranas* which describe what takes place before a widow ascends her husband's pyre. I also obtained an intimate understanding of an ancient Chinese custom from Kathryn Harrison's moving work *The Binding Chair*. Other publications that were helpful include *Women Warriors, A History* by David Jones, and Germaine Greer's *The Whole Woman*.

I would also like to thank the staff of the British Library and the Victoria & Albert Museum.

When I was a child, I saw on the cinema screen a woman who climbed upon a pyre to prove that she was pure, and who miraculously remained whole, though the pyre had turned to ash. I later learned that she was Sita, the consort of Rama. In addition to this, the culture of my village had always impressed upon me the strength of the virtuous woman.

This novel was also born because of my parents. In being close to my mother's understanding of duty and responsibility, loyalty, and devotion to her husband, children, relatives and neighbours, I was able to comprehend the shaping of beliefs that enable the human spirit to lead martyrs to their fate and widows to the pyre.

'Conscience comes from Imagination.'
Martha Gellhorn, 1912–98

'Problems cannot be solved at the same level of awareness that created them.'
Albert Einstein

In Memory of
my Mother and Father
and of
Those who climbed the pyre
And For Vishnu

PART ONE

CHAPTER ONE

A Chance Encounter

Trinidad, 1955

I WAS CREEPING through the sugar-cane field parting the long sharp leaves. I, Vasti Nadir, a St Ursula's Form Two pupil, stalked the cry. Then, crouching and peering through well-focused binoculars, I saw a brutal thing that has never left me: a schoolgirl, pinned to the ground, held fast by a man who had parted her slender legs which struggled as branches against a gale. Her voice trembled – an excruciating plea for release. We were alone in the field of sweet stems. Long cutting lances barred her from my world.

At St Ursula's Convent, the finest school for girls on the island of Trinidad, we were told that, were we to follow its rules, our lives would be filled with tradition, innovation, vitality and sparkle. Though I did try, I found that these worthy assets did not lessen the cruel intensity of that memory. The encounter has stayed with me ever since.

When I left my childhood behind, the memory of the rape I had witnessed became an invisible companion, bringing constant distress to my adult life. There was no one with whom I could share this experience, but my family did sense that something was wrong. A troubling disquiet held us all in its sway.

Stunned into muteness, I rested this heavy burden on the pages of my schoolgirl's diary where I thought I had encased it, unaware that it had a life of its own. And indeed, it did eventually erupt – at the worst possible moment of my life, flooding my sanctuary and threatening my very sanity.

Who he was flashed before me in the sunlight.

It must have been well past one o'clock. I was cycling home, taking a short cut through the cane-fields in the heat of the day. My shadow sheltered close to me, becoming small to avoid the scorching sun, which was bent on smouldering the earth. It was the last day of term. My school year in Form Two had come to an end.

There were no formal classes. 'No schooling, just fooling,' was my mother's description of the last day of term. In truth, it was the usual noisy day, in which everyone spoke at once. We twelve-year-old girls became as sure of ourselves as all-knowing adults and chatted with our form mistress, Mother Francis Xavier, about large issues: why St Ursula's lost at hockey and netball to other schools, but won the coveted island scholarships. There was the inevitable lecture on how we should conduct ourselves outside the school walls, in the presence of boys – who, it would seem, were bent on ruining us. Mother Francis Xavier heard her Form Two girls express with intense passion their dislike for boys.

Before leaving, we had to have our desks clean inside, and polished outside. Three girls had brought their cameras, and another three and I had our binoculars. Mine, a gift from my only and dear elder sister Pushpa. Brother-in-law Shami, who knew about those things, had chosen the binoculars and showed me how to get the best from them. Distance was brought so close and with such clarity that I saw with an eagle's eye; my binoculars enabled me to take flight. I could flutter on every treetop as a butterfly. What more could any St Ursula's Form Two pupil want?

We fooled about taking photographs of each other, making faces and posing. Our enthusiasm for unknown paths knew no bounds; the very roof of St Ursula and that of the nearby cathedral were searched with our binoculars, for secrets hidden high above our reach. Tired at last, we wished each other a happy holiday, followed by an exchange of addresses and heartfelt promises to write on pain of reputations lost.

And now the asphalt on the road had become soft in places, melting at the sides. I pedalled on, thinking of a cold, splashing shower, a cool cotton dress and the freshly made iced lime drink to come, sweetened with Demerara sugar. My legs were sticky; I could feel my thighs under my skirt, hot and damp with perspiration. I cycled faster.

The sugar-cane would soon be ready for harvesting; the ripe sugared stems swayed, abandoning themselves to the wild wind. 'Without shame,' Uncle Kash would have said, had these same stems been young women. 'Shame is something to avoid. It brings pain and does great harm to the family,' my mother warned when I asked her what Uncle Kash meant by women dancing without shame. As I was none the wiser after my mother's explanation I decided that shameful dancing,

5

shameful talking – or anything else shameful for that matter – was best done in private, and only if there was a strong personal desire for complete obliteration should it be done before my Uncle Kash.

A field of sweet stems continued to twist and turn, bend and lift – Nature's way – natural. Natural was good. I had learned that from honey jar labels.

The intensity of the heat sapped my energy; a stillness covered the land. The road ahead was empty save for a single parked car. At first, indistinct, then gradually my ears caught the gurgling of a nearby stream and I stood on the pedals, stretching and craning my neck to locate its meanderings, when my front tyre burst, punctured by a nail.

This convinced me that God also sleeps at this time of day. When I considered the hours of conversation I had had with the Almighty, not to mention the promises I had made – and kept – to conduct myself in such a way as to bring nothing but delight to Him and my parents, I can honestly say I expected some small gesture in return, such as sweeping away a nail – so easily done with the help of the wind. Was that too much to ask in this hell fire?

Walking home in this heat, even with my Panama hat on, would certainly be a short-cut to heaven via sunstroke. So I hid my bicycle in the bush and walked, binoculars in hand, through the canes towards the welcoming sound of laughing water over dancing pebbles.

Oh, the delight of this oasis, a clean cool stream! I cupped the water as I had seen my grandmother and mother do and washed my face again and again. My joined palms, opened as petals, refreshed my spirits as I bathed my neck and burning arms.

A lizard rushed past. A crapaud with throbbing throat sheltered in long grass. I quickly raised my skirt before him, cooled my thighs, flapping this contrived cloth fan. Then I looked around, sitting as quietly as I could under an overhanging branch. For a while I enjoyed the solitude, listening to the buzzing of tiny wings and leaves falling beside me.

Then I heard a sound – a low, deep cry of anguish. Quietly I got up. Alert. Still. Nothing but the rustling of sugar-cane. On this expansive plain, the strong wind lifted and fell as sheets on a washing line.

The next time, I was waiting for it – an unmistakable cry, a pitiful pleading, a trembling from within the canes.

Focusing my new binoculars, I saw a young girl, my own age. Her school uniform was above her waist and her intimate garment lay beside her attacker. From where I crouched I could not see their faces, but I heard her voice begging him to stop. He had parted her slender legs, now flailing helplessly as a butterfly struggling, caught in a web. In an undergrowth tone, this brute muttered: 'I will marry you.' His whole body heaved against her, as she fought against him. 'Is this the way you'll behave when we marry?' he panted. 'If you don't stay still, I will change my mind.'

A low, sobbing cry entered the swaying stems and took a path that reached me. '*Noo-ooo-oo!*' But he kept on hurting her over and over again. Suddenly her shadow moved violently, releasing a guttering sound too broken to travel. Her voice died within her.

I watched, stunned, unable to move. His ringed finger pressed against her breast. The reddish gold sparkled intermittently with the swaying sugar-cane stems. I sharpened my focus on this sun-yellow metal. Engraved upon it was an eagle, its wings spanned as if in flight. On its feathered back was a scroll. It, too, had wings.

'I will marry you,' the wind caught his whisperings. 'How many times do I have to say this?' The schoolgirl sobbed, her small palms smoothed her school uniform – crushed and soiled.

Instinctively, I knew I should not have witnessed this terrible incident and was relieved I did not see her face.

I desperately wanted to see his, however. I waited, paralysed with fear, yet hoping that he would turn in my direction so that I could know who in our midst was such a monster, but he just stood and brushed the dust off his trousers. 'We mustn't be seen here together,' I heard him warn her. 'It is best for you.' And he walked away, leaving her alone.

I knew I could not go to her; my witness to her undoing would be a shame too great for her to bear. A thought jolted me: *She may see suicide as a necessary escape from my knowing.* I waited while she dressed herself, then walked slowly away, limping.

As I hurried to fetch my bicycle, a car pulled away. Had I possessed the presence of mind I could have caught the vehicle's numberplate as it sped along. When I reached home, I thought of this again and again. 'An opportunity missed, Miss Nadir. Be alert at all times,' Sherlock Holmes, my hero, whispered in my ear.

I did not know it at the time, but I had mentally adopted this schoolgirl, wishing with all my heart that I could ensure he did not renege on his promise to marry her. How I would bring this about was not my immediate concern; it was, instead, to find out his identity. Such a man would unwittingly give himself away, I thought naively. All I had to do was remain observant and alert and I would be able to pick up the clues he left wherever he went. And in fact this did come to pass, but in a manner I had least expected.

CHAPTER TWO

On Reflection

THE OTHER CHILDHOOD experience which has stayed with me all my life and played no small part in mapping the trail I have trekked, began with the full-length mirror attached to the door of my mother's wardrobe.

I recall as a little girl dragging a chair with difficulty over to the wardrobe, climbing upon it, and with all the cunning and stealth I could muster, turning the key quietly in the lock and then springing open the mirrored door to catch *her* by surprise.

One day, I used another manoeuvre. Pretending I was not interested in *her*, I went in and out of the room, leaving the chair well placed. All the while I tried to give the impression that I was fully engaged in tidying the dressing-table, then suddenly, I rushed and pulled open the mirrored door, only to find my mother's belongings neatly folded. The perfumed scent coming from the shelves, and the touch of satiny-soft clothing, lengths of dress material, as well as small boxes and tubes of varying shapes, signaled to me that I was out of bounds.

It did not take me long, however, to realise why I could not find *her*. She was living outside the mirror in an invisible state, observing me all the while. Her antennae were attached to my thoughts, so she knew when I would spring to the mirror. She could easily compress herself within the glass, since she had the same character as air, which I could neither see nor feel even though it was there. I can say in all honesty, that she reflected me with integrity and was always promptly in her place. It was clear she felt attached to me but lived her own life.

My fascination with reflections continued through the years, offering me pure pleasure from time to time. I say pure pleasure, for it came from a wonderment of ephemeral things that appear, disappear and reappear, as well as from my partial understanding of the qualities and characteristics of different types of glass. How these change with light, the angle of the mirror, the shape and structure of the glass itself and much besides engrossed me. So taken was I with these mirrored images, that there were times when I wondered whether I too was in truth an apparition, a mirrored reflection of an inexplicable reality in the vastness beyond.

Some years later, even as a reasonably serious student over in old, multifaceted England, at London University, and with a fair grasp of the reality around me, I continued to be charmed by the simplest of mirrored glass. The faces and gestures reflected before me in the top part of the windows in London Underground trains did not belong to those sitting beside me, but instead to persons unknown, in the next carriage. Strange. Looking for a reflection's source or reality was exciting and challenging, as it increased my awareness of the silent world of living images and their diverse energies.

One late evening I discovered the moon on my window. I knew it was the moon, though I marvelled that a simple windowpane could capture such distance. It had its characteristic dappled cloudy face, which on this occasion looked more like a lantern raised high. The last of the sun's rays had bathed it with a soft glow. Leaning out of the window, I searched the sky before me, but there *was* no moon. Yet my window had captured it and was still holding it, so it had to be out there somewhere!

I went downstairs to give myself a larger view of the evening sky. Again I searched with care. Nothing. I looked up at the open window and tried to ascertain what expanse of sky it could access? Eventually, to my relief, I found the moon quietly drifting to the side of the house where it would have been lost to me had I been tardy. Had I missed it — what then? I might have thought I had imagined it all. Yet the angle of my windowpane had captured this revolving companion of our planet. And I came to the conclusion that as long as a reflection is there, its other form exists *even if unseen*.

Time enhanced my curiosity about a mirror's resourcefulness, more so with independent free-thinking ones. In the stillness of the night, I have looked closely at my grandmother's upright standing mirror and wondered whether there was a family of mirrors on continents and islands reflecting each other's thoughts as well as those received through space and time in a unique mirrored way, as mice and men are said to do when puzzling over a task.

If I could read the thoughts of the mirror in my room, I am sure I would learn that it had known better days and finer company. Being in my modest bedroom only showed how great had been her fall. For by its shape, it is clear that the polished mirror is female. Her frame and stand are of a blushing rosewood, a flow of magenta and mauve. Softly curved with graceful proportions, the framed glass holds itself haughtily aloof, like a well-to-do, well-connected Maharanee or Memsahib. She is a beauty and knows it, I am thinking. Only on closer inspection do I see that she submits herself to be held by attachments. On both sides of her waist, she is bound to a curvaceous polished stand, which is raised from the ground by an elegant pair of tigress's paws.

My great-grandfather bought the mirror at a sale in a rundown warehouse, in Port-of-Spain. He was told that it had once belonged to an old family of the plantocracy, with connections in India and the West Indies. Here in Trinidad, they had owned slaves and two sugar-cane plantations, then later with the emancipation of slaves, had sailed for England, leaving behind some pieces of their furniture which the owner, now a widower, saw as an extravagance.

When bought, a handwritten note was attached to the mirror: *This mirror comes from one of the Northern semi-arid Kingdoms of India. It belonged to a Queen who fled from performing suttee on the King's pyre, though this was her duty; she was bound by honour and loyalty so to do. When the new King was crowned, his favourite Queen sold everything this rebellious widowed Queen had left behind, convinced that it had become sullied by association. The new Queen did not wish to harbour the personal belongings of a renegade, for to have kept it in the palace, meant honouring her memory.*

So it had travelled across oceans, when journeys were long and perilous. Surely an indulgence. How had it

13

come to be made? Who had designed it? Who commissioned it – the King? And for which Queen? All this remained locked in the mirror's store of silent reflections, and I wished to know. There were times I would stand before it and my pulsating thoughts would entreat: Tell me, *please* tell me what happened.

However, as my mind then sought refuge from my impending arranged marriage, it would dwell on the intangible beauty of the mirror. Gradually, almost imperceptibly, its free-standing, upright air began to take on the semblance of intelligent life, and we connected.

When these two experiences of my youth combined and collided, they hurled me close to an abyss. Fearful, I looked down and saw a predicament, formidable in its complexity and harrowing in its associations. Thanks to the mirror, I was able to experience other perceptions of life which enabled me to have an imaginative understanding of it, though I myself was irretrievably bound, harnessed to the carriage of custom, tradition and community. There was no escape.

CHAPTER THREE

With Great Expectations

RAIN HAD FALLEN in the night. The small, white Jasmine petals were scattered on the terrazzo tiles of the Walli's home. It was six o'clock. Breakfast in his open verandah, here in quiet Green Street, Tunapuna, was usually a time of reflecting upon the business of the day. Their servant, Lola, had prepared breakfast and had already left for the open market to obtain the freshest vegetables brought in trucks from the countryside.

Sukesh Walli lowered the *Trinidad Guardian* as his son, Karan, joined him at the breakfast table; what he had to say required a father's authority. 'Devi Nadir asked me for one more meeting,' he said. 'After that, we go to the Pundit for an auspicious day.'

'Pa, we already had our last meeting. Now what did you say to her?'

'I said it was allright. We agreed on the Sunday coming, at their home.' His son said nothing, so Sukesh Walli asked, 'You want to change the time? You want to go somewhere else for this meeting?'

Karan poured his coffee. Home-grown spinach with grilled tomatoes and hot puris helped to restrain his intense annoyance at this further delay.

'Changing the place would be difficult Karan.' Sukesh warned him. 'Mrs Nadir wants to keep the arrangement traditional – quiet, no exposure to the public. I don't think she would agree to meeting at a restaurant – it is a public place. And you know we can't meet here – custom forbids it. We should be a little more understanding at this time. After all, she has recently become a widow and has to make every decision alone. This she is not used to. I could tell from her voice that she is very sensitive about her daughter being seen in public with an arrangement going, just in case it goes nowhere. She didn't say it in so many words, but I could see she wanted to do nothing that might put a blot on her family's name.'

Feeling better, Karan said, 'She has nothing on that front to worry about.'

'I told her as much. She must know how we feel about Vasti. I reassured her several times, but she kept saying that with a daughter, you can never be too careful.'

Karan could not help thinking that there might be more to all this than was being said. It was just a hunch, but he could not speak to his father about a hunch. That was too vague for a man who had set his mind for take-off. He did have some evidence, but the nature of that evidence would be interpreted as being more in his mind than in the real world, a place where his father resided permanently. So Karan kept all this to himself.

This arrangement, this prelude to circling the sacred fire with his bride joined to him by a fine length of soft saffron cotton would now be delayed even further, he mused. His natural impatience and acquired arrogance left him unmoved by Devi Nadir's concerns.

16

To Sukesh Walli, this marriage was his son's entrance to adult life, a break with his youthful adventurous past and the beginning of a well-planned future with responsibilities and obligations. The creation of wealth, the procreation of children who would carry the imprint of the Wallis on their faces and hold high the family's name and honour were a son's duties. After these were fulfilled, he could choose to retire into charitable work or, if inclined, even become a yogi. The duty of each stage of a man's life, written in the sacred texts, was known by his generation. Sometimes he wondered whether he should have done more to bring up his son according to the teachings of Hinduism, of Dharma.

Sukesh Walli was unaware of the extent to which his son's conduct was not in any way guided by moral laws. Unlike his father's generation, Karan Walli was living in amoral times, where it was far easier to slip into confusing the essence of an action with a semblance of it. One's measure was ascertained by the visible goals attained, not the dark, hidden pathways taken.

This prolonged coming and going between the families of a prospective bride and groom, Karan said to himself, this charming courtesy, with its small talk – half formal, half friendly – was a getting-to-know-all-about you exercise. It meant that your qualifications, job, skills, ambitions and potential were all opened up, albeit with tact, by the families playing the marriage-making game. It was a display of one's wares in a private place, bringing to light merits and virtues that had remained undisclosed or had been overlooked.

He picked up half an orange, freshly peeled in the traditional way. Then, without the restraint, which the

17

presence of another usually brings, he savagely bit into the juice-filled segments.

Sukesh Walli's eye had been running along the 'Properties For Sale' column in the newspaper, and now the silence following the noisy sucking dry of the fruit drew his attention. 'Is something worrying you?' he asked his son.

'This will be the fourth meeting, Pa. It means another day gone.'

'What harm is there in that? Marriage is a lifetime business. I believe the girl is nervous; her mother is trying to comfort her this way. It is just another chance for her to reassure herself of how she feels. Remember, women need constant reassurance. They are not men.'

Karan's 'youthful adventures' had taught him this. And reassurance was something he had offered in plenty, with the sincerity of a priest, when he had none. 'Pa,' he said impulsively, 'there is another side to Vasti.'

'What do you mean?' Sukesh Walli put down his paper.

'She is all that you say, Pa, and something else. I find neither restraint nor deference in her manner when we differ. She charges off as if in battle. There is none of the respect which Ma had for you. Vasti has an opinion on everything. She thinks too much.'

'On everything?' His father laughed. 'A young woman with spirit is just what we need in the Clinic. If that is worrying you, relax. That spirit is youth, son, and be grateful it is there. She has had all the time in the world to indulge herself with ideas, but with marriage, that kind of thinking, that independent attitude will drain away. Time does it, my boy. Just look around you. Strong women after their marriage bend their heads and pull the family cart, because their children are inside it, their parents too. After my first grandson, young Vasti will be like all Indian mothers. There won't be time for ideas on everything. We will be doing the thinking for her. Your aunts will set the pattern for her to follow. The waking up at nights, caring for the child, looking after you and the Clinic, will amount to total exhaustion. A tired woman does not have the energy to argue endlessly. Just let her know from the very beginning what you will allow. Speak firmly, my boy, and respect is sure to follow.'

Sukesh Walli knew that an exhausted woman presented other difficulties, but he would concentrate on the wedding plans for the moment.

As Karan did not appear convinced, his father added, 'If Vasti is going out of line, we will gently guide her back to our expectations. We will remind her of her family responsibilities, her obligations to you, to us, to her children. Don't make me out to be a blind bat, son. I'm always one step ahead of most people. And I think before I make any step, not only a business one.

'Marriage is a family affair, too. Your aunts and I know the Nadir family well. Her father was an upright man. Not religious, never pretended to be . . . had a quirkiness in constantly feeling the need to find out as much as he could before deciding on anything, even when it was clear as day to me. This made him lose out to some sharp fellas. Yet, credit him with this, he had judgement and Vasti has it, too. That is the important thing. You take it from me – that girl will turn the Clinic round into a profit-making, expanding concern.

'You need an educated girl, Karan, to run the Health Clinic properly. Vasti has a way with people. I observed

19

how she mingled with parents on St Ursula's Open Day, answering questions freely. She wasn't difficult or reserved, or full of importance because she holds a degree and was educated abroad. She was thoughtful . . . friendly. I noticed all those things and much more. I like her ways. I know how important that is in business.

'Of course, a lot goes through her head, like her father. The Clinic needs this. In that girl, Karan, believe me, you have far more than you think. Don't throw it away. Look here, daughters after a time become like their mothers, and her mother is the perfect Indian wife, like your own mother was. To Devi Nadir, her family comes first – maybe even second or third, who knows? But first is first. You are getting in Vasti someone tailor-made for our special situation. Is that not worth another visit to calm her nerves? Think about it. Think hard.'

'I have never mentioned the Clinic to her, Pa.'

'She would have to leave St Ursula. No way can we allow her to continue teaching. When she sees how much money the Clinic will be earning for her family – you, her children and herself – and when I point out to her the full potential of it, she will not refuse. What is a teacher's salary? A pittance! Just think of the challenges involved in managing a Clinic – patients, their never-ending complaints, doctors, their daily grumbles. And don't for a minute forget government rules and regulations coming at you from all sides. It is a bombardment. I have no doubt whatsoever that Vasti would take up this challenge and rise to it. You'll see. I'll bet on it. The young women today like a challenge. I understand these things, I'm not a country-bookie.'

The older man looked exhausted. He poured himself some coffee and looked into the distance. Sukesh Walli was considering whether this was the right time to express his other concerns. All around him was peaceful, he heard the milkman's call to his neighbour.

'The Clinic has not been doing well. The management is poor. This reminds me, you have to play your part, Karan, be more professional with the nurses – I mean *all* the nurses. Now that you are to be married and your wife will also be there, you have to conduct yourself at all times as befits a good husband and future father. We must be an example to my future grandchildren. I have nothing more to say. You understand me. Begin now.'

Karan became subdued. A code of behaviour had been read out to him. This tone of voice he knew. It belonged to his youth, of having to explain a poor mark in his school report and other shortcomings and misdemeanours of his boyhood. His attention jerked back to the present.

'Private health insurance is here to stay,' his father was asserting. 'The middle class is growing, demanding better care; in no time we will be expanding. Now why would I say this? Look at the public hospitals here in Trinidad. You have to be crazy or poor to decide to go in there. I hear people saying that if you intend to go into one of those places, you'd better see all your family first, for your next meeting will be in heaven.'

Sunday came and Karan took his time considering what to wear. Should he dress casually, or should his clothes and manner convey these feelings: 'I am not a man to be

21

kept waiting. When I make my intentions clear, act upon them without delay.'

He wavered. Or should he make this final meeting warm, appealing, with a promise of domestic bliss? He was good with promises, had an artful way with women. But the needs of the Clinic and Vasti's independent disposition reminded him that he must first net her with guile. Sophisticated young women, he thought, were first and foremost women, therefore vulnerable by their very nature; their needs and expectations he understood well. Experience had come his way and with it a growing confidence. Karan Walli believed that he had become a maestro in handling these matters to his advantage.

He paused again to consider the ideas now coming so fast that they were bunched and needed sorting. Should he put on the charm, heighten his charisma? 'Animal magnetism' was what he preferred to call it. What about playing the part of a young, caring priest in the Clinic? A doctor with an upright stance on social matters . . . perhaps patients' welfare? At last, the formula he would use to seduce her came to him. His manner would be amiable, thoughtful, caring; as the evening wore on, he would reveal a boldness, a strength of opinion – tempered by courtesy, of course. For a moment he wondered whether not having practised this role, he would be able to carry it through. Would his mask fall? Would Vasti's sharp eyes unnerve him? Then Karan Walli's creative energies were speedily recharged by memories of his past successes.

The potency of the idea stirred him. He revisited the mirror and was so stimulated that he removed the ring he was wearing and picked out from a small ivory box

22

the warm, reddish-gold one that he favoured. Rusha, a young woman he knew and had, with difficulty, managed to buy off, had wanted to keep it as a remembrance of their times together. Instead, he offered her a beautiful ring he had purchased at an airport. He wanted to please her, knowing that much is enriched with a grateful companion. Later, he employed her in the Clinic. This arrangement was convenient. Rusha wore his ring, content to be promised faithfulness in a love that was beyond the mere convention of marriage. Such are the attractions of the pure in heart, he mused. They will believe anything.

Looking in the mirror, Karan was pleased that his finger was now adorned by an emblem of unadulterated power, an eagle in its flight, wings lifting with the wind, though buffeted, defying the elements – its shadow sailing effortlessly. A bird of prey carrying an open scroll of ancient writ. 'And the word was with God.' The boldness of the piece, a bird of prey as the carrier of The Word, excited him. It was refreshingly honest, he felt, in depicting the real world around him.

Then for no particular reason, he decided to take it off again and wear what he had always worn on his visits to the Nadirs – a simple, well-crafted eighteen-carat gold ring. My intuitive feelings have made me superstitious, he chuckled to himself. The time to fly high will come. The mirror reflected a smiling face. Its light seeped into his steps.

CHAPTER FOUR

Guests on the Sunday

DEVI NADIR AND her daughter Vasti lived in an old fashioned spacious bungalow with polished floors, countless windows and a large shower room, decorated with blue mosaic tiles. A flowering clematis sheltered the patio at the front of the house from the intense heat of the western sky. The villagers called it the Upstairs House as it was the only concrete-built, one-storey house in Pasea village at the time, and the only home in the village to enjoy electric lights as the town dwellers did, in nearby Tunapuna. This came about because Mr Nadir had gone out of his way and purchased an electric pole.

Devi Nadir had created a restful home. Its atmosphere evoked an eventide raga, a quiet intimacy of wrapped thoughts, unfolding memories of youthful dreams and family togetherness.

With her guests due to arrive at any minute, the house was looking at its best: it was a pleasure just to be there. A tall blue glazed jar held Venetian red anthurium lilies, which kept their heads high, the better to observe the goings-on. The drawing room with its long silk-cotton curtains of running vines and wild flowers depicted a stylish elegance. The vermilion rug and the polished William Morris chairs' outstretched arms were also in waiting. They, too, had absorbed a pleasurable anticipation. Here, the human spirit sang.

Occasionally a cool breeze lifted the curtains, for the adjoining patio opened on to a range of blue mountains. And there, cloaked by the morning mist stood the Benedictine Monastery, which at night became a constellation of lights.

Devi's elder daughter Pushpa and husband Shami had already arrived, exuding filial warmth and the confidence of youth, at ease with events.

'Ma, the place is looking so nice!' Pushpa clapped her hands and smiled. 'What a cool fresh day to meet the Wallis again. Hope you're not worrying. Where is your servant girl?'

'I let Ballari go. She came very early this morning to help me. You have to give and take Pushpa. She will come back about five o'clock to help with the washing up. It is better this way. And then again, at this stage of the arrangement, I like to keep everything within the family.'

'All will go well, I am willing to put a bet on it,' Shami reassured his mother-in-law, adding, 'Uncle Kash and Aunt Sona phoned us. They are on their way.'

Devi tried to throw off her sense of unease. It was in her nature to be conventional. When her husband was alive, he helped her to release herself from traditional assumptions, but Devi no longer had the benefit of his perception or enlightened thoughts to encourage her to travel, to leave her birthplace, to see other life styles. Her daughters were aware that she had returned to the old, familiar pathways.

25

In the kitchen, Devi showed Pushpa the prepared dishes. 'Don't uncover them, Ma, I can see through the glass covers,' Pushpa said. 'We don't want to lose that rich burst of delight escaping. That, Ma we will keep for the Wallis. Let's overwhelm them!' Nevertheless an intensity of aromas reached Pushpa. She could tell that in those covered dishes there were chopped coriander and mint leaves, crushed sweet basil, grilled red peppers, cardamom seeds, cinnamon, melted ghee with the fragrance of warm jeera. Close to one of the dishes was a small white bowl of herbs, giving off a subtle scent. 'This smells really good, what is it, Ma?'

'French tarragon – the supermarket is doing a promotion. Over here I have Roman chamomile and peppermint leaves. I thought herb teas may be lighter, more refreshing after the meal, what do you think?' Devi asked

'Super idea. I can also smell incense.'

'I just did aarti – prayed for guidance and a good outcome.'

'This is a feast. Everything will go well, Ma, believe me. I just hope Karan and his family prove worthy of all this effort.'

'Don't speak like that, Pushpa. It is our duty to make our guests happy, more so since your father is not here: we owe it to his good name – our family's good name. The community looks up to us to do things right.'

'Ma, your good name will grow or die, only by how you live. Nothing else. Look how well you treat your servants.'

'Yes, yes, Pushpa, how we live *is* important, don't I know that? Tell me, are we living alone? We live in this village, we are a part of this village. We walk with a warm feeling whenever we leave this house. Why?

26

Because the villagers respected your father. His name is honoured here.'

'But if our consciences tell us we have done nothing wrong, does it matter what the community thinks?'

'The idea of a community, the how and why of it, is not so simple, Pushpa. That was a foolish thing to say. You, my elder daughter, you surprise me.' Devi looked at this fine young woman her daughter had become and her voice was gentle but firm as she spoke.

'Pushpa, I have to tell you this. I hear your father's voice in how you and Vasti speak, and this troubles me no end. Remember this: your father was a man, Pushpa. He was *not* a woman. He was a well-to-do, high-caste Brahmin and only managed to carry his kind of thinking by his quiet manner. Your father was always polite, soft-spoken. I know he had wisdom. He also knew when and where and how to speak – that is what I call judgement He was able to help many people solve their problems. But the most important thing, Pushpa, is to remember *he was a man*. We cannot live by his rules. We are women, alone now without his protection, and so we must think with care about what we say, when, where and how we say it.'

Pushpa herself had long felt that in every aspect of life, women had already made far too many accommodations, but seeing her mother's tension and worry reflected in her softly ageing, vulnerable face, all she said was, 'Yes, Ma. I will tell Vasti. I am sorry. You are right about community. It is a part of us.'

Through the open windows and doors, the incense from the puja room was escaping, yet enough remained to remind her of her mother's prayer that today's outcome would be a happy one.

'Pushpa, go now. Vasti wants to see you.'

On her way to Vasti's room, Pushpa saw her role clearly for the first time. A month ago her mother had spoken to her in confidence, but she had done nothing and now felt guilty: *'Pushpa, you know Vasti always spoke too strongly for a young woman. But since she came back from England, she speaks her mind much too plainly. We are not living in America, we are not living in England, we are living here. Explain that to her. You are her elder sister, it is your duty to help her see what is best for her now. She is not getting any younger. She is already two years older than when you got married. We cannot push the clock back. A woman is a woman. No amount of education can change that, Pushpa. You like to say travel broadens the mind: I think standing still deepens it.'*

Pushpa knocked and Vasti said, 'Come in, my guardian angel, it is open.'

They embraced. 'I am so glad, Vasti, you're wearing the right blouse. It adds a healthy glow to your neck.'

'Sensuous warmth, Pushpa.'

'Call it anything you like, but that cream one you had in mind was too plain. This has a fetching neckline and a *joie de vivre*. Walk a little, let me see. Yes, it moves well on you. Come. You need a touch more make-up on your eyes. This is so tame, Vasti. Are you afraid of him? There, you see, too much subtlety and seduction do not go hand in hand. Another thing, don't forget to smile.'

'Without cause? For no reason? That would be silly.'

'You tend to look too thoughtful, even severe at times, when they are here. Remember, you are not overseeing an examination at school. I just felt you ought to know.'

28

'I'm not sure I know him well enough . . . things have moved ahead so quickly. I feel rushed, Pushpa. I can't believe arrangements are being made for my wedding. It's as if it's happening to someone else. Strange. I am completely detached. What I am worried about is, as time brings me closer to this wedding, will I panic, will I run away?'

'Anxiety, that's what it is. Anxiety is affecting you. It is debilitating. Let's face it, this is a big step, agreeing to spend the rest of your life with someone. Maybe you should try this: a handsome doctor and his family want you to join their family. You know when Pa was very ill just before he died, and Dr Mistry was in London, Karan did come over several times to ensure that Pa was as comfortable as he could be when his asthma had got worse. So he is not a villain. His profession is a thoughtful and caring one. Just try to relax today, Vasti. If you are at ease you will say the right things. Now let's do your hair.'

Pushpa's skilful fingers wound a stylish gathering of silky hair and produced an elegant chignon circled by opening buds, revealing the nape of a neck that Old Masters could have captured on canvas.

'Look in the mirror,' she whispered.

Vasti looked. 'You always had fine taste and fingers of magic, my sister. Is this really me? Thank you!' She turned her head this way and that, and the mirror winked as it aped her.

'Pushpa, there is another thing,' she said suddenly. 'I do not want to follow other people's expectations of me. I am *me*. I do not want to manage a Clinic. The Wallis will try to push me into it. So much direct and covert pressure will be placed upon me by everyone; even

29

Uncle Kash will do his bit on their behalf, with all the trimmings of how fortunate I am et cetera. I am fed up with that kind of thinking. I don't *want* to be fortunate. One of these days, I may just tell him so.'

'Please don't, Vasti, for Ma's sake. Please just ignore him. He is not like Pa was. We expect grown-ups to be sensible, but how can they? They are not asked to consider what their own values are based on, nor do they feel the need to question them. They have lived their entire life within the same time loop. Time has not moved for them. Uncle Kash's marriage was arranged and he is happy. What can you expect from him?'

'No one asks me what *I* want to do – well, I will say it now. I want to try and help my young girls at school to begin that crucial questioning, to begin to walk the path that leads to their thinking for themselves, becoming discerning. They cannot do so without the tools to open words apart as if they were oysters, to discover them afresh, taste their true meanings.

'I want to meet with their parents and discuss the social consequences of the rapid changes taking place all around us in the 1960s. I want to engage their mothers, Pushpa, I want to show that these changes can be approached sensibly. I am hoping this may assist their daughters. I want to encourage these women to speak openly about their fears for the welfare of their daughters, the changes they can live with and the ones they cannot abide. I want to understand them better.'

Vasti got up and walked to the window. There were children jumping over puddles shrieking with laughter, but she saw nothing. A weariness, a sadness came over her. She returned quietly, to sit with Pushpa.

'I don't know what to say, Vasti.'

30

'Uncle Kash is trying to make me feel guilty. I think he suspects neither my heart nor head is in it, so he tries to win me over with tales of how good Karan was to Pa when he was ill and how grateful Pa was, and how much Pa liked him and so on. If anyone tells me this again I shall become a suttee consumed by the intensity of the fire within me, generated by pure concentrated thought.'

Pushpa said nothing, for she too had just been guilty of a similar ploy in an effort to reduce her sister's anxiety.

'I had all that bottled up,' Vasti sighed. Actually I feel better now, and will try to take the smiling on board as you suggested. Perhaps something like this.' Then Vasti winked, presenting a comical face to Pushpa, but her eyes were sad.

Both sisters laughed.

'Why did Ma want to cook only vegetarian?' Pushpa asked, changing the subject.

'Your telephone call persuading her against it won the day,' Vasti grinned. 'Her initial idea was to keep all thoughts, motives, voices, every action and deliberation of those partaking of the meal, clean, cool and quiet. That meant Pushpa, no garam massala, no animal flesh, nothing that could lead to a build-up of fiery body heat. No energy burst, resulting in raised voices and high tempers. I wonder. Is it a premonition? When I was younger, what Ma said about events to come, convinced me she was psychic.'

'Listen, Vasti. That is Shami, playing his favourite film music to cheer us up. He says Nadir women should remember this is not a trial in a courtroom but a family getting together. It is his way of helping us to unwind.

31

He has missed Pa a lot. His own father died when he was eleven. He so enjoyed the long conversations with Pa.'

'Pa enjoyed his company, too. It was good for Pa with only a wife and two daughters, to have some male company. Vasti looked at her sister fondly. 'Since my return the house seems so empty, Pushpa. Why did you have to go and get married? I'm anxious for Ma's sake. She has lived for us, her life was offered up to our wellbeing, to our future. Yet, Pushpa, I can't do what she has done, just let my life go, become an offering to custom. She wanted us to have the best possible education and yet couldn't see that that in itself meant our life goals and priorities would be different from hers.

'Oh, she knew that.' Pushpa shook her head. 'Ma is far more sensible than we think. She wanted us to have the best, whatever the consequences for her. She did not know the shape or form of the consequences, but would have felt she would manage with Pa beside her.'

'That is true, Pushpa. If Pa were here, he would have explained it all to her in his gentle way. With us, she is not sure whether our judgement is sufficiently mature or whether we are seduced by the style of New York or London. She is right to question these new attitudes to living, for she has no way of knowing whether they have enduring qualities. Nor do we, Pushpa, do we?'

'We only have the knowledge we have.'

'And dispositions, inclinations, family, community, et cetera?'

'Hmm. Ma wants you to say little today, Vasti. Please don't give anyone an insight into their character, or say something you feel they should have been told long ago for their own good. Be courteous at all times, and please overlook any indiscretions. It is a sign of maturity. I tell you what – this is a good rule: ask yourself, if Pa were present with us in the room now, and he wanted this day to go well, what would he be saying to them, and to us? For the sake of the dead and for the living, Vasti, be guided today by your good sense. You must have some stored away for emergencies, don't you?'

'And how do I, dear sister, behave tomorrow?'

'The same – until the wedding. Then surprise your in-laws with the real Vasti. That will shake them! Believe me, they will allow you to carry on teaching without another murmur of dissent.'

They laughed. And when their laughter left, Vasti and Pushpa looked at each other.

Silence brought a feeling that something precious was being taken from them and would soon be irretrievably lost. Their eyes did not meet. They held on to each other. No sound. Nothing.

'The Wallis will be here soon,' Pushpa said softly. 'Listen, that is Uncle Kash and Auntie Sona coming up the stairs. We are proud of you, Vasti. Freeing the human spirit is a longterm venture. Do not become a missionary to it. Have a life too, enrich it. Help me not to lose my sister.'

'Thank you, Pushpa.'

When the door closed behind Pushpa, Vasti sat on her bed. Her repressed tears made her eyes glisten. How, she wondered, had this whole thing begun? She wished she had been adamant from the start, had said to Uncle Kash and her mother that she was not thinking of marriage just yet. But how did one say this to parents, to uncles and aunts? She recalled her Ajee saying that *her* own grandmother escaped from an obligation to become a suttee. Unbeknownst to her family, she boarded a boat that left the port of Calcutta, not knowing where she was going.

It would appear, Vasti reflected, that the women in our family are destined to experience life-threatening challenges. Had her Great-great Ajee become a suttee, what then? Was she unique? Had there been others, mutineers all?

Uncle Kash and Aunty Sona hurried upstairs. 'We are so happy and excited, Devi,' Sona said, gasping as they were greeted by Shami, Pushpa and Devi. 'We gave ourselves plenty of time. Didn't want the Wallis to be here before us.' She was smiling, happy to be on time.

'You would think she was the bride-to-be,' Uncle Kash winked, 'so nervous and anxious, wanting us to leave too early. I told her to leave the timing to me. I know this traffic like the back of my hand.' He looked about, stooping, craning his neck, pretending to be searching for someone, playing at hide and seek. Then he said, 'Where is Vasti? Not here to meet her Uncle Kash?'

'Shhhh,' Sona warned him. 'Those people will be here anytime now, leave her alone. She needs to unwind.'

'Of course. I wasn't thinking. Sona is better at these things. I leave them to her.'

'He forgets what it is to be young,' Sona explained.

'Putting mirth and jest aside,' said Uncle Kash, 'Vasti is a lucky girl, getting married to a doctor. I am saving up all my symptoms for after the wedding. This wedding will save me a packet, I can tell you.' And he tapped his breast pocket. Their eyes twinkled with amusement.

'Uncle Kash, you are good at cheering us up,' Pushpa said. 'You are just what the doctor ordered.'

'We must not forget this,' Kash said. 'The Wallis are a very respectable family.' He lowered his voice lest it left the room, and reduced its pace, better for all to take note. 'Don't think I didn't add my bit about her education and her being abroad to widen her knowledge and so on and so on, broader vision et cetera. Oh yes. My brother is not here, but I know my duty. It is our family's name that is bringing together a match like this. All we have to do, is do nothing. Be our normal pleasant selves, nothing else. Not a single careless word; think before we open our mouths. It is a good general rule. Just so that everybody understands what I am saying, let me give an example of what I mean. Just suppose the other side runs away with saying something stupid: let it be like water off a duck's back. Take no offence. Why? Because the most important thing for all of us is to keep our eyes on the ball. Do not be distracted by petty things. Do they matter? Why attach an importance to them? We are adults. Let us focus on the big picture. Look here, the long and short of it is this. *They* want this wedding to take place. *We* want this wedding to take place. I don't have any doubt that the deal will be clinched today.' Kash clapped his hands. 'This,' he said, 'is a champion deal.'

'Devi, let me help you in the kitchen,' Sona offered. 'You know when Uncle Kash starts on this subject, he will not end till thy kingdom comes.'

As soon as they heard the closing of car doors, Uncle Kash and Shami went downstairs to welcome the Wallis.

'Namaskar' – that gracious salutation of old which honours and adds dignity to the meeting of strangers and friends alike – was received and offered by all. Uncle Kash, Devi, Pushpa, Aunty Sona, Shami and Vasti formed themselves into a welcoming family gathering. Sukesh and Karan Walli were well pleased.

Pushpa led everyone to the patio, saying, 'Come and see how the mountain mist still settles in small pockets, even now. When I was very young I once called my Pa to see this, saying, "Come see bits of the sky on the mountain, Pa. Strong rain broke the skies in the night". You know, Pa was so wise. He said, "Pushpa, only children can see what you have seen. Their eyes have a special light".'

'Pa liked standing here,' Vasti said softly. 'His spirit is here.'

Shami joined in, 'I also recall a conversation that has remained with me. He said, "We in this house are blessed". We were seated right here. I wanted to know why he thought so, but did not dare ask. He understood my reticence and said, "The mountains constantly remind us, Shami, that it is only when we are able to lift our sights high, well above narrow views, that we can see the beauty around us. What a rugged mountain climb reveals! How fresh the air! How vast the view! Another understanding comes". He later told me that he grew up on those hills and roamed about them – became close to them, I think.'

Sukesh Walli interrupted the sweet silence that enabled Mr Nadir's spirit to envelop them. 'I'm not surprised to hear this,' he said, raising his voice, 'that was his way of talking. He had one riddle after the other. He was himself a riddle.' Smiling broadly he continued, 'You never knew exactly what he was saying – I had to pretend to understand sometimes. But he was always friendly and helpful, no matter what. He knew when I didn't quite make sense of it; yet he behaved as if I had. Your father was a good man, a considerate man.'

Chilled coconut water was served and when everyone was seated at table, the dishes were brought in by the ladies: stir-fried spinach and lamb biryani, mushrooms and crisply fried okras, grilled eggplant in a tomato, butter and garlic sauce, French beans, tandoori snappers, warm silky dhal puri, fried prawns flavoured with sesame seeds. There were mango and tamarind pickles and coconut chutney. Everyone was served by everyone else. Much pleasure was received and many compliments given. The silence was inviting, full and appealing; Devi had excelled herself and was comforted by how much everyone was enjoying lunch. She told herself this special day had started well. She had played her part; now it was left to the others to carry it through.

CHAPTER FIVE

At Table

DESSERTS WERE SERVED on the patio. A bowl of rich gulabjamuns in warm cardamom syrup filled the room with the scent of sweet milk and honey, their outer coats imitating juicy crimson plums, only for spoons and forks to uncover an ambrosia. No one abstained from a second helping of these luscious indulgences. This abandonment of restraint was a compliment to Devi Nadir's fine skill with delicacies.

The early morning misty blue had lifted and though the forested mountain range playing with the light held a variety of greens, their eyes were attracted to the red caps and white coats of the Benedictine Monastery, its school and nursing home perched on the highest terrace. The grand edifices had once astonished the island peasants, the wild deer and the curious monkeys, but no more. The surrounding monastery gardens, with their abundance of fruit and succulent vegetables, had become a place to visit, in which to explore and to taste the cultivated offerings. The monkeys, birds and schoolboys all knew this.

There, it was said, the mentally exhausted, troubled and distressed sought the melody of the mountain's solitude, the chants of its flora and fauna. Some felt it was those unheard rhythms of Nature's play that slowly mended them. Others believed it was the Benedictine hymns and prayers that cradled the hills. There were a few non-believers who were sure that it had to be the fresh vegetables, fruit and large helpings of honey from the monastery's farms and apiary that eventually warmed and energised battered hopes to recovery. Everyone agreed, it was a sanctuary for sore minds and lost spirits.

A thoughtful silence enveloped the group as they looked towards the mountain from the patio, contemplating their own vulnerability.

When the aroma of coffee and herb teas reached them, they drank. Cups were refilled.

Mr Walli was contented. He saw that his son was, too. 'If anyone were in doubt of the value of women,' he said, smiling, 'I would have to refer them to this family. Today has been a perfect day. I wish to thank the women of the house. We men cannot do without the comforts they provide. Family, home and women are tied together. They are inseparable and must remain so for the civilised world to continue to prosper.'

Uncle Kash nodded his head in agreement. He was delighted that all was going so well. Indeed, a perfect day, he was thinking.

'Ma did all the work,' Pushpa said. 'It is gracious of you to say such kind things. I wish the men in the village were as appreciative as you are, Mr Walli. They do not acknowledge a woman's worth, either in word or in kind. I know families where communication between husband and wife is almost nil. I am not referring to, "Is the food ready?" or "I have to go out this evening, I shall be needing my clothes seen to. Where are the children?" '

Shami, who feared what might await Vasti in the Wallis' household, seized his opportunity. 'Men are essential to a happy family life, but their interests are seldom in the home. A woman, on the other hand, no matter how educated, irrespective of how much society is in need of her skills, is made to feel she is especially privileged if her in-laws give their approval for her working outside the house. Is there this constant need for family approval in any other culture?' He looked at Karan and smiled. 'You see, we are unique.'

'When your life is not your own, but what someone else wishes it to be,' Vasti said, 'I call that servitude. The wife becomes a piece of machinery which you wheel into one room to perform a service, then into the kitchen to perform another and into the nursery for yet another. These services are all of a kind, to give pleasure and satisfaction. But then a machine is a machine; anytime of the day or night, service can be rendered.'

Knowing that he had for a moment lost concentration, and being well-disposed towards Vasti, Mr Walli picked up on what he believed was being said: a human can be as efficient as a machine. He was thinking, in the Clinic, I need someone like this to handle the doctors who are not pulling their weight, someone to move from ward to ward checking on the services provided. Recently things have become far too lax. She has what it takes. 'The women in this household,' he said, 'are firm, clear and persuasive. This is what the country needs. However, on what Pushpa has just said: we should look at the reality. A wife may ask an intelligent question, but she is unable to take in the explanation, as it is often technical and beyond her understanding. You can have one kind of communication with your wife, but not all kinds.'

'If that is so,' Vasti replied, 'it is the duty of the husband to explain in a way she understands. Even technical things can make good logical sense. There are times when the husband is inarticulate, non-communicative, or when he himself is not quite sure of the intricate workings of what he is talking about, then he hides behind, "My wife does not understand these matters," or "My wife is not interested." I would be surprised if many wives do not feign a disinterest in the face of such husbands and with time become a decorated house servant. A household slave. Nothing more.'

A stunned silence hovered above them. Pushpa tried with the gentlest of head movements to indicate that her sister should desist from saying anything more.

'Put like that,' stammered the astonished Sukesh Walli, 'you make it sound as if women are only serving others and have no lives of their own. I move amongst women all the time. I am not in a monastery; I had a wife who sadly departed from this world, and my sisters live with me. The women I know are enjoying their lives. What can I say? The world is full of unhappiness that has nothing to do with husbands. Do all men have good wives? Many husbands work very hard for their families. What do you say to that?' His face had become hot, his ears burned. Sukesh Walli was greatly distraught.

As for Karan Walli, he was confused. He should either have been satisfied that he had warned his father earlier about Vasti, thus showing his superior judgement, or uneasy at what was in store for him as her husband. However, these emotions did not come to him. The fine meal, the sunshine, the cool mountain breeze lifting the lined curtains had done their work. Karan Walli was contented. He could see being married to Vasti was going to be fun, a challenge. To bridle such a spirit, to lead it to submission to his wishes, was an exciting and alluring prospect.

Uncle Kash's voice rolled into his reverie. 'Vasti is exposing the extreme instances, only to show what the ideal domestic situation is not.' His voice was calm and slow; it reassured.

'Oh, *ideals!* The ideal situation!' exclaimed Sukesh Walli.

'Yes, Sukesh, idealism.' Kash smiled and winked. 'It is a favourite topic among the young.'

'Oh, I see. I haven't heard that word for some time now. I didn't understand that you were thinking simply in theory, observing the entire spectrum of human behaviour. Turning to Vasti, he said, 'You are like your father – the meaning of what you say is clear in part, and hidden in part like a woman's face.' He raised both hands and sought to regain his former amiability. 'I thought you were referring to women's lives today.'

'I am thinking—,' The attempt at a reply was firm and clear, the stress on the second syllable said it all. But Pushpa was alert; she pressed her sister's feet hard. Her quick footwork had an immediate response.

'Naturally, Mr Walli,' came a quieter cool strain, 'I am also thinking of ideals. We need them. They are our lanterns in the dark: we need to raise them high on the roads engineered by men.'

Karan began to consider whether there would be similarities in the taming of Vasti and the breaking in or bridling of wild horses. He recalled that many a rider was thrown off his saddle and left broken, while the animal bounced round the paddock, its mane streaming as if it were winged, daring anyone to be so bold again.

His gaze moved along her body, engaging her slender neck, noting how well it held her bosom, which would fill out further with their first child. His thoughts left the room and he recalled a certain ripened rotundness in gauze, in transparent silk, the delicious Apsaras in the caves of Ajanta – such offerings were his ready preference. Their hips and thighs he considered to be flows of agreeableness. However his words masked his thoughts.

'Men have always engineered roads,' he said. 'We were the first map-makers, the first explorers, inventors, musicians, the lot. Whoever came after, followed in the footsteps of men. We have shown the way. These are the facts. I don't understand the need to mystify our ingenuity.' He spoke with authority and ran with the statement as if it were a flag; then his smugness overflowed and he took his smiling, searching eyes to Pushpa who lowered her head.

Shami knew his wife and sister-in-law well, and understood what had just happened. He had long observed Karan's pomposity and saw the way he took his decadent smile to his wife. The well-woven courtesy that had enabled him to camouflage his instinctive dislike for Karan, was now so severely strained that it began to unravel with a vengeance; he lifted his chest and raised his head. 'Today and for evermore,' he heard himself say, 'in the new fields of knowledge there will be women amongst the first.

43

'Times are rapidly changing. We are better informed, our new perceptions are bringing about this transformation. There shall be women engineers, and cosmologists of the highest calibre; more women mathematicians, physicists, philosophers and painters. They will surpass many in new fields because they will work harder and be less arrogant – a common failing among those long standing at the helm. An outstanding few will so expand our vision that the opportunities and secret desires of the greatly disadvantaged will come to pass.' His fury had not yet diminished. 'Sadly, to our shame, we have treated women without regard to a large part of their inheritance.'

An awkward silence fell after this outburst, and Shami could see that his wife was none too pleased with his contribution; a cosmic explosion was occurring within her which he could almost hear. 'Sorry I got carried away,' he chuckled nervously. 'As an economist, you see, I face the situation where only half the manpower is efficiently trained and utilised; it distresses me. The answer to some of our problems are to engage our women in all spheres of endeavour, but we feign blindness.'

'That is one of the main problems today,' said Uncle Kash. 'Blindness. Believe me when I say it is everywhere.' As he spoke, he was forced to restrain his anger at what was happening, but his thoughts came thick and fast: Shami is blind to what this situation demands, and should not have been invited to this close family affair. An outsider messing things up. An economist too! Sounds so much like 'Communists'. What exactly do economists do anyway? Do they know anything about arranged marriages? When you study a subject no one understands you will say so much foolishness. Dear God, I am so tired.

Uncle Kash's thoughts were racing ahead on the path lit up before him. Shami is behaving as if he is one of us. Fancy getting it into his head that he can speak for us. God help us! Please Lord Krishna help me today and I promise, if all goes as planned, I shall offer a good quality puja and feed one hundred beggars. He cleared his throat. How he wished his brother had lived long enough to marry his daughter and not leave him this responsibility. His brotherly duty held him and he had acquiesced gracefully. But now . . .

Time and again he had intimated to Sona that Nadir was far too removed from the thinking of the community. That was bad enough, but he had taken his daughters with him; especially this firebrand Vasti. Who would marry her? With ideas like this, she better call in a carpenter to build a good shelf, for that was where she was heading, hell bent. Full speed ahead is her way. Yes, she did resemble her father, had his dark complexion, too.

As far as Uncle Kash could see, this girl had no redeeming features to call on. Look at those warm, inviting eyes of Pushpa – just like her mother's. But this other one here, had the eyes of a bird of prey. Get her angry and she would forget she was a woman – would swoop at you with her razor-sharp beak. She talked about freedom. What freedom did an unmarried woman have? Did she not understand society? What freedom did a widow have? God help us all. Did I not warn them this morning? Who listens to an uncle today?

Devi should have got someone to read her palm to give them some idea of her karma. That would have saved them all this trouble and expense. At this moment their good luck was at a low ebb. Would this marriage ever take place?

O God, help me. I am trying my very best to do my duty by my brother, but as you see, through no fault of my own, things are going wrong. I would even consider not one but two pujas in your name. In fact, I'll make it two good quality pujas though things are very tight with me, but this is a desperate plea. God, in your mercy hear this prayer.

'Uncle Kash,' said Pushpa, 'please tell us what you see our other problems to be.' Her words walked softly and embraced her uncle.

'To my mind,' he said, regaining his spirit, 'the most threatening thing affecting everybody is certain ideas coming from outside. We don't mind washing machines and telephones and cars and aeroplanes, that is a different matter altogether; but ideas shaking and weakening our close family relationships should be stopped at once. Let us not forget that good family relationship is the foundation of civilisation.

'We know how our women should behave. We don't need lessons from other cultures. Our Sita from the Ramayana, is a model for all our women. The police can tell you about the kind of freedom and rights those countries are advocating. I heard about Flower Power too.

'Let us not beat about the bush, it is a licence for people to do as they damn well please. Give freedom to donkeys and see what they make of it. *Should* freedom be the main goal of life? What about responsibilities, obligations, duties, affection, caring?'

Devi's stomach fell. What is happening? She asked herself and coughed. She moved about in her chair.

46

How did this heated argument start? What is its purpose? What is the matter with my family? It is times like these that she wished she had her husband's wisdom. If he were here, she was sure, this would never have taken place.

Sona had kept quiet all the while, but wanted the present company to understand that she was also an 'educated woman'. After all, in spite of her age and background, she did go to that fine establishment, Naparima Girls' High School. Sona Teelucksingh was the first Indian girl in her village to do so. She sat tall, pulled her ornhi closer and spoke with as much confidence she could muster. She was nervous and was only making the effort to support her husband. Perhaps the name Sita reminded her of where her wifely duty lay. Sita's virtues and loyalty to her husband, Rama, had formed the very pivot of her being.

'Let me say from the start that I am not referring to my niece, who is an outstanding exception. However, I have been noticing how good young students go abroad,' she lifted her head, 'and when they come back, you will find a big difference. What do you see? I will tell you. They lose the respect and good manners for their parents and elder relatives that they had when they left. They come back thinking that three, four years abroad have made them better than us. They begin to question everything as if God had opened a whole book of truths only to them about everything in this community. It is frightening that they are so shallow, accepting foreign ways and dismissing their parents without reflecting upon the meaning of things, the purpose they serve. Our young people are trying to become somebody else. The way they walk and dress

47

and talk is painful to see. It grieves me that while they believe they are ultramodern, they are mindless, without depth, equating satisfaction from a life well lived, with having a good time, with fun. Is that a worthy life? There *are* exceptions and as I have said already, my niece is one of them.'

She looked around, avoided her husband's eyes, but turned her attention to the smiling photograph of Mr Nadir, hanging on the wall before her. 'All I have left to say is this: if using these words I hear over and over – freedom, independence, rights and empowering the individual – means losing regard for others, pushing your ideas in that proud, haughty way, which is the same as pushing yourself above everyone else, there is a savagery about it.

'Young people should have a little conscience. Their parents sacrificed everything and offered them the best start in life they could manage. It is humiliating to hear how they criticise them. Parents bear it all. They just continue quietly to give the remainder of their lives to their children and grandchildren. I can't bear it. I just can't bear it. Forgive me.' Sona broke down and left the room. Devi accompanied her.

'Your aunt talks very good sense.' Mr Sukesh Walli said to Vasti.

'Yes, Mr Walli,' she replied, 'I am fortunate in having an aunty who observes, thinks and is discerning. Yet, how to keep what is of enduring worth that our parents and grandparents have been the custodians of, requires one to be constantly thoughtful and alert. The problem arises Mr Walli when we adopt trivia simply because the rich countries indulge in it or because it is new. Also . . .'

'You are also speaking very good sense like your aunt. You will be a great asset to our Clinic.'

'You have been very patient, Mr Walli, and I wish to thank you for this and for your understanding. Please convey my regards and best wishes to your sisters.'

'Thank you, Vasti. They have inherited my mother's good looks, but me, not too much came my way. They are looking forward to meeting you, to welcoming you to our home. Well, that should not be too long now.'

Mr Sukesh Walli stood up. The tone was right, it was time to leave.

That night, as Vasti lay in bed, she completed her interrupted sentence in her head. 'The problem also arises, Mr Walli, in what to leave behind. There are many things that our parents have carried that we no longer require; they have lost their usefulness and belong to the past. Some are even harmful, in that they are limiting, forcing us to have an identity that fits into a small box, with space only for one tick. I do not want boxes, Mr Walli, I want the open skies.'

CHAPTER SIX

Exorcising the Past

THE FOLLOWING DAY my eyes opened too early. I had wanted to gather myself, knowing that after breakfast, my mother would be waiting patiently to hear that I was now ready. Once this was done, Uncle Kash would convey our consent to the Wallis. The date would be decided and both families would begin the elaborate planning arrangements for the wedding.

The altar would be freshly made, the preferred choice being a place not polluted by former use. Virginal. It would be decorated with coloured rice in intricate motifs of life-giving flowers and symbols of large meanings, compacted to an abstraction. Incense, ghee, the perfume of pitch pine, marigold and ripe red roses would bring that bouquet of distinctive scents to my wedding.

The positioning of the altar, relative to the rising sun, directs the seating of the Pundit, the placing of the bride and bridegroom and their parents. On the appointed day and at the auspicious time, the Pundit would invite the gods to join with the guests and witness the sacrament, the vows taken.

As time crept by, I felt the heavy weight of the past pressing down upon me. I wondered where was the source of the mighty stream whose tributaries flow into every aspect of life to render females less worthy than males. There was biology. There was also the denial to women of the martial tradition of power, choice and control, without which their worth is reduced and their feet directed to the common people's gate – an exit for expendable citizens.

I began to wonder how the Inca maidens about to be sacrificed on the crest of mountains felt as their time came. Were they fêted beforehand, honoured in songs and words?

How had I got into this situation? Was it through Uncle Kash's sense of duty? Or was it my mother's anxiety about her daughter reaching her twenty-seventh birthday without a husband? Had it become a weighty family consideration? Had I become a problem to be addressed?

In the dark stillness of approaching dawn, my thoughts left my room and climbed the distant mountain which my window overlooked. As I sought the source of that stream that floods women's paths, reduces our strength, impedes our steps, I found myself moving back in time . . .

In my waking dream, I am walking along plâteaux, climbing up and down hills. It is becoming colder, the terrain steep, jagged – perilous. I have joined a caravan not of camels, but of silent women burdened by the weight of the baggage they carry. Their tired feet shuffle and drag. On either side, custom-made iron bars keep the women in place. I am too overburdened. My feet are tired, too weak to lift.

On and on all day we walk. As night falls, I see lanterns ahead. On reaching them, the bars on either side have given way to glass cubicles. Young girls, young female infants are entering. I am myself attracted to one of the cubicles with a fragrant-sounding name: *Sweet Rosebuds*. I am about to enter but am forcibly stopped by two women. I peer through the wide clear glass.

I see a little girl, no more than four years old; her tiny foot is being folded as if it were an oblong napkin. A napkin is a napkin, and will fold easily, but the tiny foot of a four year old albeit tender, soft as petals, cannot be folded into two.

'It cannot be done. Leave her! Her foot is not a napkin, you silly cow!' I find I am shouting.

'Keep looking. Look there – look! It *can* be done. Watch carefully.' I am joined by a middle-aged Chinese woman. 'It needs to be broken in the middle first The breaking is about to begin.' She speaks calmly. 'Unlike the napkin, it is not folded upwards, but downwards so that all four small toes, and the largest toe, reach the sole of the heel. See?' She demonstrates with her left hand, by bending her fingers inwards to touch the lower palm of the hand, close to her wrist.

'How is it kept there?'

'By a certain thinking.'

'Are you crazy?'

'Stop talking. Just watch. This is custom. Observe the skilful tight criss-cross bandaging and sewing; it does not merely hold the folded feet in place, but with each agonising step the infant takes, the bandage will tighten and tighten further still and so, in this painfully slow way, the child is forced to crush her own toes which eventually die, becoming wasted muscle and bone. A new skin grows. In time, this shoe that is being fitted will be taken away and a smaller size forced upon her. This will continue until her feet becomes a sweet rosebud.'

With a force from the wild, the child is trying to pull her feet away, but they are held tightly by another pair of hands. She is crying out. 'No! No! No! Mama, Mama, help me. Mamamaaa.' I am banging on the glass. 'Stop it! Stop it, you fiends! For God's sake, stop it.' I am kicking the glass. The Chinese woman walks briskly away from me.

An old woman is stifling the child's screams. A handkerchief is placed firmly over her mouth and held there. The infant struggles. Stern old eyes disapprove of the infant's tears and screams. The child sobs, her voice and face are shaking. Her mother is also being held back by firm hands. Young eyes are pleading. The child now looks at the old woman who withdraws her handkerchief. 'Please Grandma, please take it off, Grandma. It is hurting me.' Her lips tremble. Tears are streaming down her neck. 'Please help me, Grandma.'

'I *am* helping you,' the old woman says. 'You will be the bride of a wealthy, successful man. You will not live in poverty or disgrace.'

'Oh, yes? But how on earth will she walk? How can this child possibly walk? You there! *You*! Remove the bandage at once!' I am banging against the glass. 'Remove the bandage!'

I stop banging and I plead. My voice is breaking. My eyes are overflowing. 'Please, for God's sake remove it! She doesn't want this. How will she walk? Please I beg you. Please remove it, she is but a child.'

The old woman looks at me with such scorn in her eyes, it is easy to believe I am a mad dog.

'She is a child!' I shout. 'She is only a child.' I rush to the entrance, banging, banging. I am screaming, 'Stop it, stop it. For God's sake stop it!' I look around, there is no one but me. In the distance I see the Chinese woman disappearing. I run and run, calling out to her. She turns.

'You again? What is it now?'

'*Sweet Rosebuds? Sweet Rosebuds?* Please explain. What is it? Why?'

She takes some time to speak, as if she were rewinding her memory. 'In Old China, the criteria of excellence for feet are that they should be tiny, plump, soft, fine, perfectly formed lotuses. Wealthy men, prosperous men, men of high status prefer their wives feet to be so.'

'Why?'

She clears her throat. Again she takes such a long time to speak that I decide she has given up on me when I hear her say, 'You know what a rosebud is, I assume? I also assume you know the shape?'

'Of course,' I reply, regaining my confidence from my understanding of rosebuds.

'When your foot is so shaped, it has lost its ability to walk, but it is now able to fulfil another function.' She coughs delicately. I am none the wiser, nevertheless she continues, 'And so, delight, bliss and ecstasy can now be offered.'

'To whom?' I ask. She has become exasperated. When I decided to use some commonsense.

'To the husband that is, is it not?' I say reassuringly. An intuitive knowing smile comes to me, though I am still quite hazy about ancient China. Then to my surprise I hear myself say, 'And what to the wife?'

I do not believe she heard me for she is really not a bad sort. Perhaps I was speaking too softly. She just moved quietly away as if I am far too simple-minded to see what is clearly there to see.

Once more I am alone. The shutters of the other cubicles are pulled down. It is dark. I see a light in the distance. There is another cubicle not yet closed. I walk quickly towards it. It is called *The Bondo Sisters*.

Sisters bonding, I think it means. I feel the need for some bonding.

There is no doubt that these Bondo sisters are important women, serious women, well dressed women with grand, flamboyant headdresses which resemble rare tropical butterflies, as the overhead fan creates wings.

'No!' they cry. They are emphatic that I cannot stay with them in the cubicle.

I explain that I would like to bond with them.

'Are you one of us?'

'Sisters? Yes.'

'Bondo sisters?'

'Is this a society? Can I become a Bondo sister?'

'She is wasting our time. One look at her and you know. She is not a Bondo sister.'

'Sorry, you must leave.'

'Can I join? I would like to join.'

'We heard you. We have ears that function.'

'And much else beside.'

They laugh.

The woman in charge speaks with her eyes to another Bondo sister. There is a hostile silence. I am pushed out forcefully and speedily. I do not qualify for bonding. So

from the outside I peer in at them. They are asking me
to leave by making flapping signals with their hands,
brushing me away as if I were a fly. Then they write in
large letters. *THIS IS OUR CULTURE. GO AWAY.
SEEK YOUR OWN.* I see a young girl being led to a
table. She is asked to lie down.

A woman from Sierra Leone joins me. She stands like
an upright candle. 'What is going on?' I ask.

'The clitoris will be removed. They will then stitch
up the labia. This is a tribal ritual.'

'Surgery?'

'No – savagery.'

'Why?'

'It is a man's world.'

'The clitoris?'

She stares at me and says nothing.

I clear my throat. 'I'm not a medical student, but I
can find out in the library.'

'The library eh?' She carries herself with grace. I can
see that she doesn't know whether to laugh or cry.
There is something peaceful about her. 'Don't trouble
yourself, sister. I understand. You need help all the way.
You are like these young women,' and she points to the
cubicle. Looking at me as if I have come from a different planet, she whispers something about the pleasure
of males, their satisfaction and priorities. I say, 'Is there
also male surgery?' She walks quietly away. I cannot say
why I seem to be giving offence, for I really do try and
speak clearly and ask nicely for an explanation of the
things I see. Yet it seems that it is my questions that are
causing a problem.

Again I look into the glass cubicle. Another young
girl is being brought by her mother; she awaits her

turn. Her entrance is being delayed. I observe what is causing it. The women are seriously engaged at the table. Two large women are holding down both legs of the young girl, who is wiggling like a crushed worm. Her mouth is covered over. A strange sound struggles out of her. Her body shakes, her thighs tremble violently. This girl is a fighting tigress. Another guttural cry escapes her. A large woman comes and squeezes the young girl's mouth; her fingers are iron pincers. I realise it is surgery without anaesthetic; when the knife is lifted, it is red. The floor is being cleaned. The sobbing patient is carried out on a stretcher.

The waiting girl is being taken to the table. I keep knocking at the glass, to draw her attention. She looks at me. I signal to her. I wave my hand. I move my head. I say, 'Leave now! Leave! Run! Hurry!' Again I am beating the thick glass. The women look up, they see me and the one with the knife leaves the cubicle and comes towards me. She raises her arm. I cry out.

I woke up trembling and shaken. How relieved I was to find myself at home in my own bed. For the first time, my arranged marriage seemed a calm affair, the process a logical and reasonable one from the perspective of those whose affections had sustained me.

I had travelled far and I was tired, but there was one other place my unconscious self, my spirit, really wanted to go. My Intuitive Feeling would fly on the wings of Imagination and I would come to an ancient time. What would I find there? *Had there ever been a time when we women were as worthy as the men?* Could I ever find out how our worth was lost? How it all began . . .

So that morning after breakfast, I went to my mother as a child would — as if I was still walking in that column of silent women. I thanked her for all the effort and care she had given me throughout her life, gladly and willingly, despite the enormity of the undertaking. She helped me to become a thinking healthy human. And I said. 'I'm ready, Ma. You may tell Uncle Kash.'

My mother surprised me. She did not immediately embrace me and say, 'You are doing the right thing.' Instead she said, 'I wish your father was here. If he were here I would not worry. It is times like these, I miss his thinking. I know you are not at ease. What can I say? I married your father without seeing him even once. I was brought up to please. I had no life that was mine. I was a part of everybody else's life. I lived as if I were a plant. I grew, I blossomed, I bore fruit. I do not know if plants think. I can see the Wallis do not think as you do. This troubles me, Vasti. But Dr Karan Walli is an educated man and your father oh so often said that education was all we had . . . I am only too well aware that it is not enough.'

For a moment I was tempted to say that Dr Walli was not an educated man. He had a vocation. Yet how unkind, how unfeeling that would have been. Would I then have given my definition of what it is to have professional skills to be able to perform a task, followed by what it means to be truly educated, in order to display some superiority at my mother's expense? How callous, foolish and arrogant can the educated young be? More often than not we acquire only an outward

58

sophistication that is but an empty shell and we so easily become thoughtless, gross, bombastic when we converse with our parents.

'Yes, Ma, education *is* the best thing we have. It should teach us to observe with care and to change our minds with the evidence.'

'Yes, Vasti, those are your father's words.'

CHAPTER SEVEN

I Speak to the Gods

MY MOTHER BELIEVED in prayer, and I, being a dutiful daughter, walked beside her. In the early mornings, within the white walls of Shiva's temple, in Tunapuna, the stillness was timeless. There the imaginative reflections by sculptors of the Omnipotent, were held in granite and marble. These varying forms of the Divine watched my entrance. I bowed. They did not speak – lost in a reverie. Cold. Unadorned – without fresh garments and flowers, with no warm incense nor softly flickering lights, the gods did not stir.

'You are the first to come,' the keeper would say. 'The temple still sleeps.' How could he turn away a young devotee? No, he couldn't. So my encounters with the gods were always intimate. I saw them in their nakedness, in the quiet of their abode. In this sanctum, my thoughts and theirs were closely intertwined. And when I left with the dawn I took their contemplative assurances and made them mine: 'The world is what it is. We are here, creations of your thoughts, and you are there. Plant strong trees, while searching for the Omniscient One. Trees that are vigorous, strengthened by the earth and your hands, that they may withstand the raging floods to come. We see nothing else for nothing else is there.'

It was my mother's idea to walk to the temple and circle its inner walls with salutations and offerings of flowers and rice. Upon each rectangular enclave where the gods stood, my warm, clasped hands poured offerings. These images made flesh had travelled over hazardous seas, from the port of Calcutta to Trinidad, endured their carriers' misery and servitude. Once more in their proper place, they were honoured and saluted in chants and epics, with ripe flowers and incense.

Amongst the gods was the demigod Nandi, calm and unconcerned – an outlook seen in fields and stables. The sculptor had raised his front right leg to provide sufficient leverage of relief to his bovine bulk. My warm palms patted his forehead, which was icy cold. Nandi looked ahead of me into the future, oblivious of the present.

For the birds, I left bananas and they flew down from the burnished copper dome with shuffling wings and sounds of satisfaction, strutting and striding, pecking and chasing. The faith of my ancestors was honoured and Shiva's temple heard my request for 'guidance in this large undertaking'.

With just over one week remaining before the wedding ceremony, much was already in place. The two men responsible for preparing the wedding feast had chosen the site for the fireplace, which had to be built sufficiently large to hold two huge iron pots comfortably. When full, four skilled arms would lift each cauldron from the burning wood with strong rope. The tarwa or baking stone for the parathas had a circumference of two and a half metres.

61

The hearth was dug; a mound of red lateritic clay bore witness. A tall canvas covering offered the open hearth protection from any unlikely tropical downpour. A truck brought pumpkins, bags of rice and flour and split peas, jars of spices and tins of cooking oil, and ghee, dry coconuts. Cars, trucks and jitneys unloaded bamboo, crockery, cutlery, drinking glasses, chairs, tables and sheets of canvas. Flowers, succulent vegetables, gallons of fresh milk and yogurt would come much later. Men and women came and went. Discussions, arguments, fury, words of thanks and appreciation danced about the yard and entered the house. My mother and Pushpa managed it all.

Fine jewellery is costly and wedding jewellery more so. It was a cost my mother was asked by me to forego. From an early age I took pleasure in travelling light, and jewellery was an encumbrance to me. As this was well known, I managed, with Pushpa's help, to get my mother to agree that I would borrow Pushpa's wedding jewellery for the day. However, to celebrate the occasion, my mother asked that I design a set of six bracelets, a necklace and a single armband. This opportunity to create pieces of jewellery occupied me for a short while. I copied an old necklace that had once belonged to my Great-grand Ajee. It was passed on to the eldest daughters of each generation. As my Ajee had no daughters, she gave the bracelet to her eldest son, my father, to be worn by his wife. My mother wore it well and it enhanced her. Pushpa wore it on her wedding day. I wanted to have a lighter version of it and I worked on this for quite a while.

I was copying from a necklace of intricate filigree-work linking gold pendants on a gold chain. Each pendant was a lotus flower progressively unfolding itself, so that perfect open blooms, with petals in dispositions to delight, circled the front of the wearer's neck, while the tiniest of opening buds embraced the nape at the back.

My sketches had been taken to SINGH'S JEWELLERY ESTABLISHMENT, which is what Mr Singh called his jewellery shop on number 68 Eastern Main Road in Tunapuna. Over the years, the craftsmanship of our jeweller brought us much pleasure, and our confidence in him grew, but with the wedding so close and not having yet seen the jewellery, my initial anxiety increased. I was particularly worried about the length of the necklace: were it a little long or short, the beauty of the pattern would be lost. I also wanted to see how my design looked, crafted in gold. The thickness and form of the armband as well as its comfortable fit were my concerns.

Old Mr Singh would have delivered the jewellery to me personally, as was the custom, but neither of his two assistants had been in the shop that week. And so rather than wait another day, and fearing that certain things might need to be altered, I said I was quite happy to visit his workshop, for which he was grateful. My mother wanted Pushpa to accompany me but the amount left to be done pressing heavily upon all, I was permitted to visit Mr Singh's workshop accompanied by two young female helpers from Pasea village. For the bride to leave the sanctuary of the house so close to the wedding day was against custom but I was thankful that my mother understood the reason for my anxiety. In obtaining her permission, I dared to think that Pushpa and Shami and I were having some influence upon her.

At the workshop, my chaperones were delighted with the pleasurable shapes of the jewellery and the multifaceted gems on display in the glass cases, and were soon in awe of Mr Singh.

He opened a box and from a parcel of soft tissue produced bright yellow gold bracelets and an armband that smelt of warmth and antiquity. He asked me to extend my arms and slipped the armband up on to the left one and then three bracelets on each arm. They were a copy of my mother's wedding bracelets, but as I had requested, thinner and lighter – a knob of gold extensively hammered, chiselled and punched into a cluster of florettes. Mr Singh was clearly a magician. The bracelets and armband made my arms glow. I indulged myself for a minute or so, allowing the bracelets to skate merrily along my extended limbs. It was the first time I had ever wished I had a dozen bracelets, for the beauty and warmth of his craftsmanship had brought to my limbs an ancient grandeur, which seduced me.

And while I played with my wedding jewellery, he took my folded necklace out of a deep blue velvet pouch. With both hands, he held it up, opening it out as if it were alive, its light form swaying with ease. Mr Singh had created a streak of light in a string. Later, in the mirror I saw that the lotus petals did not twist or turn; each lotus settled close to me, the designer of their form. The leaf veins – their pouting tips and the scalloped edges – were delicately done. The length was perfect. I could have embraced him with gratitude, so great was my pleasure. But I did as custom prescribed and thanked him warmly, saying how very happy he had made me. 'Far, far more than I can

64

possibly express,' I said, and for a moment a wisp of my misgivings escaped, camouflaged by a cloak of relief at seeing this perfection. 'This brings a pleasure more profound, Mr Singh, than anything I can think of.'

Mr Singh was overcome by this tribute so sincerely made, and though sensing that all was not well, he knew the boundaries of etiquette that not even an old friend of the family should cross.

That my own design and Mr Singh's craft should have brought me the joy that my coming wedding failed to do, and that I should have expressed this so openly was, with hindsight, the first recognised surface tremor of a large eruption that had already begun within me.

CHAPTER EIGHT

An Eagle in Flight

WITHOUT WARNING, VASTI'S distress had risen to the surface. She seemed unsteady. Mr Singh offered her a chair and while she rested, her chaperones sat quietly with her. He busied himself cleaning and polishing a number of fine gold rings. 'Whose are those?' she asked, in an attempt to regain her former composure.

He was about to place them in their separate boxes when he changed his mind and brought them to her. 'You may have seen these before, or at least one or two of them,' he said.

'I shall tell you.'

The rings were placed in a row before her.

'Fine rings,' Mr Singh said. 'I fashioned them all.'

Each ring displayed a powerful motif: a globe, a crown, two swords crossed; one was set with small emeralds, the other a single sapphire. Not knowing whose they were, she explained that she could not recall having seen any of these before but commented on his craftsmanship, which brought a smile to his face.

It was then that Mr Singh brought forth another ring saying, 'Aha! I'm sure, you have seen this one. It is liked by many I heard.'

Vasti stared at the ring as if it had turned into a cobra, slowly raising its head, its tongue, flicking rapidly in and out to reach her. She moved it at arm's length, trying to get rays of the incoming daylight upon it. Then equally slowly she brought it forward and let it lie still. There before her was the ring she had drawn and described in her diary. The very one she once looked for on every male finger, secretly becoming the youngest village detective, driven by a childlike endeavour to discover what a rapist looked like.

The passage of time and the demands of living meant that the incident had drifted into the cooler spheres of her memory. But this was a sudden seabed eruption; its depths were furiously stirred and the incident rose to the surface – whole, intact, preserved. And the heat of that terrible day returned to her and Vasti began to perspire.

There, crouching in the cane-field, binoculars well-focused: the eagle's wings outstretched, its searching eyes, beak and claws displaying a mastery of air and land. On its back a scroll of ancient writ.

'Ah,' said the genial Mr Singh, 'I can see you, too, are mesmerised by it.'

She swallowed, willing herself to take control. With a voice fearful of losing itself, she asked for a pencil and paper, then drew what was before her as accurately as she could. Several sketches were made while Mr Singh returned to packaging the rings for delivery. 'Do all these belong to the same person?' she enquired.

'Oh, so you do not know the owner of the winged scroll?'

'No! It was an unexpected find.'

'Yes. I can see it fascinates you.'

'Whose rings are they?' she asked, dreading the answer. At last she would know who had violated that sobbing, screaming schoolgirl pleading with the wearer of the ring.

'I am once more surprised,' Mr Singh said, smiling warmly, 'for the good-looking Dr Karan Walli, soon to be your husband, enjoys wearing this one. It is only a matter of days now, isn't it, before the happy occasion?'

From the age of six, Vasti had acquired the discipline of fasting, of denying herself sustenance for eighteen hours before the celebration of the birth of Shiva, when delicious savoury foods and quality sweets were enjoyed. This training in restraint, and the detective in her, masked well her inner turmoil.

'Why do you think, Mr Singh, that Dr Walli likes this design?'

'Look at the motif – an eagle is the emperor of the skies.'

Yes, she thought, primeval energy in motion, programmed to kill.

'Why the scroll?'

'You, an educated girl, asking me this? You are not yourself today, I can see that. It is the Word of God in flight from Heaven to Earth. What else? Is it not clear?'

But where birds of prey are God's carriers, Vasti thought, will power not be absolute? What has happened to the doves?

'How many rings of the winged scroll have you made?' she asked slowly.

'Oh, just the one. These are all Dr Karan Walli's. There is an agreement between us – he pays a special price and I do not reproduce them for anyone.' This arrangement was further emphasised by movements

68

from his head and right hand. 'Dr Walli likes wearing something unique.'

'Mr Singh, please think hard. Are you sure you have not made another like it?'

'I gave him my word and my word is my oath.'

'That is commendable. Tell me, Mr Singh, would you be able to say when you made this ring for Dr Walli?'

'Now let me see . . . I made it for him when he was in his early twenties, I think. It is definitely one of the first ones – twelve or thirteen years ago, perhaps, maybe even further back. And how do I know? At one time he came and asked me to make another one exactly like this; then on the very next day he changed his mind. I guessed that he would change his mind again, for he was very earnest the first time. That is why I have kept a long string on the page of that drawing, the better to find it again. It is in an old file on the topmost shelf. All my work is dated, Miss Nadir. Good accounting safeguards everybody – me, and my customers. I say this to my assistants every day.'

CHAPTER NINE

The Tide is Turning

BACK HOME, LYING in bed, beneath the pillows, that violent scene returned to her. And Vasti began to wonder whether her very sanity was being threatened. A month ago she had agreed to marry Karan Walli.

At that time, she believed she could accept this arrangement without losing the integrity of her inner voice. She would work on each day as it came. With this in mind, she was hoping to offer her marriage a fair chance of succeeding, by finding a way that would allow her to teach without offending the Wallis. After the Sunday lunch, however, she became apprehensive. Nevertheless, she moved with the rest of the family for she could not see a way out for herself. This forced her to consider whether working in the Clinic might prove to be a worthwhile undertaking. Her doubts remained, but these misgivings she bore in silence.

Vasti recalled the forceful way in which she had displayed her feelings at the jeweller's shop, even before she saw the rings. To have expressed herself so clearly, and to someone outside her intimate circle, was careless and improper. After the disclosure – that hot day in the sugar-cane field returned vividly with its mix of fear, empathy and revulsion.

It was clear that a part of her was unaware that she had agreed to go through with the wedding or was simply refusing to accept it. She wondered whether she was beginning to lose that fine grasp of judgement, of discernment, which is about knowing what and when and how to express oneself. It was a troubling thought.

Could she even now at this eleventh hour and on the basis that a decision made under intense pressure was invalid, bring everything to a halt? Yet the case against her was: why did she not *say no, on that Sunday*, when the Wallis were here? Then again it was after her nightmare that she went to her mother and said, *I am ready*.

And now to contemplate ending it? Such a disgraceful act would bring a colossal humiliation on Ma, who had taught her how to walk and talk and read and write, given her mirth and opened jars of joy for her tasting, saying, 'This is also life's blessing.'

Nothing of pain was ever knowingly brought to her by her mother; Devi protected her daughter from ugliness by being her own upright self, becoming a wall so that her child might walk in her shade at midday, and be shielded from life's many sorrows. She it was who had clapped with delight when Vasti had first recited her multiplication tables and sung *Humpty Dumpty sat on a wall*. She who, when her husband came home, asked the little girl to recite it again before him, encouraging him with nods to applaud louder. So proud was she, as if these sounds had never been made before and therefore the child's voice was a miracle.

And now, with the closing of her autumn years what would Vasti bring her?

There was no escape. For her beloved mother's mental health and physical wellbeing, Vasti would have to endure this unknown future amongst her new family, as brides had done before her.

Gradually, Vasti's troubled breathing slowed and numbness overcame her. It was as if her mind were producing its own anaesthetic to cope with what was to come. Yet as she fell into sleep, the image of the cane-field hurled itself before her again and again and time stood still. The night was long.

What could she say to her mother . . . to Pushpa? She could not give them the diary, it would merely perplex them. That she had stayed there in hiding and closely watched the rape as it happened, would seem to them inconceivable. She was of an age to discern between right and wrong.

To have seen this abomination at such close quarters sullied her. To have crouched with a powerful pair of binoculars, finely focused upon an impure act in its fullness, was unthinkable for a well brought up, middle-class, Form Two student of St Ursula's Convent. St Ursula's! A model school, its past students amongst the fine physicians, attorneys-at-law, artists and musicians, wherever they were. She was convinced that not a single other St Ursula girl would have been so foolish. What on earth could have possessed her? What had held her there? 'Oh God,' she cried, as desolation whirled round her.

Her inner voice whispered: 'Even were I to relate it as best I could, they would say: "That was a long, long time ago. Besides, men are like that. It was just a one-off thing. Do you carry no forgiveness in your heart? And then again you judge him not knowing whether he was seduced, unwittingly perhaps, but seduced nevertheless.'"

Were she to protest, 'I was there, I saw and heard. It is not as you say,' what could she do with only a week to go? The large bamboo tent had been firmly erected, the chairs and tables were in place, the vegetables and sweet-meats ordered . . . What a waste! What a loss! And the guests – the entire village. Did she have the heart to put her mother through such an ordeal? No.

There was a long silence within her. Vasti got out of bed and stood before the window, gazing at the vast darkness of space. The travelling light of stars reached her and drew her up. She was flying through space – amidst the planets, the Milky Way, distant rays like pathways, on and on and on. Her imagination reached deep into the universe to make sense of it, but infinity was too large, too cold, so strangely different in immeasurable ways. She returned to earth. Stilled.

The boundless immensity had brought a new sense of herself as a minuscule living thing, yet an intelligent life form. All living things are unique in our planet, she thought. Therefore I shall not waste my very being. I will offer it an opportunity to reveal itself. Mr Sukesh Walli wants me to work in his Clinic, but I do not wish it. He will be disappointed and unhappy if I say no. Later, his animosity and that of his sisters, and his son will heighten. The pain created will be so destructive. Why should I allow this to befall me?

I *cannot* marry Karan Walli, she thought fiercely. No one understands what I saw on that last day of term. They were not there. He is arrogant, cruel and empty. Is there not anything that a man should never do, even once? I need to be free from these cultural ties. I will ask for nothing. Let me choose the direction my life should go, the path I should walk. I cannot marry him. I will not marry him . . . such a man! I will not! My very life, they are saying, is not mine. Who decides on my life? It is mine, not theirs! Mine. This life, I will not hand it over to Karan Walli. I will not lose it. Yet how can I escape this net without entangling my mother and Pushpa? Dear God, it is too late.

An overwhelming tiredness came upon her. Vasti closed the window and went back to bed; her head ached, her temperature was beginning to rise. She sought a blanket, for despite the fever, she was trembling. Vasti Nadir was feeling chilled to the very bone.

CHAPTER TEN

A Mehndi Artist

THE NEXT MORNING, the Mehndi artist, Rojani, slowly climbed the steep, red terrazzo steps of Devi Nadir's bungalow. On reaching the front patio, she pulled at the shifting bodice of her flowered pink dress, and looked into the hanging mirror on the wall. Rojani smiled at her comely face, the middle parting of her shining hair and the neat bun at the side of her head, decorated with a freshly plucked orange hibiscus flower.

She stood erect and called, while her keen eyes seemed to be searching for something. She had in her basket, a pair of glasses used for intricate work, a book of designs and a box of cones for painting the feet and palms of the bride-to-be with henna paste. Pushpa welcomed her and explained that Vasti was unwell:

'All night she had a roasting fever and a trembling. She still has a temperature, and is feeling very weak.'

'Why don't you then, elder sister, choose a pattern for her now? It will help me when I come tomorrow.'

'I cannot choose for Vasti. What I can say that may help you is, she will choose something simple.'

'I do not recommend simple designs for weddings. A wedding is a grand occasion. You should appreciate that. Look at its full meaning. Have you thought of that? When people ask on that special day and you say it is Rojani's art, they will get the wrong impression of my work. I am a true artist. I know what is suitable for every occasion . . . A simple design for a wedding is not advisable. It may even bring bad luck.'

Rojani shook her head knowingly, then smiled broadly.

'Maybe it is cold feet, na?,' she asked. 'That is so common. Nerves play up. A lot of the modern girls are not coping well with arrangements. The problem is what to put in its place. Our custom does not allow girls to go to parties and so on, as they do overseas; how then will they meet anyone? On the other hand, at that age they are too impressionable. A fella only has to say some nice things a couple of times and they fall like ripe mangoes. So I am asking these modern reformers, who think they have all the answers – what are parents to do? Fortunately your sister travelled far and wide and has come back whole. Give praise to God as the Christians say.'

'Rojani, my sister is not well.'

'That I understand, but she is an educated girl and education makes all the difference. As a matter of fact, you should choose right now a complex and intricate pattern which would reflect her higher learning. For example, look here . . .'

'I'm sorry but I cannot choose for her. As I said, she has a strong fever – how can she choose?'

'You are looking very worried. It's nothing serious, I hope? I mean, nothing to prevent the wedding from taking place? After all, the name of this family is held in very high esteem in the village, so I can't see an educated girl doing anything foolish to bring shame and dishonour to her family.'

'This is just a strong fever which has not yet cooled down. It is worrying.'

'You think the fever will spread to her brain? Is that your concern?

'We do not know, Rojani.'

'Well, is that all then?'

'I'm sorry, Rojani, it can't be helped.'

'Is she very bad then?'

Why can't you understand? You are asking the same question over and over again.

'Rojani, my husband has called the doctor, we will see what he says.'

'I will be waiting to hear from you. You know it should be done today, but if not today, definitely tomorrow. That means very valuable time will be taken up in choosing and discussing. That is why I always put aside one day for this. I don't charge for this day. People don't know how to make up their minds. Half the time I have to help them, otherwise I am there all day.'

'My sister, when she is well, will make up her own mind with ease.'

Rojani cleared her throat 'So that is all then?'

'Yes, Rojani. I am very sorry. You must understand, there are some things we can't predict.'

A visible anxiety was flowing from the Mehndi artist.

'I do not like to have to say this, but I think it is better to bring everything into the open, just in case of any misunderstanding. I like to be straight. That way, you understand me and I understand you. You see, this Mehndi art is a complex art. A lot of skill is involved. I am a professional artist. This is my living.'

'Together we will come to an agreement if Vasti gets worse. I will inform you early.'

'Today is already late. I could be somewhere else. This is mango season. This is wedding season. It is such a busy time for me. I cannot afford to lose out.'

'If Vasti does not improve, or if her illness gets worse, we will come to a compromise.'

'Compromises are all very well, but I hope you will consider what I would be losing if I am made to suffer with too much compromise.'

'You will find you have nothing to worry about.'

'I am a professional.'

'Rojani, how can I forget that? Don't worry.'

Rojani picked up her bag of cones and books and left, but not without a gracious salutation in praise of the god, Rama.

Vasti stayed in bed. Later that day, when her temperature dropped, she became restless and Pushpa walked with her in the garden. 'Look, Pushpa,' she exclaimed, shuddering. 'We have so many slugs – where have they all come from?'

'Show me one?'

'They are all over the place. Look.' Where she pointed, there were curled leaves lying in the grass.

Pushpa picked up one. 'It is a dry leaf, Vasti.'

Then as Vasti bent down to absorb the fragrance of a white rose, she stared at something on the rose bed. 'Oh no!' she exclaimed. 'Chase that toad away.'

And Pushpa saw a moss-green piece of wood partially submerged in the damp soil, at an angle. There were two knots which could have appeared as eyes, to a fevered brain. 'It is wood covered with moss,' she said gently. 'You need to rest, Vasti.'

An urgency seemed to grip the younger woman. 'Come, Pushpa, come to my room,' she said. 'I want to show you something.'

There were two windows in her upstairs bedroom. In one of them, was reflected an octagonal roof of glass. 'What is this?' Vasti demanded. 'I know it is not next door. I can see the reflection but not what it reflects.'

'Whatever glass reflects, has to be there,' her sister said calmly.

'I know that. Well, where is this roof? Come to this window which should be nearer to the source of the reflection, but look – nothing. Yet, further away, over here . . .'

'This, Vasti, is the reflection of the octagonal roof of a conservatory which has recently been built.'

'Where is it?'

'It is in Mr Warner's garden.'

'That's not next door, it's the house next to it, further down.'

'Yes. I cannot explain why this particular window captures it and not that other one.'

'Show it to me.'

'I will, Vasti, as soon as you are better. Today, you are not well and in order to see it, we will have to go over to Mr Warner.'

But before Pushpa could stop her, Vasti climbed on to the windowsill and leaned forward. To her astonishment there it was, with its eight aluminium struts holding the glass roof of the conservatory.

The fever returned that night.

CHAPTER ELEVEN

Through the Looking-Glass

THE VILLAGERS AWOKE to thunder, wind and rain. It stayed like that all day. The morning became dusk and the evening was night. Old lamps awakened domestic shadows; swaying lanterns on bullock carts travelled as cradles of light in the mist.

At Devi Nadir's place, powerful electric bulbs shone upon the erection of the large ceremonial tent and to the moulding of the tiered earthen altar. A few wondered whether these signs – an unusually cold wind for the time of year, electrically charged clouds, poor visibility and thunderous bursts – were inauspicious. And though they said nothing, they noted that lightning had flashed again and again. Three times and then another three times, as never before.

No one spoke, but questions hung in the air. What messages were the heavens trying to convey? What could it all mean? Faces were warm and moist, inscrutable, engaged fully in preparations. The heavy rainmist and the wind brought a sudden burst of coldness. Sensing their disquiet, Pushpa and Shami explained to the women helpers that the stormy weather they were experiencing had been forecast by the meteorological office and that though it would continue for the best part of the week, the Pundit had said that on the wedding day, the sun would shine if only for a brief moment, to bless the couple.

Meanwhile, Vasti stood at her window looking at the falling rain eroding the compacted clay and gravel before her. Fierce flashes would sharply light up the depth and width of the road, then total darkness would eclipse everything. She saw the nearby embankment struck, becoming as clear as day for an instant. The light seemed strangely alive, as if it were frolicking in the mist, playing peekaboo, choosing the next place to show itself.

From the wedding tent came a melody and darkness was seduced. The night was strange, spilling sad stirrings of sitar strings upon the rushing wind. The hibiscus swayed, the parrot tilted his head to catch the flow. The scent of camphor mingled with that of warm milk and cardamom, sweet basil, roses and marigolds. At this wedding house, the bright lights warmed the expectations of well wishers.

Vasti heard laughter and could feel the women's jollity, their helping hands, the reassurances and the banter of their men. The altar was already prepared by those who knew how: intricate patterns of coloured rice, the brass goblets containing water and mango leaves, the small hearths, scooped from the earth, filled with the sweet scent of a small pyre of pitch-pine and sandalwood. A banana sapling had been planted. All this would testify to the promises made: here lay an ancient rite brought across oceans and land that would call upon the very elements of our planet and the gods to bind and bless this interlocking of lives, this marriage.

Sacred, beautiful, time honoured. Carried with dignity by the family's Pundit. As the marriage ceremony progresses, the chorus of women will explain each rite in their songs. The tears of a mother fall fast at the measure of a daughter-in-law's life. The ceremony has lost neither its beauty nor profundity. This ancient rite will sanctify and bind the body, mind and intellect of the two beings who have chosen to walk together.

Vasti felt as if she was at present on a fast train. The next station was not far away. And there the wedding guests awaited her coming.

All day it continued wet and windy; the clouds thickened and a coldness descended into the valley. By seven o'clock the clouds had begun to break, with the wind gaining strength. Then the raised lantern of the moon showed itself fully and shone directly upon her. Vasti was forcibly pushed backwards, for she stumbled and fell before the mirror, now bathed in moonlight.

The young bride was taken aback to find the mirror radiant – reflecting a blue chair that she had never seen before. It was the clear, pure blue of the desert skies; in shape it could be a carver dining chair. The seat was upholstered; the back was of cane lattice. Slatted wooden uprights held the comfortable curving arms in place. As she stared into the mirror, Vasti saw the chair begin to transform itself, to become many similar chairs, yet each one unlike the other.

Instinctively, she moved backwards in the room to ascertain what the source of this reflection could possibly be, as was her way. She could see her own reflection moving back towards the chair. So engrossed was she on finding the quaint chair that she had walked backwards the length of her room several times over, unaware of this travail.

Two reflections held her – that of the chair, and that of herself. The mirror showed that although both were close, they had not yet touched. Impatient, Vasti turned around to investigate the true distance of the reflection behind her.

Then, as if a long-travelled light, reflected by the moon, had caught her in its powerful widening gyre, she was pulled by a whirlwind force, sucked into its vortex like a spinning leaf, lifted high, defying the force of gravity, following the light. When its magnetic force shifted, her body dropped.

Face downwards, Vasti collapsed into deep unconsciousness.

PART TWO

CHAPTER TWELVE

The King's Insignia Flies Alone

Jyotika

A PROLONGED DISCHARGE of artillery awoke Vasti. It sounded close. She lay still. Again and again the guns fired. Far-sounding bugles followed; then a mighty drumming. And when it ceased – a solemn emptiness descended.

Lifting herself from the cold marble floor, she stared around. Was this an outpost? A fort? There was no end to this spacious corridor, where dusk slept. Its high outer wall was perforated with designed clusters. Only through these vents, did sunlight see the inner passage where shadows played as branches waved and wings flapped. Way in the distance, swirling winds howled, travelling across sandy dunes and steep escarpments. On reaching the Fort of Jyotika, the wind had to rise over one hundred feet to climb its bastions and parapets on this rocky hillside.

As it descended, it made its cascading call into the inner-walled circuits, swaying the lids of heavy jars, rattling open containers, empty vessels, baskets piled high with fruit and vegetables, jute bags full of grains, covered carts and open carriers. It swooped and roared at long rows of temples, their gleaming brass cupolas and gold-painted shikaras crowded with fluttering red, white, pink and yellow flags; then it ran along the soldiers' barracks, leaped over the royal stable, shaking bridles and servant quarters; wound itself in and out of rest tents, through circles of tethering posts for the common man's travelling companion. At last unimpeded it rushed swiftly over wide open spaces in the ever spreading compound of the outermost courtyard.

Only then could the lively wind enter that sanctuary of royalty, with its many courtyards of walled sandstone screens, terraces and balconies, intricately carved and pierced on all sides with harmonious geometrical designs that softly sang with the morning light.

Though Vasti was still dazed, it was the finely chiselled sandstone screens high above her reach and the nearby sculptured marble pillars with their blue, green and pink veins, which signalled to her that she was far from home. Oil lamps on tall stands kept watch.

A column of menservants marched past, their proud heads in regal turbans of Indian yellow, vermilion, crimson and emerald green. Ahead of them, another detachment wore headdresses of cobalt blue and scarlet, burnt sienna and deep red. Into the blinding light and dazzling heat they marched, stamping over the sunbaked, red-brown earth. In the courtyard, their uniforms mourned, maidservants had woven bands of soft cotton in ivory black on each arm.

The open manner in which emblems of sorrow were being offered and received led Vasti to believe that a grave misfortune had befallen the place and its people. Preparations were being made to demonstrate their grief and loss in ceremony. Voices were hushed, adding sanctity to the air. What form would this ceremony take? A strange premonition came upon her as a wave on the seashore, and then as if a raised lantern was showing her the way, she thought she knew. *She had been here before.*

Light as the mountain mist that rises with the break of day, but as invisible as air, Vasti floated along the corridor at the speed of thought. Ascending carved stairways effortlessly, she was in and out of rooms, able to hear everything; even the whispers of thoughts reached her.

Inside the Queens' quarters, soft white curtains were embroidered with long-stemmed tulips in threads of blue and gold. She recognised the three Queens. Of the two Queens from the Northern Kingdoms, the elder, Queen Meena, musician and painter, carried a perfection of beauty that sculptors tried their best to imitate. Her complexion was flawless, silky waves of hair framed her forehead and covered her dangling antique pearl earrings; her head moved as if it carried a priceless pot. She was gentle, reserved and courtly even as she engaged with the other Queens. It was her upbringing. The centre pleats of her silk sari unfold gracefully, opening into musical fans with her soft steps.

Queen Dayita, once the Northern Kingdoms' prima classical dancer, wore a simple loose court gown in which she relaxed; her shapely eyes and dispositions in movement and stillness brought alive Rajasthani miniature paintings. Lithe as a bamboo and, when not performing, she was distilled energy contained. Her long, strong hair, massaged with almond oils and marigold fragrance, was gathered into a chignon. Here she walks proudly, round and round; her superior stance colours her attitude to everything outside herself.

89

The youngest of them all, the thoughtful, reticent scholar Queen Renu from the dark South, wore loose trousers and a long-sleeved blouse. Her long veil rested on her shoulder. Queen Renu, was standing on her own balcony, pleasantly engaged in trying to familiarise herself with the layout of the streets and to identify places by the shapes of their roofs. She was smiling at her inability to prevent her veil from becoming a billowing cape in the breeze.

Being the most recent addition to the King's family, Queen Renu tried to be well-disposed to the two Northern Queens. She was also the youngest, and that could have been the cause of a biting jealousy; she was treated with cool politeness as she had come from a Southern Kingdom, an unknown world to them, a place with an understanding outside their own, far removed from their reality. And so Queen Renu was regarded by them as a curiosity, almost as a non-person.

Dark-complexioned, she was not perceived as any kind of a threat by the Northern Queens, who understood neither the enchantment nor the appeal of the shades of dusk. And though Queen Renu was wise and amiable, a scholar who had not yet forgotten the purpose of scholarship, her worth could not be instantly appreciated by a provincial or untutored eye.

Vasti believed she knew what was to come, in this semi-arid Kingdom. Why? Was she from the future? Was this their present, that she had somehow entered?

It was like sitting through a play for a second time and finding engagement pleasurable in renewed anticipation. Yet, the mist of centuries passing had meant that many a detail and precise outcome were no longer clear to her – and for some unknown reason, she felt an intuitive anxiety.

Then the sound of rushed footsteps came and Vasti turned around and saw the young slave-girl, Kala. With her was Baalaajee, a scholar of five and twenty years, who carried her daughter Sujata in his arms. The child was struggling to get down to disengage herself from this stranger. All along the corridor were sculptured gods and goddesses: the God of Creation, the God of the Preservation of Mankind, the Goddess of Knowledge and Education, the God of Strength of Purpose, the Goddess of Enlightenment and of Wealth. As these three figures hurried past, they were bathed in the warmth and glow of oil lamps. Their faces gleamed. Baalaajee tried to comfort Sujata, but soothing words and gestures were not enough. Her disturbing cries persisted.

Earlier that morning, while Vasti lay unconscious on the cold floor, the three Queens in the Palace of Jyotika were looking through the marble screens of the topmost open-air courtyard to savour the coming dawn, to watch the passing scenes of horses, camels, royal elephants from the South; to view the armed cavalry departing and injured soldiers returning from the North-West front, where several cohorts of marauding tribes had been advancing upon the Kingdom's borders. All the while, Pundits, holy men, servants, water-carriers, traders and merchants with covered goods on bullock carts, came and went. The Sanskrit chants of early pujas, temple bells and rising wafts of flaming camphor reached the Queens as they awaited the return from battle of their King and consort.

Steadfast in the biting cold remnants of the desert night, the three royal wives waited, staring into the long distance as their future drew near.

Each breath was stilled as they saw His Majesty's personal standard coming towards them. It was not unfurled, not raised aloft in triumph; instead, it was lowered as a charging lance. The King's insignia, in carmine red and gold, was billowing in the wind, its rich magenta tassels tossing in wild frenzy. Pierced by the rising sun, the Royal flag was alight, a moving flame held low by a lone soldier on a black horse.

The speed with which the dispatch rider, on dismounting his black steed, was brought to court, spoke of the solemnity of his mission. The servants noticed the black velvet saddle-cloth, tassels of black silk decorating the bridle, his turban draped in black, the absence of the chain of gold on the horse's neck. Before the Queens, his salutation was subdued and low. Then the eldest, Queen Meena asked in a steady voice that he make known the reason for his presence.

'Loyal and faithful Queens of the Kingdom of Jyotika, my errand's weight is of great sorrow. This, I am now duty bound to place before you. Yet, how I wish it were not so. It was in the battlefield that death came to His Majesty. He had led his men from the front, charging after the sun left the horizon and our shadows became giants. Though one, he sprung upon the enemy as if a raging pride of tigers once blessed him with their art. Fearless he was. His courage and daring we followed, not wanting his shadow to ride alone. Again and again we broke into the enemy's column, attacking from all sides. Our loss was large, but theirs was larger still.

'And when they had retreated, broken and dispirited, when once again we were in command of our Kingdom's borders, we did not rejoice, nor did we praise God for killing our enemies. Instead, we returned to His Majesty's tent in silence. On his way, the King had asked that we respect and honour the soldiers who had given their lives for their country. Our deaths were to be remembered in the reporting, but all deaths, both our enemy's and our own, were to be respected in our silence. We were related to all we fought. His voice was faint, as he said, "Brothers in blood, we can use theirs in our veins and they ours. Peace," he breathed out. "We both need peace with honour."

'His voice seemed filled with the desert sand. It was then he fell off his horse and for the first time we saw how mortally wounded he had been, for he had made little of it and kept us going until victory was ours.

'Then death, jealous of life but generous with him, claimed him; just before, His Majesty called the second-in-command, and our serving Pundit. Slowly he lifted his head and asked that his brother Mahendra be crowned. His Majesty's dying words were, "May God's blessings be everlasting upon the new King, upon my own three Queens of Jyotika and upon the People and the Kingdom of Jyotika"

'The Royal cavalry escorting the King's carriage will be here in a day's time. I have been honoured to have ridden through the night on the Kingdom's fastest steed – His Majesty's horse Chapala, who seemed to understand after I shared my mission with him. Then he galloped with the wind as if it were his sails. Chapala offered his all that I may be here. Long Live the King.'

*

93

The Queens' deep affection for the King heightened their private grief. He was, as monarchs go, more generous and wise than most. And yet now, his widows must somehow disentangle their loss from the dire consequences of his death?

The bonds of marriage for the two Northern Queens must hold, not only 'in times of sickness or in health' but in death too, they must not be parted. However, this suttee – this immolation of a widow on a burning pyre with the body of her dead husband – had never been a custom in the Kingdom of the South-West from which Queen Renu hailed.

Queen Meena and Queen Dayita had always known and accepted that their affection and loyalty to the King must one day be sanctified by their becoming suttees. This had been the culture of their birth. It was in the nature of things, they would say, that men experienced the joys of natural birth, but not its pain; likewise, by virtue of being men they did not become suttees. It was a way of thinking, passed on through the years. It did not imply knowledge – for it might be only an assumption or a prejudice of antiquity, or of priests – but the rite of suttee was greatly respected for it wore that honoured cloak of custom.

The three women moved slowly indoors. Queen Renu, absolved by her tradition and culture from this ritual of death, felt very distressed as she walked back inside the Palace with her two sister Queens. It devastated her, to think that the courtly, gentle Queen Meena and the creative, vibrant Queen Dayita would soon be overcome by flames, suffer indescribable pain and then perish in agony with the dead. It made her limbs tremble, to look at them so alive before her and

94

then picture them as ash, at one with sandalwood and pine.

Being the only child, brought up almost as a son by her father, she rode in the forest with him, accompanied by the Royal Cavalry, joined the hunt, could shoot with precision, attack and defend by sword, could drive a carriage and two horses, and was permitted to attend official sessions of the court. This meant she had acquired another attitude, a freer, more masculine way of thinking.

Something had to be done, she decided, to remove the Northern Queens from this terrible obligation. But the obstacles were considerable in this Kingdom of chanting high priests, of proud fighting men, whose valour and fortitude in the face of death were celebrated and sung in lyrics, and whose women vied with these heroic qualities to exhibit their own un-sullied affection, their own inner strength to face a burning pyre.

This Kingdom's flag, when held in the wind, symbol-ised for all who saw it, friend and foe alike, that unique combination of the most dauntless of warriors and the purest of women.

Given that she had only two days at most, Renu was faced with an almost impossible challenge. All she had in her armoury was this other way of thinking.

Queen Meena's grief took her straight to His Majesty's dove-cote. She spoke to his birds, bidding farewell to them, wishing she were feathered too as she fed them. Like Queen Dayita, she was aware that becoming suttees on the late King's pyre further enhanced his stature, honour and prestige. She knew she must climb the pyre and was already mentally preparing herself for the ordeal. Her own family's esteem would also be magnified, her honour would become above suspicion. They would take pride and comfort in her memory. These thoughts became a soothing balm.

As Queen Meena made her way back to her own quarters, to breakfast in private as was her custom, Queen Renu approached her. 'Big sister, first and eldest Queen, I have an honourable and righteous proposition to put before you and Queen Dayita regarding this suttee approaching us.'

'Youngest Queen and sister, let us meet after breakfast at my quarters. I look forward to hearing what you have to say. However, bear this in mind, you have come from the South, thus your ways of seeing things will be different from our own. We will listen and will let you know if the way you perceive our custom can be accommodated by us. Sacrificing our lives is what is expected of us. Our sacrifices offer us worth, dignity and respect which form the breath of life. Remove self-esteem from any life and it dies.'

Queen Dayita, who had joined them, listened and nodded gracefully.

'We are born to serve,' Queen Meena continued, 'and it is only through our thoughts and the way we live and die that we are able to bring God's blessings to lives unborn, lives yet to come. God looks favourably on those who gladly make large sacrifices to please Him. He cannot be fooled. He will not be satisfied with mere symbols of sacrifice by the cunning and the sophisticated to protect them from pain. The teaching of our sages: "Blessed are the pure in heart" is constantly before us, and—'

'Yes, big sister, eldest and wise Queen Meena,' interrupted Queen Dayita, 'you speak our truth clearly.' She was irritated and resentful of the fact that Queen Renu, the swarthy newcomer, should dare to initiate a meeting. 'We do not know *your* truth Queen Renu, and if we did, would not feel compelled to comment upon it, for that is not the way of royalty here. Whatever you do say, try not to anger our pundit, for we need his blessings throughout the ceremony; we need his mantras and good will. To have an angry pundit, our only connection to God's words, as we leave this earth, will dilute the very essence of our suttee. It is important that you understand our perception – for it would seem that you do not: it is through the yearnings of the spirit for purity, for untainted devotion to the supreme ruler and King of the Kingdom of Jyotika, that the past Queens have become suttees.'

She looked imperiously at the younger Queen, her eyes narrowed, vixen-like.

'There is also a belief of ours which I have found people from the South – perhaps even including the royal families there – do not understand. Our divine ones have made it known that only the love of goodness for its own sake ought to prevail in the hearts of suttee wives. I cannot stress this sufficiently, for the slightest thought of personal interest, of rewards for family and self, pollutes the offering to God and makes this dedication of our being null and void.'

Again she looked at Queen Renu and flames leapt from her eyes as her unspoken thoughts raced on: I trust pure, untainted goodness will be large in our hearts as we climb the pyre, though I have my misgivings about you; but I leave you to Brahma.

97

The two Queens listened, astonished at her passion. Queen Meena turned to Queen Renu and said, 'It is only right and proper that you be heard, if you wish to speak. We may all benefit from your scholarship. What harm can come of it? In the short time that remains, we should comfort each other. It is agreed. We will meet in my apartment in one hour.'

CHAPTER THIRTEEN

In the Kingdom of Jyotika

QUEEN DAYITA'S GROWING resentment of the King's recent choice had finally gushed forth. Until Renu came, she had enjoyed the status of 'most favoured one' and remembered well King Paresh's whispered indulgences, his delightful surprises. To have a competitor for first place in the affection of His Majesty was not only new to her but was intolerable. Besides, there was something inexplicable and disturbing in his finding pleasure in someone so dark, so unlike herself, in fact more like a young man in the way she walked and talked.

Those hostile to Queen Dayita's aloof manner felt that her rapid rise in the world of classical dance was not due solely to her creative performances of the epic tales but also to her ability to manipulate her old guru and the officials who ran the Temple School of Dance from whence she came. Many a lady at court kept to themselves their belief that when she was there, this classical dancer used her youth, charm, and sensuous beauty to engage in subtle coquetry, thus ensuring that her duties, both public and private, became more advantageous to herself.

However, of late, Queen Dayita was unable to show that quiet dignity which came naturally to Queen

Meena when the latter had faced the loss of most favoured status. Queen Dayita remained proud and alone, removed from others. Over the years her autocratic manner had barred any affection from her ladies-in-waiting, although their loyalty was well-rewarded. Today, the sudden news of the King's death had led her pent-up energy to ignite into a blue flame.

On returning to her own private puja room, Queen Dayita placed fresh garlands of flowers on the King's painting and spoke to his smiling visage. 'You, who caressed my pains, calling to me with murmurs of "soft eye" and "cloud-sprung." "A Rajah's choice," you whispered, as your gifts covered my nakedness. Your strength and courage have sustained me, at no time leaving my thoughts. My memory of our times together will keep you eternally youthful, as you were when you first undressed me here in your chamber.

'I have lived for you. My life had no other purpose but to please you. I know that you would not want me to climb the pyre, but be comforted that I shall dance for you again in that most pleasurable way, which you have called for again and again, so thirsty for my beauteous warmth. "Fair-faced and beautiful" were amongst your welcomes to me. "How you fill the King with pleasure" another.

'Although my nature is delicate, I shall not abandon my duty and will gladly offer myself. My spirit rejoices knowing you will await my coming; you understand my rhythm, my most intimate feelings and have touched them so.' Queen Dayita clasped the framed King to her ripe fullness and was aroused by the thought of the joyous reunions to come.

Meanwhile, Queen Renu walked along the spacious corridor to her own quarters, the enormity of the task she contemplated weighing heavily on her mind. Pundit Krishna, the royal court's pundit, would not be easy to persuade, she reminded herself. A man of faith in uncertain times clings to his faith; to see the Queens through the rite of suttee was also his duty to the Royal Family of Jyotika. Only they, as suttees, could mirror his devotion, his contribution to his King's passing.

What will my position be when this is over? she thought. Pundit Krishna's resentment of my disobedience, my scholarly challenges, will cut deep within him – he will be unforgiving. And what will become of me from day to day? Here, a widow's life is a living death. I will be shunned and placed at the rear of the palace. We, who were once someone's daughter, sister, mother, servers to all, by custom moulded, are ill-equipped for a self-propelled life. Maimed by outmoded ideas from the past we hop about with damaged lives like wounded birds.

She shuddered. To live to that fullness of her being, she would need to remove herself from this Northern Kingdom. She could not return to her parents – that would place too great a burden on them. According to custom, she must stay here – come what may – even if her sanity or her very life were being threatened. Oh, the tyranny of such traditions! I will *not* submit to this barbarity, she thought fiercely. I will not! My observation of the natural world and the society of men gives no credence to this belief of life after death, and so each suttee becomes for me a human sacrifice. I will not bow to ignorance and bullying by priests, saints, or so-called

101

holy men. My father encouraged me to debate with God. I cannot let him down by consenting to this Northern custom. Yet, I am afraid of what may befall me. The powerful never allow themselves to lose face. They create the rules, and even Faith bends to comply. They alone decide when and how they are to be obeyed; what we should think and how to think. They keep the keys to Freedom here and in the hereafter as well.

Queen Renu gave a deep sigh. She would have liked to get to know King Paresh better. When they travelled together from the Southern Kingdom, he was so thoughtful and affectionate. There was wisdom in what he said. Smiling, she recalled how he conducted himself was simply charming. To have known such a man was a beautiful thing.

Now she would pay her respects to the King in private before he lay in state, but first she needed to call her loyal servant Manu, brought with her from her father's court. 'Take Manu, he is the most able,' her mother had advised. 'Treat him well. He has no relatives, they died at sea. Never neglect him. He is your other pair of eyes and ears. In a strange place you need also to guard your back. If a time comes when you can trust no one at court, then use him to find a way out. He knows all the routes from the South to the North, from the East to the West.'

'Ma, the time has come,' she whispered. 'I shall arrange with Manu to leave by night. If I ever come out of this whole, I shall write to you and Pa. Bless me, my parents, bless me.'

Kala, the young slave-girl, was thin. Her small, round head was well covered, though her clear, bright eyes

102

were not reached by the sari border that framed her face. She kept her voice low, explaining herself to Baalaajee whose thoughtful face was neither handsome nor plain but mirrored his thinking in a refreshingly youthful way. He walked beside her with quiet dignity, his regal head-dress adorned with its ribbon of mourning. A trained, erudite pundit by the age of nineteen, in the vast compound surrounding the palace, he was perceived more as a friend, than a priest.

The pair were making for the inner sanctum of the royal court. Kala had received a summons from the royal pundit, on behalf of Queen Meena. Kala and the other slaves of the compound were so fearful as to what this could possibly mean for her and them, that Baalaajee was asked to accompany her.

Sujata was still crying loudly and she stretched her arms outwards to her mother: 'Mama, Mama,' she sobbed. Seeing that Baalaajee's soothing words and gentle rocking did not comfort her daughter, Kala took her from him. Instantly, Sujata snuggled close, clasping her mother's thin neck tightly. The corridor of shadows and lamps was silent.

As they hurried down the unending passageway, Vasti floated along, keeping them company. They were unaware of her wraith-like presence, picked up no traces of her, and she put this down to their anxiety and grief. Soon Sujata fell asleep, and Baalaajee carried her once more.

They reached a place where two soldiers guarded a heavy ebony door on which was carved a Khamadhenu: a being with a peacock's tail, eagle's wing, cow's hind- and fore-legs, a woman's head and breast. Six necklaces and two large hanging earrings adorned her.

It seemed the guards were expecting Kala and Baalaajee, for they not only opened the door but their manner was most reverential. And yet Kala's sari was of poor quality cotton, albeit clean, and on her feet she had the plainest of sandals. Her wrists were bare, apart from a single pair of thin silver bracelets; little Sujata had the same.

One of the guards left his post and walked on ahead. They followed him. On reaching a heavy door embossed in silver, he knocked. The door opened and Kala was greeted by the keeper with a slow genuflection.

Baalaajee became anxious. He was concerned about the guards' attitude towards Kala. Their earlier deference had now become reverential, and this undisguised veneration of the slave girl was dramatically out of keeping within this strict, hereditary-caste society. He observed that the closer they were to the inner sanctum of royalty, the throne room, the more heightened was this adoration. His earlier suspicions were now confirmed. The purpose of the Royal summons was tied to the fate that awaited this unprotected young slave-girl, mother of Sujata.

Twice daily, when the sun began its ascent and descent above the horizon, Baalaajee chants his understanding of life both before and after deep meditation: 'We arise out of the elements and unto them we return. There is no consciousness after death, for we are our beginnings and shall return to Prakrit. We are part of everything and everything resides within us.'

The full implication of this thinking not only to reincarnation but to the core beliefs of world religions was too devastating to contemplate. Baalaajee chanted the belief of all Charvakas. The root of their under-standing came from the ancient atheistic Sankhya school of thought.

As he walked beside the slave-girl, he was overcome by fear at the fate that awaited her, and a sharp pain shot up from his stomach, reaching his throat. The sleeping Sujata was soft against his cheeks. How well, they had chosen their victim! How deep was their cunning! Baalaajee knew all about the absolute power of the Royal Court, how its decisions were made and carried out. How could a lowly slave-girl deny the Royal Court its request? To help Kala do so was the formidable task before him.

The power of a royal summons, the tenacity of cus-tom and the sagacious Pundit Krishna of the Royal Court, all strengthened the 'request' that would be put to Kala. Baalaajee's thoughts were combing the Shastras diligently, seeking even a hairline opening – a passage out. Suddenly an idea came to him, he held it reluc-tantly, for it seemed too lithe. Could he grasp it, follow where it led? It might be the entrance to many pathways.

He also had a hunch that because of the early domin-ant atheistic thinking on the origin of the world in ancient Hindustan, the old sages and scholars, cognisant of the degeneracy that comes to kings and the priestly class, would have found a clever way of inserting a clause or two, which would give some measure of protection to the victims of their power. If his thinking was right, a neat exit clause was what he should be looking for. But in which book of ancient writ would it be found?

The learned and experienced Royal Court Pundit might entangle him in a web of orthodoxy. In addition, Baalaajee was aware that the weight of this custom and the strong conservatism of the province might crush him.

Baalaajee's other predicament was, that he would have to reveal his unorthodox thinking to assist Kala, and if he failed as was likely, they would both perish. She would be led to the pyre; he would lose his position at court and would have to leave the province, dishonoured. His thoughts returned to this worthy exit clause he sought; what form would it take? Would it be thinly veiled? he wondered. His anxiety was growing; time was of the essence and Kala was in grave danger. What would become of Sujata, he asked himself if Kala was sacrificed to an ancient design, glorified by the priestly class?

Royal horses and elephants were being scrubbed and washed in the stables, their glittering trappings and adornments made ready. The nature of the procession to come with the Queens and the King's body was explained to the animals; this ensured, their carers said, that by their countenance and movements they would convey the sanctity of the occasion. When they encountered sceptics, they replied, 'The elephants have had a previous life: what understanding, hidden from us, do they now carry? Who knows? Do *you*?

Voices in the royal stable overflowed and joined the stream of emotion issuing from the corridors of the palace and the hushed anticipation of the procession forming in the courtyards beyond. The desert wind took these feelings and, rising high, scattered them throughout the kingdom, to men and women in the fields, in the crowded marketplaces, in the vibrant villages and the poor districts.

Expectation was growing of the spectacle to come; the royal funeral would be more deeply moving than a royal wedding, with its pomp and splendour. For there was something about excessive joy, the abandonment of restraint, the feasting in delights, which, when they passed, left an emptiness.

The people of Jyotika were in awe of the grand spectacle that awaited them. Many were leaving their homes and their workshops to ensure a close view of the Queens, of whom they had heard much but never seen. Already the jostling and pushing and shoving were taking place; anger flared here and there. Children were restrained.

In less than two days, they would witness this sacred event as their grandparents and parents had done. A few old heads amongst them whispered that they vividly recalled the suttee ceremony of King Haresh, father of the late King though that was thirty years ago.

Then, the beauty of the Queens they said, in that knowing way, almost rivalled the gods, so blessed by Brahma were they; their unveiled faces glowed with happiness and devotion to the King. 'It was a privilege to have seen the Queens' royal sedans lifted high, slowly moving along the main venue,' they stressed, 'and to witness their public offerings of jewels and other ornaments. So much purity, innocence and feminine grace,' they continued. 'It was a heavenly sight, an intense devotion, unrivalled – not of this world,' was their pronouncement. 'They sat like goddesses and awaited Paradise to open to them; all the while fierce flames raged upon them. Our eyes were blessed to have rested on this vision of womanhood.'

At no time did these elders reflect on the vulnerability of a live human body on a flaming pyre. At no time did they say, 'I heard piercing cries of agony. Undisguised by ghee and sandalwood I smelled the terrible stench of burning flesh.

Thirty years on, this same expectation fanned the air. The people of Jyotika were looking forward to seeing the Royal Queens paraded before them: the classically beautiful first Queen Meena, the celestial dancer and second Queen Dayita, and the dark Queen Renu from the South. Men and women alike were particularly interested in the third Queen. How did fine scholarship sit upon a woman? Did it make her happy? Did it destroy her motherly qualities? 'If she thinks and talks as a man,' an old woman remarked, 'it is not something that we should copy. Two masters in a house leads to fights. And by the way, are men comfortable in her presence?'

'Well,' some young women were saying, 'it has done her no harm. The King chose her, so she must have excited him greatly. Besides,' they whispered amongst themselves, 'he saw beauty in that strange, unfamiliar South.' In an unguarded moment another asks, 'What does that tell us about the King's tastes?' The older women were silent, the younger ones amused, others embarrassed.

On the day of their supreme sacrifice, the spectacular sunset colours of the desert would be reflected in the grand pageant of royal elephants and camels in their glittering finery. Thoroughbred horses, the finest specimens of speed and beauty, clad in gold and velvet trappings, would carry them to the pyre.

The widows, their vermilioned bodies covered in celebratory garments, would slowly approach the fragrant gums and resins of the pile of cedar and sandal wood steeped in oil that awaited them. Ahead of them, bells and drums, ancient incantations, gongs and cymbals, the blare of conches and trumpets and sacred Vedic chants would cleanse the path, make it holy for their passage to the other world. The King's private regiment would march alongside, guarding each Queen's royal conveyance from the large bands of jostling subjects, who had come to have a closer look at an unveiled Queen. This royal privilege, this blessing comes but once in a lifetime to the common man.

Everyone would be on foot except the Queens and the body of the King.

It was believed that their deaths would, on that day, break through into the world of infinite possibilities, far beyond the limitations of human thought and its observed realities.

The patiently waiting crowd had come to see these spoken words of their priests brought to life, for here faith asserted that the sacred Sanskrit writ, further purified by the raging flames, would bring about the promised transformation. The power of God – creator of all things – would turn dust, ash or the carbon of the pyre into its former living human forms. The Omnipotent One would return the Queens to their former wholeness, a miraculous completeness. Reborn, the widows would be endowed once more with their former beauty, youth, memory and mind; their tastes and loves unsullied, to enjoy conjugal bliss once more in heaven. Thus was the interpretation of the written word. It was the nature of belief.

When the four corners of the pyre were alight, tongues of fire would swiftly spread, racing inwards and upwards consuming all. A deafening clamour of shouting spectators, drums, cymbals and bells would drown out the women's screams.

While the embers of the burning pyre slowly subsided into ash, the people would head for home, taking with them these written promises of the sacrifice revered in ancient texts, mantras, chants and ragas; in epics and classical dance.

Such a spectacle would remain in their memory, and in the retelling, it would become society's understanding of the ultimate form that a woman's purity, loyalty and devotion can take.

So ends the marriage that began when husband and wife were joined together as they circled the sacred matrimonial fire while Sanskrit chants called upon Agni, the god of fire, to witness their solemn vows.

CHAPTER FOURTEEN

Queen Meena

OF THE THREE Queens of Jyotika, it was Queen Meena who carried a regal dignity more suited to the character of the Northern Kingdoms than His Majesty's younger Queens. Her Royal birth, private tutoring, natural grace and aristocratic reserve, as well as her quiet delight and pride in wearing beautiful clothes and elegant antique jewellery, reflected her disposition and that of the people. In private audiences, she behaved as one would have expected; she listened well, said little and her amiability was finely measured to suit the occasion.

Had you come to her with a petition, you would have left uncertain as to whether your cause had found favour with her. In the event that you had, and on her sharing this view with King Paresh, who then offered reasons why you should not be assisted, Queen Meena would take no offence. She would accept his judgement wholly, at no time suggesting that there were other positive qualities she had observed which he had not considered and should be given attention. Her acceptance of the King's advice was based on the belief that her upbringing and cloistered life did not qualify her to have the discernment required to evaluate the masked characters of men, nor their hidden agendas.

With the King's death, Queen Meena knew what awaited her. She would be accompanying him on the pyre as custom prescribed. The belief of life after death and its connection to reincarnation and one's Karma, the cumulative results of one's actions, she accepted in good faith, as she had accepted her role of being an obedient daughter and later of willing wife. She was the first of the Queens to visit the King's temple, where in its inner sanctum, the late King's Paresh's body, like his father's before him, was being prepared for cremation.

At so early a stage, it was not necessary to oversee the preparation of the bathing and dressing of the King, yet Queen Meena felt that though her devotion to His Majesty would end on his pyre, it should begin by ensuring that the preparatory rites of his body were faithfully carried out. Queen Meena was also conscious that her early presence and the length of time spent with the late King honoured him, enhanced his name, strengthened his stature and lineage. This was in keeping with her opinion that the courtesies the King received at death should reflect his life.

Queen Meena was particularly pleased to learn from one of the old matrons that the water used for bathing the King had been taken from the confluence of the two streams of Jyotika, mixed with water from the Ganges.

Later in her own puja room, the eldest Queen prayed silently, asking that the King should forgive her growing inner weakness and that the spirit of Saraswatee, the Goddess of Knowledge, should bless her with the wisdom to prepare herself for what was already so close.

Queen Meena no longer recalled that there had been a time when the young King called her 'Love's Delight' and 'Sun's Rays', when her classical beauty and her graceful form brought pleasure to those in her company and when she had entertained him with her sarod, vina and sarangi playing. Those times had long since left her. It was at the age of fourteen that the King had sought her hand in marriage, thus disrupting the idyllic life she enjoyed at her parents' home where, privately tutored, she learned to read Persian and the sacred Sanskrit texts, to paint, to play the flute and stringed instruments and to compose her own poems on life around the court.

As the years came and went in the Kingdom of Jyotika, she resigned herself to the mirror's tale, accepting with uncommon grace that the bewildering pomp and dizzy splendour which flowed upon her during her first years at the royal court, as well as the King's too frequent favours and calls upon her, would one day close as the hibiscus does before its petals fall.

CHAPTER FIFTEEN

A Parting of Waves

QUEEN RENU ENTERED the softly lit pink marble inner sanctuary of the King's temple, its outer court-yard, was guarded by his private regiment. The high priests of the temple were in deep meditation, lost to the world. She came with the same steps, the same attentiveness and courtesy as if the King had returned from battle and his server had invited her into His Majesty's presence.

Taking the aarti, a plate of burnished bronze alight with camphor and fragrant pods, she circled his body, allowing the flames she carried to flicker its warmth and light upon his face, and the scent to bathe it. She recited her own personal mantra, given to her by the family's pundit when she was seven. As she stood beside his corpse, her thoughts left her to reach him:

'King Paresh, King of Jyotika, defender of the faith and the Kingdom of Jyotika, I bid you farewell. May your spirit live amongst your people and may the brave manner in which you fought remind them to persevere against life's tribulations. Tonight would have been a festival of lights with your homecoming. And as you had promised that our first meeting should be on your return, I am here. It was your good taste and understanding of me that prevented you from a fulfilment of pleasures, intemperate in its haste, when we travelled in your carriage from my parents' home. Though together and alone, you conducted yourself with the gracious courtesy of a host with his guest.

'It is strange that I should love you so well in death, when after our too brief meeting at my parents' home, you surprised them and me with your request. I was suspicious of a man who could make up his mind with such haste on what was for me the future of my life, my growing maturity – the cultivation of my mind.

'Now that I seem to know you better, my affection for you would have made our first meeting in the privacy of your chamber a sweet melody as we prepared each other for the beautiful gift of our beings. I would have welcomed you with warmth, creativity and joy. But such pleasures may have made the gods jealous and so it was not to be. I, here and now, bid you farewell for this custom of suttee is unknown to us in the South and so I am unable to join you on the pyre.

'In addition, my years of learning and scholarly observation, as well as my father's encouragement that I should participate in debates with young and old philosophers have directed me to use reason as the main ingredient of belief, and so I say with all honesty that I feel none of the inspiration deemed necessary to the sanctity of this sacrifice.

'I have been reflecting on your asking my parents for my hand in marriage, I am ashamed to say that it is only with hindsight that I am so deeply moved by my parents' foresight and affection for me. I am overwhelmed with admiration for their courage and

115

astuteness, for they only agreed to your request after your reply to their concern. They wanted to know whether in the event of your death, your being a soldier King, I would be expected to join you on the pyre. You said, at no time would I be asked to do what was alien to my custom, my inheritance. My parents then said that in order to ensure their daughter's good name and that of her family, you should call together all the pundits of the royal court and affirm this edict openly in their presence before me. This you promised to do with all the solemnity and earnestness of an oath. Sadly, the large incursions by your neighbours, descending as hungry wolves on the borders of your Kingdom, took you by surprise and prevented you from attending to this promise.'

Queen Renu bowed again before the King, and then with a more relaxed voice and a budding smile said: 'I had thought of placing with you, at this meeting, the jewellery you offered me. But I am aware that it will please you more, were I to use it to the good, as you used your last energies. I salute you King Paresh, Supreme Lord of the kingdom of Jyotika. I, Queen Renu, beg to take my leave of you, my Lord.'

She stood, head bowed as if awaiting permission to leave.

It was the silence, the cloistered atmosphere, the presence of the dead that spoke. The room was cold, her stay long. It was time for Queen Renu to leave.

As she walked away, her footsteps silent along the corridor, sunbeams entered the patterned screens and brought designs, true and complete, reflecting a moving path upon which she trod. Recollections of another time when she was surrounded by the comfort, security and good sense of her home returned; a sense of anxiety gripped her.

Her thoughts opened. The curtain of time and place was lifted and she heard her mother pouring tea. The sound was distinct, and so was its aroma and sunshine colour. This cupped flow had interrupted the quiet contemplative silence of her parents which followed their shared heartfelt farewells and tearful good wishes. She saw her father standing up, her mother too.

Their daughter princess who had become a Queen of Jyotika understood it was their way of showing that the King should not be kept waiting any longer, for the journey was long and hazardous. Again her mother's voice: 'Renu, I have something to say which is as important as the King's recent promises. You must endeavour early to ask him to offer a choice to his two other Queens, on the event of his death. They should decide whether they wish to ascend the pyre. It is important that King Paresh announces the promise he has made to you and the choice he offers his elder Queens at the same time; this would help you to gain the Queens' trust and perhaps with time you will be blessed with their affection.'

Her father spoke next: 'It would not have been courteous for us to ask any more of the King. His Majesty must see the welfare of his other two Queens as his concern, not yours, his youngest, most recent Queen from the South, so I want you to be aware of the delicacy of your request; choose the time with skill, and prepare it in such a way that it appeals to his compassion and his sense of being seen to be impartial to his consorts. Do remember, my daughter, that to ask a King and be granted such a large favour, when your affections for each other have not yet woven the threads of integrity and trust to form a oneness, will be no mean accomplishment.

'Tread with care, my daughter, do tread with the utmost care. I am hoping,' and he began to smile, 'that your practice of debating with our philosophers at court will be of some assistance to you, though it is preferable for a wife to be charming than to win an argument. Yet, if you can have both, you are your mother's daughter.' He smiled even more broadly and added, 'Also, never forget that even upright men must be made to feel that they are masters in their own home. Your mother is very good at this, I can assure you.'

'Your father chooses to make fun of me, Renu', her mother replied. 'Go in peace, my daughter, and may the good fortune of our Kingdom remain with you always, and may the spirit of the good wishes of all our people continue to support you. I feel a little less troubled now that Manu has agreed to go with you.'

She bowed down before her parents and they blessed her with tears.

Queen Renu found that she was in need of a handkerchief, and her steps hastened to the privacy of her quarters.

CHAPTER SIXTEEN

A Way of Thinking

THOUGH ONLY A mere ten minutes had passed since Baalaajee began his mental search through the Shastras, it appeared an eternity to him. His anxiety was growing, for as each minute passed by, his footsteps took him closer to the royal court. There, Kala's fate would be irrevocably sealed. He was desperate for a way out. Baalaajee slowed his breathing to concentrate, and with his despondency gradually receding, he meditated.

He was resolute. He persevered, yet nothing came. Then with the all-consuming intensity of a human mind struggling in the dark, he called upon the spirit of his late tutor and also on that primeval energy of the birth of the universe, its erupting waves creating stars – to enlighten him, to guide his thoughts through aeons of ancient writ – to sanctuary. He opened his unconscious to all that he had summoned.

Slowly, he felt strangely light and what he sought appeared before him as if it had always been there. Wait. It came – a true find. He began muttering it to himself in order to memorise it: According to the rules, *She must give her consent*. Another clause rises from the Shastras: *The slightest intrusion of a self-interested motive is fatal*. He is aware that though not stated explicitly it refers to her husband's salvation and her own. *Divine promises are turned to dust – where hopes of posthumous rewards are taken to the pyre. It becomes an unclean sacrifice.* Again he knows this is so because then, it has become a mercenary calculation of profit

He had interpreted it correctly. He now saw why past suttees would not have wished to cite these verses. In most instances they would not have known of them, and of the few who did know, they would have found them double-edged. How could they *not* give their consent willingly and in a spirit to ensure that their motives were untarnished by personal gain? If they did, they would be damned amongst the living. It was better to leave this life with honour.

The contradictions were large. Baalaajee had no doubt that this came about in part from the layers of mistranslations, false readings, blunders and misinterpretations carried through time by interested parties, who in their telling reflected their own limitations and preferences. He would have liked so much to know what was originally said and the thinking behind it.

This young man of goodwill, felt driven to ensure that the human sacrifice of Kala did not take place. Why Kala? he asked, and wondered whether the wives had declined to follow custom or whether the court's Pundit wanted to enlarge the image of the King's worthiness by this degenerate extravagance of another's life to boost the numbers. Were there not accounts of hundreds of lives – wives, concubines and slaves – upon the pyres of some kings and rulers?

But why Kala? he mused again. This slave-girl had apparently once been an exciting, attractive female. Such a beguiling flower left unguarded in any garden would be plucked from her branches to delight others and later left to wither. Who did actually rape her? Did they believe that she would become as radiant in death as she had once been in life by entering the cleansing fire – a suttee on the king's pyre? He could not fathom it and so decided to desist from surmises that led nowhere.

A deep misgiving tugged at him; he wasn't sure whether what he had in mind would work. It depended on what they presented to her, how she reacted to it. Who would say no to wealth, and honour? Who could resist them? A poor slave-girl? His anger mounted. Was there another place in this vast universe where men displayed such blind egotism, such overwhelming conceit and gross selfishness? Were there other places where innocent subjects were expendable for the glory of kings, rulers, heads of state?

What manner of God was this that men had created? Why would a God, a Super Intelligence, creator of all things, demand so much suffering, penance, humiliation and debasement of the human spirit, when lesser beings had been known to seek nothing, ask for nothing in return, on offering their affection, compassion and understanding? See how freely this iniquity, this thinking, flowed into other deep channels of subservience in which women must swim in order to live! And we call it custom, he thought, as his contempt for the Kingdom's religious leaders rose. 'We call it tradition,' he cried out in pain. Kala looked at him. Talking loudly to oneself in anger, she understood, for she herself did it.

If this woman who had harmed no one, he thought, was put to death by fire, she would die in unbearable agony and her child would be left without a mother and

121

he, with his lifetime of learning and of study, could do nothing to prevent it. Baalaajee was once again overcome by an acute pain that shot up from his stomach into his throat like a flaming arrow. He was lost to the present. Once more he called upon the spirit of his late tutor, for he felt that the enormity of the task before him was about to engulf him. And Baalaajee recalled his last day with him for the comfort it brought, for the reassurance he sought, to fortify himself.

'There is nothing left that I can teach you, Baalaajee,' the old man spoke softly. 'Go forth and teach yourself – this way you will learn more. You will learn most by observing everything with care. Even a standing piece of granite on the roadside has an interesting life story to tell. Be open to it. Ask it! But by far the most difficult to do I shall now demonstrate.' The tutor showed Baalaajee a tall, beautiful, pink marble vase on a raised stand. He then went out and picked a scented red rose which he placed behind it. 'Now,' he said, 'from where you stand, Baalaajee, can you see the rose?'

'No, Punditjee. The marble vase is in the way.'

'If you keep standing there and do not move, would you ever see the rose?'

'No, Punditjee. It cannot be done from here.'

'What then, if you wish to see the rose, to hold its fresh stem, catch its beauty, receive its perfume, must you do, Baalaajee?'

'It is clear. I must either walk around the vase, or remove the vase.'

'Very well, remove the vase.' Baalaajee walked to it with the confidence of youth and attempted to lift it and found he could not.

'Why are you unable to lift the vase Baalaajee?'

'It is far too heavy, Punditjee.'

'And if your feet were firmly fastened to this comfortable divan of mine, would you be able to walk around the vase and see the rose?'

'Not unless I was able to untie my feet.'

'Now you see, the vase and the divan are obstructions – our very own prejudices – cultural and personal impediments – to a better understanding of all that is around us. They are almost immovable; not easy to lift out of ourselves, not easy to untie ourselves from. I have not managed it myself.

'Look, Baalaajee, look at this Kingdom of Jyotika. You can see that it is our corrupt court and its politicians, middle-ranking officers and clerics who form a cohesive barrier to what should be the simple message of living: *Treat one another kindly*. Religious rituals are comforting to the spirit but they are also self-serving to the officiators who control the direction and quality of our lives.

'We are told what meaning words should have. To abnegate such a large development of our thinking process to another, undermines the glorious potential of the human spirit.

'If your conscious self is aware of this, you will have that beautiful compassion for all peoples – humanity. It is ourselves at our very best. Hold on to yours. With it, you are never lonely, for then your life connects with others, becomes beautifully composed ragas of varying moods and tempos, colour and melody . . . Go now.'

Baalaajee bowed down before his tutor's feet and saluted the humanity within him. 'Bless me again, Punditjee. Bless me again. And whenever you think of me, wish me well for I am afraid of the court, its rulers and their power. Before their might, I am like a leaf engulfed within a tsunami wave. You will be the source of my strength. I have no one else. Do not leave me alone. Even in death, when you return to prakrti, part of a newborn star, flicker your light upon me, Punditjee.'

The old man gently rested his hands on the young man's bowed head, closed his eyes and concentrated upon *all that was good that he knew*, wishing it to come to Baalaajee's aid, to protect him. 'Though neither you nor I know your parents,' he said, 'remember this: they offered you their blessings at your birth, and once more when they parted from you with tears and anguish. When you were brought to me, the young pundit asked me to give you a name, for the name your parents gave you was lost by the midwife. He could not tell me the exact time of birth, so I offered you my own.' The young man and the old man embraced.

'Each day I tried to offer you the best of myself,' the old man said. 'Now at our parting, I offer you myself, my spirit, my thoughts of good will. Call upon the good spirits of *all* our ancestors whenever in need, and you will be enlarged for you have the capacity to carry much that is good. You have my blessing now and always.'

As Baalaajee's footsteps faded, his aged tutor sat down to write the true account of his student's birth. When he had finished, he placed it in an envelope and addressed it: *For Baalaajee. To be opened on your return from my burning pyre*. It rested at the bottom of a drawer near his bedside.

Punditjee died. A month later.

What happened to that letter?

Baalaajee never received it. How it was stolen and later sold, shall be revealed.

CHAPTER SEVENTEEN

The Water-Carrier

KUNWAR, THE WATER-CARRIER, lifted the large lid of the copper jar. Pundit Baalaajee Senior, whom everyone called Punditjee, had not used the water for bathing which he had brought earlier. This presented Kunwar with a problem. There was no empty water storage jar ready at hand to receive this second quota of water and not knowing exactly what the Pundit would like him to do, he knocked. Again he knocked and waited. Coming closer, he pressed his ears to the door and listened closely. Nothing was stirring within. His fingers gently pushed the door, all the while greeting the Pundit, enquiring if he was well or needed anything, aware of the possibility that some recompense might be offered or good will earned, were he to be helpful.

'Punditjee? Good morning, Punditjee. Good morning. This is Kunwar, the water-carrier. Where do you want me to pour this second quota of water?'

His enquiry went ahead of him, into the darkness; a ray of light followed. On seeing the Pundit lying down, he approached his divan saying, 'Punditjee, I brought your water for bathing at five o'clock Are you not feeling well?' It was the nature of the stillness that encouraged him to touch the body. The face of death was well-known in the compound. Yet a mere water-carrier touching any Pundit in the absence of his wakeful presence he knew was forbidden; he hesitated and looked round the room carefully before extending himself.

That the Pundit had died during the night became clear. Near to him was a fully opened drawer; an envelope was peeping out. He could see that the Pundit had been trying to remove it just before he died. He pulled the drawer out, took the letter and reported the death to the court.

Later on, when the day's work was done and he sat alone in his small dark place, he removed the envelope from his belt and opened it with care, expecting to find inside, something of value – jewellery or money. However, on finding a letter he was greatly disappointed; he could not even have the pleasure of knowing its contents as he could not read. The thought of taking it to someone who could read, he quickly dropped, seeing that such a step would implicate him, and his job in the palace compound be lost.

Besides, he pondered, how would he know that what was told to him was the true content of the letter? Supposing the letter indicated where some money was hidden – would the reader let him know? Kunwar knew no one could be trusted. So he simply returned the letter to its envelope, and attempted to re-seal it. It could not be done. What should he do now? He decided that it was not a pressing matter, so he removed the old jute bag from the centre of the hut, dug a hollow in the earthen floor and placed the envelope inside it. Then he firmly pressed in the loose earth he had removed with the soles of his feet. The jute bag was replaced. No trace was left of the old tutor's letter.

CHAPTER EIGHTEEN

A Scholar's Dilemma

LITTLE REMAINED OF the Queens' meeting save the crumbs of ladoo on tea plates, the fragrance of Muscat grapes lingering in drained cups, which were refilled again and yet again by Queen Meena, who poured her special warm brew of tea leaves from the cool flanks of the Himalayan hills. It was pale gold in colour.

This crucial gathering had already become a memory. Each Queen, now in the stillness of her quarters, recalled that gathering in her own special way. But it was Queen Renu who actually wrote an account of it:

When I entered the room, the two Northern Queens were already there. I could see they had been discussing the suttee. And though their eyes were alive with curiosity about what I had to say, I sensed the strength of their honour, duty and obligation to the King, to their family, to custom.

I had come with the underlying confidence of youth, certain of my position which I saw as both rational and compassionate. But I sought to mask these; instead I asked questions and listened carefully to their replies, watching how their limbs and head, neck and eyes spoke, noting what they kept to themselves – their pride, their conscious omissions.

My sister Queens said that I already knew their position and asked me to state mine. They listened while I pleaded with them to leave with me, for my faithful servant Manu, had already alerted me to his plan for my escape.

I could see that beginning life anew in a strange land, on the other side of dark threatening waters, was not something they could embrace. And yet, there was no time to spare, to grow used to the idea. They had to decide *now*. What was unsaid was their preference for the pyre, rather than leaving the Kingdom, scuttling away like a lowly animal in the dark, their reputation in shreds and their family's name dishonoured for all time.

The fact that they would not be around to experience this shame was something I dared not suggest, for one's name may be likened to one's inner light: to lose it is to die.

How then might they escape the pyre with honour? It was self-contradictory. It may just have been my sensitive imagination at work, but the simple thought of leaving them, knowing that they would soon become ash, jolted me towards an idea that held its breath, unsure of itself, hesitating at my door of acceptance.

Like many childhood stories, wishful thinking was its carriage and I said to myself, while there was that outside chance that an imaginative strategy could save them, I would be willing to reveal it even at the expense of my own safety – although I was quite clear in my own mind that I would never willingly step upon a pyre.

129

At that point, Queen Dayita stood up to assist Queen Meena with the pouring of the tea, and she did so with such grace – rising from her chair, lifting the silver teapot, while her eyes and arms, her entire frame, appeared to attend to the pouring of the delicious warmth, that it gave me thought.

After we had drunk, Queen Meena brought us the letter she had written to her parents. Her handwriting was exquisite. It was a form of straight lines and curves so skilfully intertwined that it gave way to meaning, to music, to sound.

There and then my former impetuosity which I believed had left me, propelled itself with such a feverish haste that I heard myself say: 'We have amongst us three, the talent, the skills and the accomplishments to save not only ourselves from the pyre but to bring about a change in direction in the lives of widows of the Kingdom of Jyotika. From this may come a change in the thinking of all women in this vast land of ours. We can avoid death on the pyre with honour, with our names respected, even recalled with affection and admiration in a more lasting way than having the palms of our hands and the soles of our feet imprinted in stone.'

I spoke as if I were my father's Chief Minister proclaiming a new Order at court. They looked at me earnestly and waited. I knew that I needed to compose a stirring raga that I must also now play. It was my only hope of carrying them with the essence of this measure.

And so it was I began:

'Sister Queens, we are told in the Rig Veda, that the suttee act was purely a symbolic one, denoting the

130

coming to an end of the connection with one life and the beginning of another. In those times the pundit would bless the living and the dead – the widow and the body of her husband – lying on the pyre. Her husband's family and her own family would come together to bless the occasion of the parting.

'It was a symbolic acknowledgement that what had once been brought together in marriage had now come apart by the death of the one. The gods were called upon to acknowledge and bless the separation.

'Well before it was lit, however, the widow was wisely raised from the pyre by a male relative of her husband, to affirm it was the family's wish. Thereafter, she was greatly respected for herself and was allowed to enter into any or all aspects of her former life when she so chose.

'Consider this: no man in the Kingdom would wish to exchange his life for that of his wife. It is no mystery why this should be so. He sees her life, her very existence engineered by custom to serve his. Is this ordained by God or by men? A married woman's entire life is one of daily duties and sacrifices. She brings comfort to all around her: her children, her husband, her husband's family and, before marriage, her own family.

'When her husband dies do you think that the Supreme Being, the Creator of All Things, would ask that she be put to death in that most cruel of horrors – burned alive on a pyre – pinned down by logs while the priest, her children and family watch and listen to her shrieks and cries for help before she is painfully consumed? What manner of God is this when a human, a lesser being, can have more compassion, more affection for the powerless, the disadvantaged? What manner of

God would accept such a cruel sacrifice? It is our power-seeking priests who have created this and given it significance.

'Do we not know that it is not the gift that pleases God, but our motivation, our intention in the giving. It has been written that a single fruit, if offered in good heart by those who consciously seek the path to Dharma, pleases God. I am proposing that together we direct the remainder of our lives to another path to dharma, to discovering, like the Buddha, the truth about living the good life.'

'How? How can that be?' asked Queen Dayita. 'Must we become yogis?'

'What is the nature of this new path?' questioned Queen Meena. 'Has it been built? Is it close by? Is it steep, strewn with cutting stones?'

'I propose that we set up a school for young girls in this royal compound. Sister Dayita will teach them dance—'

'And poise,' Queen Dayita interrupted. 'And movement, composure, form, disposition, rhythm, measure and . . .'

'And much, much more,' I said, smiling at this unexpected burst of enthusiasm. 'Our eldest sister would be the chief administrator of day-to-day matters. She will be the principal of the school, while all other large decisions we will make together in a School Council of three. I am aware that Queen Meena will teach them to read and write beautifully, to paint, to sing accompanied by her veena, to make music, to put their thoughts into metre and—'

'Many other things. While you, Sister Renu,' again interrupted Queen Dayita, 'will teach them to think

132

clearly, to question, to be discerning, to learn how to read the sacred texts and put their thoughts down in some invisible order. We will need help to do this. Who should we ask? Who can be trusted to see, as we are now seeing with Sister Renu's help?' she wanted to know.

The silence was long. Everything seemed to have come to a standstill.

'I would like it to work, Sister Renu, it is the better way,' Queen Meena said, rising from her seat, 'yet how can these aspirations be fulfilled? How could we possibly manage without the help of the royal court and the High Priests? And what would their reaction be to our undertaking?

'I can already hear and feel their hostility, their anger: "The King has given his life to save the people and the Kingdom of Jyotika, while the Queens of Jyotika are dictating that this same King should for the first time in our history leave his palace, his Kingdom, alone – unaccompanied, as if he were a commoner, a lowly subject." Would we be able to live with silent taunts, with being made to feel unclean, unfit to be Queens?'

Again and again they spoke, and all in all I was able to appreciate more fully that we would not be protected by the royal court, nor supported by persons of authority amongst the priestly class. We would be shunned by the newly crowned King and his wives, our ideas remaining stillborn.

Again Queen Meena expressed her stifled anxieties: 'When Prince Mahendra is crowned, our lives will be miserable. If there happens to be any wife who sympathises with us, she would be foolish to make this

133

known.' Queen Meena stared at us intently. 'The quarters we will be assigned, the foods and diversions offered will be so monotonous, plain and simple that our lives could easily be as dreary and as cold. Much that we now have will be seen as property of the Crown. I refer to our jewellery, our finer garments and other belongings. Because of what I have said,' Queen Meena strongly suggested, 'we must put it all down, write it out fully: A comprehensive case, for ending the custom so that other Queens, other wives and widows would understand the thinking that led us to choose another path to Dharma. Otherwise, those who would not welcome this change could so easily dissemble what we are saying to their advantage, that our reputation is irretrievably lost.'

'Another reason for having it written down,' I said, 'is to help the younger priests to articulate with reason, with support from the texts, another path to Dharma. This may encourage them to defy the pressures from the temples and so bring to an end this human sacrifice. Shall we call it "The Enlightened Way"?' I asked with smiling eyes.

Both Queens said to me over and over again, that what would be brought into question was their loyalty, their devotion to the King. Queen Dayita was particularly vehement that wagging tongues belonging to ugly, mean women might question her faithfulness when her thoughts had seldom ever left the King.

Queen Meena turned to me: 'Where do you think,' she asked, 'I, the eldest, amongst you, would be placed by the incoming Queens of Prince Mahendra when he is crowned?' As I was unable to say, she informed me that she would be allocated a small dark, rundown part of the palace, and whenever she left her room, she would be accused by the silence of the royal wives, and other silences would follow theirs, 'and I would become an outcast. It would be like being buried alive. With whom would I speak? I may lose my mind.'

I could see the shock of her changed position, its suddenness, her unpreparedness and the full weight of those tragic consequences she would have to carry with dignity and little royal means of comfort for the remainder of her life. She would prefer the burning pyre to such daily humiliation. It became even clearer that our proposition, a worthy school for girls, must be supported by the Crown. Its very existence was dependent on the Crown becoming its patron. Oh, how the two Queens wished they had discussed these matters with the late King. To negotiate with an unknown was always so risky. What was Prince Mahendra's view likely to be? Was he like his brother? It was hard to tell.

All this while, Queen Dayita was thoughtful. If she was planning anything she kept it to herself. I couldn't help feeling that she greatly favoured the plan, for at no time did she say anything to discourage me.

We were facing an impasse. Who would assist us? I silently wept, thinking, I shall have to leave them to their fate.

There followed the sound of silence that beat upon the windowsills and carried its own strain with the wind. There was no way out. Our idea was before its time of harvesting, in a place where its fruit was unknown.

Sister Dayita rose. She walked round about us.

'In a room with no company or diversions,' she said, 'we would be like caged birds with little water or food. Is this life? Why should we save ourselves for this when on the pyre we gain dignity, respect, honour, our name sanctified for all times. Besides, Queen Renu, we were expecting to be there and so we were prepared by custom.' She paused. 'But if we succeed, our lives and those of others, would be transformed just as you have said, so it is most crucial that we manage to persuade the Royal Court Pundit, the most honoured Pundit in the kingdom to join with us.'

'To have such a person, so respected, would be a gift from heaven,' I declared, 'but surely he is more likely to offer you a full cup of soma so that you would be unconscious when the flames consume you.'

'That he will not do, Sister Renu,' Queen Dayita said, 'for we are expected to stand and make offerings of our adornments, fineries and jewels. We are expected to bless those who hail us, and come to us – those many who even now patiently sit and await our coming. He has to be wholly with us, not in part.'

Queen Meena poured us more tea and reminded me of what rewards awaited her on becoming a suttee. 'Do not take lightly, Queen Renu, that promise of thirty-five million years of bliss in a place where there is no want, no pain, no ugliness, where we may even see the gods in person. And in addition, having become suttees, we would become male in our next birth. That would be my preference.' She spoke as a child who grew up in a protected place and had learned to trust those around her, believing whatever was said to her, where obedience was praised and encouraged with gifts and outward displays of affection. It was the comforting simplicity of believing what others say, be they parents, tutors or priests.

In the absence of doubt, an overwhelming trust had formed the pivot of her life. Isn't it strange, I thought, that she would question the quality of the tea or the fabric that she had requested, yet defer this rigour of questioning on the direction of her life? I knew that had she had my parents and I, hers, I would be her and she me, and this thought brought me closer to both my sister Queens; all the more so when the desire to persuade them not to end their lives in this customed way surged within me forcibly. I felt I was in truth trying to save another reflection of myself.

Queen Dayita had listened attentively and I could not help thinking that unlike Queen Meena, she enjoyed being a woman. Of course it was just a fleeting feeling that passed my way. Once more Queen Dayita brought up her idea, repeating that Pundit Krishnajee seemed our best hope. 'Pundit Krishna has more influence in court than any other priest and were he to look favourably at our School for Girls, we would be well on our way.'

Queen Meena felt the same and so in her quiet subdued way, emphasised that this route should be pursued with skill and care.

'Well then, who should approach the Pundit?' I asked, knowing that I, a newcomer from the South, couldn't do it. I looked at the two other women and Queen Meena directed my question to Queen Dayita who remained still for a while though it seemed everlasting.

She then picked up this request as if it were a personal challenge in which her negotiating skills would be

137

severely tested. 'Now that we have much to live for,' she remarked, 'I would certainly try to persuade the Royal Court Pundit, the most erudite of them all – Pundit Krishnajee – to look kindly at our undertaking.' It was agreed, therefore, that after the meeting we would all be having with the Pundit, we would leave Queen Dayita to begin negotiating with him on her own.

Since I believe the teachings from the Brihad-Aranyaka Upanishad that clearly states there is no consciousness after death, Queen Meena's understandable preference to be a male in her rebirth did not hold the same significance for me. Yet I did understand it, for if I were her, I would wish the same.

Though my father brought me up, his only child, as a son, there were still handicaps. Were I male, I would have been allowed to ride into the forest alone and enjoy the serenity of Nature – allowing my unconscious self to leave, to move about, becoming one with the other primeval energies present. I would have been permitted to travel, to take up arms, moving with the frontline, to hunt on my own and to choose my wife. Instead, here I was, chosen by another and placed neck-deep in this quagmire of Northern custom.

How I longed to be known for endurance, courage, fortitude, not first for chastity and purity, then later for faithfulness and gentleness. I did not want to be a reflection of a man's dreams. What of my own? Oh, I had been born at the wrong time. How I would have liked to be a woman warrior like Queen Masaga. Her army and I would have stopped Alexander in 326 BC at the Battle of Hydaspes.

And two hundred years before that, how I would have liked to have ridden beside Queen Nayanika, ruler and military commander of the Satavahana Empire, nearer to my home in the Deccan region. Today, where are our Padminis? When Padmini's husband was captured by an enemy commander in a skirmish outside the walls of Chitor and taken to the Mogul's camp, did not wring her hands and weep, or contemplate death, fearing rape or abduction into another man's harem? No! On receiving a most obscene letter from the Mogul, who suggested that he would return her husband alive and unharmed were she to join his harem. She bided her time and planned a reply to his gross insolence. After choosing with care fifty-nine men, she advanced a surprise attack against the Mogul's camp, killed him and returned with her husband to safety.

Why is my time so different? Why did it change? How can we regain our self-mastery? Give me trumpets and horns when I come through the gates, my face bare in the wind, not veiled. Am I a silkworm, to be so cocooned? I want my strength of character to be tested amongst men and giants. I cannot bear meekness, and I have had to feign it.

There was a time when our women debated the sacred texts in the councils of rulers and scholars, sages and priests. We wish to regain those former customs, those lost opportunities, and put aside others that extinguish the divine sparks breathed upon us at our beginnings.

These days, what is demanded from us women – a continuous denial of self and a repression of ambition – constrains our innermost desires. Yes, Queen Meena is right to choose to be male at her next re-birth, to have opportunities aplenty to seek valour, to propel herself to heaven by hurling spears and wheeling swords.

My Ajee promised to come to me and tell me what it is like after death, and she has not done so. We agreed that she would confirm the believers' belief by returning and she has not. She promised she would ring the temple bell at midnight exactly to alert me. And she hasn't. She asked me to say this to no one, for if I did, the chances are that the temple bell would ring but it would not be her. All this was said with the seriousness of contemplation, and since the integrity of my grandmother is unsullied, I believe the sage Yajnavalyka's understanding stated in the Brihad-Aranyaka Upanishad: 'We have arisen from the elements and unto them we return.'

Here in the North, I would soon be known as a disloyal wife. I would work with my sister Queens for our 'School for Girls' but if we fail I shall leave. Once again I shall attempt to persuade the other two to come with me, but I can see that that would not be possible. It would be the pyre and honour rather than an escape in disgrace, their family's name brought low and spattered upon.

And yet I am asking myself how and why I can enable them to change their minds. Manu tells me there is a port where ships leave, travelling to far places, taking all those who are prepared for a new life with opportunities to remake themselves and gain in prestige and wealth. I am prepared to begin anew.

'May you prosper,' are Valmiki's last words of farewell in that much loved epic, the Ramayana. How I wish it would be so for us all. Oh, how tyranny has woven itself within the very weave of custom, concealing itself within custom's thread.

CHAPTER NINETEEN

Two Crafts Meet

AS THE CAVALRY accompanying the King's carriage approached the outer gates of the palace, a medley of sonorous Sanskrit chants and mantras – the grandeur of ancient orthodoxy – awoke the land. Flowers were strewn and sweet scents sprinkled where the King's body rested momentarily. Royal elephants trumpeted their welcome to the King and horses neighed, while clashing cymbals met the horns and bugles. The conch shells of the temples raised a call from ancient seas.

It was the Pundit Krishna, Most High Pundit of the Royal Court, who conducted this symphony of His Majesty's final homecoming, the Kingdom's ceremonial rite of arrival and departure of kings.

The Queens' anxious minds were full of these passing scenes. Their quarters had lost the welcoming sounds of life – music, conversation and laughter. Instead, an uneasy silence moved within their screened walls, as they attempted to accommodate the speedy preparation of the King and his pyre, while adjusting to their new thinking. Would they survive? *Could* they survive? Would Chance play them a favourable hand?

*

141

Pundit Krishna had battled for two hours yesterday with the smoke of sandalwood, incense, camphor and ghee. His limbs were weary, his eyes sorely red; his strained throat is losing its metre. Yet that night, he did not spare himself. Gathering his texts with urgency, he studied and prepared himself for this Royal meeting – his sacred duty to the Royal Family

The appointed time came and Pundit Krishna hastened to his audience with the Queens.

His position was an enviable one, much sought-after: not only was his remuneration large, but his influence at court was second only to the Royal Family and the highest echelons of the military. His father previously held the post and whenever an opportunity came his way, would take his only son, a mere boy, to the grand palace. The old man realised that by just being present in the room during a negotiation, his bright eager apprentice would learn much. And so it was that Pundit Krishna, with paternal care and direction, arrived at this most high office that would now prove more demanding of his skills of diplomacy, of self-discipline, compromise and scholarship than his father could ever possibly have envisaged.

Pundit Krishna approached the seated Queens; he had denied himself the warmth and joy of colour. His flowing white apparel carried no adornment, even his angochar which was usually an alluring mix of raw sienna and gold, or crimson with silk tassels of deep orange, is today softer, and though its rich satin-lined white, is daintily embroidered, and it is only with the narrowest of delicate lace that it is fringed. The Pundit's expression was sombre, his salutations reverential; his humility clear. He believed that these royal widows would soon be in Paradise with the King, looking down upon him, and he wished to gain their good will.

The Pundit was far-seeing. He knew perfectly well that when the new King was crowned, His Majesty would have his own trusted servants and loyal priests. Nevertheless, Pundit Krishna hoped to be offered a position not entirely without prestige or honour. He would therefore prepare the dispositions of the Queens and in addition conduct each phase of the suttee ceremony according to custom. Orthodoxy would direct him. By carrying out his other duties of loyalty and erudition with meticulous care, he hoped the incoming Royal Family would be favourably inclined to trust his judgement.

The overhead bell struck a pure sound, and as it circled the cool, serene space, Pundit Krishna called on the gods to witness the proceedings. He recited a mantra with a contemplation carried by the will and the sanctity of the occasion, chanting with fervour the glory of God in Sanskrit. Then he addressed the Queens.

'Your Majesties, Royal Queens of the Kingdom of Jyotika, wives of our courageous and compassionate King Paresh, who died in making our borders safe, I come to you as is my duty to prepare Your Majesties for this sacred ceremony which has come down to us from the first fathers of mankind.

'You, by your courage, your ardent devotion, purity of thought and constancy to your lord and King will once again, by your sacrifice, bring forth one of the greatest miracles of the Omnipotent. No mortal power can nullify this divine mystery, this sacred ordinance;

143

yet it could not come to pass without your womanly courage and superior chastity.

'Today, once again, our concept of unsullied honour and the divine relationship sealed by marriage, is being publicly renewed. Your becoming suttees is the ultimate act of devotion and loyalty which cannot be rendered even by the elements. I, with the people of the Kingdom of Jyotika, salute you. I, as well as the hundreds of your subjects anxiously awaiting you, am blessed to have lived to witness this glorious day of the salvation you will bring to all those intimately related to you.'

Pundit Krishna, who bowed only before the gods and the Royal Family, once again bowed low, moved by what he had said. The majesty and dignity of this finely sculptured room of the Trimurti was empty of sound, save for that of his voice. And there was this unusual calm, he sensed, of these fine women. Their peace had brought a sacred solemnity to their role. Their dignity touched him.

It was not without difficulty that he bowed so graciously, for age and its ailments were creeping upon him. The sculptures of Brahma, Vishnu and Shiva observed him with thoughtful deliberation. On this occasion, as on others, the Pundit's pressing concerns meant that he had at no time looked closely at the Trimurti, and so had not benefited from the sunburst of the sculptor's imagination.

'Tomorrow you will honour the Crown and the Royal Family of Jyotika.' he went on. 'You will be following in the footsteps of those women with a sacred devotion to their deceased husbands. I recall the presence of Sita, Savitri, Damayanti, Uroondhootee – all will be close to you as the blessed flames enable you to depart from us.

144

'Thirty years ago, my father performed the last rites for King Haresh, your father-in-law, who was accompanied by his six wives to the gates of Heaven. He explained to me that though the Kingdoms of the North know of the valour of our men, it is the high concept of honour our women hold, that has increased their esteem of us many fold.'

The Pundit was proud of this and paused. With care, he unwrapped a fading cloth of vermilion, opened a Sanskrit text so fragile that a number of pages were beyond repair and becoming dust. Straightening his bearing he read:

' "She that goes with her husband to the other world purifies three generations, that is the generations of her mother's side, her father's side and husband's side; and so she, being reckoned the purest and the best in fame amongst women, becomes too dear to her husband, and continues to divert herself with him for a period equal to the reign of fourteen Indras or three and a half cootee years (thirty-five million years) which is equal to the number of hairs on a human body".'

The Pundit paused, then lifted the tone of his voice for he believed that what he was about to say placed a heavy responsibility on widows. The consequences for husbands, were serious, for in the advent of wives failing to become suttees, this would adversely affect their husbands' future rebirth.

'Though the husband be guilty of slaying a Brahmin or a friend, or be ungrateful of his friend's past deeds, yet the said woman is capable of purifying him from all these sins. Hence after the demise of a husband, there can be no other duty for a faithful wife than to take herself to the fire.'

Queen Renu closed her eyes, covered her indignation with her palms. Queen Dayita touched her, appealing for patience.

The Pundit cleared his throat and drank from a brightly burnished bronze goblet. As his trembling hands cradled it, he saw a contorted reflection of himself. Something ill-defined from within him had briefly unlocked itself; a nearby moving lantern had made his features dance within the bronze. The distortion he recognised as a part of the vessel. It was so, it had always been so, yet why it should be so had never interested him.

The Pundit had come to an end and was showing signs of weariness, but his loyalty drove him on to say: 'The Royal Family to come will permit the people of Jyotika to pay homage to you before the King's altar. Your names will be inscribed lest the imprints of your hands and the soles of your feet will, with time, be eroded – lost like an aging memory.'

He closed the text and, looking at the graceful forms, the beauty veiled before him, was overcome with pity and sorrow, but custom is powerful and the Royal Pundit found that he had said to them: 'Only a wife who performs suttee can get rid of her feminine body.'

Though his account of what would come to pass was complete, there was a strange feeling in the air. Something important was absent: an emptiness encircled him. It was as if all that he had just said was unrelated to the Queens. But how could that be?

A respectful silence filled the room as Pundit Krishna waited patiently for permission to take his leave. There was much to be done for the day to come.

The Queens had not expected the suttee proceeding to have a life of its own – moving to its finality as if it were a natural phenomenon. At no time had they been asked if they agreed to it. This haste increased their anxiety and they were greatly disturbed.

The two younger Queens, by the slightest of movements sent their confirmation to Queen Meena to proceed. All three stood.

Pundit Krishna was relieved; permission to leave was here. He waited, but instead of dismissal, Queen Meena indicated that the Pundit should approach her. He was astonished to receive a scroll stamped with the royal seal. Satin ribbon, impressed with the late King's insignia enclosed it in a bow.

This was most unusual. Pundit Krishna hoped it was a pleasant surprise, some reward for his services, perhaps, before they departed. As a Brahmin priest of longstanding, living in comfort, performing divine rites, surrounded by those who respected him, he expected nothing less.

The Pundit looked at Queen Meena who affirmed that he should break the seal in her presence. The three women sat and awaited his response:

The handwriting on the scroll was beautifully formed; this erudition made him uneasy. At first his eyes saw the letters but he could not read them. A film of dazzling light seemed to be covering them.

He wondered suddenly whether a younger priest had already found favour with the Royal Family and whether he was to be ousted. His heart sank. However, he was a disciplined man and not without wisdom and knowledge of the etiquette of court. The Queens, seated, were waiting so he took hold of himself and began to read.

*

147

'We, Queens of the Kingdom of Jyotika, wish to thank Pundit Krishnajee who has performed his duty of encouraging us to accompany the body of our courageous, compassionate and wise Lord, His Majesty, King Paresh, the late King of Jyotika. You have elucidated the rulings and ancient customs of our Kingdom as befits your erudition and prestigious position at court. We acknowledge your guidance to us this day.

'However, after much study and careful consideration, and with the help of the wishes of our late King, as well as the scholarship and wisdom proffered by sages and scholars, we have decided that on this day we would like to begin to walk upon another path to Dharma. Our chosen path is not narrow. It will enable us to use the remainder of our lives to bring that which is good to the King's name, to his relatives, and to our family, as well as to the parents and children of Jyotika.

'We, Queens of the late King of Jyotika, find we are unable to take it upon ourselves to terminate God's gift of life that honours us so. This divine offering – life – is the most worthy of miracles we hold, and therefore we embrace it with honour, dignity and integrity.

'Together, we have formed an important plan. We would like to open a school for young girls – children of the Royal compound. Queen Dayita will teach them poise, movement, form, rhythm and measure, for as you know she was trained at the renowned Shiva's Temple of Dance and became the prima temple dancer of all the kingdoms of the North. Queen Renu will teach the girls to think, to question, to be discerning. They will learn to read the sacred texts and write their own personal mantras. And Queen Meena will teach them to read and write beautifully, to paint, to sing with her veena and make music. We are hoping later, to supplement these arts with other useful skills.

'This new Kingdom of Jyotika where eventually there will be many schools for girls came to us in recurring dreams. Again and again we were visited. We believe Saraswatee, the Goddess of Education is the source of our inspiration and will not be comforted unless we do as she so plainly wishes.

'It is a new path. We are hoping that you will use your good offices to enable this vision to come to pass. Our late King Paresh, the Wise, the Compassionate, discussed this with us, and did solemnly ask us not to become suttees as his mother, Queen Sanjivani, had had to do. She had no choice but to join with the other Queens, though, we are told that she had plans to impart her erudition to the young.

'When a mere boy, the late King on one of his sojourns through the Kingdom with his father, by chance witnessed a widow's death by fire. The shrieks and cries of agony by the woman calling upon him for help stayed with him always.

'It is in part for these reasons that we know we have the encouragement and the King's blessing for this endeavour, and are hoping to name our school after his mother, Queen Sanjivani. Once more we ask that you join with us, most honoured Pundit of the Royal Court, to enable the flowering of this good.'

Mercifully, it was short. The scroll curled upon itself and closed its contents, for Pundit Krishna had released it.

The water carrier sat on the jute bag. Of late Kunwar had become anxious, wondering who to entrust with the letter buried beneath him. He was in a quandary. Should he approach the young Pundit Baalaajee? Kunwar knew he had to be careful: a wrong move could mean losing his livelihood and with it, that little bit of self-importance that his water carrying duties gave him. Besides, working in the Royal compound itself had a certain standing in his district. He must tread carefully.

The right move, he pondered, could lead to a betterment of his situation. The problem was, he had no way of knowing what was the right move. Kunwar was convinced that the letter was important, for the old Pundit was trying to reach it. A dying man would only be trying to get hold of something of worth. To whom could this letter be of value? But answer came there none.

Daily, Kunwar had sat on the jute bag. This had caused the soil to compact. So with the sharp end of a piece of wood, he cautiously probed the sides, loosened the earth and retrieved the letter. He had not yet decided to ask others in the royal compound whom they thought could be trusted. To whom would they go, if they needed good advice? In the meantime, he would work out what he should say in his defence, knowing that he would have to explain how the letter came to him. These things needed more thought. Could it be, asked Kunwar, that God was beginning to smile upon him? He had at no time shirked his duty, nor cheated on the quantity of water he measured out for each priest. These acts had obviously not gone unnoticed.

Pundit Krishna was baffled, his thoughts confused. Most of all he was stunned. Was this a ploy on the Queens' part to ascertain the strength of his loyalty to the late King? Or were they so stricken by grief and fear of the unknown that they had lost their senses, and their troubled minds sought to offer them sanctuary in a school? He then considered that since it might be a temporary reaction to the suddenness of their grief, he would maintain a normality which in itself would assist their return to their former selves.

As he looked at the scroll, he was in no doubt that it should be destroyed, lest it fell into the wrong hands and they were brought low.

A school for girls? What an idea! Would they then become good daughters and wives? Or would they develop ideas unsuited to their sex and create an imbalance in the home and outside of it? He frowned and asked himself who would provide slates and pencils, a blackboard and chalk for such an idea? Where would it be? How could they possibly bring children of all ranks and castes and ask them to sit side by side every day? Impossible! It was the work of a fevered brain, he decided, and thought, I will offer opium, and will ensure that cloves and cardamom, the soothing of the one and the comforting scent of the other, are added. This compound of my making may prevent their complete unravelling before the pyre is lit.

The Royal Pundit had seen the anxiously awaiting crowd, their expectations growing, the lines and columns swelling. The masons were even now preparing for the imprints of the Queens' soles and palms. All other pundits of the court were making ready for this grand procession and spectacle. The King's soldiers would be present. Should the widowed Queens not appear, what would his brother, the Prince Regent, Prince Mahendra, make of this? And his wives?

151

A time-honoured custom being put aside by dreams? More like a weak mind seeking solace, seeking shelter in fantasies of its own making. It was piteously sad.

Pundit Krishna felt he had no choice but to try and bring them back to the pyre, that path to salvation for widows, more so for those who wish to be reborn male. He owed it to the King, the Royal Family and the people of Jyotika.

He bowed low: 'Your Majesties, I have read your response to the ancient custom of the Kingdom of Jyotika. You are Royal Queens and your life has been an example to the virtue of womanhood; thus let your passing be the same. It is likely that His Majesty's wishes to you were directed by concerns for your distress rather than expressing his innermost desire. He was hoping that your devotion and your purity of thought would of themselves be sufficient to persuade you to accompany him. I know that you are aware that to ask for what is required is not the way of Kings.

'Imagine his joy on seeing his three Queens! His Majesty knew that you would honour him in death, as he favoured you in life. In this Kingdom, we know that it is from duties and obligations faithfully carried out that we earn our worth. We are defined by our responsibilities to society – nothing else is there.'

Queen Meena was visibly moved. Queen Dayita felt challenged and Queen Renu admired his skill.

'As a long-trusted servant to the Royal Family,' he went on, 'I am duty bound to inform you of the consequences, should you decide not to join your King on his pyre. Most Gracious Queens of Jyotika, I am pained to say that you will be shunned by all. Living in a state of neglect you cannot possibly imagine.

'I do not have to remind you that you are unable to return to your parents, and were you to move out of the Royal compound, you would have to hide your identities permanently. Your beauty, fine form and grace would greatly endanger you. I implore you Most Gracious Queens of Jyotika to reconsider your position.

'You would be choosing a wretched existence, instead of taking the departure that enables you to be transformed, becoming sacred and holy, immortal. Men and women will come from afar to worship at your sculptured soles and palms. I beg you, Royal Queens of Jyotika, to reconsider your refusal to embrace our long-held tradition that has served us well, lifted our esteem beyond our boundaries. Would the people of Jyotika not ask themselves, "What does it say about the King of Jyotika, who has given his very life to protect us, if his wives will not accompany him on his last journey?" '

Queen Renu was fascinated by this cunning, Queen Meena deeply concerned. Queen Dayita reflected on the position he held and his brilliant mind.

'Because of this,' the Pundit went on, his voice lowered, 'I am willing, even at the risk of my honoured reputation, to offer you sufficient opium, indeed to administer it myself, when you have satisfied the jostling, shouting crowd, and are safely behind the protective enclosure. I shall ensure that you will be in too deep a sleep to feel the flames as they engulf your mortal remains, your immortal spirit having already left its casement.

'I would make it attractive for the undertakers to look another way as well as pay for their silence later. This is my duty, if you so wish it. You may prefer to consult with each other now, as time approaches us, unimpeded. If this meets with Your Majesties' approval, I shall take my leave. However, I most humbly plead with the Queens of Jyotika, to consider with care what are the full consequences of their proposal, for the King, for their own families, for the people of Jyotika and their own rebirth.'

CHAPTER TWENTY

The Queens' Scroll

THE QUEENS LOOKED at each other and Queen Meena responded: 'Long-trusted and faithful servant to the Royal Family, we thank you with all our hearts. We want you to know that whatever becomes of us, we would leave behind, for the incoming Royal Family, a well-deserved commendation of the highest order pertaining to your loyalty and faithfulness to the Crown. We shall ensure that all know our chosen path was ours and that you did try to direct us to the pyre.

'However, we trust your intellect and judgement and it is for this reason and no other that we would prefer you to walk with us. Your valuable practical assistance, your wisdom, will enable us to lay a foundation that will arouse the admiration, wonder and esteem of generations to come. Your name would be remembered. You would be seen as Pundit Supreme, with a vision blessed by Brahma, denied to many.

'You would be immortalised not only by the entire Northern Kingdoms but throughout the full length and breadth of this vast land, for the courage you would have shown in supporting the betterment of half the lives in every Kingdom. Your qualities of courage and integrity would be praised in song and mantras and in the telling by many, handed down from generation to generation. You too must therefore choose. We trust you will be with us, enabling us to create this good.

'Our sister Queen Renu would now speak on our behalf. Her view will be our final word on this ancient custom and will reveal why we are unable to willingly destroy our lives in so perilous a manner. After this, we ask you to assist Queen Dayita to the state room. She needs your support, for her disposition is frail. We implore you to do all that is in your power to strengthen her to face this most painful of burdens that would be placed upon us and of which you have judiciously reminded us.'

The Pundit bowed low and his inner self offered him the solace of his personal mantra which he now recited without sound. There was pain in his stomach, his age was also affecting his stamina. And now he saw Queen Renu rising. He noted that she had taken up a position of advocacy.

For Queen Renu, this was the field of mental battle and in her mind's eye she knew she was facing columns of fierce guardians of religious beliefs – religious warriors, past and present, experienced advocates of tradition, unequalled in learning. Such an army watched her closely. Well equipped, they awaited any evidence of chinks in her armour which would be extended, then pulled apart.

Before addressing him, Queen Renu acknowledged in full his royal position by the appropriate salutation as was the custom in the South:

'Pundit Krishnajee, most worthy, faithful and trusted servant, I, Queen Renu, third and youngest wife of our late King, was taken from my father's

Kingdom in the South. I have been a guest in this Northern Kingdom of Jyotika as well as in the palace itself. I have been met on all sides by your richly endowed customary courtesies accorded to guests. My presence at the court has not been long. I accept that I cannot be offered the privileges granted to one of its own. I, therefore, being a guest, cannot address you as an advocate of our position without first seeking your indulgence, your permission to participate before you at this meeting.

'Though my marriage to the King makes me one with his other gracious Queens, neither I nor the people of Jyotika have had time sufficient in duration to knit closely these newly formed ties. I therefore need your good will to proceed.'

She awaited his response.

The elderly man was moved by her courtesy towards him, and he, with the dignity of antiquity, gave her a gracious bow.

'Most worthy of pundits I thank you,' Queen Renu said. 'My bow is well strung and you will receive from me four shafts of light. I now shoot the first. I ask your forgiveness for sending it, as this first shaft comes from your own quiver – the Shastras – which are full of inconsistencies. It enables one to make a strong case against, as well as for, this practice of suttee. In addition, this sacrifice is not practised everywhere in this huge sacred land of ours, which was once the abode of the gods. There is no evidence that the gods favour the Kingdoms which perform it; is it not clear therefore, that it is not needed for our salvation?' She paused. When the Shastras can negate as well as support the same practice, it brings it into a sphere of ambivalence and uncertainty. Serious scholars must reject an idea that demands the very life of another when the support for such a sacrifice is itself a matter of conjecture.

'My second shaft of light has its source in the eternal flame of the Shastras, which, if it says anything, says one thing loudly and clearly: the paths to God are many. We are merely selecting one that harms none; we are choosing one that brings light to the hearts of men, reduces suffering and adds joy not only to one's family but to all. This, is what we are proposing – seeking Dharma, seeking the good, by walking another path.

'My third shaft of light comes from the late King's character. We know that King Paresh would have felt humiliated had his soldiers thought he could not gain salvation by his own actions, but had to sacrifice the lives of three women to attain it. He trusted that his soldiers knew and the Kingdom understood that it was his example on the battlefield that honoured his name, *not* ourselves on his pyre. To seek his comfort by the discomfort of others, was not our late consort's code of practice in life. Therefore, to see us turned to ash in so cruel a manner would bring him such discomfort, that whoever performed such a task would earn his justifiable anger.

'To knowingly court the anger of a just man will not be viewed kindly by the gods. It is in the light of this, to protect you from losing your high caste status in your next rebirth, that I have felt duty bound to reveal this to you. Royal Pundit most High, consider this: what does it say of the moral strength of our men, when they ask their wives, whose entire life has been sacrificed to their welfare, to save them from the just punishment of God for their crimes, in this most barbaric and savage way. In so doing, does such a man not cheat the law of Karma? Are our priests, philosophers and scholars, so tied to rituals that they have lost that profound understanding of the purpose of life – which is to care for one another and to enlarge our consciousness and with it our imagination for the good?

'You in your wisdom have seen that time would erode the sculptured imprints of our palms and soles. What we hope to engage in will have a life of its own. Knowledge grows, develops; old understanding gives way to the new.

'My fourth and final shaft of light is the strongest, and though it has already been alluded to, it lies at the very centre of Sanatan Dharmic principles. Since without it we will regress to the most primitive of life forms, the need to bring it before you once more is compelling. I shall now so aim my arrow that it rests upright, one step before you.

'As long as our men are able to satisfy their appetites, indifferent to the pain, distress and dishonour they bring to others; as long as such men are able to gain Heaven without compensating their victims; as long as such men are not seeking forgiveness and are without the need to live better lives, but instead await their salvation by sacrificing the lives of others on their pyre; these men will have no incentive to live the good life that pleases God. Such a combination of rewards for men is repugnant to all human feelings everywhere and is also at variance with the ways of Heaven. Any kingdom that continues to practise this ignominy will bring the wrath of God upon it and will remove itself from men's vision of what is enduring, worthy and honourable. It shall become a nothingness that not even the wind feels or sees.'

Queen Meena became restless, troubled, wondering whether Sister Renu's tone should not have been softened, even a few lines altered. We need the Pundit's help, she was thinking. This is not the way to entreat him. Oh, where is her restraint? Does she not understand our true position now? Scholarly restraint is such a fine tool in negotiations between unequals. If used deftly much can be achieved. Why does Sister Renu not employ it?

Queen Dayita, felt admiration for this archer; she was somewhat jealous, but most pleased to be included in this scholarly repartee, for in Queen Renu's defiance, she found strength and comfort.

The weariness of the day came upon Pundit Krishna, as a mighty wave, hurling him on to the shore. Aware that the next incoming wave could drag him back into the ocean deeps, he rose. 'Your Majesties, if you faithfully intend to carry out the declarations you have made here, there is nothing more to be said. I humbly ask your permission to depart and shall wait upon Her Majesty Queen Dayita, outside, in the company of the King's guards.'

Queen Renu approached Pundit Krisahnajee and offered him a sealed scroll, a copy of her personal address which included additional reasons for their position, but which she had felt were inappropriate to openly assert there and then. The Queens believed that in his private moments of quiet contemplation, having these scrolls would enable him to reassess their perception and beliefs.

The two Queens departed, leaving Queen Dayita to prepare herself with the utmost care before approaching the well-guarded, colossal door.

CHAPTER TWENTY-ONE

The Measure of a Temple Dancer

AS QUEEN DAYITA approached the grand door, the guards opened it and bowed in deep reverence. The perfumed air which her passing had stirred, raised the sleeping folds of their garments.

Once more, Pundit Krishna offered his salutations. The Queen's veil in shades approaching dusk, embroidered with silver threads, was more transparent, or so it seemed to him. It might just be that he could now see as never before; her presence was for the first time within his visible reach.

They walked alone along the royal corridor that led to the King's body lying in state, their steps quiet and unhurried. Only a fragile delicacy of shifting light came through the floral tracery in sandstone. All else was still. After a while, Queen Dayita spoke. In a voice schooled by her guru and dance tutor of the Temple, she whispered that she would like to rest, to gather herself awhile, before facing His Majesty, her consort and Lord.

'My sorrow has so overcome my spirit Pundit Krishnajee that I am not myself,' she murmured, seated on a cushioned chair. 'I wish to thank you for agreeing to accompany me.' Her veiled voice, carrying the warmth of spring, ensured that he was conscious of this privilege to have been chosen to walk with her. 'After my sacred duties are performed, I would like to consult you, for now more than ever the Queens of Jyotika are in need of someone most trustworthy; one who also understands the larger nobility of our cause and respects the traditional etiquette of the royal court, to advise us.'

The Pundit could see that the task before her had taken its toll, for she closed her eyes and her breathing slowed. As he looked at her, his eyes followed the threads and pattern of her garment. He discovered that, though in mourning, her outer apparel was appealing: a border of silver lotuses following the curves of her fullness. She moved as in attitudes of dance to adjust her partially lifting veil better to protect herself – a lifelong habit.

As their steps continued on, Queen Dayita spoke to him of her need for a guru. Her royal protection, which had arisen from being the King's temple dancer, and later his wife, was now being brought to a close. Her guru and tutor at Shiva's Temple of Mysticism in Dance, she informed him, had died six months after she became the second Queen of Jyotika. She was therefore now more than ever before in need of a trusted friend and spiritual guide to whom she could turn for solace and a more profound understanding of the divine purpose and joys of life. 'I wish to be strengthened, to live with affection for those around me once more.

'Affection,' he thought he heard her say, though it was scarcely discernible, 'comes to us, if we are prepared to offer it to others.

'These attributes I have mentioned are more likely to be fulfilled by a younger pundit with a less ascetic attitude to life. I have in mind one who is amiable, with a larger willingness to listen well,' she explained, her voice softening. 'Someone from the royal court,' she explained, 'had suggested Pundit Baalaajee. They spoke very highly of him.' Despite this, Queen Dayita said, she would be happy to be guided by him – the Royal Court's Pundit – on a matter of such delicacy. She would await his recommendation.

At that point, the royal widow left Pundit Krishna and entered the privacy of the King's temple, where the dead King of Jyotika lay in state.

The King may have requested, or it may have been Queen Meena's choice, for he was not dressed in the elaborate gold cloth, rich satins, chiffon and crepe de chine of a crowned monarch. Instead he was wrapped in embroidered white silk. His turban in carmine red and gold, adorned him, while holding in place the family's insignia – an eagle and a dove. It was an exquisitely sculpted piece of jewellery inlaid with rubies.

Queen Dayita had never envisaged this day. She knew the King intimately and seeing him so still, his eyes closed, radiating no light or warmth, awakened her resolve to live and offer her rapture of movements in dance to the young. Queen Renu was right, she thought. They must create something of worth for the children with the remainder of their lives. They would take this path; it would be pleasing to God. Their success would encourage other wives to forgo the pyre and to climb life's other paths.

While Queen Dayita was taking aarti round and round the King, she was also quietly offering the sanctity and protection of her personal mantra to his spirit

163

which she felt hovered above him. She noticed that a tub of honey had been left open on a corner table and a family of bees was feasting. Thinking that they might come and settle upon the King, she covered it, but not without difficulty as the bees disliked her disturbance and tried to buzz her away. She asked one of the guards to have a maidservant remove it.

Meanwhile Pundit Krishna was striding up and down the corridor deep in thought. Moved by her beauty and grace, he felt as if she had been performing a sacred temple dance before him, her movements had attained a purity of form. The King's second wife had always been aloof, and certainly beyond reach of those without royal connections; her ladies-in-waiting had found her so. Even here and now, her steps were within an ancient vase of royal courtesies. Pundit Krishna had seen her previously, but only from afar. Fine veils protected her from the searching gaze of commoners and unfavoured eyes within the palace.

From the characteristics she stipulated as her requirements for a guru, it was clear Queen Dayita had ruled him out. He would very much like to recommend himself, but that was a matter of some delicacy. The Royal Court Pundit wondered what he could do that would favour him before others. To become her guru, to meet with her in private, to be in such a favoured position, comes to him with a pressing urgency. Then misgivings struck him. How could he enjoy this royal privilege of being her guru, and at the same time meet the growing expectations of the anxious, jostling crowd outside the palace gates? And what about those royal emotions of Prince Mahendra for his brother? Although Pundit Krishna had not met the Prince

Regent, he assumed that the ruler would be seeking loyalty, an enhancement of prestige and esteem for the Crown.

The Queens, seemed unaware that they needed first to become acceptable to the priestly class, who could so easily undermine them. They sought freedom to walk a new path, one that was sure to arouse hostility and suspicion. To be free, yes – but with honour. His astuteness alerted him to the fact that the more acceptable the Queen was, the less compromised would her guru be.

Could all this be accomplished? It was a towering challenge. Nevertheless, he was feeling energised. It was then that he reminded himself that he, Pundit Krishna, was the royal pundit supreme. No pundit would dare to challenge him. Respect for his seniority as well as his influence on their future prospects might enable him to satisfy the anxieties of the establishment. Meanwhile, he would try to offer an opening to the Queens to begin their school. If he could perform this balancing act, he would become indispensable to the Queens and therefore become the ideal choice for Queen Dayita's guru.

Then a shadow fell upon him. A deep misgiving hovered above him. It was an impossible endeavour, foolhardy! He should do nothing to sully his fine reputation, his life's painstaking creation. It was an intoxicating dream but a dream it should stay.

Yet his mind would not let it go, on the contrary, it became enlarged and his ripened imagination illuminated a perfumed path for him to take.

For some time now, it had occurred to him that the slave girl Kala had been taken forcefully *not* by a royal guest, which was what she said, but by the King himself. The evidence appeared compelling. By the age of fourteen, Kala had blossomed into one of those sensuous forms of joy, sculptured in the sacred temples. When she became pregnant, bearing in mind that Queen Meena and Queen Dayita had not yet been with child, Pundit Krishna, observed the King's self-confidence blossoming. His Majesty's demeanour appeared enhanced, he was at peace with himself; his eyes acquired a confidence, his steps a calmness.

Private arrangements were made by someone in the palace; every month, without fail, the Pundit was given a substantial offering of clothes, food and toys to take to Kala. He knew he was trusted to assume the role of the sole giver of the gifts and he played that role well. Loyalty to the Crown was his supreme duty.

There could be no other explanation for such generosity. Therefore, he believed that in the absence of his wives, the King would not be displeased to have the company of Kala. As the sacred ritual of suttee consumed all physical ugliness of age and sickness, the slave-girl would regain her former self – that exciting springtime of joy. Were this choice of his to be questioned by the other pundits, he would take the most vocal of the dissidents into his confidence, explaining this royal folly, which his priestly brother would see must remain within the boundary of discretion and so be undisclosed.

In addition, he would explain that it was the King's private wish to have his Queens lay the foundations of an honourable school for girls in memory of his mother. He would simply remind everyone that the sacred fires of the King's pyre would purify Kala, and she would be made whole again. Her present imperfections of caste and the wear and tear of time would leave her; these were the just rewards of pure devotion. To lay down your life for another had from the beginning of time, pleased the gods and brought honour to those devotees and their families.

Again the enormity of what he was attempting to do weighed heavily upon him. This dilemma of the Queens' making preyed on him, sapping his energy.

Kala's young daughter Sujata would certainly become a pupil at the school for girls in the compound; she might even become an accomplished musician, dancer or painter, serving the Royal Family. Without her mother becoming a royal suttee, Sujata would not gain entrance to the royal school. Pundit Krishna felt a sudden pang of longing for the privilege of seeing Queen Dayita dance. But this rested on being able to carry out an impossible task.

His opponents would be the Brahmins, the Royal Family, and the people whose expectations would be disappointed. He must face them, but with what? He had only his powers of persuasion, his knowledge of men, and his present position, which itself could be irreparably harmed were he to make an error of judgement at any time along the hazardous way before him.

It was clear to Pundit Krishna that no one was as qualified as he was, to become the guru to a royal widow. Most pundits he knew were unfit to be in the same room with Queen Dayita. He certainly did not think that Pundit Baalaajee was suitable. Yes, he was young, alert and erudite. His features were agreeable, but he was nowhere close to understanding how to conduct himself in the presence of royalty. He could not recall Baalaajee ever having a single meeting with any member of the Royal Family. The very fact that he was unschooled in royal etiquette and diplomacy made Pundit Baalaajee unsuited for the royal court. The young man would be at a loss – conducting himself without finesse. In addition, Pundit Krishna had noted time and again that this young man's views were far too lax on religious concerns.

His thoughts moved restlessly backwards and forwards. Despite what had been said, he was well aware that no one could terminate without warning a strongly held custom, sanctified in ancient writ. The repercussions were going to be far greater than the Queens, in their cloistered quarters, could ever have imagined. They had no idea of just how rough, uncouth and ordinary, the common people were. Did the royals think their subjects were the way they saw them? Their pupils would have to be handpicked from the compound. They must come from ambitious, well-to-do families, who would appreciate the worth of the school, in improving their daughters' marriage prospects. And no doubt it would be these beneficiaries who would be spreading the good name of the school far and wide.

The Pundit's gentle smile faded as he acknowledged once more that he would not have an easy time of it, putting the Queens' ideas across to his colleagues. They would be aghast. What small gesture could he make to the traditionalists like himself? Maybe if Queen Dayita could be persuaded to offer the Brahmins a sacred temple dance once every full moon, they might, albeit reluctantly, soften their disapproval. Maybe offerings of freshly made delicious sweets could be taken to them, as part of the ceremony when they left.

He knew that any dissident of the plan, once taken into his confidence about Kala, would in turn take others in his confidence; soon everyone would feel privileged in being the sole possessor of a Royal secret. Quietly they would withdraw their criticism of him. He needed to think it all through again! There was so much to do and so little time.

The elderly Pundit made up his mind. He would send a summons now to Kala, to meet the Queens in the throne room. Then he would offer her three fine pieces of jewellery, the contributions of the three Queens, and ask her to become a suttee for the King. It would be an honour to be chosen – she would know this. Besides, Kala trusted him, believing that the gifts he continued to bring her were partly a result of his generous nature. The servants' compound was well disposed towards him; all knew of these charitable acts.

He would explain to Kala that her wise decision meant that he would adopt her daughter, bring Sujata up as his own. The jewellery she would be given could become her daughter's dowry at fourteen. Yes, he would speak to Kala, explain everything. It would be a closely guarded private meeting.

A slave-girl would surely not deny herself such a privilege, especially as the bliss that awaited her was far greater than she could possibly have imagined. By this selfless act, she was ensuring that she would return in her next life not as a mere slave-girl but as a woman of the Kshatriya caste. So powerful was the act of becoming a suttee that were she to climb the pyre willingly, full of purity of thought and devotion to the King, he would not be surprised if she even became a Brahmin woman.

Pundit Krishna perceived no flaws in his plan. He was pleased with his imaginative response to this intricately complex labyrinth through which he would be leading the Queens. His understanding was that he would harm no one while enabling all to attain worthy goals.

CHAPTER TWENTY-TWO

A Contrivance Conceived

IT WAS HER perfume that reached him first. Pundit Krishna awoke from his reverie and was reminded of a heavenly nymph, a fresco in a cave, he had once explored in his youth.

The Pundit explained his arrangement. Kala's rise to the upper rungs of the caste hierarchy was emphasised. After the cremation, he would become Sujata's guardian and later use the royal gifts of jewellery as her dowry. He pointed out that the people's expectations were growing. Many were sleeping out in the open so as not to miss the colourful funerary procession that should accompany the King and his Queens. How could expectations of that magnitude not be fulfilled?

'If the King were to be seen unaccompanied, he would be severely compromised in the eyes of his subjects. Prince Mahendra may in turn feel its repercussions on his reign, but what is certain is that the newly crowned King would see your choice as an omen that the strength and esteem of the Royal Family here were being weakened.

'It pains me greatly, yet we need to keep in mind that your own positions as the King's widows residing in the royal palace could so easily become untenable. Your present aspirations may then not come to fruition and your lives gradually dwindle to a withered shadow of your present passions for the good. Your only hope of success lies in this compromise. We shall meet in the throne room. I shall send a despatch to Kala by the King's messenger. This should be sufficient, adding urgency and aura to our request. I shall inform the guards to expect her and to welcome her as she walks to the throne room.

Queen Dayita could see the madness of this contrivance, its breathtaking inconsistency, its inherent ugliness and dangers. For the first time she felt her feet move involuntarily. Yet all that the Pundit had said was true. There would be difficult days ahead, but these she had anticipated, and had felt that she would be able to overcome them, given time and the chance to win over the new Queens and the higher echelons of Brahmins.

What the Pundit had suggested made faint-hearted cowards of them all. He had read their written reply to suttee, had listened to Sister Renu's reasoned arguments, but had understood nothing. If the King did not require their deaths to gain his salvation, he certainly did not require Kala's. It was true that both she and Queen Meena had had difficulty at first in comprehending the fullness of what Queen Renu was offering them. Their Southern Sister Queen was overthrowing an entire library of beliefs. Queen Dayita had found this strangely exciting. Of course they were being asked to move from a belief of death on a pyre, to one that offered them an opportunity to become the means of children's enlightenment; their widowhood was given a dynamic and worthy purpose. They were bound to be in favour of it.

It was too much to ask of the Pundit, Queen Dayita told herself: his beliefs, reputation and his future were at stake. They were asking him to leap across a yawning crevasse, at such a vulnerable age. None of them had time on their side. If they had even a whole year, they might still have failed to convince him, so why did they think they could do it in the time of its telling?

The Queens intended to meet with Prince Mahendra before his Coronation, to explain their plans. They would also be speaking to mothers to encourage them to send their daughters to the royal school. She was hoping that, given time, mothers and the Queens of King Mahendra would come to believe that what they were doing was beneficial to the compound and to the good name of the Royal Family, and that climbing the pyre would have been a loss, a waste of human endeavour. Queen Dayita was also hoping that a few of the younger Queens might find comfort in their idea. It was so important that the school got started – that it be given the blessing of the priestly class.

Though full of misgiving, Queen Dayita decided to go along with his proposition, outwardly at least, while secretly devising a way to save the slave-girl. Her life at the Temple of Dance had taught her to be bold, to take risks. Even if she had to do it herself, she would save Kala. To do otherwise would send a message too ghastly to contemplate, too far removed from their motives and their new understanding. To send Kala to her death would be far worse than their climbing the pyre. The hypocrisy and deceitful compliance of the act would destroy them.

173

This plan of hers she must keep to herself, disclose it only to her sister Queens, for it was clear Pundit Krishna would not agree to it. How could he? It was the very essence of his strategy.

Queen Dayita said that she would leave the matter in his capable hands and would inform her sister Queens immediately of this arrangement. They would join him in the throne room and the gifts of jewellery would be made ready.

'Before we part, Pundit Krishnajee,' she entreated in a softer tone, 'I know you are aware that these trying circumstances have made it all the more pressing for me to find a guru. I must now take consul, for my new life is about to begin and I shall be needing assistance in giving it direction. An early consideration would offer me peace of mind Krishnajee. Have you thought of anyone? Please ensure it is someone blessed with the attributes of trustworthiness and loyalty.'

'Trustworthiness, Your Royal Highness, is all-important as well as understanding the strict etiquette of the royal court, being at ease with royalty yet maintaining standards of professionalism is not easily attained. The relationship between a guru, one who offers a deeper understanding of life, and he or she who is prepared to receive this enlightenment, must be of the highest order. Please beware, especially of the young, Queen of Jyotika.'

Suddenly there was a sound – a bee trapped in her veils was seeking a way out. Queen Dayita gently lifted the layers of rich lace, but the bee climbed higher; she had no choice but to raise her arms high, and yet higher still. The bee was now well above her forehead, entangled in her hair. Her veil must rise still further.

174

The bee in its bewilderment darted about. Queen Dayita remained calm, an enchanting form – rhythmic – unruffled. The Pundit was too close. He had become the most privileged of commoners, seeing her beauty uncovered in this intriguing way. It was done. The bee sped away.

The veils were lowered once more, but her scent had escaped and now encircled the Pundit. These artful movements of arms and lace drifting upwards along her warmth, so far beyond etiquette, had led his imagination where it was forbidden to go. Here, another world was opening before him – an unspoken revelation of joy, of life itself. To a man, no longer young, such a vision was devastating.

Pundit Krishna was visibly moved. He needed to ensure that he *and no other* would have this heaven, this living Apsara. His temples throbbed. 'Queen Dayita,' he began, his limbs trembling, but the compassionate cover of his garments protected him. Moments passed. Pundit Krishna regained his composure and with it – himself.

'I, Pundit to the royal court, bearing in mind the circumstance of your need, and time being of the essence, would be happy to consider myself in the honoured role of your guru.' He noted that she appeared neither visibly happy nor even relieved at his offer and wondered whether she was disappointed. He continued, 'I would ensure that you are shown the best paths to walk in the maze that you will all too soon encounter in your new life.'

'Pundit Krishnajee, Royal Pundit of the Court,' Queen Dayita said, bowing her head gently, 'I accept your concern for the new path we have taken. I am pleased that you will do your utmost to enable our goals to come to pass. Your long experience with the Royal Family, your understanding of the etiquette and demands of the royal court favour you. Having so graciously offered yourself, I here and now accept you.'

She paused as if in prayer, closed her eyes and then on awakening said: 'Bless me with your favourite mantra, Gurujee, and pray for me. Think of the large work we have to do together and of the wonderment of our rich heritage. We will offer a fine selection of its erudition, skills and accomplishments to the young. As my guru, you and no other may with time, be favoured with that privilege of seeing my uppermost veil folded when we are in serious discourse pertaining to the welfare of our school. Such a time can only come when we three Queens are safely established in our endeavours.' She lowered her head. The movement was unhurried and thoughtful. She was royal; he had become her guru. In this situation where she could not be publicly seen, her veil was allowed to fall on her shoulders.

With eyes closed and doing his utmost for his voice and words to have a significance and strength that would appeal to her and the gods, the Pundit rested his hands upon her head and blessed her. Caressing the parting of her hair thrice, he offered solace and a genuine empathy with her new, troubled life ahead. As his voice came to a halt, she drew her veil over her face before lifting herself and was hidden once more.

CHAPTER TWENTY-THREE

A Ghastly Masquerade

BAALAAJEE'S STILLNESS WAS complete, his thoughts concentrated but getting nowhere. Finding a response to the royal summons that would save Kala was proving beyond this scholar.

A growing apprehension enveloped him. It touched Kala. 'Baalaajee why is this? I am a house-slave in the compound, living in the servants' quarters. They know me. Now they think I am close to God. Baalaajee, tell them I am Kala. Tell them, please.'

'Wait! Yes! Yes!' Baalaajee seized on it as it came to him. He repeated it to himself, the better to hold what the texts prescribed: '*According to the rules, she must give her consent. The Hindoo divines assert that the love of goodness for its own sake ought to be the sole emotion of the woman. Her mind and thoughts must be pure. But were she to take to the pyre, not with a pure heart but with hopes of posthumous rewards or even the slightest intrusion of an interested motive, then her sacrifice is without worth and is of no significance, for it has been transformed into a selfish bargain with God for calculated profit, and all is forfeited. The sacrifice loses its name and so itself.*'

Baalaajee whispered, 'Kala, you must listen carefully to what they say. Whatever they promise you, accept nothing, agree to do nothing. At no time say yes to anything even if they offer you Heaven. Just be quiet and listen. Please remember, Kala. Never say, "yes, I agree." If you do not understand what they are saying, it is better to say nothing.' Suddenly he stopped and said with an urgency that troubled her. 'If they say, "You are silent, it means you agree" always remember to say, "I agree to nothing".'

'But if they offer me Heaven, why should I say nothing?'

'Because Heaven is not theirs and so they cannot give it to you. Can you give away something you do not have?'

The woman was thinking: 'What is Baalaajee saying? Heaven is what everybody wants. Why does he think I don't want to be with God for ever as other people do? Instead, she probed: 'You say they do not have Heaven. Baalaajee, they are Brahmins reading the Shastras every day. Is the way to Heaven not written in the Shastras?'

'Kala, you will go to heaven without their help. They cannot promise you Heaven, only God can. Whatever they offer you, however precious, do not accept today. Thank them and say you need time to make up your mind; say that you will give an answer when your mind is pure. Your state of mind is not pure, Kala, if when they offer you something, you would like to have it.'

'Baalaajee. Look at me,' she said, saddened by what she heard. 'I need good fortune.' Kala was distressed and thought of her youth, when she was broken into by one of the royal guests; that was when she was beautiful, when her hair danced and her eyes laughed. She had struggled to protect her good name but was held down.

178

Torn apart. Dishonoured. When she found she was with child, and had become what men call a 'used leaf', she walked to the riverbank to give what was left of herself to the swift currents below. Her courage failed her. The thought of struggling alone, drowning in the cold stream, held her feet on the warm, solid bank. The fact that she was alive, was witness to her fear in the face of death. Later in the quiet of the night, a part of herself returned, 'You are a mother.' it said, 'one day, your daughter and you would become sisters.'

'I must ask you one favour,' Baalaajee said. 'It is so large that you may not be able to manage it. If so, I will understand.'

'Baalaajee whatever you ask, if I am able, I am also willing.'

'Very well, Kala. It is this: whatever they say to you, whatever they bring to you, thank them and say your thoughts are not pure. You are thinking only of the gifts and the good that will befall your daughter Sujata.' He knew that no other reply could loosen their grasp on her. Kala would be facing the most sophisticated and erudite of priests.

'I will do as you say, although I do not understand everything you are saying. Stay with me and help me for I am a simple slave-girl. I am Kala. I trust you.'

'Promise me before God that you will do as you have just said.'

'I, Kala, slave-girl to the Palace of Jyotika, promise before God to do as Pundit Baalaajee tells me. May I perish if I do not do as he says. I promise this with my whole being.'

Sadness walked with Baalaajee. He knew he had used his position and her vulnerability to get his way. He had behaved as a bully, forcing her to promise when he knew she could not do otherwise. He told himself that it was for her own good, and that he had been forced to do this by the royal court. And yet, how he wished it were otherwise. He stretched forward and took the sleeping Sujata from Kala.

At last the swirling clouds on the carved door of the throne room were before them. The door opened and they entered. The room was strangely still. Its walls were lined in raw silk, and hung with rugs of colours from an early dawn to a setting sun, displaying a completeness – life with its circularity, its simultaneous beginning and end, repeated through time.

Giant, pink vases, carved from magnificent blocks of marble, stood like statues. Garlanded with sweet jasmine, the gods and their spouses were thoughtful in granite, and stone, marble and limestone. Embroidered tales, painted scenes from the great epics the *Mahabharata* and *Ramayana* hung on the walls. On another panel, framed by gold leaves, royal hunts were relived by a row of former kings who gazed at the paintings of their chase.

As Baalaajee adjusted the sleeping Sujata on his shoulder, he was drawn to a sculpture of two beaming faces of mother and child at play. The warmth and affection that flowed between them reached him. The child stretched his hand to pull at his mother's dangling earrings; she restrained him by touching his arm and turned her smiling face out of his playful reach.

Gongs were struck and conch shells blown. Three holy men chanted from sacred texts. A carpet of peacocks and cranes, small birds on graceful vines of tulip-shaped flowers, comforted their soles. All bowed low before Kala.

The three Queens were seated on high, rubies, diamonds and emeralds embossed the geometrical patterns on the royal thrones. Lamp-black saris framed the milky complexions of Queens Meena and Dayita. Though her sari was also black, Queen Renu's had a border of fine embroidery in silver thread which lit up a face long caressed by the sun.

A stuffed tiger leaped towards those below, its mouth open, bearing long incisors. A swooping eagle held a baby turtle in its sharp talons. A falcon awaited a royal bidding.

Baalaajee and Kala bent low before the Queens, their hands clasped in gracious salutation. The Queens sat with folded arms, which indicated they were ready to receive those attending the court.

A gong was struck and a single conch shell blew a low prehistoric sound of a new-born sea. The Royal Pundit of the Court, dressed in white with a garland of frangipani, climbed the stairs to the throne and sat on the rug. In centre-stage, a small pyre of sandalwood was alight.

'OM . . .' the omnipotent, the all embracing syllable was carried long and in its fullness, by the Pundit. The gods were asked to sanctify the meeting by their presence. He blessed the throne and the throne room and offered prayers for the well-being of past and present Kings and Queens of Jyotika, calling upon all that was divine from the beginning of time.

Again he called, and now it was the elements of our planet – earth, water, air and fire – that must witness what was being asked and promised. Water was brought.

181

A few drops, held by a leaf, were offered to Agni. The God of Fire moved with the wind.

The warm air from the burning camphor, ghee and sandalwood lifted itself high, floating out through the intricate carvings of the sandstone walls. The mingled scents slowly spread throughout the throne room caressing the senses.

A sadhu entered. He carried a chair and placed it before Kala. It was the identical blue chair that Vasti Nadir saw, reflected nearly two hundred years later, in that upright standing mirror, in her bedroom in Trinidad. The Pundit blessed the chair with jasmine petals and asked Kala to sit, explaining that what he was about to make known was the divine will of God, meant only for the ears of the chosen one. He was angry that Baalaajee, the uninvited, was here before him, standing beside Kala and holding the sleeping Sujata.

He approached the empty chair: 'This request, and no other, that I am about to make to Kala, lifts her high above the common people, above her present Karma. It is fitting that from this instant, she be raised above the ground to receive the royal request and hear the words of the sacred texts that will bless her affirmation of consent.'

Kala did not understand. The warmth, her closeness to the royal Brahmin and his incense-burning altar, a proximity never before experienced – for it was not allowed to outcasts – had left her unable to think clearly. This was all outside her daily experience. Fear and her recognition of the power before her, held her to that stance of waiting to do some bidding.

Once more the Pundit indicated to her that she should sit on the chair. He now pointed to it with his right hand and affirmed this with a nod of his head.

Raised above the floor, seated on the chair but well below the elevated throne platform, she looked at Baalaajee. The young Pundit gave her a reassuring nod to indicate that so far she had done well. Pundit Krishna observed this communication

'I have already indicated to you that what I have to say is only for her ears,' he told Baalaajee.

'I shall not listen, Punditjee.'

'I am asking you to leave the room with the child *now*. This is no longer a request; this is an order from me, the Royal Court's Pundit.'

'Pundit Krishnajee, are you able to confirm that the Queens will be listening to what you have said is only for Kala's ears?'

'You are not a simpleton, do not behave as one. It does not become you. Your words and actions are not befitting a Brahmin employed by the royal court. I am warning you, as it is my duty to do, that if you continue in this obstructive manner, so devoid of courtesy, I will have this court dismiss you from its service. You seem not to know who provides the high standard of living you have been enjoying. There will always be some amongst us, thankfully only a few, who seem to think they can change the customs and beliefs by which men live to suit their own interest or ungodly convictions. I have also observed that these very men are inclined to show little gratitude to their benefactor. I trust your elite education has enabled you to understand the working of the law. I do not have to reply to your insolence, but I am a man of custom, of law. I prescribe and follow it to the letter. Where there is ignorance it is my duty to enlighten; it is in this vein that I offer you an explanation.

183

'The Queens are here, as you must know, simply by virtue of their positions. Firstly the deceased is their husband and by custom his name, titles and spirit, and his Queens are the guardians of the throne until the coronation of his successor.' He paused. 'Secondly, they need to be here, for in truth, it is they who are making the request on behalf of the Crown. I am merely speaking on their behalf. So once more I, Pundit Krishna, the officiating Royal Pundit to the Court of Jyotika, command you to leave the throne room with the sleeping child now. You are holding back a most important procedure. Petty wrangling is an indulgence, time does not allow. The King lies in state and the royal astrologer has given the most auspicious time for the King's departure. It is tomorrow before noon.'

'Pundit Krishnajee, I too am bound to remain here. I here call upon Lord Krishna to hear my plea: Pundit Krishnajee, you are commanding me to dissolve herewith, my word as a Brahmin, my oath taken before the Geeta, given to Kala willingly and freely that I would stand beside her and at no time leave her. Now that I have informed you of this oath, you must know that to falsify my word, to reduce its worth to dust, is too great a sin for my Brahmin spirit to carry. To have to endure Lord Krishna's great displeasure is not, I am sure, what you would knowingly wish upon me. It would not reflect favourably on the priesthood. I inform you of this, for in so doing, we continue our tradition to uphold the integrity of the words of Brahmins.

'Secondly, it is only fitting that I remain with this girl child Sujata, whose immortal spirit should hear the request you are about to make to her mother Kala. The implications for the child's entire life, this one and

184

others to follow, will not be small. The order you give, the requests you make will affect her greatly; for this too you will be called to account, from the greatest arbiter of our lives – our Karma.'

The Royal Court Pundit did not believe a single word he had just heard, but he was unable to say to a fellow Brahmin, 'This is but a ploy, you are a liar, I do not trust your word.' Brahmins must respect each other's words, for if they did not, why should others?

He knew he had been outwitted with an adroitness that he could not help but admire, but because the Queens were present, he was angry. His pride and pomposity had been bruised. However, there was a long way to go yet; he was confident he would have his way. The promises he made to the Queens and the interpretations he formulated to them would enable this suttee rite to come to pass.

Pundit Krishna decided to continue: 'Our King Paresh of the Kingdom of Jyotika has died. Prince Mahendra, our Prince Regent, has been travelling far and wide to discover and learn new thinking and new methods. So far away from the Kingdom of Jyotika is he at present, that even on the fastest steed he could not be here at the appointed time to light His Majesty's pyre. His two sons, aged seven and ten, will stand in for their father and perform the sacred rite of setting the pyre alight. The Prince Regent is now travelling to Jyotika.

However, to fill this intervening time, before the Coronation, our Queens must be here to maintain the continuity of the Crown's authority. It would be unthinkable for them to neglect the Kingdom and for anyone but the King's honourable wives to hold this royal position of Head of State. This absence of the

Prince Regent, has placed the Queens in a perilous predicament.

Unknown to Baalaajee, pundits, sadhus, Sanskrit scholars and holy men were sitting behind him in the Public Audience Gallery. They arrived some time ago, without sound, as visible ghosts with a lightness of being. Pundit Krishna was furious that they had been allowed to enter. Now, he could not consider stopping the proceedings nor would he ask this following of elderly holy men, these close colleagues of a lifetime, to leave; nevertheless, his anger at their presence exploded within him.

The arrangement he had placed before Queen Dayita was based on the assumption, crucial to its success, that he would be speaking to Kala, and the only audience present would be the three Queens. The resourcefulness needed to convince a young slave-girl was entirely different from that required to satisfy a public gallery of priests and scholars.

Unforeseen circumstances had found him unprepared. Here and now he must make every turning the correct one, for there could be no going back on one's word.

With his confidence much ruffled, Pundit Krishna strove to formulate an honourable exit clause for the Queens, whose situation had changed this very instant, before him. It was only his astuteness that turned a potential disaster into a well-reasoned case favourable to the Queens. However, the enormity of the strain was taking its toll.

By lowering his voice, Pundit Krishna hoped that much of what he said would be missed by the elderly audience sitting in the public gallery, and by those who even now were in a state of perfect contemplation, seeking a path to eternity. He needed a sufficient measure of ambiguity, confusion and uncertainty to save this strategy. The Pundit was energised by a lurking secret pride that the Queens had just witnessed a maestro among priests at work.

He comforted himself, by thinking that what Kala was about to say would please the audience. After that, he would have to present the Queens' plan – a school for girls in the compound. He thought of Queen Dayita. But here before him, was the compelling present, its outcome was crucial. He had regained his confidence, his dignity.

'In view of the Queens' troubling predicament, already alluded to, they have decided that so worthy and honoured a position of performing suttee with the King of Jyotika be offered to Kala. While she resides in Heaven, I will become Sujata's guru and will ensure her well-being. At the appropriate age, her duties will be in the honoured venues of the Palace. She will be taught the skills of a lady-in-waiting as a tribute to her mother becoming a royal suttee. The Queens will gladly guide her upbringing. The daughter of a King's suttee carries a most honourable place in the province.

Kala understood what had been said. The future of her daughter would become larger than any child of a slave, could ever hope for. Suddenly she felt cheated. She had promised Baalaajee to accept nothing. For the first time, she regretted having trusted him. She felt that she and her daughter have been denied positions of great honour and worth which she could not possibly have earned in many a lifetime. Why would Baalaajee do such a thing?

She remembered what she had to say – it was meant to give her time, that is what Baalaajee had said, but she knew she did not need time to think of accepting Heaven, honour, worthiness, respect, a favoured life. Could it be that Baalaajee disliked slaves? No, no. Maybe he *did* explain and she either missed it, or did not understand. Would God punish her if she did not keep a promise to one Brahmin in order to obey another Brahmin who held a higher position? Pundit Krishnajee would not ask her to do something that would harm her. Or was a promise a promise no matter what came afterwards? She did not know the answer. She was not a scholar.

Kala was distraught that she knew so little. She could not ask Baalaajee or Pundit Krishnajee now, could she? She was unable to make her promise public, though it would explain her difficulty to Pundit Krishnajee who had been so good to her.

To have a royal privilege placed upon one of humble origin was such a great honour. Oh, to have been asked to sit with the King on the pyre, alone! What could she have done to deserve this? Could she break the promise to Baalaajee? It was too large a promise. He had made her step upon her daughter's future. What a thing to ask a mother to do!

Queen Meena nodded and a royal server brought a silver plate with three pieces of jewellery on it. These were placed before Kala. There was a torque necklace forged from gold, extensively hammered, chiselled and punched. Beside it was another gold necklace, set with rubies, diamonds and emeralds. Also a pair of gold upper arm-bands, revealing nine auspicious gems: ruby, diamond, pearl, coral zircon, blue sapphire, chrysoberyl, cat's eye, yellow topaz and emerald. These ancestral jewels appeared as strings of pure light throbbing with life. Here were fragments of beauty and perfection crafted in another time, when a jeweller's vocation was to offer pleasure to the wearer and to those around her.

There was a long hush. Kala was dazzled by the flickering light emitted by the pieces.

The time had come. Kala must respond.

Everyone looked at her. The audience thought they knew what she would say. So sure were they of the outcome that all but a few old heads got up and left.

The younger pundits who were leaving, had officiating duties to attend to but they also wanted to be the first to give the news of Kala's good fortune to the servants of the compound, who had been waiting at the Palace gates to hear the outcome of her royal summons. They themselves were not quite sure why she had been chosen, but only Pundit Krishnajee was privileged to know the thinking of the Royal Family. At present they were not troubled, confident that he would explain it all in good time. They were carriers of important events to come. Their voices would lift the royal request for Kala to the blowing wind.

Meanwhile, outside the royal compound in the servants' quarters, the letter-carrying water-carrier, Kunwar, was thinking of how to approach his other water-carrying brothers to find out who amongst the learned pundits was trustworthy. It was difficult to know how to bring up the subject without awakening their suspicions.

He started feebly amongst his friends by saying how the pundits in the compound trusted them to bring pure water, and what a good job they did. They were trustworthy water-carriers, he declared.

'Of course we are trustworthy,' said one, affronted.

'We are more trustworthy than many other water-carriers,' asserted another.

Then they all chimed in, one after the other.

'Trustworthiness is a most valuable thing. This we are also carrying with our water.'

'Trustworthiness is everywhere. If it wasn't, the whole world would stop. Nothing would move.'

'I do not believe everybody is trustworthy. We are, but not everybody is.'

'There is too much to gain by cheating, especially if you believe you will not be caught.'

'That is a difficult one.'

'The poor are trustworthy.'

'If we are not, they will throw us out!.'

'Yes.'

'Still, considering the temptations we are faced with, all in all, we are trustworthy.'

Kunwar found this was getting him nowhere.

It was then they saw a large group of pundits leaving the Palace. They were talking amongst themselves, and the word 'Kala' drifted over to the water-carriers.

'Kala trusts Baalaajee,' one said.

'Kala trusts Pundit Krishnajee,' said another.

'Of course she trusts them both.'

'I wonder what is happening to her?'

The small group of water-carriers looked at each other.

'Of the two men, if you *had* to choose,' said Kunwar, suddenly becoming excited, 'whom would you choose?'

There was silence.

'Both men are good,' said one, sure of himself.

All heads nodded.

'Pundit Baalaajee listens well. He is friendly and wise too, my mother said so.'

'Pundit Krishnajee,' another pointed out, 'is the more powerful.'

That set them off again.

'Yes. He was close to the King.'

'Yes, he is in a position to grant favours,' another said, smiling, his eyes widening.

'What a stupid question!'

'Yes. Who are *we* to choose anything?'

And with that, their short break ended, the water-carriers' feet hurried away as if they were rabbits being chased.

Inside the throne room, Kala turned to Baalaajee. Queens Meena and Renu were uncomfortable. They could see that Queen Dayita's idea of a rescue plan for Kala was made on the spur of the moment as the only way out of this horror. But the details had not been worked out – there had not been sufficient time. This made Queen Meena and Queen Renu anxious. Queen Dayita was not unaffected, but she had acquired a much stronger disposition, having lived through the harsh Temple School training; even now as she sat there, Queen Dayita was weaving a specially chosen yarn into the fabric of escape for Kala.

Round and round, questions chased through Queen Meena and Queen Renu's minds: what if it did not work? What if the crowd discovered that they had been cheated? Where would they hide Kala and a young child after this event? What would the consequences be for the Royal Family and for their own plans to open a school when this intrigue was revealed?

They did not ask why the Pundit had done this? They left to him the appeasement of the priestly class, believing that he knew what he was doing. Perhaps he could not divulge all his reasons. After all, they had not told him of their plan to save Kala.

Baalaajee nodded and the slave-girl rose. Feeling the need to see him and knowing that she must also address the remaining few in the gallery, Kala turned sideways. Taking her time and pausing where she must, she spoke clearly. She was terrified.

'I am Kala, mother of Sujata, slave-girl to this royal court. I speak the truth. I am ashamed to say that my thoughts are not only with the King. I am sorry he is not here, but the truth is, I am thinking of the jewellery. It is so precious, so beautiful I cannot help it. I see my daughter wearing these gifts, living a life in the court far above any slave-girl's thinking. I, Kala, slave-girl to this court, need time to make pure all my thinking which, as you see, is not pure enough today. I would be no good to the King if my thoughts were not clean. I thank all the Queens for thinking of me and honouring me in this way and for their kindness to Sujata. I also thank Pundit Krishnajee who has always been good to me and Sujata. I cannot thank him enough.'

The young woman quickly glaced at Baalaajee and took comfort from the steadiness of his countenance. She pulled her cotton ornhi so close to her face that it partially hid it She continued: 'One thing is worrying me. I am not learned and so I do not know the answer to many things. What will the King say when he is waiting on the other side and sees me, a mere slave-girl, and not his Queens in Heaven with him? I do not know if he will like this. Will the King be angry with me for coming? What will he be thinking? If Pundit Krishnajee is *sure* that the King would not be angry to see me, instead of his Queens, I ask him please to let me know, for I am an ignorant slave-girl. I will always do my best to please the Queens and Pundit Krishnajee. I am so very sorry about everything. I ask you all to forgive me, if I have disappointed you. Please advise me later, Pundit Krishnajee. Let me know what is the right thing to do. I need time. I need time. I must not say yes to anything until I am clean.'

Baalaajee looked at Kala, unable to believe his ears. He had to use all his willpower not to display any exultation. Taking Sujata to her mother, he whispered, 'Good, Kala.' He thought it best not to look in the direction of the Pundit of the royal court.

Queens Meena and Dayita were stunned by what Kala had said. They were mortified. No one had ever done this. No one would have dared to think like this, let alone express it so simply before so many.

'What the slave-girl has said is incredible,' Queen Dayita breathed. 'She must have been primed by that rogue, Baalaajee.'

Was this their end? Was there no way out? The Queens would have to speak to Pundit Krishna immediately, for the pyre would be lit the next day before noon.

The body of the King had been washed with spirits and incense; massaged with oils, herbs, spices and perfumes of myrrh. The midday heat was intense. The suttee ceremony must be carried out before the body began to deteriorate. Additional incense was already needed. The astrologers said that in this lunar cycle, tomorrow was the last auspicious day for the funeral.

Queen Renu looked more closely at Pundit Baalaajee, for the first time. She was intrigued by his gentleness with the child, by his composure throughout. All could see that he had tutored the slave girl. What could have persuaded him to take such an unusual stand? He had irrevocably exiled himself not only from the Palace but from the Kingdom. Why? She saw that he had placed them in an untenable situation and felt as if she were drowning. Although she was in no danger herself, Queen Renu could not bear the thought of Queen Meena and Queen Dayita being burned alive and was enraged that what separated her from them, what gave her protection and not them, was a belief in something that called on faith to give it credence – and not humanity – compassion one for another.

CHAPTER TWENTY-FOUR

The Water-Carrier Seeks a Buyer

IT WAS A busy time in the royal courtyard. Kunwar the water-carrier had waited long to meet Pundit Krishnajee; he had the letter tucked neatly into the folds of his turban. There was much coming and going all around the palace; like a colony of bees buzzing in the open fields, searching for a new hive. Earlier, a slow-moving column of pundits and holy men had gone into the palace and he saw a large number leaving. But the Royal Court Pundit was still inside.

Rumours came to Kunwar in small fragments, but even when put together they did not make sense. The Queens were now ruling the Kingdom. A slave-girl had been chosen by the Queens to be honoured on the King's pyre. Her daughter would become very wealthy and would be looked after by Pundit Krishnajee. Pundit Baalaajee had spoken about Lord Krishna and the need for Brahmins to be true to their word.

The water-carrier understood none of this; he had never tried to make sense of things that did not concern him. He had a job. He knew what he had to do and this he did. Purity was a concern that took priority. Everyone knew this from childhood, and he did his best to ensure that his water was all that it should be. He had not met many pundits on his morning and evening rounds. He simply delivered their water, nothing else. They liked their water delivered early so that the fresh rays of the sun at the birth of dawn might further cleanse the water, removing any impurities that could have entered his containers on their passage to the compound. Besides, the early morning sun was best – the purest of lights.

Kunwar was hoping that the reward he might get for the letter would gladden his day. His spirits were high, for once more he reminded himself that any letter a dying man was trying to reach must be worth much. He had said this to himself over and over again until his temples throbbed with the sounds – 'worth much'. He had chosen to bring it to the Chief Pundit of the royal court who was the most powerful man there. Something as important as this letter deserved to be in the best hands, if he was to be amply rewarded. Those most blessed by God had to treat others fairly, or else they would lose out in their next life. God would expect him to be treated fairly. God understood why he did it. He was a very poor man – a man with nothing. Besides, someone undeserving might have stolen it. He discovered it because he had come in to help the Pundit.

When the Pundit finally arrived. Kunwar began to waver for there was something about the mood and the stride of Pundit Krishnajee that was fierce and troubling. He appeared unapproachable. The water-carrier's tough life had taught him that anxiety was a common feature of life. Besides, he did not wish to return the letter to its burial place. There it was of no worth to him. He just had to do what he was about to do. Saying a prayer for guidance Kunwar then, as befitted his lowly position, humbly approached the Pundit.

After bowing and greeting the Pundit, he began to tell the tale he had carefully prepared: 'That morning, Pundit Krishnajee, was like all other mornings except that I found the door of the late Senior Pundit Baalaajee open. This did not surprise me at first, I thought little of it as it was a windy day. This letter was rolling about outside in the compound as if it had wheels. I believed it belonged to Senior Pundit Baalaajee because of the open door, but I could not be sure.

'Through no fault of my own, I was running very late so I just picked up the letter and hurried on to make my rounds. It was only later in the day, when I untied my turban in my room that to my surprise I saw it on the ground. I had completely forgotten that I had it. I panicked, for I had later heard that Pundit Baalaajee had died and was afraid of being accused of wrongdoing. However, I am a little calmer now, although still very troubled. I knew that I should not continue like this and felt it was time to explain what had happened.

'I bring it to you, Pundit Krishnajee. There is no one else I would take it to.' Kunwar produced the letter and the Pundit took it. He Immediately recognised the hand of his late colleague and rival – a man he had secretly admired, envied and disliked. He asked the water-carrier to wait outside, saying: 'I shall let you know whether it is an important letter or not.' He closed his door, sat down and read the letter.

Dear Baalaajee,
    May the spirit of the good build a nest upon you. My blessings I bring you.

I have given much thought as to whether this letter should be written. There were times when I told myself there was no need. It is only after long meditation that I have decided to write it.

When you marry, and I hope you will soon, try and find time to educate your wife. Few tasks you will perform as a pundit will carry such a large worth. Educating oneself offers an opportunity to have a deeper understanding of a few of the things that affect our daily lives. Much has been gleaned through time, in every sphere of knowledge, and this is why to educate oneself is a lifetime's endeavour. But there is also another reason. It constrains our passion for the prevailing fashions in dress, behaviour and thought, and permits a constant rethinking and resifting of what we believe to be truths. So you see, Baalaajee, why it has occupied us both so fully.

You are a learned man, an educated man with the manners and behaviour of a high-caste Brahmin. I brought you up as I would have my own son.

At birth, your parents were given that most weighty of burdens to carry. The word 'Untouchable' was tied round their necks by the midwife. It is a mere word, a sound. Yet we judge men by the sound we play before them at their birth.

It was on the pavements of Calcutta. Night had already fallen when I heard you crying loudly, for you were hungry. Your mother had already given you all that she had, which was very little. Having visited my brother and his family, offering them as many gifts as I could afford, I was now standing before a shop, waiting for the rickshaw I had arranged to meet me. As it was late, there was time to look around and your loud crying attracted my attention.

I had three bags of sweets which I had bought for the poor children who live outside our compound gates. Taking gulabjamun dripping in syrup from an enamel container in my bag, I offered it to you. You placed much of it in your mouth. I smiled and you smiled. To this day, I do not know why there and then – on impulse – I asked your parents for you. There are times I tell myself it was the way you smiled at me, the pleasure in your face, like the heavens opening, but I know that the true reason may well be my unfilled yearning for a son.

Your parents looked at me, pretending they had not heard me. I had nothing to offer them save my three bags filled with delicious sweets, the best quality ladoo, peera, jellaybi, ras gulla, rich kurmas which I had purchased in the section of the market that receives its custom only from the well-to-do. Taking the best to the wretched ones gives me so much pleasure; it is my way of bringing them morsels of the Heaven we luckier mortals experience daily.

I explained to your parents who I was, and promised to bring up their son as my own. There and then I called upon the gods of the Vedas to witness the oath I was undertaking and to ensure that I fulfilled it.

Your father asked, 'Will you educate my son as if he were your own?'

I promised to do so.

'So, my son will be able to read and to write? Will he sit with you at prayers?'

I said I was bound to do so, as no son of mine could possibly be without those skills. All that I knew I would offer you. Your mother said she heard my words, but could not let you go. After a while she said that if I would promise once again before the gods that were I to fail to keep the promises I had just made, I should be returned to this world as an Untouchable, only then, did she say, she might consider answering.

All this while, you looked at the bag and then at me, awaiting my response with such appealing eyes that I offered you another. Your mother said that was enough and she took all three bags from me with such a firmness of grasp that I had no time to resist and then when it was done, protesting seemed such a wretched thing to do. Your father wanted to know where I lived and if he could visit me and see his son from time to time. He also asked, 'Is a boy child worth only three bags of sweets?'

I answered that one boy child and one girl child together were worth the whole world. He smiled, but your mother was not to be won over by words which did not cost me anything. She intimated this first by her posture and after considering what was before her, questioned me. 'In this price,' she spoke slowly as if making a calculation, 'are you taking into account the amount of work our son would do for you? Besides, what of his loyalty to you in bad times? When you and we become old, you will have him in your old age. What will we have? If you add these things up, what should you be offering us?'

I was taken aback by her shrewdness To be honest, I was unhappy to be losing the argument. To my shame, I began to think that I ought to let the whole matter drop. In part it was because of my wounded pride – an arrogance I would have denied I possessed. With it came all manner of doubts. Were you really their son? I had only their word. If I were to let them know where I lived, would they not come again and again because of their desperate circumstance and ask much more of me?

Your parents detected a cooling of my enthusiasm, and there and then my rickshaw arrived.

Your mother followed me, holding you in her arms. I asked her to wait, while I asked my driver whether he knew your parents. He said he did not know them well, though he believed the child was theirs as they had had you for several months. I saw the need to put aside my pride for I knew that were I to leave you behind, your eyes seeking my bags of sweets and your smile and cries would haunt me. So in truth, I took you for my own peace of mind and not for any altruistic motive.

I explained to your father that I agreed you were worth far more than three bags of sweets, but that was all I had. Though it was not the truth, I had already given my brother more than I could afford. What I was left with, had to meet many obligations. Your mother wanted to know whether my wife and family would not be unhappy to see their son. I pretended that I was married – said that my

201

wife would do as I told her, and I was sure that she would do as I do, that is, to bring you up as her son.

I was afraid to say that I was not blessed by children, for this meant I or my wife were in some way cursed, paying for some ugly act done in our last lives. Oh how the law of Karma wields a double-edged sword. The idea that one's destiny is determined by one's actions is commendable. It enables us to look inside ourselves to seek self-improvement. But as you know, Baalaajee, I was never able to come to terms with the idea that the wretchedness of the poor or the misery brought to others by disastrous events, natural or manmade are to be interpreted as a punishment for devilish actions in a past life. It is too cruel to contemplate.

Besides, it impedes us from properly challenging the Brahmins. As you can see, my one untruth to your parents was joined by another. Untruths are so like us – social beings. They like company and very seldom walk alone.

Your father pressed me again, wanting to know where I lived. I said that I lived abroad but every year at noon, on the birthday of Shiva, if they would come to the temple of the Court of Jyotika I would arrange that a gift of my thanks and goodwill, be presented to them. Your mother asked whether they would be able to see you. I said, I could not say now; I was afraid, that on seeing you they might take you away again. Then she blessed you and your father did too. I took you from her. But as I was about to climb into the rickshaw, she took you from me and embraced you, asking me to keep to my promises or else God would punish me

202

most severely. She said that you were a very good boy, and that if I treated you well, much good luck would come my way.

I took my time to tell her that she and your father would be proud of you. Once more I called upon the gods, asking that their wrath be upon me, were I to harm their son. A silence came upon us: it was as if the gods had come and were listening to my oath. I asked her how old you were, and she said one year and four months.

When I asked her your name, she said, Punditjee, you must give him a strong Brahmin name. Is he not now your son? What will it be? What will you choose for your son?' At the time, weary and worried, I could only think of my own. I shall call him Baalaajee I said. Your father, turned away to hide his tears. 'You are a good man,' your mother said, covering her face in her sari. A deep anguish shook her frail body; the rickshaw pulled away. The driver told me that she stood there all the while looking at us. Her anguish came to me and I wondered whether I should not return you.

The bright tone of the driver, so matter-of-fact, so practical was what helped me to decide that I would keep you. 'Punditjee, I know a very good shop,' he said. 'You need to go there to get some good quality Brahmin clothes.' After I had bought you three changes of clothing, that number recommended by my driver as well as three bags of sweets, for I could not bear to look at the disappointment in the faces of the children at the compound gates, I found I was very hungry.

The journey ahead was long, and fearing that

you too would be hungry, and wanting you to begin your new life on wholesome foods, I bought a bag of savouries: baras and kachouries, a jar of mango chutney, and a container of excellent warm dhal, which you know I swear by. Surrounded with so much that was good, I headed back for the court. Later, when I brought out the container of warm dhal, I drank first. As I drank, you watched me in silence, your eyes sad. You were accustomed to seeing others drink before you, knowing none would come your way. You watched. I stopped. I brought the warm bowl to you. You stared at me and I nodded. Your eyes and face simultaneously became alight. It was the most beautiful sight I have ever seen. Pure joy. You drank too fast; all the while you looked at me. What was going through your head, I cannot say. Perhaps you were still unsure of what was happening.

The satisfaction I received from looking at you filled me. It was the beginning of a new life, one that was greatly enriched from that day forth. The pleasure you brought made me young in heart and limb. I even contemplated finding a wife, for a certain fullness returned to me.

It was at a late hour that I arrived back at court. But first, I stopped beside our main stream, knowing no one would be there, and bathed you myself. You kicked and screamed, your body battling against mine, for the water was indeed very cold. You screamed and bit my arm I was taken aback by your reserve of energy, but I held you firmly and did, I think, a good job. Your new clothes fitted you so well, I was amazed, and struck by the

204

extent to which, how we cover ourselves also dresses our thoughts.

I watched as the stream took your old clothes away. Then I carried you back to the buggy. Its rocking soon cradled you to sleep.

I told the court you were my brother's son and brought you up as my own. I wanted you to be closer to the concept of Brahma than our brother Brahmins are. Your knowledge of the sacred texts and the great epics is considerable. At first I wondered whether you would be able to manage such erudition, but the way in which you took to the sweet melody of the Persian and Sanskrit languages removed my initial doubts. Your application was astonishing. You were thirsty to imbibe much; to drink long at the fountains of knowledge. You studied with the same enthusiasm and enjoyment as you ate. I enjoyed watching you eat. You made eating look like a divine gift. The massages that the old lady I employed gave you in the morning and in late evenings, delighted you. A beautiful, sensuous little boy, my memory records. You were a ball of joyous life, reminding me daily, that life can be a blessed thing.

Later I taught you a few fine mantras, and of your own accord, you would recite one loudly before your meals.

I was aware that you had to make a living so I prepared you to officiate at our ceremonial rites of passage, as well as to expound to the public the essence of the teachings of the Upanishads, the Vedas, the Mahabharata and the Ramayana.

There is little left to say. Keep this letter to

yourself. The court is not yet ready for change, and thinking like this undermines it. The Brahmins and the Kshatriyas have most to lose and being powerful men in powerful positions would not go gently.

And now, my son, I must tell you that your parents *did* come to see you. They came every year. On each occasion they were so happy for you, so overcome with joy to see their son grow into a scholar, a Brahmin, a fine young man, that I felt ashamed I had once nursed the idea that they would take you away or that they would bargain further for a greater compensation from me.

By the time you were eleven years old, they had ceased to come, so I must assume that they are no longer with us. Think kindly of them, for they did what they thought best. It would not have been easy for them to give you up. I think your mother used all her knowledge of psychology and religious belief, to frighten me into behaving as I had promised. Later she blessed me. And I returned the honour she had bestowed upon me, adding that you were the son of very fine parents. She wept and would take no credit. 'It is all your doing,' she said through her tears.

Now destroy this letter, lest it falls into the wrong hands.

I have brought you up as my own son and so cannot abandon you, for it is my duty to be with you even after I have returned to the stars. On any dark night, I shall shine upon your path. This I promise.

From your dear old friend,
Baalaajee.

206

An Afterthought

I think you ought to be aware of what is happening in the South. My brother has informed me of a new sect from overseas, preaching there. In much of their thinking they resemble the Brahmins, in telling us what is right and what is wrong, except, while the Brahmins do not seek converts, they do. Unlike the Brahmins they say we have all sinned and that their God has prepared a hellfire for us. This sin we are supposed to have is like an inborn illness, an inherited disease, for even a newborn child carries it. What a dark and terrifying thing it must be to have to say to a babe-in-arms that he is a sinner.

The imagination of men has never ceased to astound me, Baalaajee. I would be surprised if there are many converts, since the only way one can be saved from this sin, my brother informs me, is to drink the blood of their prophet and eat bits of his body. Such cannibalistic thinking, even in symbolic form, will not travel far amongst vegetarians. The very imagery of flesh and blood would be offputting.

Man's yearning for immortality has widened his imagination and greatly deepened his creativity. Our sages, scholars and pundits have provided us with a comprehensive plan for living; they have even considered the comforts of their gods, providing consorts for many.

I trust you will continue to observe your fellow men and also examine yourself well: by these methods, you will learn about the thoughts of others, their motivation, needs and interests, and have a better understanding of yourself. These observations and self-examinations will enable you to direct your life to a more fulfilling path.

From time to time remember me, for it is only in the memory of others that man gains immortality.

Affectionately,

Baalaajee.

Pundit Krishnajee could scarcely believe what he had just read. Was this a hoax? The handwriting was that of the late Baalaajee Senior, but the letter itself must be the work of someone's imagination. The reason why it must be false was that the young man Baalaajee was an erudite, fine pundit — the best in the compound; Pundit Krishna did not include himself in this valuation. After all, the wisdom and judgement that comes with experience could not be compared to that of a young man, however good.

Could he for a moment bring himself to believe that someone like the late Baalaajee, with a lifetime of experience and accumulated wisdom, could transform an Untouchable? No, he couldn't! Only God could transform people. The human mind cannot develop overnight. It took centuries, a gradual improvement through many reincarnations, to attain scholarship and enlightenment like his own.

He tried to predict the consequences if the letter were genuine. Did it mean that the entire court, the Palace, the throne room, courtyard, the compound would need to be cleansed? An Untouchable had walked into the most sacred places! He recalled how he himself had held the child so many times. In fact, the late Pundit Baalaajee had so often encouraged him to allow his charge to officiate at small private functions where he, Pundit Krishna sat with him, albeit as the senior partner. Surely he would not do that, would he? Besides, were this young man really an untouchable, Pundit Krishna was sure that he would have known something was amiss, he would have felt Uncomfortable, sitting that close to him, touching him. He might even have become ill.

Could it mean that his colleague, the late Baalaajee, had no respect, no regard for anything? Was nothing sacred to him, a Brahmin? How had he thought he would face God? Did he really believe he could become a star without God's help? Such utter foolishness! Had it come from an ageing mind – rapidly falling apart?

Yet, who in the compound would now wish to play such an unwholesome trick? It was not worthy of a grown man and could only come from someone with an immature disposition – a young man with no understanding of how things worked and certainly with no responsibility for anything.

The timing was most unfortunate for him. Pundit Krishna had grown suspicious of everyone: was this meant to further reduce his confidence so that he began to lose a grip on things? Was one of his colleagues wishing to see him go, so that they could take his place within the new Royal administration? He recalled that it was Pundit Baalaajee's name that Queen Dayita had put forward. To have a Queen bowing before an Untouchable, to have had an Untouchable as her guru . . . He felt faint and closed his eyes. A dizziness came upon him. Pundit Krishna bent his head in anguish. On regaining his composure, a thought tugged at him. Had he been so neatly overruled by an Untouchable in the throne room! This alone convinced him that the letter was a hoax. It was meant to cause him distress.

It was true that their name was the same, but it was customary for brothers to give their sons the name of an uncle who had done well. In addition, the late Pundit Baalaajee had at no time been discourteous to him; why would he write this letter to cause him pain? The letter was addressed to the young Pundit Baalaajee. It was a calm, affectionate letter. Nothing about it was revolutionary. It was a simple tale told by a storyteller, the work of his creative mind. *There was a moral lesson in it: just as an Untouchable can become a Brahmin, so too a Brahmin can become an Untouchable.*

Maybe it was written to ensure that the young Baalaajee continued to behave with compassion to all, to be courteous at all times. It was being sent as a warning to him that, were he not humble before God, he could become an Untouchable.

Maybe the late Baalaajee had seen in his nephew, the first indications of an unwholesome pride. That was it! The letter was a disguised moral lesson to his nephew. The Pundit sighed with relief. He had examined a number of explanations and at last had understood the implication of the letter. He would keep it and hand it to Baalaajee himself, and observe his reaction. Now he had to decide what to say to this water-carrier.

In the meantime, outside Pundit Krishna's abode, Kunwar's hope for a good outcome was rising. The Pundit had taken a long time. Only an important letter took time to consider, he mused.

The door opened. 'I must let you know the truth,' the Pundit told Kunwar, 'the letter is not as important as it looks.' The water-carrier had a large emptiness in his stomach and this was not entirely because he had not eaten. 'However, you did well to bring it to my attention, so I am rewarding your judgement. I believe entirely what you have told me. I must warn you, however, that no other pundit would have done so. They would have called you a thief and you would have lost your job. In your own interest I am warning you to remain quiet on this matter. Say nothing to anyone, not even your closest friend.'

'I have no close friend.' Kunwar said, with conviction.

'Well, there are times when this is an advantage; it so happens that this is one of them. I have decided to reward your judgement as I have said, and to say that in future, if you find anything suspicious rolling before the homes of the other pundits in the compound in the manner you have described, it would be in your interest to bring it to me. I will at all times treat you fairly, as this is what God expects of me. However, you will need to trust me, for understandably, not every paper that rolls past you will be important.'

'Yes, Punditjee. I understand everything you say and will do as you say. God knows why He told me to bring it to you.'

Pundit Krishnajee rewarded him handsomely, knowing that he was in fact paying a small price for an informer. He needed to know what and how the other pundits were thinking, especially after today. He needed to become better informed.

CHAPTER TWENTY-FIVE

What Life Remains for Us?

THE THREE QUEENS sat in silence.

It was a silence of disbelief and of bafflement, of hurt, shock and hopelessness that came tumbling upon them as a mighty wall. After a while the pulse of the silence changed into an atmosphere of concealed reproach. Queen Meena lay sobbing. Queen Dayita went to comfort her, but her two outstretched palms kept all at bay.

Suddenly, Queen Meena reared up. Sensing fury, her sister Queens awaited the smashing of the stillness: 'I have never in my life been so humiliated – never!' she stammered. The inadequacy of words to express her turmoil frustrated her. 'We are now wicked in their eyes – our behaviour that of dishonest women. Are we? Are we? Look at what we have done to the good name of our family, the Royal Family of Jyotika, but most of all to ourselves. What will become of us? I was so ashamed, I wished the earth could have taken pity and swallowed me up. I want you to know that there and then I decided I will go on the pyre. It is the only honourable path now open to us. Our plans were founded on our characters of good repute, on the prestige of royalty. Who will now allow us to come close to their daughters?'

She looked through the latticed screens into the courtyard beyond. 'The palace has too many people who act impetuously on weighty matters, no matter the consequences to others. I cannot live this way. I cannot cope with this mountain of ugliness. I feel hemmed in; I am in the dark, cut off from the light.

'Yet now I see clearly. There is no choice. We were fooling ourselves – it cannot be done. How can we now live the life we had hoped for – running a school, preparing our lessons, instructing the children and seeing how they grow. It was a dream. Women can't dream in the Kingdom of Jyotika! It was a wild wish.

'After what the slave-girl said before all those sadhus, holy men, brahmacharis and pundits, our life will be unbearable. To be known as the Queen who wanted a slave, with a child, to go where she herself would not . . . this I could not endure. Those who accuse us with their silences will be the worst; we won't know what they are thinking. Then there will be the hurried scatterings of gossiping women whenever we enter a room, avoiding our eyes, moving away as if we're defiled.

'A kind of emptiness will enter our soul and reduce us. We shall be alone. Always alone. Unseen. It will be as if we are not there. We shall become as nothing – invisible.

'Who will our friends be after this? Will they not ask, are we worthy of protecting? We tried to do something and we see its time has not yet come, and when it comes, it will not come first to Jyotika. Let us not fool ourselves, sisters. Pundit Krishnajee is not with us. How can he be? He does not even listen when we speak, let alone understand what we are saying. If he had really understood, this situation would not have come upon us. I am sure of

213

it. He belongs here. He is a part of the Palace like its old hunting trophies, armoury and museum. He cannot be moved by what we think, by what he does not believe in. His design has brought us to this.

'A pundit who does not share our belief cannot do what we asked . . . We made such a stride forward, we had courage; but he is what he is. I am sorry to have to say this, I may regret saying it, but I have to for my temples are throbbing with it. Sister Dayita should *not* have agreed to his madness. And when she told us, we should have forbidden it. I cannot recall now why we didn't. Can anyone remind me? I am weak and confused about everything. Why did we agree? Why did *I* agree? Was I afraid to be alone? I have nothing more to say.'

Queen Dayita saw the depth of Queen Meena's hurt, and felt responsible:

'I agree fully with all that Sister Meena says. It is right that she should speak her mind. I prefer her openness to a grudging concealment. I too realise I should not have consented to Pundit Krishna's plan when it was put forward. Yes, Sister Meena and Sister Renu, I saw it was wrong to ask the slave-girl to sacrifice herself on the pyre.

'On the other hand, we were asking Pundit Krishna to go where he would be undermined, and ridiculed by his own priestly class. His plan backfired because of Baalaajee. It was a compromise he was making on our behalf, based on beliefs we no longer hold.'

'We understood this,' Queen Renu said. 'It was a risk we took. We misjudged much. We were rowing against powerful currents of religious tradition.'

'Yes, Sister Renu,' Queen Dayita encouraged, 'the Kings of Jyotika had never been on their pyres alone.

Pundit Krishna could not bring himself to preside over a King's pyre without his consorts. Failing this, he was attempting the best possible combination, as he saw it, taking into account his beliefs, the priestly class and our goals.'

'The question he envisaged being hurled at him,' Queen Renu added, 'was: "What does it say of the King, whose valour on the battlefield, and compassion at peacetime was an example to all men?"'

'Pundit Krishna was fearful, Sister Renu, you are right. Fearful of being reminded by his fellow Brahmins that though the King met his death on the battlefield defending the Kingdom's borders, the Royal Court Pundit was unable to defend the King's honour in death.'

'Yes, Sister Dayita, such an observation by the priestly class,' Queen Renu stressed, 'would be a humiliation he could neither face nor live with, all the more so when it was his own firm belief that His Majesty was being greatly dishonoured. It was our enthusiasm to bring to life a beautiful thought,' Queen Renu spoke slowly, looking at Queen Meena, 'as well as to anchor everything in place, in the time we had, which in fact was no time at all. Pressed in this way, we overlooked a crucial aspect of our own plan. Pundit Krishna's first loyalty is to the King. His duty to the Royal Family is his vocation.

'What we were asking him to do the impossible. We wanted to build upon what we saw as an imaginative enterprise that would change the lives of all the girls in the compound. We wanted so badly to give the idea a start. We were child-like in thinking that Sister Dayita could change the Pundit's vision, his approach to life, and so we ran on with our plans in hand, heedless of the dangers pressing in upon us. We were inexperienced and naïve. We also asked Sister Dayita to do the impossible, but she would have pulled it off, had Pundit Baalaajee not accompanied the slave-girl Kala.'

'What was especially foolish of me, Sister Renu,' grieved Queen Dayita, 'was to think that saving the slave-girl Kala, could be done without Pundit Krishna knowing and without my action being disclosed to him or the people later. Had I been successful, what then? Had I failed, what then? It was an error of judgement for which I cannot forgive myself. I am to be blamed totally. Forgive me, Sister Meena. Forgive me, Sister Renu. I too was unhappy with what was proposed, yet seized on the only thing that was available and it was not good enough. Forgive my stupidity.'

She turned her face away, and Queen Renu came to her and embraced her saying, 'You judge yourself too harshly. I would have done the same.' This togetherness, this receiving of each other's suffering, the comfort, forgiveness and sympathy the one brought to the other in her time of need, opened a path of communication between them that would not have been thought possible.

Queen Dayita approached the eldest Queen: 'Sister Meena all that you have said is correct. I ask your forgiveness. I regret with my entire being that it has come to this. It could have been so different.'

'How very true,' Queen Renu said, nodding in agreement, 'if there had been no audience. Pundit Krishna was surprised, just as we were, to see so many people, as well as Pundit Baalaajee there. He saw his well-laid plan pulled apart before him, yet he courageously battled on, all the while sensing he was in combat with a younger man. He could see that Baalaajee had prepared Kala, to respond as she did. Obviously, she had rehearsed her reply. No one could have foreseen this, not even Pundit Krishna.

'I so felt for him at one stage,' Queen Renu confided, somewhat embarrassed with the manner of her admission. 'His age and tiredness combined to make him so vulnerable before the youthful Pundit Baalaajee. Look how he tried desperately to explain why we were unable to go on the pyre. Consider the reasons he gave to protect us. There and then, he was forced to think on his feet, for he had never envisaged having to present reasons in detail to an erudite priestly class. The strain must have been enormous. He is worthy of his position as the Royal Court Pundit.'

'Yes, the initial tussle with Pundit Baalaajee caught him offguard,' agreed Queen Dayita. 'Bearing in mind the position we placed him in, his plan was not entirely without merit, for it was clear that when the slave-girl saw the jewellery, she was moved. And who would not be? Sister Meena's gold necklace is enamelled on the back and each ruby, diamond and emerald is set with gold foil. Your torque gold necklace, Sister Renu, dazzled like a golden plait; my pair of upper arm-bands with their gold foil skilfully inserted between each precious stone as well as its mount, I did not part with easily. I had asked for each band to be fitted with a pair of fine cords. These were of silk and metallic threads for binding my arms.'

'What do you think was going through her mind then?' asked Queen Meena, brushing her curly hair off her moist forehead and adopting a more relaxed position.

'I can only think,' Queen Dayita, attempted by way of explanation, 'that she was under oath, having made a promise to Pundit Baalaajee to do as she did. I say this because I saw how dazzled she was by the jewellery. Something very strong kept her from agreeing to Pundit Krishna's plan.'

'Is this the attitude of pundits?' asked Queen Meena, aroused once more. 'Pundits, because of their beliefs, are only too pleased to commend other people to the pyre. Maybe he has a personal grudge against Pundit Krishna or against the royal court. Such men have no place here. His main purpose was to humiliate us all and he succeeded.'

'Sister Meena is right, it is puzzling,' Queen Renu observed, 'yet I can think of no other explanation for her stance, other than what you have said, Sister Dayita. Bearing in mind her own beliefs and the sheer magnificence of those pieces, could there be another explanation? Pundit Baalaajee did not look like a knave. He carried himself so well.'

'He is a knave. The common people trust him and he is using their trust to settle old scores.'

'How can we know for certain?' Sister Renu asked.

'Our ancestral jewellery would have presented her with a terrible dilemma,' Queen Dayita acknowledged. 'On the other hand, as I have said, had she accepted it, I would have been faced with a most horrendous predicament.'

'The slave-girl was terrified,' Queen Renu explained. 'Her reply that humiliated us, came from her genuine fear. She would have asked herself that simple question, it is without guile. When you consider what was being demanded of her it was a reasonable question. Let us try to think as she did: the King is expecting the Queens and sees only her. How would he react? Clearly she did

218

not want to be the cause of his anger and disappointment. It was a genuine concern.'

'I believe Pundit Baalaajee told her to ask that question,' Queen Meena said firmly.

'Yes, that is clear,' Queen Dayita agreed. 'She is a slave-girl – how could she possess such sophisticated cunning? It was her question that was so simply put, to Pundit Krishnajee that did the damage. This question effectively undermined the very reason for her royal summons. Consider what she did. This slave-girl turned the attention away from herself and placed us in a—'

'Formidable predicament,' Queen Renu helped, adding, 'a part astutely played.'

Queen Dayita looked out into the distance, her eyes were open, yet they saw nothing and then she said, 'It now seems as if it never happened, as if it were all a bad dream.'

'Yet Sister Dayita, we three were at court and heard the request and the reply,' said Queen Renu, thinking aloud and pacing the floor. 'Something crucial to our understanding of what took place is missing. Just consider again what happened: a slave-girl refuses an opportunity that she is aware will never come her way again. Wealth, status, an opportunity of a far better life for her daughter, and for herself, Heaven with the King. What does she do? She turns down this royal request. It is unheard of. Then she places her misgivings before us in such a way that it has disgraced us. An extraordinary feat!

'What I would so much like to know, is what is going on in Pundit Baalaajee's head. Why did he do it? He left nothing to chance. He bound her with an oath, for he felt that strongly. What is it that stirred this Northern pundit so? What directed him?'

'I too have been asking myself, what could his motive be?' Queen Dayita said slowly, as if exploring the question. 'If that young woman were beautiful or if she were high-born, I could understand, but to have such a lowly subject refusing the King . . . what would the thinking be that forbids it? It is an action that says a slave can refuse a King. It is humiliating to a ruler. It is also curious, disturbing. Had I not been present, I would not have thought this possible. As for Baalaajee, it cannot be he has his eyes on her. He remains an unknown.'

The Queens were puzzled, each pondered on why Kala was chosen, yet nothing was said.

'It is our own beliefs that condemn us,' Queen Renu answered 'and this is why we are rightly so aggrieved. It is not Baalaajee nor the slave-girl's question that has damaged us. We are also greatly troubled that it took place before such an elite audience. It portrayed us and the Pundit in an ugly light. We became false beings, as Sister Meena has intimated.

'No one present there could have guessed that this was not what we wanted, nor of your plan, Sister Dayita, to prevent Kala from becoming a suttee. How could they, when we presented valuable gifts to her? It turned us into three cunning manipulators.'

'Genuine fear or not, if the slave-girl was primed to say what she said by Pundit Baalaajee, he should not be employed by the royal court,' said Queen Meena. 'He should be dismissed immediately, for he sought to humiliate the Royal Family and discredit us before the influential men of court. It is unpardonable. He thinks as an enemy of the Crown and so continuing to have

220

him here is foolhardy. Pundit Krishna must dismiss him at once . . . Our problem arose from the fact that, despite all that we said to Pundit Krishnajee, he was a non-believer. It takes time to change a lifetime's convictions. Had he believed, he would have thought of another way.

'Sister Meena, your judgement is correct,' Queen Dayita said, nodding.

'I thought along similar lines,' Queen Renu concurred. 'I must let you know that, like Sister Dayita, I also had a personal plan which I discussed only with my trusted manservant Manu. It was because of this that I went along with our initial agreed strategy.

'My plan was devised very early. It came out of our initial meeting in this very room. After we presented our reasoned analysis on suttee to Pundit Krishna, I was hoping to explain to the crowd why we three Queens had decided not to go on the pyre, but instead would open the school. I wanted to point out the good of it and, reveal how their own children would benefit and how indeed a large number of kingdoms do not practise suttee but instead allow their widows to live useful lives with their children, grand-children and great-grandchildren.

'Manu was against this. He said they would think I was only saying this to save my own skin, and he even felt that an angry, disappointed, crowd could easily lift me and throw me on the burning pyre. Even when I suggested that I would have the King's guards protecting me, he said that they would be reluctant to shield me, believing that I was discrediting the King by not becoming a suttee. His view was that the only person who could possibly face the crowd with our plan was

Pundit Krishnajee himself. No one would wish to kill a Brahmin priest, let alone the King's Pundit of the royal court. He could also see that Pundit Krishnajee might not wish to risk his reputation nor his future prospects with the incoming Royal Family and therefore might desist from doing this.

'I am a little suspicious, perhaps wrongly, that Manu who promised both my parents that he would protect me at all times, felt that of the options open to me, leaving the Kingdom was the safest. He would not be interested in higher causes, risking one's life for the greater good. He would, like Pundit Krishna, be interested only in carrying out his duty to me and my parents. My safety would be his concern, nothing else. So whether he is right or not I have no way of knowing, save to say, he argued his case well and did put doubt and fear into me.'

'Maybe it is our Karma to go on the King's pyre,' Queen Meena whispered. 'We have tried to resist it and failed. The gods do not wish it.'

Queen Dayita and Queen Renu said nothing. A soothing, breeze was playing its way through the sandstone screens, when Queen Renu spoke her thoughts: 'My position has not changed, sisters. I will now leave the Kingdom with my faithful manservant, Manu. I would be so very happy if you, Sister Meena, and you, Sister Dayita, would journey with me . . . seeking a new beginning together in a new land where we would establish our own rules and live by them, not follow those of other men which lead to our destruction. There will be room for us all. Take only what you cannot part with, what you would grieve for. Thereafter we will establish our own rules and live by them.'

No one said anything. Hope was once again being offered. Old fears, beliefs, intuitions came and went. Their heads ached, their shoulders and neck had become as stiff as iron rods with the strain of it all. Personal images of the unknown and how each would cope were shifting. Was it too early for the other two Queens to aspire to and pursue yet another concept of change for the good life? They did not have time to mull over opportunities and risks in a more informed way.

The path to the pyre was the easiest. It was all prepared. They just had to move along from one ritual of preparation to another as the Pundit had explained, with the old woman he had chosen coming to assist them.

The two Queens embraced their sister Queen Meena with tears, overflowing with anguish. Queen Dayita promised to let her sisters know of her intention. Queen Meena would ascend the pyre; Queen Renu would leave.

Alone, Queen Meena stood behind her closed door and listened as the footsteps of the other two faded along the corridor. As she walked to her chaise longue, she was overcome by dark emotions of helplessness and guilt at having said too much in anger, in disappointment and in haste. She lay down and wept silently.

Queen Renu had already turned her attention to the escape plan. How should she sneak away from the jostling crowd? How could she get through the gates of the inner courtyard? Manu would have been working on that. There were only two gates to the fort – the one at the front where the crowds were waiting, and the back one, quiet and forlorn but well-guarded. He had said they would take the latter.

223

CHAPTER TWENTY-SIX

Queen Meena Struggles

A DEEP LONELINESS descended on Queen Meena and she fell asleep. On awakening, she looked around the room. There were too many shadows; her eyes rested on the veena, the white border tiles with their deep crimson and yellow tulips, the finest rugs on the floor, the peacock screens, a painting of the late King and herself, her trunks containing jewellery, clothing and gifts. Distressed, she opened the outer window to allow the patterned light to enter.

The courtyard was busy with carts and people, with merchandise coming and going. It all looked so normal, and yet her secure world had gone. She was still aware that she could change her life and travel with Sister Renu. Facing the unknown with the young woman, somehow seemed less painful after their openness with each other. But she must make up her mind. If she wished to join her, she must act now or else it would be too late. She wondered what Sister Dayita would do. Perhaps she had been too harsh towards her. Would Dayita keep her word and let her know of her plans, or just leave her to climb the pyre alone? To be alone on the pyre suddenly seemed such a cruel thing. A horror.

The ceremonies that awaited her in preparation for the pyre, came pressing down upon her.

Sister Renu, she thought, I shall miss you dearly. How I wish I had your strength. The unknown frightens me. My life has been closed, I have not your understanding of the larger world outside. I did not know that anyone could question their parents, husband or priest, or as you once told me, God Himself. All this is so strange, and on first hearing it, I found the ideas disagreeable, but no more. Were I to come, I would be a burden to you since I am unfit for many tasks. Our plan, this school for girls, would have suited me so well and this is why I was so overcome with disappointment and anger at the manner in which we were forced to give it all up.

Working in the open, the public sphere, is an unknown in all its aspects. The world outside the palace gates is apparently harsh. Pundit Krishna is right. How would I know who should be trusted? Being outside of the world for so long makes my entry more difficult. I would be like a child playing along a cliff, not recognising the dangers.

And then again, what if I were to choose to become a lady's maid in some wealthy home? Would that not be open to abuse by the master of the house or any of his blood relations who fancied himself to be irresistible, believing it was his right that I comply with his wishes? Here no one would have dared. We were the King's. Only his. I feel as if I have lost my very skin and so cannot last long.

Suddenly, we three are vulnerable, exposed to all the uncertainties and all the dangers that falls upon the weak. How do I defend myself? To whom do I go when

I am wronged? Who will understand? Where is shelter? I have never had to ask these questions.

Yet, I do know I could not now face the raging fires that await me. To stay and perish when all that is within me is saying: 'Get up! Run! Escape!' This much I know: I would not be allowed to leave partially burned. Would they not hold me down? Why are we not like the people in the South? How does one ask a people to change? How do beliefs change? Where do beliefs come from?

Why can't we be treated as men? Are we not vessels for the unborn? Do we not enable life itself, that most precious of things, to be created and cradled for nine months? Should that not be honoured? Why is it not? We provide comforts, sanctuary and joys. Are these of no account? Why? Why is it that whatever we do is insufficient to gain the power to direct our own lives as men do? Why is it so?

I can see from here that large crowds await my performing suttee. Dear God, be merciful. Help me. I know not what to do. Make sure I am not alive when the fires are lit upon me. Dear God, please save me from perishing alive in an open furnace. Give me the strength to do what is right – what will please You. How will I know what pleases You? How does Sister Renu know what is best? What drives Sister Dayita ?

Should I not ask them? How have I become the person I am? I must begin to think for myself, but how does one start? Is there some way of knowing that the direction one is travelling in will eventually take one to the good life?

It is strange; already I am feeling different. I ask questions that would be unrecognisable to my former self. I want to continue in this way so that I do not just ask but also learn what to ask and how to ask. I wish to work at understanding more, opening all that was closed to me. I will contact Sister Dayita; we have the same culture, she will understand my disposition better. I do so regret I spoke to her in haste. I am learning how to live without power.

I know that I am betwixt and between the orthodox beliefs of the Northern provinces and the ideas of Sister Renu. I may continue to be so for a long time, but I must learn to give myself direction. It is frightening and exhilarating. When in the past, saddened and depressed, or when I desired something, I turned to the gods. Now to whom will I turn? To myself? Will I ever be that strong?

CHAPTER TWENTY-SEVEN

Baalaajee Leaves

BAALAAJEE KNEW THAT he would no longer be able to live in or near the precincts of the palace. No one had ever refused a King. Had he said nothing, Kala would have had a short-lived experience of what it was to be greatly honoured. Was this experience worth her life? Maybe her daughter would have risen to become one of the senior ladies managing the daily working of the palace and may have married well. With such a dowry many higher castes would have been tempted. He smiled to himself. The priestly class needed help. Maybe. Maybe. But when the fire surrounded her on the pyre, what then? He knew that he could not, believing as he did, have done anything else but what he did.

He could see that Kala would, for the rest of her life, accuse him of denying her and her daughter the opportunity of a lifetime. What should he do now? He had done the best for her and now he must leave . . . Had she become his responsibility? He had decided to leave almost immediately to avoid the need to explain himself, to escape the torrents of accusations and intense disapproval. He wished to be on his own. He would leave Kala where she was, he told himself, for she would not trust him again.

This was sufficient for him. He would travel more quickly alone. No man could have done more to save her. After all, he had put himself out for her. He had made a name for himself both in and out the compound, but because of her, he must now leave as the wretched do – quietly, unseen, no farewells. No human contact. His reputation lost. What had he gained? Peace of mind – that he was certain of, but he was ill-at-ease that peace of mind should be so costly. A life's work diminished.

She would remain here. This was her life. He had done his best for her. No more should be expected of him. She would cope.

The miserable existence of an outcast will be her lot – but it had been her lot before. Nothing had changed. For his own inner tranquility, he would tell her the truth. He was going to the port where he would leave with others on a ship to make his fortune in another land. Manu had explained to him that after five years, he would be able to purchase land. Kala would too. Would she like to come? If she said no, he would not try to persuade her, that would be that. If she said yes, and he was hoping she would not, she would have to get ready quickly and they would leave at about four in the morning to avoid any nastiness. Baalaajee was greatly saddened. He walked about in the space where his guru had taught him, and then bent down and saluted the spot where his guru had sat all those years. It had become holy ground to him. How he wished there was another way.

Kala was not happy. Everyone around her told her the advice she had received had not been good. She should have broken her oath: God would have understood her dire situation. Was He not offering her an opportunity to better herself? It was too late now, of course. She had paid the price for being foolish and ignorant. It was the story of all their lives. They still did not understand why Pundit Baalaajee had advised her so.

A few servants maintained that Pundit Baalaajee was an upright man, a worthy man. The only explanation was that he knew something they didn't. Maybe he had learned that all the promises and the jewels might not really come to her daughter Sujata after all, and that the King would have been very disappointed. She would have lost out and Sujata too. On hearing this, they all agreed that it was so, for the late Pundit Baalaajee's Uncle and Pundit Baalaajee himself had time and time again been helpful to them and their children on how to approach a conflict, whether a bargain was fair, what to take when they were ill, or who to go to for further advice on health matters when he couldn't help. They were unable to count the number of times he had come to their assistance.

It was comforting to Kala to hear all this; besides, he was highly recommended to her by the slave elders, and they knew best. So when Baalaajee approached her with the chance of five years of hard work overseas, with a piece of land to her name afterwards, it was the next best thing to Heaven itself. The very idea of owning a piece of the earth here in Jyotika would never have occurred to her. She was convinced that Baalaajee was a good man after all, just as the elders had said he was.

Early the next day, long before dawn Baalaajee was taking his possessions and some of Kala's on his back.

He left the inner courtyard, then the outer. The guards recognised him and saluted him with clasped hands and bowed heads. There was understanding in the silence of the parting. Nothing was said. One of the guards wished to touch his feet, but Baalaajee restrained him and blessed him.

The road ahead was long, the night was cold. Sujata was sound asleep, covered by a threadbare blanket. Kala did not know where they were going. Nor did Baalaajee, yet he headed for the port. Manu had told him it was the place to go if you wished to leave for work overseas, to begin another life. They had once talked idly about going together, and Manu had described the route. He remembered much of it and his feet were guided by this memory.

CHAPTER TWENTY-EIGHT

A Dancer's Recall

AS THEY WALKED along the corridor, Queen Dayita stretched out her hand and delayed Sister Renu. 'Let us stay here awhile. I know our paths will not cross again, and parting like this is too abrupt. I want you to know that I feel responsible for our present humiliation. I cannot help thinking over and over again that had you been to see Pundit Krishna, things would have turned out differently. You would have persuaded him to move your way. This I truly believe and want you to know it.'

'You pay me too large a compliment, Sister Dayita. When the Pundit and I meet we are two strangers, courteous but not at all interested in each other, while I have noticed that with you, there is a definite attraction, apparent in his eyes. This would have given you a favoured place, helped to make a task impossible for an orthodox believer, become something that he could possibly consider, to please you.'

'You do not see clearly in this instance, Sister Renu.'

'Maybe, Sister Dayita. I too, carry no small burden of guilt. It almost numbs me when I think of it. My deep regret is that I was not more thoughtful. On that morning when we stood together and watched the King's Standard, lowered in the breeze; His Majesty's insignia approaching us, lance-like, piercing its path, you and Sister Meena would have had your faith to console you. Going to the pyre with faith would have offered you considerable reassurance and a resigned acceptance of your role, but to go now, with disbelief, is suicide; to be forced, ritual homicide.'

As she was speaking, something flashed into her mind – an idea presented itself, as the missing piece to the enigma of the young Pundit Baalaajee. But she distrusted this flickering thought and discarded it. He was a Northerner, a Brahmin, a junior pundit of the royal court. To have him holding concepts of disbelief like her own? No! No! This idea had no foundation. How my mind plays games when my energy ebbs, she thought.

How could such a seed take root and grow in one so young, in this compound of orthodox beliefs?

'What are you thinking, Sister Renu?'

'That I am responsible for Sister Meena's present anguish. At this moment, she may be changing her mind minute by minute until it rests where some plausible justification beckons.'

'I intend to do my very best to save her. Three times I have been blessed by women without whom I would have become so distraught, so depressed that I would have been driven to take my own life. I was greatly helped, now I too must play my part.'

'To be fair to Sister Meena, she was anxious and unhappy throughout. She could see the yawning inconsistency of our position which Pundit Krishnajee, with his competing loyalties, failed to comprehend. As far as he was concerned, we were going to do something useful with our lives while Kala, on becoming a suttee, could attain two commendable things – better her caste in death, and establish her daughter's future. His beliefs made this a neat arrangement.'

Dayita's voice then carried a gentle understanding: 'Sister Meena went along with our plans, because she trusted us, Sister Renu. Once upon a time I too trusted in that total way. Later I was helped to realise that trust should be taken away when it is abused. In the Temple of Mysticism in Dance, my tutor, who was also my guru, the senior swamis and chief pundits were spinners of a vast and complex web, masters of intrigue.

'It was the incense, their upright postures and flowing garments, sonorous Sanskrit chants, the rituals and sounds of pujas that seduced us into trusting them, believing they were our conduits to God. So we gladly offered them our respect and quietly submitted to their authority.

'As I was the Prima dancer of sacred classical dance, the chief pundits and senior swamis of the Temple of Mysticism in Dance used me to gain royal patronage. I worked very hard for them all. Before Kings and Princes I danced and danced, and the Temple prospered and flourished.

'As my reputation travelled, my tutor was much sought after; fine royal gifts came to him. He soon became overbearingly arrogant and spoiled, far too complacent. Gradually his former uncompromising discipline left him. So much praise diminished him. It even affected the way he spoke and walked. He began to induce me to favour him, to become his handmaiden. This position, he advised, was much sought after, and to hold it was an honour, never before bestowed upon anyone.

234

'Fearing for myself, his power being considerable, and in an attempt to temper his ardour, I said I could not accept this honour, as I had made certain promises to Shiva, the God of Dance. The god had kept his promises and I could not do otherwise but be faithful to my obligations, for to cheat Shiva would bring disaster to the Temple of Mysticism in Dance.

'Some time passed by and then my tutor began to say that I owed him a great deal, that I was being ungracious not showing my appreciation. This made me realise that my departure should be imminent.

'To repay him was impossible, he would whisper to me. What he was being forced to request, arose from the discourtesy I had shown him. At no time had he ever confronted such an absence of gratitude from a dancer. His finest dancers in the past were young girls of great repute, outstanding in beauty and grace with an incomparable understanding of the needs of dance.

'It was explained to me that my art would attain heights of perfection that could not be reached in isolation, for when a student and her guru of dance are able to share the undisclosed, an unparalleled beauty surfaces; fresh images are reflected in her every movement. This was his mantra.

'Once, on seeing me alone in the Temple's garden, soon after it had rained, he led me to the pagoda tree; its reddish-orange blooms were feeding their sweet scent to the wind. With trembling hands he carefully chose each flower and decorated my hair. It was what he had done when I was seven and about to make my first public solo performance. I should from time to time ponder, he said, his voice gentle, that it was he who had used every aspect of the energy of his youth, his sensuous

235

and intellectual being to give me form. He was my sculptor. I had become a magnificent piece of his art. Being close to one's creator was one of Nature's most satisfying tasks. Therefore in the quiet sanctity of night, he urged me to meditate on these things. I thanked him, all the while keeping my distance with the respect due to his high office and reputation.

'He saw I was moved, yet I could not offer him what he desired. My strength to resist him came from a kind matron of the Temple, whom we called Big Sister, a mother figure to us all. She had observed much. One day she asked to see me, and in the domestic comfort of her room, explained that any intimate relationship, I might desire or be induced to have with the swamis, pundits or tutors of the Temple, would lead to my ruin.

'With affection, she warned me that my career in dance and my ability to attract suitors of high renown would speedily come to an end, were I to lose my honour. She had spoken in so caring a manner that her warnings were my rudder. Without her maternal guidance I am sure I would have been caught in the carefully laid snares of the Temple's hierarchy. I used her as my shield whenever I felt at risk.

'I disclosed that I was overcome by pity for my tutor, but she explained to me that in my circumstance it was a dangerous emotion which reduced my defences and I should not harbour it. Yet I was not without compassion for him. This once fine, disciplined, erudite and handsome tutor of dance who had attained the pinnacle of his creativity, provided his audience with varying imaginative forms of interpretation in movement, was now driven to a wild shamelessness.

'I confided in another woman, a hardworking assistant to the administrators of the Temple who had suspected something all along. She divulged her feelings openly: his advances were forcing me to become a bird in the path of a tornado. Far too many fine girls with enormous potential had been caught in the Temple's web, she said, unable to disentangle themselves with honour. A few committed suicide, seeing it as their only graceful exit. Despite bringing such shame and ignominy to these skilled dancers, who were but young, unsophisticated girls, the powerful men in the Temple continued in their exploitative ways and had become addicted to unrestrained sensuous delights. Their "priestly power" formed their protective cover.

'That woman helped me to plan an honourable escape. Together we bided our time.

'The Temple funds had been brought low by the excesses of the chief priests and swamis. And so when I was taken to dance in a newly completed grand Temple, close to Jyotika, she managed to get my tutor to agree that I should perform before King Paresh. My tutor was well aware of the royal gifts and praises that would come his way. The fact that he was my guru would make him the envy of the rising, young tutors who were challenging the old order. He could also see that the senior swamis would be eternally grateful to him, and this would soften the persisting sense of insecurity that had come to him with age.

'It was all arranged. At the appropriate time, with my administrator's help and that of her trusted servant, who had contact with the palace, I managed to convey to the King that as the dances were being performed in his honour, I would like to discuss with him in private, beforehand, his preferred choices from my repertoire.

'It was an unusual request. But being a Prima dancer carries a certain attraction, even to royalty. In addition, my far-seeing administrator had earlier ensured that His Majesty knew of my fame and acclaim through the erudite in dance in Jyotika.

'So it was I was able to induce the King to meet with me in private. My tutor was told that it was the King who wished to see me before the dance to make a personal request. He was not happy about this, but when the administrator reminded him of the desperate financial situation the Temple was in, and the added strength he would gain in the Temple's hierarchy by donating a few of the gifts that would certainly come his way here, he reluctantly allowed the meeting.

'I engaged the King of Jyotika with the artistry of the dances of the Apsaras, frescoed in the Ajanta caves. After he had chosen, I let it be known that the final performance of the evening would be my own composition, dedicated to him. I alluded to the fact that this creation had never been performed before, nor did I think it would be repeated, as it was a dance that would be performed for his eyes only. I hinted that as King of Jyotika he had it in his power to request the Prima dancer to dance in the inner sanctum of his private Temple at certain times – either in the eventides of quiet shadows or as approaching dawn flickers its first soft rendering of itself. He replied, "It is the time when earthen oil lamps call to be replenished."

' "The prestigious Temple of Mysticism in Dance would understandably not wish to lose their finest dancer," I warned, "and may come to you with reasons why the Temple must continue to be my abode." I indicated that I was in a bind. There was the Temple with its ever-increasing demands on me, while I would prefer to dance for small exclusive audiences, even an audience of one as this facilitated the performer's enrichment of the mystery in dance. Before a large unschooled and distant audience, much was lost and less was offered. The beauty and grace of tones and rhythms when combined are as fragile and intricate, as silk lace patterns, and demand serious concentration so that the artistry and the emotions they evoke are cradled as one.

'I explained that the thought of dancing solely for the King of Jyotika had first come to me after an early morning puja. More recently in a dream, I said, the God, Shiva, had asked that His Majesty be assisted in the further understanding of the complex motions of his cosmic dance, inspired when time was young and earth's elements pure.

' "I am ill at ease to disclose," I whispered, "even in confidence to Your Majesty, something that brings a considerable disappointment to the Temple. Nevertheless, to fulfil Shiva's request would be an esteemed honour, Your Majesty. The power and the right to bring this to pass belongs only to you and to no other." '

'You are, Sister Dayita, a most remarkable woman,' said Renu, smiling, 'my life did not have your colourful exuberance or warm intrigues, though it had pleasures, challenges and excitements.'

'Tell me just a little. I have told you my all.'

'You know I was an only child and brought up as a son. I was allowed to question everything, to move about with a greater freedom than most, to join the royal hunts, to participate in debates with the scholars and pundits who frequented our palace. My parents would answer any question I put before them. I was made to feel that they were my friends, not parents.

'Despite my upbringing I am a daughter, not a son, and have certain obligations to my parents. I cannot return home: I would be taking too great a humiliation to them. We are close to the Northern Kingdom in this aspect of marriage. Once a daughter marries, there can be no turning back to her parental home; no comfortable place is kept for her there. This aspect of our tradition diminishes us.

'We are both lucky, Sister Dayita, to have nurtured that spiritual strength which circumstance enabled us to exercise further still, but Sister Meena's life was lyrical, a poem. Understandably, she lived a life to please others. There was no pressing need to challenge anything, no one to encourage her to think about things differently. She was a true flower of the royal courts.'

'Yes, Sister Renu, she trusted those around her and walked on the rugs they provided. I agree. We have to save her from her circumstance.'

'At present she does not know what to do and will go wherever custom leads.'

'You either believe or don't. You can't do both. With your help, Sister Renu, she and I have moved our thinking from where it was. She walks where we do, but it is unfamiliar ground to her.'

'Yes, Sister Dayita, unlike you, she does not yet know the comforts of reason, the exhilarating challenges of doubt, nor the language of disbelief. She needs more time, which none of us have now. But it will not always be so with her.'

'We are still superstitious here, Sister Renu. Who knows, she may be waiting for a sign.'

'And will interpret it, Sister Dayita, as her needs allow. Will she climb the pyre? It is not that I am wiser, it is just easier for me since I was not brought up with this belief. There may have been occasions in the past when this human sacrifice served some higher purpose than the glorification of husbands. But now? It belongs to the past. I too am superstitious and I indulge in wishful thinking. Perhaps the difference is, I tell myself that it is wishful thinking, not an observation.'

Now Queen Dayita felt much better and she said, 'I have not yet decided what I shall do, but I will send a message to your manservant. It is safer that way. These walls may have ears and eyes. Tell me, where are you heading for?'

'I shall ask Manu to map out our route for you. Later, you can follow us. I hope you do. There is a stable boy, his name is Datta, he is trustworthy, knows everything about horses and travel. He has studied Manu's map to the port. They have discussed it. When you are ready, go to him. He sleeps beside the stable.'

'You think of everything.'

'No, my mother did – and Manu always provides alternative plans. Datta was to take me, if Manu was prevented. We shall keep him on the alert for you. I shall let you have some opium I brought with me. Give it to Datta. He may have need of it in order to assist you.

'With regards to escape, you will dress as a travelling merchant who has just delivered his merchandise and must leave the compound early to journey on. Leave in

241

the dead of night, when the compound sleeps. Keep inside the covered carrier, give orders from within, disguise your voice. Merchants say little except when negotiating their merchandise. Travel with an imperious manner from inside – grandiose gestures to the guards at the gates should work.'

'I cannot promise that I will manage it all. I shall have to see.'

Both Queens then handed gifts to each other. Dayita's gift to Renu was an enchantment, a gold chain of forty five lotuses. It seemed to have been the work of a botanist expressing the miracle of the natural world and a jeweller's understanding of it. Queen Renu's gift to her was a pair of bracelets of fine gold. 'It is a copy, Sister Dayita, of the geometrical pattern of the sandstone screen on our windows – so intricate – it looks as if a bird's beak had created this fine interlocking tracery. We were caged birds.'

'But your jeweller has made it look beautiful.'

'The pattern is.'

'It is so like you, Sister Renu, to say in your own way, "It should have been kept for jewellery not windows".'

They hugged, not knowing if their eyes would ever rest upon each other again.

Sister Renu walked away slowly and then turned back. 'Sister Dayita, I beg you, this is crucial. Do *not* trust Pundit Krishna. He is a believer; he has everything to lose. He needs to regain his self-respect and honourable position more than you think; he can only do so by having us put on the pyre. Remember, he cannot do otherwise. He is the King's Pundit of the royal court and will be faithful and loyal to the end.

Again they embraced, lost to all that was around them save each other's breathing.

As Queen Renu hurried to send a message to Manu, Queen Dayita decided that she must now come to the assistance of Queen Meena. Helping was contagious. All at once she found that her mind had been made up and she would now make arrangements for escaping. She would get in touch with Datta to learn his strategy and hear his advice as to the best time to leave the compound.

She did not wish to hold back Sister Renu. A small party was less likely to arouse suspicion; besides, the earlier Renu left, the better. How long it would take her to persuade Sister Meena to leave with her, she could not tell. Dayita was aware that, by arranging to take Sister Meena, she would be compromising herself; two women leaving the compound will trigger suspicion . . . so with their disguises, there will be two travelling merchants.

This escape frightens me, Dayita thought. I am not as young or as fearless as I once was. With hindsight, I can see our last plan never had a chance. What would happen to us if we were caught? How would I ever face Pundit Krishnajee? We *must* succeed. It *must* be done.

Tomorrow when the sun rose above the horizon, King Paresh would be placed on the pyre. Knowing Pundit Krishnajee, as she did, Queen Dayita predicted that it was only when the sun had attained its full glory would he officiate, not before. This exactness by the Pundit may work in their favour.

PART THREE

CHAPTER TWENTY-NINE

How Far We Had Drifted Apart

As I knocked at my sister Vasti's bedroom and waited, I was smiling to myself for this small courtesy I had taught her many years ago. An elder sister, my parents explained, had certain responsibilities to the younger; it made good sense.

Though I was her senior by five years, having been at the same primary and secondary schools gave us much to talk about. This was also a time when the world moved at the pace of a Sunday afternoon stroll, when there was a common understanding. People, food, clothing, hairstyles, houses and gardens remained faithful to expectation. Teachers behaved as if they were encyclopaedias; textbooks, as well as the school tie, could be passed down through the family.

Our close sisterly relationship was helped by parental direction and encouragement, and so we grew up together in an atmosphere of trust, affection and dependence, until she went abroad.

Vasti returned an adult, independent, with a changed outlook and a good degree. She saw the world as if she had come from the future and we were just behind it. She talked constantly about changing her pupils' attitude to learning, to everything in fact.

Nevertheless she was contented, happily teaching at St Ursula's when this arranged marriage came upon her.

With hindsight, she must have felt that by displaying an indifference, not participating in it, the arrangement would peter out. But she had underestimated Uncle Kash's and Aunt Sona's enthusiasm. I myself am not without blame. I should have alerted her to what was happening. As men go, Dr Karan Walli was all right, but that is simply not good enough for young women today. Why should it be? They have placed a higher value on their own lives. This idea has been long in coming and is yet to be embraced fully by the village elders.

The problem was also elsewhere. Village culture says being in love is neither essential nor a necessary condition for beginning married life. Love will come with time and has to be earned, worked at. The working at part was apparently the task of women. Such ideas are incomprehensible to the young and the educated. They are suspicious, for they see love being bartered for whatever attribute their elders are happy to offer in its place. This could be wealth, family connection, education, profession, good character, a person's manner and style or good looks. There is also that indefinable influence brought to bear by uncles and aunties. It has its own soundings – 'I can feel he is right for her, will fit in well with the family. I know the family well. I can feel it in my veins, it will be all right.' Which niece would dare to say that her aunt's veins were a poor conductor of her own feelings and perceptions?

Come to think of it, Vasti compromised primarily because she wanted to please Ma. Since Pa is no longer with us, she could not bring herself to be the one causing Ma pain or distress. And to be reasonable, she could not be entirely removed from our village thinking. After all, we brought her up, all of us. Our community was our metronome and we stepped in time.

Here in the village where girls marry in their teens, primarily because their parents are trying to protect them from being awakened by the wrong sorts, and where it can be seen that to be present at your grandsons' weddings is the only time the village encourages you to dance as never before, and applauds your free style; well then, to be in your middle twenties with no marriage on the horizon becomes disquieting.

Things were moving along nicely, I believe, until she went to collect the jewellery. I did go over and try to glean from Mr Singh what actually took place. He was not very helpful . . . merely said something as trite as she was not well on the day. The jewellery afforded her much pleasure, he emphasised. I saw none of that when she brought it home, and wondered whether he was a reliable witness.

He spent some time explaining what a beautiful piece it was. There was also something about showing her the rings that Karan had sent to be cleaned. I wanted to examine them, to see if there might have been a swastika symbol or some dreadful design on any of the rings that could taint his character, and said as much.

Mr Singh was furious: 'Pushpa, how can you say a thing like that about my work?' he exploded. 'You think I have no morals? I, Anjit Singh, designed those rings. In fact, it is my family's tradition that guided the creation of those rings. We Singhs, the jewellers, have earned a reputation for craftsmanship of the highest standard. Those rings are special, finely worked and that is why they stand out. Once you see them, only once, mind you, you never forget them. Never! That is what craftsmanship is about.'

Anjit Singh said nothing more for quite a while, then on regaining his equanimity, spoke calmly, though peeved that I could have thought the way I did, furthermore expressed it in his presence.

'Making an impression on the mind, Pushpa, is what style is about. You should know that. Dr Walli enjoys style. And to crown it all, no one else has any of those rings I have designed for him. He is very particular. I cannot emphasise how much he likes a designer ring to mark him out as an individual.'

After Mr Singh's lengthy self advertisement, I was sorry that I had missed seeing them. The Wallis had already called for them.

What sent me to the shop was something I had observed but kept to myself, not mentioning it even to Shami. On her return from the jeweller, despite what Mr Singh said, Vasti had lost her spark, her laughter which she carried in her very stride. Normally she would have lost no time in enthusiastically pointing out the fine filigree work of her new bracelets and the necklace – the varying inclination and size of the petals, blooms and leaves. She would even have fooled about, putting them on Ma and then on me and, if Shami allowed her, on him too. Vasti would have displayed a sense of delight that the jewellery she had designed had turned out as she had imagined and hoped for.

On that evening she simply showed them to us as courtesy obliged her to. There was no sense of pleasure, instead, a hint of gloom. Vasti is always concerned about not causing anyone pain. She worries for everyone, and for herself too. I think she has a particular sensitivity. Obsessed by the idea of chance and probability from quite a young age, her fears were both large and small. A new school, a new form teacher, Sports Day. Later, it was examinations and whether she was university material or not. These were all spoken of in terms of the probability of this or that happening in her favour.

When she returned home with her degree and a head full of ideas as I have said, she nevertheless seemed more composed, and serious about wanting to play her part in the community's welfare. She threw herself into teaching and was beginning to regain her comic, mischievous ways.

My growing anxiety for Vasti meant I could not rest until I interviewed the two young women helpers from the village who had accompanied her to the jeweller that day. I did not tell them why I wanted to see them, for I needed to know what actually happened, not the fabrication of two young heads. I interviewed them separately. One had little to say. The other replied in a most fascinating way. This is a part of what she said: 'You asked me what I saw, right?'

'Yes.'

'But you did not ask me what I was *feeling*.'

'No, I didn't.' I was mystified by her words.

'All right – tell me what you felt.'

'From the way Sister Vasti kept looking at one of the rings, and the many questions she asked about it, even I realised that something terrible had happened. It looked as if somebody wearing a ring like that had done something bad . . . *very* bad.'

251

'Like what?'

'I don't know. But very, very bad.'

The girl kept quite still for a while, and suddenly without warning, held on to her own throat pretending she was wearing the ring on one of her unadorned fingers, which she indicated by waving it at me. Her strangling hand was placed over a gasping, struggling throat. This young woman was a born actress.

I said to her, 'That's enough, thank you. I understand.'

'And Vasti, I believe, saw this ring on a finger doing this terrible thing.' She supported her act with those words.

Well, I told her that Vasti would have had to be so close that the person would then have turned round and killed her too. She agreed it didn't make sense. Then she came out with, 'This is why I haven't told anyone. I know it doesn't add up . . . yet something very worrying is there. I have a nose for these things – I can sniff them.'

'It was a sensible decision to keep quiet.' I attempted to persuade her to remain silent and to keep her feelings to herself. Fancy sullying Karan's character like that, suspecting him of murder! Village girls are using this new-found freedom to speak their minds too openly.

After that, I realised I was on the wrong track. Yet I had seen Vasti's health deteriorate so rapidly after the visit to Mr Singh that the young woman's words remained with me. A deep sadness came over me when it was obvious that whatever had caused her anguish and loss of will to go through with the wedding, she had kept to herself. How far we have drifted apart, I thought, regretting that I had lost her. I was also

252

reminded of how little we really know anyone, even those closest to us – let alone ourselves.

As her door was not locked, and not hearing anything, after repeated knocks and pressing my ear to her door, I entered, calling to her.

She had been forcefully thrown to the floor, as if struck by a car.

The impact was on her forehead. Her face swollen, discoloured; badly bruised as if she had been lifted and dropped more than once. I thought the worst. The window was wide open, the wind had kept the curtains aloft as a kite, moonlight was rapidly leaving the window's ledge.

I could not feel a pulse. I looked closely, bending over her, holding my own breath to hear hers. To my relief I detected a slow quiet rhythm. To ensure it was not my imagination, I checked again.

Then I began to wonder how much longer she would remain unconscious. How long had she been on the floor?

CHAPTER THIRTY

On the Road

KALA CARRIED THE sleeping Sujata on her shoulder. She and Baalaajee had been walking through the night. It was now dawn and they were both tired. Sujata awoke and started to cry, as she was hungry. Her mother knew there was not much food and tried to coax her back to sleep, but the little girl kept on crying. Baalaajee offered her a piece of his naan. She stretched out her hand eagerly and took it.

They were attracted to a roadside shrine offering shelter. It contained a life-size sculpture of the god Vishnu and they paid homage to it. Baalaajee saw a concept of Divinity expressed in granite. Compressed thought was reflected in the god's face, and though a surge of energy flowed along its limbs, yet the sculptor had exerted a restraining calm. Power was contained. In the soft dawn, Vishnu's face shone, and as the celestial light moved, a thoughtful tranquillity was revealed in its entirety.

Baalaajee recognised that the sculptor was offering another concept of power: knowledge, control, mindfulness; balance. Stillness. No thunderbolt from the heavens, no charging cavalry full of passionate righteousness; no trumpet-blowing celebration of wars with banners hoisted high. Here was displayed a symphony of other virtues to strengthen the weak, the silent ones. Here the disadvantaged were offered rafts of virtues with in-built oars to cross the floods of life. This sculptor had fashioned a form of power that Baalaajee knew would be difficult to find again.

He did not search for the artist's name; he knew that the sculptor had left his work, not his name. This was the custom.

As they gathered up their belongings, a well-covered carriage on wheels pulled by two fine horses stopped a few metres away. It once carried the royal insignia, this he could tell, for he knew where to look. Baalaajee suspected that they had camouflaged themselves, had come to take him back to the royal court to make an example of him. He stood and waited. He would offer no resistance, nor would he attempt to escape. He hoped they would give him an opportunity to defend himself, albeit aware, that this might serve no useful purpose. A non-believer speaking to the sycophants of the prevailing power can only give one verdict. Then the driver climbed down and approached him.

A familiar voice spoke: 'Punditjee Ram Ram. It is me, Manu. We are going to the port we once talked about. Queen Renu would like to offer you and Kala the hospitality of her own Royal Family. This carriage and the horses were exchanged for gifts her parents gave her. You and Kala and Sujata could travel with us perhaps for a part of your journey if you do not wish to go to the port.'

Kala was delighted by this turn of events and Baalaajee knew that he must think of her and Sujata and keep whatever feelings he may have about royalty to himself. He was very tempted to decline. His proud spirit urged him to refuse with courtesy. He was about to do this, but Kala was way ahead of him with Sujata. He would have to stop her, ask her to come back. He found it difficult to take away this comfort offered to the child and her mother.

The sun would rise higher still and, when it did, the intense heat would not be good for the infant. Yet he did not think he could face the Queen, not after what she and the other two had been planning to do to Kala; he was about to call her back when Manu said, 'We are in need of a pundit. Your presence will enable us to deter bandits and robbers. Our swords may not be enough. We need your help.'

Climbing aboard, he was taken aback to find Queen Renu dressed as a young man, complete with sword at her side and turban; she carried both well. With her clear, keen eyes, Queen Renu looked at the man who Manu said did not believe in life after death and who had used his understanding of the ancient texts to save a slave-girl from the pyre. She was curious. How had this come about?

Baalaajee was wondering: What does this intelligent face see when it looks at me? He was unable to say, for Queen Renu was equally courteous and welcoming to all three. He saw that Manu had tied her turban in the style of the South. Without a veil, and the colour removed from her hands and her nails short, she looked the part. Queen Renu was wearing a young man's kurta, her trousers well fitted, the same as Manu's. Both had dispensed with the stylish waistband and long tunics of court. The very material used was meant to camouflage the status of the travellers. It was cotton. Manu would have been observing the dress of travellers, of merchants, for a long time. Baalaajee wondered whether the Queen had prepared herself with this outfit long ago, in anticipation of the King's death, and her flight with Manu. Not knowing about her upbringing as a son, he guessed she had tried it on several times, for her movements were manly. If he hadn't been aware of the disguise, he would have been taken in.

Baalaajee understood that now was not the appropriate time, but there were a lot of questions he wanted to ask. If they had been avoiding the pyre, why allow Pundit Krishna to coax Kala to join the late King? He would ask Manu first – the Queen confided in him.

Queen Renu was happy to have the company of these three, and showed it by providing fruit and water for everyone. The carriage was commodious. Kala and the baby were given a place inside, while Manu and Queen Renu shared the driving of the horses. Baalaajee had never before held the reins of a horse.

All day the horses' hooves pounded the rough earth. On and on, the carriage rattled and shook. Many miles went past. Dusk descended and they travelled on. Night fell. Both they and the horses were in need of food, drink and rest. On seeing attractive stalls before a rest house, it was halted for the night, planning to leave early the next morning. Before alighting, it was decided that Queen Renu and Kala would say nothing. Manu and Baalaajee would attend to any nosy questions. Their cover would be that Manu was working for a merchant, who had sent him with a load of sandalwood to the Fort at Jyotika. He would soon be back with another load of merchandise – sugar, rice and saffron from the South. His passengers were hitching a ride to their distant relatives. They would refill their water bottles and purchase more fruit from the stalls.

Manu was left to see to the horses. Baalaajee, with the remainder of the party, was about to enter the rest house. A young woman with a sleeping child was tending one of the sweet stalls. Sujata pointed to the baby. Queen Renu, decided to make a purchase and then to stroll round about the rest house, in keeping with her new role as a young merchant. 'Please keep the change for the child,' she said to the young woman at the sweet stall. 'It is too much,' replied she, 'half is more than sufficient.' Again Queen Renu graciously offered it, insisting that it belonged to the child.

It was flattering to have received so much attention from a handsome dark young man with perfect manners, his sword dangling from his waist, its attractive hilt reflecting high birth and status.

Queen Renu walked around and as she was about to enter the rest house and join the others, she once again smiled at the baby. It was then she noticed that the young woman was trying to catch her eye to tell her something – but was clearly constrained by the presence of the other stallkeepers. Youth and affection found a way, and it was with subtle use of eye and head movements, that Queen Renu gathered she was being warned not to enter the house. Nodding her understanding, she went round the back to find Manu.

There she saw two men with lathis approaching Manu, who had unhitched the carriage and with his back to them was feeding the horses. On seeing Queen Renu, who unsheathed her sword, and with Manu alerted, now equipped with a sturdy piece of wood, they pretended to be simply passing through.

Manu whispered that three of their horses were from the royal stables of Jyotika. 'We are in a den of robbers. This means murderers too, using their roadside rest house as a spider does its web. We can leave straight away but the horses need rest. I can negotiate an exchange of fresh horses with them, but I am loathe to leave my horses to such men. For me it would be an act of betrayal. Then again, they can bide their time and on our leaving, accuse us of stealing their horses. Our carriage and horses must be watched. Baalaajee and Kala must be warned.'

The too-helpful, chuckling landlord, was all smiles, enquiring if there was anything he could do to ensure their stay was comfortable. A hot meal would soon be ready. Even water for bathing could be arranged to ensure they were refreshed for their onward journey. Their welfare was his concern. 'Where are you good people travelling to?' he enquired genially. 'You are strangers to the place – we can always tell, so let me advise you, Punditjee; when the road forks a few yards further down the road, do take the right turning. The left one will lead to your being robbed by roadside bandits. We, the local people, have studied their ways. I have an obligation to my customers and it is also in my interest to ensure their safe onward journey and with it their recommendation of this homely establishment. I must tell you that I get particular pleasure from hearing that we have been recommended.'

It was said with so much sincerity that Baalaajee knew he would have been taken in, had he not been warned. He had worked himself up to such an extent that he was afraid to take the drink offered and refused the food when it was brought, although he was both thirsty and hungry. Baalaajee sensed they were all being closely watched. Maybe, these bandits knew more than they were letting on. He said as much to Manu, who reassured him that news of escaping Queens from Jyotika would not yet have travelled this distance. He was not sure when the people would know.

Manu and Baalaajee took turns to keep watch. Early that morning as the horses were being harnessed, the same young woman, the stallkeeper, came out of the dark and shyly whispered to Queen Renu that they must not stop the carriage for any reason. 'Whatever happens, do not stop!' She hurriedly explained that one of the many ploys used was to have one of their men blocking the road with an ox-drawn cart, pretending to be a farmer in distress examining a damaged cart-wheel. Were they to stop, they would be overpowered by a band of robbers.

She said the proprietor believed they had suspected something and would do just the opposite of what he had advised. Queen Renu offered her a gift of money for this advice. She refused it, saying the risk she had taken to inform them was her thank you for their kindness. Continuing in this soft tone, she pointed out that the owner of the rest house had become a gross man, ugly in every way, unlike them. She wanted the pundit to bless her and the baby and to pray for them. This Baalaajee solemnly did, and promised to remember her in his prayers.

When she had gone, Manu asked how were they to know that she had not been set up to say what she did. There was silence. As they had no choice but to travel on either one road or the other, they were in a quandary as to what to do. Kala said they should chance their luck and do as the young woman said, for it was plain that she had an affection for Queen Renu, thinking she was a young man, and would not wish to see her robbed or killed.

As nobody had any other suggestion they decided to trust the young woman and take the very road the proprietor had suspected that they, having become suspicious of him, would *not* be taking.

Manu, with rested horses, raced full speed ahead. At the forked junction, he turned off to the right. Kala took hold of the lathi, Queen Renu unsheathed her sword. After a mile or so, moving like the wind, they could see a beggar standing in the middle of the road. He had but one leg and appeared to be hopping about in agony. Manu said it was a set-up. He decided to make it clear that if the man did not remove himself quickly, he would be run over. Baalaajee blew his conch shell, and Manu an old bugle. The horses, understanding this to be an encouragement to gallop faster still, surged forward. Queen Renu came out brandishing her sword which caught the first light. Closer and closer they moved to the solitary figure; they could see him more clearly now. On and on the horses' hooves, went pounding, pounding the earth. The horses understood Manu's determination. The reins were loose, allowing a greater freedom. The cart-wheels rolled effortlessly. This man, still in the middle of the road, would be run over. Everyone was watching. What would the outcome be? Manu had become a man possessed. Nearer and nearer still, the horses were flying past . . . when it happened. The man speedily scrambled out of the way

261

with two perfect legs. The tension dropped. Everyone was relieved and they fell about with laughter.

Baalaajee said he could see that he needed Manu more than Manu could ever need a priest. Both men laughed. 'What made you so sure?' Baalaajee asked him.

'I felt that a one-legged beggar would not stand in the middle of a busy main road,' Manu answered, 'and were he to do so, he would have begun to take a few steps to save himself, not to circle round and round. His acting was poor.'

The journey took almost three weeks. They stopped several more times at rest houses and at markets to purchase food and water. On reaching the port, Manu and Baalaajee left the others in a sheltered spot and moved along the crowded streets of merchant shops to try and get a fair price for their carriage and horses.

Baalaajee asked how Manu knew he and Kala were on that road. 'We had no problem leaving the Fort. The guards knew me. No matter where I am, I always culti-vate a good relationship with gate-keepers, those of earth and of Heaven, aware that one day I may need their assistance. It was when we were leaving the court-yard,' Manu explained. 'One of the guards at the gate told us you had left with Kala about two hours before, taking the right turn. I had a hunch that you were also more likely to take the road to the port because of our past conversations. We were so pleased to find you at the roadside.

'Besides, you and Sister Renu think alike on the mat-ter of suttee. Queen Renu says it is foolish to continue to address her as I once did; we are to call each other

262

Sister or Brother. It is safer that way.' Without his asking, Manu told Baalaajee that the intentions of the Queens, had been both to save Kala and to open a school for girls in the compound.

Baalaajee was saddened to think that now there would be no school for girls in Jyotika; he believed the plan to save Kala, would have failed. No one could have done it without being found out. Manu interrupted his thoughts: 'Baalaajee, if we are together and behave as a family, we will be kept together when we land overseas. We should settle in the same place. Together we will do very well – I am sure of it.'

'Whose idea was that?'

'I suggested it on the way. I also said you and I would be able to build a house and plant vegetables around it as my father did when I was a child. Two men can make the women's lives less strenuous.'

Having disposed of their conveyance at a price they wished were higher, Manu purchased clothes for Sujata and Kala and kitchen utensils, blankets and cotton sheets.

They were spotted by a man who was recruiting labourers for plantations abroad. He led them to the local magistrate, who registered them. The recruiter, all the while, continued to reassure them that this was a good move for the entire family. Soon each of them had their certificate of registration which stated their age, caste, occupation and gender. But when Renu heard the magistrate informing the man ahead of her in the queue that he had now to go to the depot where he would be examined by a physician, she decided to come clean, explaining to the magistrate that her brother had persuaded her to travel that way for her own protection.

263

The magistrate was far too busy to be bothered with any brotherly advice given to a Sister and replied with impatience, 'Whatever it is, tell the doctor.'

Sister Renu did explain. The doctor was aware that the plantation owners were asking for more women to be recruited, to stabilise the labour force, to provide some domestic comfort and family responsibility to the men, in the hope that this would make their hardships easier to bear and ensure that their contracts would be renewed. The doctor thought a family of two women and two men was an ideal one.

At the crowded depot, they joined the long line. Behind them were two brothers, who said they had been told that after they completed their five-year contract they would be free to go and get rich, if they knew how to manage money and spot the right opportunities. They could open a shop and, after that, nothing would stop them. They would return as Maharajahs. They were looking forward to the future. Sister Renu and her group listened. Kala was excited and a feeling of well-being came over her for the first time since she had left the royal compound of Jyotika.

The man ahead of them in the line was also listening. He turned to Baalaajee and said, 'Punditjee, there is not going to be much work for you. People do not have money for prayers, as there is barely enough for the belly. The work is very hard and you and your family do not look like field-hands. It is hard labour from dawn to dusk.'

'How do you know this, my brother?'

'I have been there before.'

'Why are you returning?'

'There is work over there. Here there isn't. This time, I will manage my money differently. I only wanted to let you know the truth, so that you will not be disappointed on landing. If you are prepared, you will cope better.'

'It is good of you to let me know. I will work in the fields, and I will also do pundit work, but when I am doing pundit work I will not ask for payment. We have to keep our spirits up when far from home, especially when the going is tough.'

'You speak as a real pundit. I hope we will be sent to the same sugar estate. May I say that I am related to you, so that we *are* sent to the same place?'

'Yes, brother, but feel free to change your mind. You do not know us, and you may find a family more to your liking on the journey.'

Manu came over to Baalaajee and whispered, 'Whom do we believe?'

'A little of both to begin with, and when we reach there, we will make the necessary adjustments.'

'Baalaajee, he is looking at Sister Renu. He has his eyes on her – this is why he wants to be "related" to us.'

'You mean dressed as she is?'

'I believe he overheard what she was saying to the doctor.'

'I always felt you possessed a good imagination, Manu. Now you should consider writing poetry. I promise to read whatever you write.'

'Tell him that she is your wife. It will protect her. Explain to him why you told her to dress like this.'

'I cannot do that. I think you should begin to compose your thoughts straight away, for your brain is unusually active, but . . . how can I say this and not

265

offend a dear friend? "Manu, I have changed my mind, I may not wish to read everything you write." '

Both men laughed On seeing this, but not knowing the cause of the laughter, Sister Renu and Kala smiled too. Sujata slept.

Not long afterwards, with Baalaajee carrying the child, they were all holding onto the rail, climbing up the swaying steps of a ship bound for either the West or the East, they were not quite sure. They were hoping it would be a place where they would be able to begin new lives.

CHAPTER THIRTY-ONE

Changing the Tides of Time

I WAS ON the telephone to Dr Mistry, asking him to come at once.

'Yes, Vasti has a high temperature. Her breathing is very weak, as in deep sleep.' . . . 'No, I did not try to wake her.' . . . 'Thank you, Dr Mistry.'

Ma and I placed her on the bed. Ma caressed her face and hair with her comforting worn palms, but to no avail. We were unable to reach her. Dr Mistry had said that her conscious mind was elsewhere. When one loses one's consciousness, where does it seek shelter?

Ma and I took turns to keep the temperature down by wiping her face and arms with cold, wet hand towels.

When Dr Mistry arrived, he checked her breathing, her pulse, her throat for constrictions, opened her eyes with one hand, and shone the light of a small torch into each. With a patella, he tapped her knees and elbows, with his knuckles, he tapped her toes. Then, using the sharp pointed end of the patella, he scraped the bottom of her feet; though she responded, she remained unconscious throughout.

He turned to my mother and said, 'Mrs Nadir, there does not seem to be anything physically wrong. I can

267

see that she has injured her forehead and face, but it is not sufficiently severe to bring about this prolonged, loss of consciousness. It may just be that she is undergoing a severe mental strain. Prolonged worry leads to stress throughout the body and can so easily lead to all sorts of ailments. What we must later ensure, you, Pushpa and I working together as a team, is that once we have identified the cause of the stress, we remove it. There is really no other way.' Dr Mistry then asked for his favourite drink, a cup of Darjeeling tea.

As soon as Ma left the room, he said that he wanted me to come clean with him. 'Vasti is experiencing a depth of unconsciousness that is disturbing. The cause is in part psychological. You know I have the greatest respect for tradition Pushpa, but when it brings so much misery and pain, one needs to re-examine it. We cannot sacrifice our mental health to ideas that are no longer relevant. Nor can you send your intelligent sister abroad for an education in a country where women have much more freedom than here and expect her to return and behave as a pliant village lass. Now, Pushpa, are you still that strong young woman I knew, or has that husband of yours begun to wear you down?'

I smiled. 'Shami is a good husband.'

'Well, he is an exception. But then again, you are a charmer.'

He had grown old, but was as good a doctor as ever, offering light banter to prepare me for the worst, or so I thought.

'I think it is the wedding that has brought this on.' he told me soberly. 'I have seen this sort of thing before. Vasti will recover fully only if the source of her distress is removed. If you and your mother are able to sit down and consider what other events could possibly have brought this about, let me know, and we will confer. She does not wish to go along with the marriage I believe.'

'How do you know that the wedding is the cause of her condition?'

'Be honest with me. Is she happy to be getting married in a few days' time? Or is she going through with it because it is what will please everyone? Sadly, this situation is far too common. The village girls barter their entire lives, more often than not taking on a lifetime of misery, in order to give members of their family peace of mind. Brides in this village are sacrificial lambs.'

'That is so wrong, Dr Mistry. *Every* bride? Living itself is a strain. Marriage shares that strain. Tell me what is *not* difficult in life?'

'Well put, Pushpa. Let us say then that a spirit as sensitive as Vasti's is going through an anxious phase. As I came in I saw all the preparations moving at full speed ahead downstairs. But I must emphasise, if you are convinced it is the wedding, as I am, it is better to save her now. It is only too late when she is dead.' I looked at him in amazement and wondered as to the nature of the brutality within marriages that he had seen, for it was clear that he felt very strongly. He went on, 'If the marriage had taken place, and this had occurred, I would have recommended a separation. I could speak to the Wallis about how ill she is, in order to make the enormity of this strenuous task less onerous for you. I am serious, Pushpa.'

'I know you are. Let me also be frank. At this twelfth hour — and that is what it is — postponement or cancellation are not options. It cannot be done. You should understand the limits of every culture, beyond which you go at your own peril. Family shame can be devastating. There are some families where suicide would be the lesser evil in a case like ours.'

'Take your time, think it through carefully. Try and recall everything she has ever said to you about the Wallis. I'll leave it to you.'

When Ma brought the tea, he said, 'Mrs Nadir, your daughter is experiencing extreme anxiety. It is important that you understand fully how serious the condition is. A change of environment is what she needs, but more importantly still, she requires a change in her present circumstance. Her body and mind just cannot cope with the strain. Her illness needs healing of a different kind. I know a fine psychiatrist of the old school – we were at medical school together. His name is Dr Anjum Shah. He lives abroad, but is here spending time with his family. I am sure he would be happy to treat her.

'You have lived long enough, Mrs Nadir, to know that marriage can so easily become a ball of misery yarn that lengthens each day, entangling limbs and slowly suffocating life itself. Bad marriages occur not only deep in the sugar-cane belt, they also exist in more privileged homes where the families are educated and well-connected. There, the mental pain inflicted is far more sophisticated.

'I have also seen members of an extended family goading the parents of a young woman – whom I will continue to call "a victim of tradition" – to bring more orthodoxy into their lives than commonsense warrants. Day by day, they poison the thinking of their own

270

brother or sister in the name of custom. Custom is not sacred in itself. It is simply a way of doing things that has been handed down.

'This kind of thinking, keeping to custom, has no place in this house, Mrs Nadir. Your husband's spirit is today greatly saddened that his daughter Vasti suffers so. He wishes you to do what he would have done.

'With regard to your daughter, you just have to be strong in the knowledge that you are able to give her back what she had, the joy of living. If you approve, I will ask the psychiatrist to call round. Give me a ring if you think she is becoming worse. No matter what time of day or night, ring me. Keep her comfortable, use cold compresses whenever her temperature begins to rise. Closely watch her pulse and breathing. Let me know if you observe any change. It may be the body's way of seeking refuge from an extreme build-up of nervous tension. From time to time, try to give her a drink of water. If she continues to be in too deep an unconscious state and is unable to take it orally, I will ask my nurse to set up a drip. Give the surgery a ring, if you are not able to get liquids down her.

'On an equally important social front, what is required of you may be likened to changing the tides of the time, Mrs Nadir. But you will not be needing the wisdom of Solomon, only your own and that of your husband.'

He pointed his finger at me.

'Pushpa, never forget you are your father's daughter. He would have done the right thing, whatever it took, and so must you. You will do it well, if you believe you have to. You owe it to your sister and your father and dear mother. Be patient and courteous with the Wallis.

271

If they say unkind things, it is a small price to pay for her release. What we are asking of them is catastrophic. It is much worse to have to face them, than it is for them to receive the news. It will not be easy. If I can be of use, let me know. We will discuss psychiatric help when she has regained consciousness fully. You must be able to give her the good news of her changed circumstance when that happens.'

CHAPTER THIRTY-TWO

The Making of Conspirators

WITH THE TIMELY warning of why Pundit Krishna was not to be trusted, Queen Dayita retraced her steps along the corridor to Queen Meena. She was surprised to find her return so welcomed. Queen Meena explained that being by herself, without any support, had forced her to think in a way she had never done before.

It was the knowledge that the late King would not wish her to be on the pyre, Queen Meena said, that forced her to ask: What should I now do? What could I do? What would I *like* to do?

'Sister Dayita, I have decided that I want to leave with you. When I came to this decision, my old life left me. I felt strangely light and free, as if something that had bound me had loosened its hold. I have listened carefully and have had to learn quickly. I am now walking away from one world of ancient designs into another world with other designs. I want to be useful, to help carry out our escape plan. It is not going to be easy, so tell me what to do.'

The two women talked as conspirators. They decided to keep this strategy under cover, with every move controlled solely by them. And so the two Queens from the

North spun a web to constrict others and to facilitate their escape.

'It will have to be done before the first cock crows.'

'We need two horses and a two wheeled covered carriage, not one of those heavy goods carts. Anything smaller would do, but it needs to be well-covered, pulled by sturdy horses. Datta will know what to do.'

Together they sat and prepared what should be said to Pundit Krishna. Queen Meena realised that their future safety depended on her being able to convince him. This would entail a masterly piece of acting. It formed the very pivot of their strategy. Queen Meena had charged herself not to falter.

'I must leave now to make contact with Datta,' Dayita told her. 'Be prepared. You cannot fail. We two men-servants will leave these quarters tonight.'

'I can tie a turban well.'

'Me too, but travel light.'

They embraced and parted.

Alone again, Sister Meena wondered whether she could transform herself sufficiently to carry out the perfect performance. Making herself pleasurable to be with came naturally to her. Her allurement and personal style were not too far removed from the Pundit's beliefs and understanding of the purity, meekness and beauty of womanhood. These ancient concepts would help her.

Sister Dayita had once sat next to her and said, 'In the Temple of Dance, whenever we were about to offer a public performance, our tutor would say, "You will all dance as never before, because you wish it so. You are special, for you are eternal. In your branching limbs, in every part of you, there resides the strength and majesty, the glory and wonder of all the forests, mountain ranges, stars, oceans; the might of typhoons, the delight of soft breezes, the beauty and fragrance of ripe flowers. You are a combination of all that you see — for you are the eternal way of Nature, you are the eternal way of being. There is no other. Tomorrow you too will reflect this, and the audience too will come to this understanding".'

With that memory, she heard herself say: 'Today, Sister Dayita, you and I will call upon the spirit of Queen Padmini and Queen Nur Jehan and will reinvent ourselves, becoming whatever we need to be. Who can tell what two Queens with a new beginning in a new land will do?'

The matronly sadhuine sent by Pundit Krishna explained to Queen Meena that although she understood the Queen had just bathed, it was not sufficient. Bathing in preparation for her husband's pyre was not only different but formed an integral part of the other preparations for her being with him.

In the bathwater prepared for the seated Queen, soothing clove oil and warm, invigorating cinnamon sticks. Reddish-orange petals of frangipani floated, giving up their scent and colour to the water, which was poured over her neck and shoulders by the old woman. The petals tumbled upon her breasts, and fell to adorn her undressed lap.

Her hair was cleansed with yoghurt, wild honey and cactus juice. It was combed, each strand given a lustre with fragrant oils poured at its root and taken to the very end of its full length. Her body was dried, then massaged with the oils of both sweet and bitter almonds; any excess was absorbed on a small white cotton sheet; and then the finest quality saffron, taken from purple and bright yellow crocuses was brought to her. The Queen was asked to lie down. No part of her beautiful form was denied the colour of saffron, the aura of the sun. Her thighs and bosom, face and back and neck, were well massaged.

Queen Meena was helped into one clean garment, then a second garment was placed over the first, fully covering it. The sadhuine said: 'Now I am done. It is my duty to say this: it may just happen, I am not saying it will. As the procession comes closer and closer to the pyre, or when you see the huge mound, you may feel frightened. If that should happen, bear in mind that the body is always afraid to perish, but never the spirit; you should then repeat your mantra, the one your guru gave you when you were about to leave your parents' house. I hope His Majesty comes swiftly for you, brave and courageous Suttee Queen.'

She bowed low before the Queen and asked to be blessed, conscious of the privilege, of being so close to a body that would soon be ash, would soon walk with the King in the Heavens and see the gods in all their magnificence.

As she was about to leave, the Queen called her back and placed a fine gold coin on the folded white cotton sheet that had absorbed her oils and scents, saying, 'This I give to you.' Again the sadhuine bowed low, her forehead almost touching Queen Meena's feet.

Her aged body then turned to the offering made to her and she bowed before it too as if it had become alive, endowed with the suttee spirit of the Queen. Then her wrinkled hand clasped it to her bosom. The old woman knocked on the door to be let out. It was opened by the Queen's guard. This woman with failing eyes and near crippling arthritis, must take her time going down the carved stairway, along an exclusive royal corridor of ancient armoury, to Pundit Krishna's private temple where he awaited her confirmation that Queen Meena had been properly prepared for the suttee rites.

In the meantime, Queen Meena was undressing, re-arranging herself for the role she must now play: she removed the garments that had been placed upon her, and put on white silk, embroidered in silver threadwork. Her eyes and hair were attended to, her fragrance enhanced. She had become a messenger from God. Her natural inclination, classical features, and tone of her skin helped her to play this part. So would her other attributes.

As she approached Pundit Krishna, her steps were without sound. She was veiled.

Queen Meena, of her own accord, faced East as she had been taught from childhood. He offered the sacred Kusa grass, and into her cupped palms poured water from that part of the Ganga where the water is nectar to the spirit. This she sipped. Sesame was brought, her palms were filled. Once again, she bowed to the East – source of the birth of all matter – then to the magnetic North. All this while Pundit Krishna, chanted 'OM.' His voice carried her to the doors of the unseen.

She closed her eyes. Oil lamps flickered, incense burned. Shadows fell. Dusk tarried awhile. The temple was cold, too sheltered from the sun:

Queen Meena's soft voice now followed the sounds of Pundit Krishna; it was barely discernible as she repeated the oath:

'On this month, in this lunar cycle, on this day, I Queen Meena, widow of King Paresh, King of Jyotika, here prepare my spirit to meet the pativratas and reside in swarga that the years of my stay may be numerous as the hairs on the human body, that I may enjoy with my husband and Lord, King Paresh, the felicity of Heaven and sanctify my paternal and maternal progenitors and the ancestry of my husband's Royal Family, and that, lauded by the Apsaras, I may be happy with my Lord, King Paresh through the reigns of fourteen Indras, that expiation be made for all my husband's offences whatever they be.

'I call on you, ye guardians of the regions of the world – sun, moon, earth, air, fire, ether and water as well as my own soul; I call on Yama and his twin sister Yami. I call on day and night. Thou, conscience, bear witness that I will follow my husband's corpse on the funeral pyre.'

The Pundit blessed her three times.

As she was lifting her veiled head, he heard her whisper, 'Royal guru of Queen Dayita, the Prima classical dancer of the North, I, Queen Meena, in this blessed position, both widow and suttee, both in body and in spirit promised to the King, confirmed by you in this sacred ritual of dedication, bring an important message of truth. It is meant only for your ears.'

The old woman was dispatched, by Pundit Krishna and told that she would receive further instructions from him later on.

Queen Meena was offered a cushioned seat. The Pundit saw a gracious form carrying a quiet dignity. All was calm around her. The ceremony he had performed had transformed her to part saint, part prophetess. Queen

278

Meena explained with care that her sister Queen Dayita was at present overwrought by what she now saw as her duty.

'This change came after praying fervently to the Trimurti. When she fell exhausted, she was advised to climb the pyre. It was the God Shiva that came to her. She first heard his arrangement in the room, and found her steps being led to her bronze sculpture of his Nataraja. As she stood, offering her spiritual thanks for the gifts He had so generously showered upon her, Shiva spoke to her. He requested that before she climbed the pyre, she must dedicate her last dance to Him.

'His favourite amongst her compositions is her bridal concept of Nritta. This is to be followed by the Nrittya form. It was fitting that a microcosm of life's songs in movement be rendered by her and dedicated to the God of Dance – her spiritual guru – before she is consumed by the fierce tongues of fire.

'It is also fitting therefore, that this, her last dance be performed in her guru's temple one hour after the breaking of dawn, when the energy of the sun, climbing to its zenith, will effuse her limbs; Shiva will undress her earthly movements and so enhance her, that she will become the essence of life before the pyre changes her form.

'Queen Dayita, the proud Prima of dancers, requests this indulgence.

'She also requests that you ask the guards standing before our quarters to take their leave now, so that the rehearsal of her special offering to Shiva can take place as is fitting, in complete isolation. My only request to you which I make as a suttee, before I climb the pyre, is to be allowed to extend our steps in and out of our quarters, in quiet contemplation, unseen except by the Divine awaiting us.

'These last moments on earth are holy to us, and are of special significance. We wish our quarters to become our last sanctum unsullied by the steps of others, as we move like holy men along the royal corridor for the last time to absorb our life's memories and concentrate in solitude upon the good that awaits us.

'We wish to experience on our last night, the deeper yearnings of an ascetic before we depart. This noble indulgence, I a confirmed suttee, ask on behalf of Queen Dayita.

'Here, the God Shiva and you will see how her dance transforms her to an Apsara, or whatsoever is most satisfying to the hour, to this temple and Shiva's indulgences.

'As the King's suttee, I now bless you, and hereby prophesy that were you to meet the requests of Shiva and those of Queen Dayita and myself, you will have an enlightenment beyond that of any other pundit in the royal court. You will discover a new world, and these sacred dances of Queen Dayita, here in your temple, will remain with you and comfort you not only now, but also in years to come when loneliness becomes a frequent visitor.'

Queen Meena slowly lifted her veil and said: 'Most Honoured Pundit Krishnajee, this privileged moment comes only once in a lifetime; it has come to you, prescribed by your position. You will not see me again. I am unable to unveil myself to the public. That would be a disclosure my modesty and family custom forbid. So I, Queen Meena, Suttee Queen, honour you, and hereby take my leave.'

280

Pundit Krishna saw the loveliness of Rani Padmini, an exquisite sculptured form, radiant. He saw before him what was worshipped each day in holy shrines, and knew that he had become the most privileged amongst the living. Dazzled by the wonder before him, his personality and beliefs helped him to perceive that he would soon receive enlightenment, a revelation unknown to all other pundits of the royal court.

Pundit Krishna promised to fulfil all the requests made by the suttee Queen Meena, and his bowing low, in respectful silence, was an affirmation of this.

His imagination took him to tomorrow, when he would meet a proud Queen, her former disdain subdued – a convert to his thinking – though still walking in a sphere – outside his reach – sublime and gracious in her joyous movements. It was a combination that stirred him. Only a fool would deny himself the sight of a Prima dancer offering herself to Shiva in lyrical movements, opening like an unfurling leaf, revealing Shiva's essence through her moving forms. Then and only then, the Royal Court Pundit said to himself, would life's meaning be understood. Such an experience would silence the voice and evaporate words.

Later, as dusk fled at the approach of night, he began to wonder in the quiet of his room, whether their natural feeling might recoil with fear at the eleventh hour. He would now attend to this.

Pundit Krishna knew he had been outwitted by Pundit Baalaajee at the royal court. It must not happen again. 'I could not hold my position nor my head high were this humiliation to be repeated,' he muttered out loudly as he paced the floor of his comfortable abode.

CHAPTER THIRTY-THREE

Datta and Sakuni

PUNDIT KRISHNA SLEPT well in the knowledge that the renegade, Baalaajee, had chosen to leave the Kingdom of Jyotika. Self-exile, he thought, was the noble thing to do after his insolent behaviour, which showed that his allegiance was not to the King but to his own pride. He was prudent to have judged himself and found he could no longer expect to be employed at the palace.

His taking the slave-girl and child with him was the appropriate burden for him to bear. 'God's justice is being played out,' Pundit Krishna murmured to himself, believing that to be continuously in the company of a person of low caste would inevitably sully one's character. Baalaajee had brought it upon himself. No one escaped the law of Karma.

The Royal Court Pundit was also pleased that the dark Queen of the South, with her clear questioning eyes that always appeared to be looking through, rather than at him, had left with her manservant Manu. Her life would have been intolerable in the palace, the other two royal wives having become suttees. In addition, her unorthodox understanding of the Supreme Being and unsympathetic attitude to their customs, would have led to her receiving little consideration from the Prince Regent Mahendra and his wives.

He wondered whether Queen Renu might have asked him to do something to help alleviate her sorry neglect by the palace. Though there was nothing he could have done to assist her, merely trying would have meant compromising his own position with the new royals, thus her decision to leave has made his life less problematical.

The Royal Court Pundit also slept well in the firm belief that the situation had miraculously changed in his favour. Earlier, he had been despondent, and on seeing his plans come to nothing at the royal court, a deep depression had overwhelmed him. Then the King would have had to be on the pyre alone, as a nobody. Now Queen Meena and Queen Dayita had seen where their true duty lay, and would be on the pyre with the King tomorrow.

Before noon, was the time the royal astrologer had prescribed for setting the pyre alight on all four corners. It would be a most fitting farewell for such a brave monarch who had served his people well. The irrigation he had introduced to the fields meant there was more food for all. God bless the King and his Queens. Tomorrow would be a day to remember.

Pundit Krishna had been humiliated and wished to ensure that the experience would never again recur. Nothing was left to chance. More than ever before, he paid attention to the smallest detail. Soon after Queen Meena had left him, a wary feeling had come upon him. Later, this unease once again tugged at him and he decided to pay attention to it. Just in case the Queens' courage were to fail them in the dark stillness of the night, when the spirit is most vulnerable, he had taken certain precautions at the stables.

Queen Renu had the use of an old, spacious royal carriage which was in good working order. So he told the two senior stable hands in charge that no royal carriage, nor royal horse was to be made available to anyone. Were they to fail in this duty, they would be taken by soldiers to the border of the Kingdom to seek their livelihood in another place.

As an added precaution, he also sent a message to the guards at the giant gates of the outermost stone fortifications. At no time must they permit royal horses, or royal carriages to pass through. They must be thorough in their examination or be dismissed from their post.

Much later, when those pangs of misgiving once again returned, he felt driven by impulse to go to the Queens' private quarters, or better still, to place an undercover to keep a check on their movements. He was on his way to arrange this, when he hesitated. He had given his word to Queen Meena at her suttee ceremony that their surrounding quarters would have no worldly intrusion. Should he now break this solemn promise and court a Suttee Queen's anger?

He reminded himself of the incident with the droning bee, furiously seeking an exit, and how Queen Dayita had removed her veil in an act that was both controlled and daring. He would not therefore like to be cursed by her, before the large gathering of royal pundits, as she climbed the pyre. She was proud and aloof and could, if provoked, decide to dance only before Shiva in the privacy of the King's temple.

He would not do anything to endanger this once-in-a-lifetime experience. To receive her offering, her last sacred performance before the demise of her form by fire, was an honour worthy of trust.

Thus comforted, he removed his sandals and returned indoors, taking pleasure in preparing himself for his night's rest, anticipating her soft call to him, his leading her to the inner sanctum of the temple. This brought an ethereal feel to his senses. At the rising of the sun, when Queen Dayita would be dressed in soft silks, satins, and ritual jewellery, his temple would become one of the innermost Ajanta. caves, with its burning incense, flickering earth lamps, musicians and Queen Dayita, the Apsara of the temple. After tomorrow, each day on his visit to his temple, he would relive this intoxication.

His elderly head sank into the soft pillow and sleep came.

The Queens had packed and were ready to leave. They looked like two young men in their turbans. A lifetime of practising the cosmetic art had enabled them to disguise themselves well. Queen Renu and Manu had provided them with trousers, long-sleeved coats and attractive cloth sashes for their waists. They opted for modest beards and moustaches and practised a merchant's stance in front of Queen Dayita's mirror. They walked and moved their heads to acquaint their bodies with this new identity, at the same time imagining their first encounter, their conversation with the guard. What would their small talk be? Should it be of the perils of the life of a merchant: bandits and robbers, scheming traders? Or the hazards of dust storms, mountainous terrain, strange customs, obliging women?

Careful! Queen Dayita's fine standing mirror warned, its echo reverberating and connecting with the Queens' inner voices: '*Do not try so hard. Do not labour at it so.*' Then as Queen Dayita studied her reflection and its vulnerability, her mirror again advised, '*Merchants would not rush to offer information not asked for by officials; they would be thoughtful, not overtly amiable. Merchants give nothing away; custom has taught them the art of surviving amidst hostility. These travellers from afar are shrewd observers of what a situation requires. They will often speak with silences and looks, their pinched watchful eyes attuned to seeing far, through dust and perils. We, the reflecting class, see all, but seldom disclose all.*'

Once more, both Queens looked into the crystal-clear mirror. The two travellers before it were erupting with nervous tension and the mirror was absorbing it. The soft light of the room came closer, the better to see for itself. 'Is the mirror weeping?' the light asked. 'It is so moist.'

And yet the mirror remained calm, motionless, despite the two Queens' restlessness.

On closer observation, the mirror was *not* still; a million tiny stirrings, connections, were being made within its depths, which registered everything. Again and again it reflected a deep sadness it could not contain. Queen Dayita wiped it with an old veil and ran the soft palm of her hands along its upright form. She was recognising its presence, saying good-bye. It had served her with integrity; it had offered her insights into herself, invisible to her eye. *Thank you*, she said.

The Queens had decided to be slow in pace and pensive in outlook before officials on this perilous journey.

Their faces were pressed against the stone screens. The courtyard was still, the desert wind cold. Then, movement – coming their way. They backed away from the wall. It was Datta: he had come to the outer wall of the Queens' quarters. He raised his lantern; three times he raised it high and held it. It was time to leave. Queen Dayita turned to the eight different yogi postures of Shiva, and paid homage, she then approached the mirror to look at herself for the very last time in the Palace of Jyotika.

Queen Meena did as her sister had done.

Stealthily the women moved, not stopping to look around for the last time at the paintings of the ancestors of the Kings of Jyotika observing their leaving. They were acutely aware of the danger they were in and they felt at one with the deer, the rabbit, foxes and birds – with the hunted – moving cautiously, their eyes and ears finely tuned, the hairs on their skin standing erect.

The strength of purpose of the Rani of Jhansi had entered them. In this darkness, they moved silently as the moon behind the clouds; their understanding of virtue was not gentleness, timidity or purity as defined by men for women – instead they carried the warrior legacy that honours strength, courage in battle and cunning. In reinventing themselves, they had embraced a merchant's stance, energised by the warrior's prerogative – power, choice and control – subscribing only to the necessities of battle.

Tonight their path was clear. Passing the sleeping Pundit Krishna's abode, they arrived at the far end of the stable. Datta explained what the Pundit had done and that Sakuni had become suspicious of him. Queen Meena suggested giving him opium and taking him with them, for that would ensure his silence for at least six hours. The first cock crowed; dawn must not find them here. They dispersed.

From the darkness only Queen Meena approached Sakuni and Datta. The former became suspicious. He saw this merchant had come to negotiate on behalf of the Queens, to make a deal with him and Datta. She asked them to sit with her, saying that she had a proposition to put before them. Sakuni said firmly he could not help, and were this merchant to insist, he would have to awaken the other stable hands. Datta was silent, pretending to be interested in what was in the box that Queen Meena had with her. She said to Sakuni, in a low voice, 'Do not refuse until you have seen what I have to show you. Here is an opportunity that has never before come to a stable-hand. It could be yours.'

As she was alone, Sakuni was thinking he could easily overpower the negotiator, have both the jewels *and* the Pundit's approval. Queen Meena opened the box. It was mirrored, filled with velvet pouches of the deepest blue, scarlet, gold and green. There were also brocade pouches of intricate floral designs. She carefully held up a scarlet pouch. 'It is all gold,' she said. 'Before opening it, weigh the worth of this piece in your hands.' She passed it to Sakuni. His naked palm and fingers experienced a touch, softly comforting, and scented. It offered no resistance but rested upon him. He was enjoying the sensation, which was new to him. Queen Meena indicated with her hands that he might open the pouch. He hesitated. She encouraged him with her head. Sakuni was out of his depth. He concentrated on the cord. A delicate perfume came his way, which he thought was rising from within the velvet pouch as he carefully loosened the cord of silk. Sakuni opened it with extreme care and deference. Then a dancer's step, that barely touched the earth, brought a lathi to the back of his head. Queen Dayita's measured blow was well placed. Datta held him down and Meena administered the opium.

The commotion had made the horses restless. Datta called to them, his voice reassuring their sensitive spirits. Sakuni was bound and placed in the well covered, strong cart, watched over by Queen Dayita. Two fine horses were hitched to this wagon. Everyone was on board. Slowly, quietly the vehicle rumbled out of the courtyard. Datta, disguised as a merchant trader, held the reins.

At the gate of the inner courtyard, he was stopped. He yawned widely, pretending to be half-asleep and in an irritable mood. 'At this hour when all honourable men are with their wives,' he said, 'I must make an early start. It is the curse of my trade. I must meet a caravan before the sun awakens or my debts will ruin me. The road is perilous. Would you care to join me?'

'What do you trade in?'

'I, Zaman, trade in spices, the finest dates, wool and the best karakul skins.' He held on to his rein and clicked at the horses as if the interview was over and the guards allowed this breath of clove and cinnamon to pass.

The cart now approached the gates of the outer courtyard. His irritable face, hurried manner and an appropriate bribe to the senior gate-keeper enabled the cantankerous merchant to leave without hindrance. The cart wheels turned; the horses clopped slowly into the inner circle, the circus of stone fortifications. As they left, it was decided that the Queens must become pundits at prayer when they reached the giant gates. They prepared themselves; a plan was born.

As they approached their only way out, this skilled stable-hand knew that he must become a far more convincing merchant. He narrowed his eyes as he neared the gates, muttering to himself. He stopped, slowly and sulkily, pretending that he had no time for all this officialdom, and bent as if arthritis was getting the better of him. He would say nothing. Yet if asked, and why should they, he was on his way to the crossroads to meet the overland camel caravans. Fortunately, his lungee and chapan were genuine. This he was told by Manu.

The Queens, in low muffled voices, began to recite Sanskrit prayers. Two well-built guards were on duty at the great gate of the fort defended by turrets on either side. One opened the gate partially and stood before it. The other examined the horses closely, he said they were royal steeds. Datta thanked him and said, it is not the first time that his horses had been paid this compliment. He himself treated them as royal guests; he had no choice. Fine horses were considerable investments and must be kept in a good condition for hazardous journeys. He had learned this the hard way. But . . . he hesitated and displayed a superior smile. 'These are not royal horses, they are not trained for royal parades or the King's carriage; they only *pretend* to be regal. They are wild horses with handsome faces, brought from the Great Mountains of the North where the gods once lived.'

The guard was not convinced. 'I cannot allow you to leave,' he said, and bent to look for the distinguishing mark of two eagle wings. All horses from the royal stable were thus dated and inscribed. He knew where to look and was intent on finding the royal wings. The guard was convinced he was right and meant to show he knew what he was talking about. His job was on the line, but equally important to him, was his pride in proving that the horses were royal.

Datta's anxiety was mounting: 'I shall explain only once more. These are wild-spirited horses and will not tolerate too close an approach by strangers. I must leave now. I do not have time for this fooling about. To wait any longer means I shall lose too much; already, I am late to meet the caravans at the crossroads.'

The examining guard, crouching low, was creeping closer still to examine the horses better. 'I cannot allow you to leave, until I have examined the underbelly of both horses,' he shouted.

Suddenly a loud din erupted from within the cart of bells, drums and conch shells. This, and the guard's proximity made the horses lift their feet high, and raise their heads. Neighing in alarm, they attempted to bolt. The cart was tugged violently forward. They tried again. Had it not been for Datta's skill with the reins, the guard would have been trampled to death.

As he lay on the ground, too terrified to move, or speak, he shut his eyes in prayer, the horses' hooves mere centimetres away. The other guard at the gates, seeing that Datta was now directing the neighing horses towards him, hurriedly opened the iron gates wide. The horses rushed past and the covered cart rattled out into open space; a bundle of dried dates, Sanskrit chants, and the frenzied shouting of the merchant reached the standing guard. The two men watched the cart recede.

291

Once again the gates were firmly closed and they tried to make sense of the pugnacious merchant. Their understanding was that he was hurrying to reach a caravan of merchandise. Two Brahmins were hitching a ride and were angry that they were also being delayed. The guards sat and enjoyed the dates, surprised that the bundle was scented. They smiled that knowing smile of men, believing the merchant to be something of a ladies' man. Yet the one guard was still convinced that the horses were not fully broken in, and that they were royal steeds. However, the quality of the dates and their perfume brought him pleasure and forgetfulness.

Too much time had been spent at both gates. Distant cocks were crowing, the precursors of light. Datta lashed out and those fine horses displayed the speed of winged hooves.

The young pundits through habit were offering thanks to Something, some unseen, unknowable Presence of good will. Feelings of relief, and of gratitude, enveloped their limbs. Sakuni slept on like a babe as the cart rattled forwards. Datta spoke fondly to his horses, leaned over and caressed their heaving sides and tossing manes.

CHAPTER THIRTY-FOUR

A Daughter of Marriageable Age

THEY WERE GRATEFUL that Dr Mistry had come; relieved too when he reassured them that there was nothing physically wrong with Vasti. She would get well. Pushpa could almost hear her own thoughts: We will follow his advice to help her recover, but we cannot accept his suggestion to cancel the wedding with only a few days to go! That just goes to show how out of touch Dr Mistry is with reality. Incredible!

Devi's strength and quiet way of managing her feelings surprised Pushpa. She had thought her mother might have cracked under the strain of it all. Instead she simply made tea for everyone and Shami and Pushpa went and sat with her. Pushpa knew that her mother believed in doing the right thing. To cancel the wedding would devastate her. But to go ahead with it, believing that Dr Mistry was right, would chip away at her sanity.

'Ma, Dr Mistry does not have a daughter of marriageable age,' Pushpa said. 'How can he understand our concerns? He sees things with the eyes of a doctor handing out prescriptions at his surgery; they are not the eyes of parents. Will the biological clock wait for us?'

'Pushpa, how many good families with professional sons do we know? Now with your father gone, who will remind the public of us?'

'Ma,' Shami said gently, 'what is important to keep in mind, is that the Walli family wants this marriage to take place. Mr Sukesh Walli is very happy with Vasti. That is a positive thing. It is a good start to married life.'

'Not the way Dr Mistry sees it,' Devi replied. 'Vasti was always so sensitive about her own failings, she might be wondering how to cope with children, her teaching job, pleasing her husband and Sukesh Walli's two sisters, and then there is the Clinic too. That is a difficult one. Anybody would go under with this kind of worry, let alone Vasti.'

'Yes, Ma,' her son-in-law Shami agreed. 'We do not know the number of things that are bringing this about. For some time now I have sensed that she has become withdrawn. We have to keep telling her in many different ways that we are here to assist her.'

'Ma is right. When you consider how sensitive Vasti is, I wouldn't be surprised if the concerns she mentioned have not been piling up on her.'

'Do you remember Pushpa how she cried when she saw the neighbour's dog knocked down by a car? She expected the car to stop, that the driver would get out and ask whose dog it was, and she was only seven at the time.'

Her expectations are too large, the frame she has to live within is small, Shami observed to himself.

'Yes, I remember,' Pushpa said. 'She sat down and cried and demanded that God bring back the dog or else she would not believe in Him. She then threw a stone in the direction of the car, although it had long since gone.'

'She felt strongly, you see, Pushpa; she had to do something to vent her anger. Otherwise, as her father said, Vasti's rage would have set her on fire.'

'I can believe that. Aunt Sona once told me that they couldn't have her helping in the shop because she always gave extra weight to poor people, especially with butter and cheese. When they asked for one ounce, she gave them one and a half ounces for the same price. They caught her doing it.'

'She told Aunty that God would give her blessings because the poor needed proteins.'

As these three opened themselves to each other, trying to make sense of what had happened, they gradually began to relax. While Devi refilled the cups, Pushpa went to have another look at Vasti. She took her temperature, cooled her brow with a damp face towel and opened the window slightly after arranging the cotton sheet carefully around her.

'Ma, her temperature is much the same, but just looking at her I know the worst is behind us. Her face is peaceful now.'

Shami looked at his wife: 'I hope this is not wishful thinking. Should you not inform the Wallis?'

Devi said, 'Yes, I too have been wondering whether it would not be a good idea to explain to Sukesh Walli that Vasti has a temperature and is unconscious, but that Dr Mistry says it is nothing serious.'

'I think we should, Pushpa,' Shami urged.

'Let us wait for one more full day and by then we will know whether recovery is definitely on its way. Only if it isn't will we contact them. No use saying anything now.'

'Why not?' her husband asked.

'Because we have already had to have them here more times than is usual, thanks to Vasti's uncertainty. They may see it as wavering yet again. We do not want them to think that she is unreliable, because she is just the opposite of that.'

Pushpa gave a deep sigh. She still felt shaken by the doctor's outspoken opinions. 'Dr Mistry seems to think arranged marriages are a source of pain and nothing else; at no time performing a useful social function. Does he ever ask himself how on earth young people can get married if their culture does not provide the venues for meetings like drama societies, poetry groups, neighbourhood clubs and so on? Only at parties in respectable homes can they meet. And on those occasions, all the "aunties" in the house adopt them as their own. Ten pairs of eyes could be looking at them at any time. In these nice homes they will only meet the buffoons they already know. No unfamiliar ones.'

'Buffoons, eh?' Shami said.

'Look at the case of Anil,' Devi said. 'A very quiet boy, dull even.'

'Very dull and boring, Ma.'

'Yes, but a good car mechanic.'

'Knows nothing, is interested in nothing else but the working of a car. He is permanently under a bonnet, while the world passes him by.'

'There's nothing wrong with that, Pushpa – not everybody has to be a scholar. Let me tell you, people say he is the best mechanic they know. Anyway left to himself, would he be married?'

'No way, Ma.'

'But he is married today with a nice wife and a sweet little boy.'

'True Ma, yet I can't help thinking, Pearl could have done better for herself.'

'That is neither here nor there. What I am saying is that it is all thanks to an arrangement. Of course, you have to know what you are doing.' Then Devi turned to Shami, 'I agree with you. Vasti is going to join a good family, marry a professional man. They are both educated and should be able to find a way to live well together.'

'I think the trouble comes when you force people,' Shami said. 'Nobody should be forced into anything. If a girl or a boy do not want to marry why make them?'

'It is not easy for parents to withdraw,' Pushpa observed. 'Especially if you believe the family is right, the boy is right and you hear the biological clock ticking away and the Pundit tells you that the stars are in agreement too.'

'It is certainly painful, Pushpa, to lose face in one's community. To let them see that your child's voice is stronger than your own, that you have no authority, that your views do not matter, it is too much to bear. You bleed quietly inside. Your reason for living drips away with the flow of time.'

'What happens, Ma, when your child wants to marry somebody you believe is not right for them?'

'You tell them what you think and why, Pushpa. If they still want to go ahead with it, have a small ceremony with only the immediate family present. Pray that God will bring them good sense. You still have to give them your blessing – after all, you are asking God to do the same, na? If it doesn't work out, they cannot

297

blame you, and if it does work out, show that you are happy for them. It is a blessing to have a good marriage, for a good marriage, Pushpa, makes life worth living. What else is there? Someone you can always trust, someone beside you, no matter what. Someone to listen to your voice. What else can anyone want from life?'

CHAPTER THIRTY-FIVE

The Awakening

PUNDIT KRISHNA GOT up suddenly as if startled. At first he thought he had overslept, but the distinct shade of darkness reassured him. He could hear the rattling of milk carts, the hurrying carriers of curds and ghee, the heavy weary movement of overworked yoked cattle, the refreshing steps of the first water-carriers.

It was early. Only distant cocks heralded the dawn. He could have taken his time in rising from his bed; instead he rose briskly as if it were already late. A nervous anxiety possessed him. He could not explain it.

The Pundit prepared himself well, for the priestly class believes cleanliness to be the first and last step to godliness. His skin glowed healthily, his white flowing cotton garments enhanced his Brahmin features, his disciplined stature. A single mala of frangipani offered him its sweet scent. He was ready for the most exhilarating event of his life.

When Queen Dayita's musicians arrived, he led them to his temple which had been prepared and then returned to his rooms to await the Queen. The two tabla and two sitar players were moved by the care the Pundit had taken. Fragrant orange and yellow flowers from the cultivated royal park lay on Shiva's altar, a mass of scarlet blossoms adorned the sculptures of Brahma and Krishna. Burning incense hummed; on tall stands, freshly made cotton wicks in earthen oil lamps were lengthening their reach. Floral scents mingled, contributing to the heightened stimulation the musicians were beginning to experience. A rich aroma of delicious sweets made of ghee, honey and nuts, curds, essences of flowers and fruit, came to them, although there were none in sight.

They took their seats and waited. Amongst the temple hangings, the large figure of Krishna, and his spouse Radha, caught their eyes; it was painted, dyed and stamped with gold. The senior sitar player could see why Queen Dayita had chosen this place above all others for her last mortal rendering of dance. The temple with its white-veined marble pillars, huge and intricately carved, replicated the celestial assembly of the gods. This Prima dancer would move between the pillars as a vine, and face each god, offering a distinct posture to revere, to supplicate, eventually to celebrate with graciously restrained allurements of movement.

Knowing the structure of her compositions, the sitar player was aware that it was before the God of Dance, Shiva, that Queen Dayita would attain a culmination of purity and simplicity, interwoven with lyrical variations to portray the essence of woman. All the while accompanied by the younger sitar, its melody climbing upwards, increasing in momentum, lifting expectations, ascending higher and higher still.

The musicians were happy to have time to contemplate upon these pieces again.

Pundit Krishna did not want to open his door nor leave it ajar, that would show his anxiety. He would await that soft knock, that intoxicating scent that rose to him, the moment her veil fell upon her shoulder as her head, neck and shoulder were lowered before him to receive a guru's blessing.

Once more he checked that his appearance was favourable. The Queen was late. Temples were now awake and the day's activity had grown loud: Brahmins were blowing the conch shells, sacred verses hung in the air. He could hear the movements of goats, asses and mules, but the encouraging voices of the senior stable-hands to the elephants and camels were absent. He was upset that they had overslept, when they were needed to begin the lengthy and elaborate preparation of the animals for the funerary procession. He imagined that the horses, not yet brought out from the royal sheds, were becoming nervous. Skittish horses were unsuited to a dignified procession. Yesterday, he had discussed with Datta and Sakuni and the junior stable-hands, the colours and symbols to be used in their adorning.

It was then that Pundit Krishna heard a knock on his door; it was not the gentle tap he was expecting but an urgent, rapping. Nevertheless he approached the door smiling.

Four junior stable-hands stood there, all speaking at once: 'Sakuni and Datta have gone! A pair of fast horses are missing too. All gone, Punditjee. There's no sign of any of them.'

After a conversation with the Pundit, the boys returned to the royal stable; their understanding was that they were now in charge and would be promoted, if they conducted themselves responsibly. The camels, elephants and horses were to be made ready for the procession immediately. Their promotion depended entirely on how well they carried out the Pundit's instructions.

They were told that, if in doubt, they were to come back to him. Pundit Krishna promised to return soon to offer further advice and guidance. He admitted to them in a low voice that for some time now, he had felt that Datta and Sakuni were unsuited to be senior Royal stable-hands and was neither surprised by their behaviour, nor the manner of their going. The very spirit of the King's procession would have been tainted, had their hands prepared it.

The stable-boys hurried joyfully: here was an opportunity that came but once in two lifetimes and they would not fail to make good use of it. They were determined to show their mettle; after all, in the past it was they who did all the hard work anyway, while Datta and Sakuni, merely gave orders, fussed over the smallest details and never shared any of the gifts of appreciation they received from royal guests.

Pundit Krishna slowly made his way to the musicians. He had asked the royal kitchen to prepare mouth-watering royal sweets, which he had intended to bring to them at the end of the dance. It was to be his gesture of appreciation. He had been moved to do so when the senior sitar musician had said to him, 'Punditjee, you will be experiencing, the interlocking movement of two giant waves of creativity – music and dance – and you will know ecstatic joy.'

The Pundit conducted himself in silence. He carried two plates at a time from an adjoining room, and placed them before Lord Shiva's altar. The gift of sweets was covered in vermilion silk.

The men could tell that something appalling had happened, for desolation walked with their host. He handed the musicians delicious sweets on polished brass plates that acted as mirrors, increasing two-fold, the delights they held.

The sweetmeats had been prepared by the royal chef, who was instructed that they should appeal to all the senses. 'Your sweets are to be offered to the Queens before their transformation at the burning pyre. So let the many pleasures of being mortal come with the tasting of your sweets,' he had advised.

The musicians awaited him.

'You four are Queen Dayita's most accomplished and favoured musicians,' he said. 'I take comfort in this, for I have news that may disturb you; yet you are men who have a cultivated control of your emotions. Over the years, you have trained yourselves to measure with precision, the pitch, colour and tone required to convey the spirit of a piece. You will need this art today. These sweets I bring you have come from Queen Dayita. This is her way of expressing gratitude for your untiring service to dance.'

He paused; what he had to say next was the hardest thing he had ever had to do. He was solemn. A minute passed.

'Last night, after praying to Shiva, she found that both Queen Meena and herself could not, despite our custom of suttee, do otherwise than faithfully follow the request of the King, which was that his three Queens should not join him on the pyre. At first they were fearful of the wrath of orthodoxy and remained unsure as to where their duty lay. They were a long time in deciding, but in the end, it was the desire to honour the

303

King's wishes that has prevailed with them. I had, on oath, promised to bring her gifts to you and to inform you, here at this temple, but not before the time. The Queens expressed the wish to leave quietly, without regal farewells, in the discreet anonymity of night.'

Immediately there were protests.

'Punditjee, Queen Meena performed a religious act.'

'The sacred ceremony was a solemn oath taken in the presence of the gods.'

'The anger of the gods will fall upon her as a thunderbolt.'

'It is not as you say.' Pundit Krishna was blunt.

'This is what the pundits teach.'

'Is it not true then, what the pundits are teaching?'

Pundit Krishna raised his voice. 'God in His wisdom is aware of the frailties of men and women. If Queen Meena lives a life of charity, even this large wrong would be forgiven by the All-Seeing, All-Knowing Creator of the universe. We should not forget that the Creator knows more about Queen Meena's motives than we could ever discover. Is He not in a better position to judge her than we are?'

'It is a sad day when such a brave and loving King is abandoned in his hour of need by his Queens.'

'This Kingdom has always had most faithful, loyal and courageous Suttee Queens.'

'We can understand the dark Queen of the South being unable to rise to so sacred an obligation as our own Northern Queens.'

'Even so, when one is married, one gives up the culture of one's parents and adopts the culture of one's husband. His culture is then the one to honour.'

'Yes. That is custom.'

'One should be very careful when changing honoured customs.'

'I have found there is always a good reason for customs.'

'In all the Northern Kingdoms, there was no better King than our King Paresh.'

The Royal Court Pundit had listened well. He had allowed them time to express themselves. Now it was his turn to speak.

'You are musicians whose skill lies in listening with care to even the most delicate stir of sounds, yet you speak as old men devoid of hearing, for you have not grasped a word I have said. I have answered your questions, but you have chosen not to hear. It is the way of scoundrels. I shall repeat: it was the late King's wishes, *that the Queens should not climb upon the pyre.*

'You have conveniently forgotten what the great ragas of divine love say. In the stillness of night when your music flows, it has brought tears to men's eyes. It is well-known in the courtyard that travellers in a hurry, on hearing your playing, have tarried, forgetting their urgent missions. Yet sadly, the wisdom and the healing emotions of those ragas appear not to have touched you.

'Your own expectation and disappointment have led you to deny the integrity of the Queen, who did not forget you even as she was departing. You have allowed your thinking to be devoid of the poems most loved by the gods – those of compassion and understanding.'

Pundit Krishna saw that he must now try and calm himself, despite the crumbling of everything around him. Yet he would pick up the shards and build another vessel.

These musicians were men with independent minds, yet their disposition to custom was fixed and firmly held. Before leaving they took their gifts, but nothing else.

Along the route to the Mahasati, the place of burning, were thousands of people, jostling for a better view of the procession. The villages were empty, the fields too. A loud bugle cut through the air, signalling that the procession had begun.

'The elephants and camels looked resplendent in necklaces of semi-precious stones, silver bells on their ankles and sumptuous brocades spread across their flanks. They glittered and sparkled, their heads bowed as they moved. Another burst of bugles sounded along the procession route. The crowd was silent, their expectation, large. Four rows of sadhus blew conch shells, row upon row of pundits recited mantras, a few rang bells, while others with eyes closed remained in quiet prayer. Foot soldiers played a lament on their drums.

All the while, on either side of the procession, the royal cavalry in the King's colours of carmine red and gold, rode along keeping the crowd ten rows deep, comfortably at bay. The saddlecloths were eye-catching – velvet, embroidered with silver gilt thread and appliquéd with sequins.

The procession moved slowly along. The crowd was silent, watchful. A few were looking at the sky. The auspicious moment for the King's cremation was approaching, the sun now swiftly climbing in the Heavens.

At last the King's bier in an open royal carrier left the palace – it was garlanded on all sides and drawn by two black horses. A royal pundit dressed all in white, recited passages from the sacred Shastras. The King's personal flag with its coat-of-arms – an eagle and a dove on a bough of rhododendron blossoms – was carried unfurled and lowered by one of his personal guards. Pundits, sages, ascetics and holy men formed an inner circle surrounding the royal bier. They in turn were protected by foot soldiers. The cavalry remained closest to the crowd.

As the King's carrier took him on his last journey, the watchers bowed their heads; many prayed, giving thanks to the Almighty for this privilege of witnessing their brave soldier King, their enlightened monarch being taken to another world. A few women were weeping quietly, older men wiped their eyes. Those overcome by deep emotion were supported by younger members of their family. A quiet dignity prevailed. Again the pundits blew their conch shells and the holy men recited their mantras.

Now came the Royal Court Pundit, regal in white, solemn and dignified. He walked alone. A large retinue of the King's menservants, the high and the lowly followed.

The crowd awaited the Suttee Queens, their expectation rising. The people were looking behind at the long procession yet to come. There was a surge forward of feet, shoulders and chests; a craning of heads towards the slow, steady stream.

A few who knew a little about the protocol that should be followed were wondering aloud: 'Why are the Queens' sedans not behind the King?' They were expressing their anxiety at this error to their neighbours, partly to impress and partly to display their concern. 'Silence!' an old man reprimanded. 'How will I

307

hear the blessings of the Suttee Queens? My own ear must hold that sound. The strain of a suttee voice was a unique privilege to receive, for her blessing is the last mortal sound before her ash will mingle with her husband's.'

There began a silent pushing and shoving. Mothers with ailing children wanted the shadow of the suttees to fall upon them, for this would bring if not a cure, substantial relief. In many instances, they were hoping to be able to take home flowers, jewels, other personal adornments, grains of rice, or anything the royal suttees had touched. Such a relic would bring good luck. The more daring were trying to come close enough to the suttee sedan steps, to touch it and so gain a more favourable outcome to their lives.

The more knowledgeable had joined the procession from the outer palace gates and would walk all the way to the Mahasati. They believed that in so doing they would be rewarded as if they themselves had performed a great sacrifice of enormous physical and emotional self denial. The suttee sedans they had not seen, but they assumed that they had missed them, and that the Queens were way ahead.

However, there were a few who were even better informed. Still greater blessings were to be had in being as close as possible to the Mahasati. As the flames rose and enveloped the seated Queens and the King's corpse, those in a position to place their offerings of sweet sandalwood, ghee or garlands would earn merit far exceeding ten-million fold of that of a great sacrifice. This was the belief.

In their desire to gain merit for themselves and their offspring, parents lifted up their young children.

The sun was rising in the heavens; it was becoming hotter and these children needed be protected. A few were already uncomfortable and had begun to cry loudly. Fathers were encouraging their older children to move forward in order to see better; everyone was surging forward. The King's guards, on horse back and on foot, raised their lathis and horse-whips as a sign to the public to retreat, warning that the horses might trample the children.

One cavalry soldier, feeling sorry for the crying children and seeing that tender babies were being burned as the sun struck mercilessly upon them, declared, 'Good people of Jyotika, there are no Suttee Queens. Go home and pray for the King.'

It was as if he had spoken in a foreign tongue.

He repeated it. 'I said, good people, there are no Suttee Queens on the procession. Go home and pray for the King.'

Those close to him were stunned. They still did not understand what he meant. A young girl of no more than eight, told her mother what the King's soldier said. As he had moved on by then, with the rest of the procession, there was no one to verify what the girl said. Her mother paid no attention to a child's foolish utterance.

The distance between the King and the Suttee Queens had become too wide. A middle-aged man cried, 'The Queens, the Queens – where are the Queens?'

A younger man joined him, relishing this intervention which would draw attention to himself. 'Where are the Queens of Jyotika? Where are the Suttee Queens?' Higher up, the waiting crowd heard the word

'Queens', and, thinking that they were at last in sight and were being greeted by the crowd, also began to shout, 'The Suttee Queens! The Suttee Queens!' Everyone was straining their necks.

A few now understood and they informed others. The discipline of the crowd began to fall apart. People were rushing about everywhere, men and women trying to join the procession from all sides. The cavalry and the footmen were holding them back.

Senior cavalry men moved slowly along the procession line, speaking to the crowd. 'Loyal and patient subjects of the King, the Royal Court Pundit is about to speak at the Mahasati. Listen to what he has to say. He will explain what you want to know.'

The Mahasati was enclosed by tent walls. The King's bier was removed and placed on the pyre. Pundit Krishna and two older pundits officiated. Sanskrit hymns and mantras were sung. The canvas walls were removed and the people pressed forward, towards the unlit pyre, which was heavily guarded.

The Royal Court Pundit approached the crowd of mourners. A loud solitary bugle was sounded. One drummer played a lament. Senior pundits cried 'Shanti Shanti. Shanti.' Silence came. Pundit Krishna addressed the people:

'Loyal subjects of the Kingdom of Jyotika, I stand before you on this day and at this time prescribed by the court's astrologers, to bring you an understanding of how our late King Paresh wished to depart from this world and what he requested from his faithful and honourable Royal Queens.

310

'Our late King, as you know, was not only a soldier of daunting courage, but also a traveller and an innovator. In his travels, His Majesty was interested in the ways of thinking and of doing things that brought prosperity, good health and happiness to people in faraway places, so that he might introduce them into his kingdom. As you, the people of Jyotika, know full well, he brought irrigation to the fields and new practices in the growing of food which have increased our harvest more than tenfold. In this semi-arid land, we have been shown how to make the best use of water, and how to preserve it in the soil by mulching.

'Likewise, he observed in the South West, deep South and many other places, that the custom of suttee was not practised, indeed had never been their tradition. In those places, widows lived long, useful, happy lives, helping their children and grandchildren, being much respected, well cared for and held in deep affection by their family. This is a way that also pleases God.

'His Majesty was moved and wished to introduce this custom of a greater compassion and care for others to our Kingdom. He realised that he must be the first to set an example, the first to bring about a change in our thinking. It was with this in mind that he asked his faithful wives, his honourable Queens, to assist him in his large reform, by not accompanying him on the pyre.

'From this day forth, His Majesty wished that all widows, having paid homage to their husband on the pyre, should return to their homes, where they should be comforted by relatives and friends. He asks that the widows of Jyotika continue to help their children and grandchildren, who in return should treat their parents

311

and grandparents with affection and care, as people do in other lands. It is a way that also pleases God.

'The loyal and faithful Queens of Jyotika were greatly saddened to have had to leave; they explained to me that their deep affection for the King and their great loss were becoming too much for their spirits to bear in a palace of beauty, so filled with memories of him. They left quietly without pomp, out of respect for the late King, the Prince Regent and his wives. They wanted this day to be one where your adoration for a King, so kind, gracious, and brave as our King Paresh, should in no way be compromised by their presence. This day, they insisted, must belong to you, the fine people of Jyotika and to their King.'

The people listened. No one moved. They were not sure they understood everything. The majority were dazed. The few who understood what had been said, were uneasy, unconvinced, as never before had a King broken with custom nor his Queens shunned pomp and splendour.

The soldiers who had fought side by side with the King, now came forth one by one and saluted him. The King's personal flag dipped low. The two sons of the Prince Regent, with torch in hand, circled their uncle's pyre three times, bowed deep and low before the King. Together they approached a corner of the pyre and before setting it aflame, turned to the bier that cradled the King's body, asking the King's spirit for permission before they set it alight. A gentle bow of affirmation leaves them. Consent has been given. This is requested three more times. Beginning at the east, the young princes move with their flaming torches in a clockwise direction. With the four corners alight, the wood, steeped in ghee, yellow sugar crystals and incense, began to burn, moving upwards and outwards with the wind.

The desert wind came upon them, fast and fierce. Women held their veils. It was not long before the flames' fury enveloped the entire pyre. It had become a furnace and the people retreated. The heat had become unbearable.

A young girl, no more than ten was thinking of what would have happened to the three Queens had they been there, when a sudden gust of wind pitched up a red-hot glowing piece of coal and, not unlike a comet, hurled itself outwards. Flying high, it gradually lost momentum and came down smack upon a middle-aged Brahmin priest.

He stumbled backwards. The hot coal struck his face first, then fell on his neck and entered the opening of his upper garment, where it lodged. A young man hesitated at first, then seeing the Pundit fall, his body writhing, lifted his white apparel and removed the burning coal with his hands well-wrapped with the end of his turban. The Brahmin was yelling in pain. Instantly his skin changed colour becoming more and more inflamed. He began to chant mantras, but could not continue. 'Fire. I am on fire!' he screamed. 'My entire body is in great pain! Bring me cold water, bring me cold milk. Hurry! Everyone help me! I am a pundit! Hurry. Cold water!'

A woman had some water in a jar; it was for her baby. She would have gladly offered it, but she was not of the right caste. The pain became too excruciating; he cried out that flames were rising within his very being. He began to unravel his own turban and fanned his face. Already the scorched skin was filling with a watery fluid and the skin had become a bubble. Two pundits came to his assistance with thin Sanskrit manuscripts, and fanned him. 'He will need a paste of the aloe plant,' one said. The priest's face was covered and he was lifted and taken away by two younger men of the right caste. 'Remove the cover,' he pleaded. It was done. 'Fan me with cool air. Faster please – blessings will come your way.'

In the silence that ensued, one or two present were strangely relieved that the Queens were not there, roasting on the pyre. A few were looking to see if anything more had escaped from the fire that they could use as relics, believing they would have the power to heal or bring good fortune to their household. Relics from such a fine and noble King were of great value.

The fire continued to rage. Slowly, quietly the people dispersed, their steps leading them homewards. They walked in contemplation, saddened at the death of the King and hoping that his brother would be equally concerned about the people's welfare. They were perplexed at what they had witnessed. What other aspects of their customs would alter, what would it mean for their daily lives? They would return to these questions another day. Today they would have liked to see the three faces that carried so much beauty, the eyes that mirrored so much affection for the King and his people, with little regard for themselves.

Yet, if it was the King's wish that it be so, there was no need to worry unduly. All that could wait. The artisans, the peasants, the large landowners, would be cautious; they would wait and see what the new King had to say. The suttee ritual did not affect the agricultural labourers, since they were long ruled by the necessity of having the hands of the entire household at work out in the field to ensure a daily meal.

The next day, the common people of Jyotika returned to their stalls, their shops, flocks and fields, but in the inner courtyard, the footsteps of conspirators met. It was a conspiracy of the priestly class. The pyre was still burning when one of the senior pundits decided to move against Pundit Krishnajee. He had devised a plan to undermine the Royal Court Pundit's authority, knowing that this would force him to resign. He laid bare his scheme before three like-minded pundits, drawing their attention to the large discrepancies between what was heard at the funeral address, and in the throne room both by those who left early and those who remained. The musicians were also asked to relate to this small group of conspirators what Pundit Krishnajee said to them, before and after the distribution of sweets, and they gladly obliged.

The Brahmins were uneasy about what Pundit Krishna had said at the Mahasati and about what they understood he had said to the slave-girl, Kala. It was agreed that where there had once been faith, order and clarity, the Royal Court Pundit had brought doubt, muddle and confusion.

These priests were also troubled at the thought of so many young, attractive and indeed mature women living an active, normal life after the death of their husbands. There was something disturbing and full of potential for unseemly conduct, alas, even amongst the

315

highest caste. Temptation should not be placed so openly before men. The entire business was alarming. They began to suspect that the late King had at no time suggested such a thing, that it was all the work of Pundit Krishna's failing, arrogant mind.

They even suspected he might have wished to save the Queens. To what end, they asked. And after pausing to consider, rapidly retreated from further contemplation of it, in order to restore their sanctity.

Three days later when the Prince Regent arrived, four senior pundits sought an audience with him. They explained the strange, unorthodox happenings that had occurred, the dishonour and the humiliation the late King had had to endure, going unaccompanied on the pyre, as one of low birth; the escape of the Queens, the yawning inconsistencies of what had been said in the throne room and the far from honest conduct of Pundit Krishnajee in both small and large matters. He had disgraced the office of the Royal Court Pundit, was their charge, had brought dishonour to the royal court, and sullied its workings. They had no way of knowing if the late King did indeed want their age-old custom to be replaced by customs from the South. The new King must decide.

Not long afterwards, Prince Mahendra summoned Pundit Krishna and asked him to explain himself. The Pundit, offered the scroll that Queen Meena had given him, including the plea that Queen Renu had made, written in her own hand. He explained what, faced with this unexpected situation, he had sought to do and the part Pundit Baalaajee had played in undermining his plan. The King, having read the scrolls, asked the Pundit to state exactly what was said before the pyre

316

was lit. Then Pundit Krishna was asked to return the following day.

When Pundit Krishna left, Prince Mahendra could not help but admire the tact of his brother's trusted Pundit, his mental dexterity, courage and loyalty. Yet, he could not keep him, for he had already promised the post to another loyal and faithful priest. He could see that Pundit Krishna's senior colleagues were envious of him. It was likely, the Prince Regent thought that Pundit Krishnajee had unwittingly brought this upon himself. The unhappy dispositions of the four senior pundits towards him had reached this sorry state partly because of his powerful mix of arrogance and erudition, and his ability to cope with other men's intrigue, and to manage his own effortlessly. He had neglected his colleagues at his peril. A cultivated camaraderie with them, accompanied on occasions by favours freely given, might have defused their envy.

Prince Mahendra roamed round and round the room, not knowing what to do. He called upon his favourite wife, who advised him to make a clean start. 'It is preferable not to have to hear, "your brother did it this way, Your Majesty," or to listen to, "the late King Paresh would have preferred it that way". After your Coronation, you will decide how to rule the Kingdom without perpetual guidelines from others who have been too successful in introducing daring new ways of doing things.

'Perhaps we need to return to familiar pathways. You lose much prestige by changing things too quickly; also, the common people may be tempted to ask for more and yet more. That is the nature of the lower castes who outnumber us. Rapid changes lead to

317

instability. Change upsets the established order, dear husband. At present men know their place and women too. What more can a future King wish?' she purred. Her last coquettish words, though she did not know it, were an untimely overindulgence and ruined her whole argument.

When the Queen left, Mahendra knew she was wrong. Like his brother, he too had travelled widely and had seen other, better ways of doing things. He had followed his brother's advice and paid particular attention to such matters. During his journeys he had asked questions and made valuable contacts. His own Queens had lived protected lives so he had learned to keep the business of state to himself.

He truly wished he were able to hold on to so experienced a priest as Pundit Krishna, yet was aware that his own inexperience and immaturity would have led him to become too dependent upon him. Without him, he would be forced to listen more carefully, to ask more questions, to become more involved in the management of his Kingdom. He would make errors, yes, but he would grow. And yet, with care, he could learn much and learn it quickly, were he to retain this sophisticated man of state. What should he do?

He found Queen Renu's ideas and her fine hand alluring. The restrained appeal for change by his late brother's three Queens had genuinely moved him. His brother, he mused with a smile of pride, had chosen his Queens wisely. However, he still had to decide. Should he ask Pundit Krishna to leave?

CHAPTER THIRTY-SIX

Creating a New Path

WHEN VASTI FINALLY opened her eyes, she stared around at the curtains lifting in the breeze, the wardrobe, the bookshelf, the standing mirror. Then she realised where she was and who she was. She was herself again, no longer a floating consciousness in the Kingdom of Jyotika, a silent observer from a future time. A being without footprints. She could be seen, be touched and spoken to. Vasti was both elated and relieved.

As her thoughts began to move outside herself, the hub of activity and the voices of the workmen erecting the tent, drifted into the quiet room. Dear God, her wedding! What could she do? Making the best of a bad job had its limitations. Her spirit sank. A huge wave of tiredness overcame her and she slept.

An hour later when she awoke, it was her mother's hands she felt cooling her forehead. Her loving family were around her. Pushpa and Shami were smiling. After a glass of warm milk with a dash of brandy and nutmeg, a hot shower and a change into cool fresh cotton, she began to feel her energy seeping back.

Her mother's care, her courage and quiet dignity flowed around her, together with the familiar scent that had enveloped Vasti as a child on returning from school. Vasti knew she must remove the anxiety etched on that beloved face of her lone parent. She must do what a daughter from such a home was expected to do and embrace the fortitude, discipline and wisdom of her parents.

With only a few days left in which to heal herself, she became quietly determined to overcome other feelings and let the wedding be as her mother and sister would wish. She had learned a few important things from the scholar, Queen Renu, and would bring her temperament and wisdom to her own situation. I will decide, she thought, which wedding vows I promise to take and so direct the path ahead. This in itself will place markers that Karan will have to note.

Rojani the Mehndi artist found that an exuberance in pattern and design was quietly, even warmly accepted, not frowned upon. This was not what she had expected, judging from what the sister Pushpa had earlier indicated. It just went to show, she thought, how foolish it was to think we know our brothers and sisters.

On the following day, Pushpa brought the family box of gold jewellery handed down from mother to daughter for four generations. Vasti must choose what she wanted to wear. The Sirbandi for her forehead was a string of tiny bells attached to a chain of open lotuses in fine filigree. The matching nath for her nose she would have to consider; the hathphool, an adornment for the hand, however engaged her. There were five rings for her fingers and each ring was attached by a thin gold chain to a carnation in the centre. The pair of anklets were particularly attractive with their fine threads of gold woven into loops from which minute pearls hung.

Amused at this indulgence – a toe-ring – she picked it up and tried it on her thumb.

The necklace and earrings had been worn by her mother on her wedding day. They were grand, elaborate works of craftsmanship. Attached to the earring was a string of stars which would rest on the outer lobe of the ear – beautiful, heavy to carry, yet she would wear them. It would bring her comfort to have these pieces that were close to her mother. To wear all these to advantage, she pondered, smiling, one would have to walk in a certain prescribed way; these adornments were not made for running uphill, skirts lifted, hair dishevelled in the wind.

'Before I try them on, Pushpa, I want to go through the wedding vows with you,' she said. 'Of course you know them well. How often do married couples live by them?'

Pushpa could sense that the old questioning Vasti had returned and she knew it was crucial not to be pulled into a controversy. Time was of the essence; it was already late in the day for changes.

'Seven vows are requested by the bride and five by the bridegroom,' she said. 'If you look closely, Vasti, you will see that they rest on the highest Sanathan Dharma principles.'

'Yes, I know. To be honest, on reading these ancient marriage vows I was struck by the status given to women. Considering how old these vows are, we must blame the interpreters of our sacred texts for the low position women have been forced into. Reading it has helped me. I respect it. There is wisdom here.'

'So you will keep some things?'

'Yes, and remove what is no longer applicable. I have written one vow for bride and bridegroom. If anything of worth has been lost, let me know.'

'We will have to inform the Wallis.'

'Of course, Pushpa. It would not be right to spring it upon them on the wedding day. I wouldn't do that. This is not guerrilla warfare, is it?'

They laughed.

'Believe me, Vasti, there are times when you do need guerrilla tactics to get your way – when you have little power, as is often the case with us women. Very well. Now let me see what you have.'

'Wait a minute. I will show it to you. But I want you to understand what I have written, and why it makes sense to me.

'I have deleted *the bridegroom's need to assist her parents if hard times befall them.*'

'Why?'

'This sort of help should not be forced; it should be willingly offered or not at all. When compulsion takes place, the bride may not hear the end of it . . . I helped your parents and you are now not doing as I wish you to do etc. Pushpa, I shall help Ma if she is in need. I intend to be economically independent. Now let me see . . .'

'Vasti, will you keep the last bride's request?'

'That, Pushpa, cannot be upheld by a promise; it will come within a marriage or not. How on earth can I ask the bridegroom *not to allow any unworthy motive to come between us?*

'This is fascinating. The bride's status is emphasised in the Bhavar – the bride and bridegroom circling the sacred fire seven times offering grains to Agni. Observe, it is the bride who leads first and who leads the bride-

322

groom four times out of seven. I take comfort in this. We lead first, we lead more often.

'Do you think our past offered us worth that we did not know how to utilise and so we lost it? Or do you think other aspects of the culture were not conducive to the bride retaining the esteem offered at the marriage ceremony?'

'Vasti, I shall have to explain these changes to Ma.'

'No. I will do that, Pushpa. You will have enough to do to call the Wallis.

Now, regarding my promises. You may delete the first. I will not promise *to conduct myself in society as* never *to bring* disgrace or dishonour *to his honoured name.*'

'Ma will want to know why. Surely there is no harm in this.'

'It is double-edged. I am unhappy with *never*. If his family or he or both begin to abuse me – physically or psychologically or try in any way to demean me privately or in the presence of others – I have no intention of staying, and were I to decide to leave under those conditions, I will not have the words never thrown at me, mind you, they will be interpreting my leaving as a disgraceful and dishonourable act, blind, of course to how they behaved. Under those conditions, why should I promise to uphold *his* honour? Honour indeed! I will be trying my best to maintain my *sanity*. On the other hand, I shall not dishonour him, in the way we understand the meaning of the word.'

'I can see that.'

'Good. You have an uncommon clarity of vision. It is for these same reasons I shall not promise to be punctual, regular and careful in my domestic duties *so that he may not suffer inconveniences.*'

'Vasti, you are aware that I have to explain all this to the Wallis.'

'You, Pushpa will soon be handed a good marriage vow to take to them.'

'Hmmm. We seem to be crossing out quite a lot.'

'How can I promise that he will not suffer inconveniences? Be practical, Pushpa. I may not at all times be at home when he is there. I may be at a staff meeting. He will merely have to help himself to the nice meal I would have prepared. I can't always be at home to serve him. He will have to be modern, realistic, take the rough with the smooth. I mean conveniences as well as inconveniences.'

'I wouldn't know how to put that before Mr Walli. You will have to help me.'

'Do not be so timid, Pushpa. Oh, how marriage has changed you! I intend to be alert to its softening process.'

'Next removal, please.'

'Oh, I will keep the last promise.'

'That's good. But you have left out two.'

'Those are related to what I have already said. I do not need to promise to be *a good host to his friends in his absence and in accordance to their status*, nor will I *walk out of my marriage at the least provocation and seek a more comfortable home*. But as I have said, if events offer me no choice but to leave, I will have to go.'

'Our marriage ceremony is moving Vasti,' her sister said gently. 'It has a quiet dignity, an accumulated wisdom gathered from experience. It is also more symbolic than most, this may be because of its ancient beginnings. It was clear to the priests that the people couldn't follow the ceremony by listening to the

Sanskrit chants but they could by what they saw. This may account for our being joined together, by a weave of cloth.'

'And there is Kanyadana, Pushpa. I have seen old and young women at weddings wipe their tears away when this is being performed: the bride's parents cup their palms together to support their daughter's hand, then ask the bridegroom to cherish, love and care for her according to Dharmic Principles. This request touches me deeply. They await his reply, and it is only after the bridegroom consents to this that in my case, Ma, and Pa if he were with us – will remove their palms and enable mine to rest on Karan's. You see, Pushpa, we have to continue to give words their worth.'

'I have no trouble with that,' her sister said. 'It is because of this, Vasti, that the Wallis will be furious at the omissions.'

'They shouldn't be. Here is what I would like us both to promise.'

Pushpa looked at it. 'It is short, Vasti. Is this taking the place of twelve promises?'

'Read it, Pushpa.'

'On this auspicious day in the presence of the gods, the spirits of our forefathers, our parents, family, friends and our community, we, Vasti and Karan, bride and bridegroom, do solemnly promise to live our lives with courtesy, respect and affection for each other. In times of hardship, we promise to comfort and assist one another. In times of good fortune we promise to share our joys and show compassion to those less fortunate.

'Decisions that will affect our lives, be they large or small, we promise to discuss openly and in good faith. We also promise to consider the concerns and judgements of the other with care.

Where there continues to be serious disagreements between us, we promise to clarify them before members of both families. We promise to do so neither in haste nor anger for we are aware that the breakdown of a marriage is comprised of many small steps. The path of separation is not consistent with the domestic history of our forefathers which we promise to do our utmost to uphold.'

That night, as Vasti laid her head on her pillow, she felt as if she were attending to part of her unspoken anxiety – her deep misgivings. As sleep approached, she welcomed it to relax her mind. Through the open window, the light of the glowing moon moved softly upon her, enabling her to leave herself behind and join a radiant stream of reflective thoughts, mirrored through time.

CHAPTER THIRTY-SEVEN

A Spirit at Ease with Itself

PRINCE MAHENDRA WAS conscious that he had
not yet matured or gained in confidence, as befitted a
monarch, and was reluctant to let the Pundit go. He
reflected long. Then he said to himself, 'I must do
without my brother's Royal Court Pundit. Circumstance dictates it.'

He could see that the Pundit's vast erudition,
experience and sagacity would be too great a match for
his own personal attendants. They would instantly dislike each other. Already there were the enraged senior
pundits of the palace were too envious of him. Some
things cannot be returned to their former state. He
reminded himself that he had promised the position to
another, not in so many words, but there was an
understanding.

It was sad, Prince Mahendra pondered to himself,
that a man could lose his job because he was too skilled
at what he did. However, he would treat the Pundit
according to his status and his worthiness. He should
have the freedom to choose his manner of leaving and
be permitted to take with him all his royal gifts; he
would also be offered two menservants of his own preference. The Prince hoped that the Pundit's dismissal

would not colour his recollections of his life at the royal court of Jyotika and that he would leave without regret.

Pundit Krishnajee did as he was asked. He gathered his things together, chose a worthy carrier and two fine horses. Instead of two royal menservants, he chose two of the bright, strong stable-hands with amiable dispositions to go with him. He told them that together, they would travel to seek their fortune in a land overseas where, with hard work, they could become rich and return as maharajahs. This he knew would appeal to them, because going abroad to make one's fortune was what the royal compound had heard from the Southern merchants.

How much of this hearsay was true, and how much merely gossip spread by the ship's merchants and their recruiters of labour, he could not tell at this distance. He himself was not fit for harsh physical work, but he had promised these lads and would keep an open mind.

Pundit Krishna, the Royal Court Pundit, said good-bye to no one. He dressed modestly so as not to attract bandits and robbers, and closed his door for the last time, taking his sacred texts with him and gifts of silver and gold medals that he could exchange for money, if the need arose later. He sat with the stable-boys who took charge of the horses. They were neither of a high caste nor a low caste. This brought him no discomfort. Instead it was his silent leave-taking, the heartbreaking memories of his life here that held his thoughts. He was thankful that his gentle father had not lived to see this day. More than once he had contemplated on his retirement, it was a position to be envied, that is to say, to have status and privilege and little to do, amongst familiar surroundings of beauty and order. Yet it was not to be.

Tears came to him as he saw the place where he had stood, to perform those rites of welcome to the late King and then tired and weary had to face dissenting Queens. He had tried his best to grapple with opposing beliefs passionately held, and at the same time to defend the integrity of the Queens. Now he was at peace with himself

At the tall, iron gates the new guards did not recognise him. He made himself known by a letter given to him by Prince Mahendra. On seeing the royal seal, the guards were embarrassed. They bent low before him and pleaded that their large ignorance be forgiven. Then the gates opened for a man who once did the same for those he served.

The three travellers were in no hurry. One of the stable-hands said with enthusiasm that he knew the way to the port. The Pundit too knew part of the way. They would alight at roadside rest houses and try to get as much information as they could as they refreshed themselves with short naps and hot meals. Maybe the Queens had done the same. The Pundit would ask discreetly to ascertain the route they took.

The morning was bracing, the wind cold. A family of cranes was flying overhead. Doves cooed, bullocks at the wayside watched in silence. They passed a village where two oxen were ploughing the land. The houses were made of wood, reeds and mud bricks, thatched with straw. The wheels rattled on. Fields were separated by narrow foot paths and rough roads. Everything was quiet; one man pumped water into his field, another tended his vegetable plot. No longer did tigers and

329

lions stalk the land. The wheat fields moved with the wind.

After a while Pundit Krishna stood upright and looked back. All that was visible now were the seventeen- metre thick and sixty eight metre high walls of hard sandstone of the Fort of Jyotika that he knew bore the marks of many a siege and had withstood them all. Impregnable with its turrets, defiant on its steep hill. He smiled to himself, thankful that he had once lived there, where life in its infinite variety had spilled over him and taught him much.

Once upon a time, he too knew little and was as keen as these two boys. The travelling Pundit opened a bag and offered the stable-hands some delicious sweets. They were the very sweets Dayita's musicians might even now be enjoying. A feeling of camaraderie joined the three men, ordinary stable-hands and the most erudite of Royal Court Pundits from the Kingdom of Jyotika.

The fine horses had taken them far. Now, no one looked back. Had they done so, they would have found that even the giant, impregnable walls of the fort of Jyotika on its steep hill were no more.

Their own thoughts touched Vasti. She pulled the blankets closer, for the morning air in Jyotika was so cold, frost glistened on granite and on an aircraft wings. She was returning home.

CHAPTER THIRTY-EIGHT

Pruning an Ancient Tree

'HELLO, MR WALLI. This is Shami here. How are things moving at your end?'

'Couldn't be better. Everything is in place. I have to say tradition treated the boys' side good.'

'Yes.'

'Compared with what you have to do, we have less than half the worries. It is your side that has the major headache, I know that, man. Fireworks at your end, eh? Preparing for our coming with all our guests as well as your own – that takes a lot of pulling together. The facilities must be in place and so on. But the women, you know, they are masterful. So everything going like clockwork at your end, eh?'

'They don't tell me anything. I am just an errand boy here, if there is anything simple to do, only then I am asked.'

Sukesh Walli laughed. 'Is that so? Relax. Take no offence, that has advantages.'

'I wanted to talk to you about the wedding vows.'

'Is Vasti worried about that? Tell her nobody troubles themselves with that. Half the time they don't know what they are promising.'

331

'True. She wants the guests not to have to wait too long for the wedding feast. There are some mouth-watering dishes at this end, and with all the aromas while your stomach is grumbling, it can become too much for the young children and the old too. So she has tried to move things along without losing anything.'

'I don't understand.'

'She has taken out a few old-fashioned things from the promises. Some of these promises, you know, are very out of date – like Karan having to seek her consent when he is going on a pilgrimage, or when he is erect-ing a temple, as well as his promising to allow her to join him in prayers. She says he does not have to make such promises because she knows he will.'

'Well. I must inform my sisters. This shows that Vasti understands that a man must feel like a man in his own house. That is a good move.'

'It is. She has added a few things too, like they must pull together in all important matters.'

'Of course – intelligent girl, thinking ahead. Karan and she will be running the Clinic, putting their heads together to get the place moving. I can see she has a business disposition.'

'Yes, she is thinking ahead as you say.'

'Naturally. Modern women are like that. The engine of progress and prosperity, you know.'

'So I will tell her that the one promise they will make together is all right?'

'Of course. Nothing to worry about. Promises? After the wedding who will remember them? She will know what is expected of her and will play her part. She doesn't need to worry about promises. If she is in any doubt about anything, we will explain everything.

'When she comes here and meets my sisters, she will realise straight away that those promises are not important. She doesn't know us. My sisters will be guiding her all the way. The least of her worries would be promises. They are part of the whole thing, na? You just go along, man. Tell her not to worry.'

'You see, she believes the key to success in marriage is to come clean with your husband, not to spring something on him. She calls it courtesy.'

'Of course that is what it is, courtesy, good manners, concern for other people. We know all about that.'

'I told her so – not that she had any doubts. She wants you to know, Mr Walli, what she thinks. It is her way.'

'That, Shami, I say is a good, good way. I like it.'

Mr Sukesh Walli was contented. At the back of his mind he was aware that he was more keen on this marriage than his son was. He could see that Karan flirted with the nurses, girls not in the same class, without family background and a good education. He would prove to Karan, that no matter he was a doctor, his father was right all along. A bright-thinking girl was Vasti, just look at the quality of that family.

He was happy to inform his sisters of Vasti's modern approach to promises. The two women feigned contentment at their brother's wholesale approval of something he had not seen, but when he left the room their alarm went off.

'Our brother is far too trusting,' said one.

'Do you know of anytime he wasn't?' her sister replied.

'Approving of something you have not even seen – my God! Going along with everything they tell you on the phone, then again, it is only the parts they want you to hear. This, to my mind,' she sneered, 'is his behaving like a foolish old man when a young woman smiles in his direction.'

'Before you know it, she will have him marching to her beat.'

'Eating out of her hands.'

'I can see we have our work cut out. We must go about it carefully though.'

'Don't I know. Slowly, slowly pull the net round her. I know how. That girl has to be firmly held back. She wants to tell us how to think and what to think.'

'We have to show her who is boss, then again she could decide to live away from us. She will be the new madam, na?'

'How can she keep Sukesh's grandchildren from him? Besides, what does she know about bringing up children? Book-learning tells you everything? Leave it to me. I will prepare Sukesh for this kind of . . . of family transgression. That is the word. This is what people call wholesale transgression.'

'True. Who does she think she is? Changing the sacred promises!'

'Unbelievable. Is she still Indian?'

'How to know that?'

'No concern for culture? No feelings for the elders?'

'She is Miss Know-All, na? We can't have people saying that she is ruling us.'

'We need to work on her for our brother's sake and we must not forget the name of this family.'

'I wouldn't be able to bear that kind of shame . . . having your daughter-in-law, an outsider, ruling us?' And the elder sister held the end of her ornhi to her eyes.

CHAPTER THIRTY-NINE

Mother and Daughter

DEVI NADIR WAS the last to know. Vasti brought the old text and showed her the changes. And though Devi was sensitive to the underlying thoughts that had led to the changes, she said, 'I have no worry, Vasti, with what you have here, especially as Shami says the other side is happy with it too. I can see it is a good guide for a happy marriage. One thing I want to leave with you. Tell Karan early in your marriage that if you happen to do something that displeases him, he must tell you quietly and that you will not do it again. Let him know that your father never struck me and that you wish to continue in this vein. This is our family custom.'

'Yes, Ma. But there is something else I completely forgot to mention. I have only now remembered. Look, here it is.'

'You mean what the bride's father asks of the bridegroom?'

'Yes. I do not want Uncle Kash to make these requests or for that matter any requests on my behalf. You know what Uncle Kash is like. You will have to be firm with him, Ma.'

'I see why you can't have it, Vasti. It belongs to a family of old sentiments you have already removed.'

'Yes, Ma. I am relieved you can see that it would look foolish for Uncle Kash who will be standing in for Pa to say, "*My daughter is of a tender age and very inexperienced with the intricate path of the world and will need all the advice and teaching you can give her.*" '

'As well as all the rest, na, Vasti?'

'You mean, "*If her ways and habits are not in accordance with yours, it is for you to change them to your own way of thinking by gentle administration and a good example.*" '

'Yes. Let me say now, Vasti, it is not good to speak of your Uncle Kash like that. He is trying his very best for you in the only way he knows. It is not your way, but it is the only way he has. And let me explain: in those days there would have been occasions when the age gap was clearly too great. But the opportunity to marry your daughter to a respectable wealthy old man and so ensure she had a comfortable life was a good thing. Even some young women today I believe think the same. Do you want to keep the remainder?'

'What remains is: *If I were to commit any wrong, my husband should exercise forgiveness and by mild reproof endeavour to prevent further recurrence rather than adopting the harsh and cruel method of putting me out of his love and protection.* In a way I have kept that, since it is included in the promise I have put together.'

'Very well. I will explain it all to your uncle. Remember, Vasti, your Uncle Kash can be very helpful and nice. He has always treated me with great respect.'

'You are kind and generous to him and Aunt Sona, Ma. Besides, it is easy for anyone to respect you.'

'Do not be so rational, Vasti. There is a harshness to it. Life is about give and take. So what if sometimes you lose? You are a young woman. Be softer, more like a plant than an iron rod . . . more welcoming. Do not expect everything on your terms, Vasti, even when you are sure you are right. Life is a large, beautiful thing. Do not get tangled up in small things. Let some things pass over you, my daughter. Be a little like the Buddha from time to time.' Devi looked at her daughter. 'There are one or two other things I want to leave with you, Vasti.

'If Karan purchases something for the house which you do not like, treat it well, show your appreciation of it, especially if he has bought it for you. Much time must pass by before you explain to him in the most indirect way that you have other preferences, just in case he continues to bring home many of the same.'

Between mother and daughter the gentle silence of trust hummed. And after a long thoughtful pause, 'If you are unhappy, Vasti, tell him so and say why, and tell us too. Pushpa and I are here. Never forget this is your second home. When you are married, you become someone's wife and later someone's mother. But you will always be my daughter. Nothing can change that. And your father's spirit will walk with you always. You were his favourite. He will help to keep you calm, prevent you from saying anything you would have wished you never said.'

'Yes, Ma. I will remember.'

And Vasti bent low. 'Bless me, Ma.' Her tears flowed while her mother called on the gods that wisdom be bestowed upon her daughter. Vasti slowly touched her mother's feet with the soft of her fingers, three times, taking it to her forehead, asking that the affection of her mother should walk with her.

It was an acknowledgement of the divine in her mother, Devi Nadir, who was standing by her and would do so in the future no matter what befell her. It was one spirit honouring the other with grace and affection. Her mother had confirmed that this home, the home of her birth, of her childhood, would be her sanctuary in times of persecution, in times of sorrow. Home was home; becoming a wife did not alter this.

An inner vacuum was slowly beginning to close within a troubled, young, questioning spirit, seeking a path for its healing and its growth.

CHAPTER FORTY

The Drums Beat

FROM AFAR, THE ceremonial tent looked like an Arabian Nights' desert shelter. Within, it was a royal palaquin reflecting colour and light. The breeze refreshed all. Sun-gold, silvery and ruby red baubles swayed. Strings of glitter mimicking distant lines of stars twinkled in play with light and shadow. A few potted plants were attracting attention by their perfumes, others by their running tendrils, while bouquets of abundance decorated the altar, filling vases and giant jars.

The drums were beating and the village knew it was the ceremony's call. The urgency of the beat said, 'Good people of the village, hasten. Time is near, the Pundit is here.'

Under the wide white tent, chiffon and organdy, raw silk, near silk, satins and soft cottons flowed from the women as they took their seats, dressed in their most attractive saris, long skirts, salwar kameez, beaded blouses. The heads of older married women were covered with an ornhi; others who called themselves modern, who said they were moving with the times, wore their veils on their shoulders. It became them for they carried themselves well. The reddish-gold jewellery on burning brown skins so flattered the gold that their wearers looked prosperous; hair ornaments of petals, buds and leaves attracted the eye.

The men, not to be outdone, wore their silk embroidered waistcoats, Nehru shirts or smart shirts with collars and cuffs well starched. The bamboo frame of the white tent gave a forest-green flavour of an ancient freshness. Time passed, whispers, greetings, smiles and laughter embraced the gathering. Devi, Pushpa and Shami were at the entrance to greet their guests.

Old Mrs Cuthbert, the village Grande Dame, who some said was older than the spreading gnarled mahogany tree in the savannah, walked through the covered entrance decorated with coconut palm leaves, garlands of coloured bulbs and hibiscus flowers, their opening petals pink, yellow, near-white and red. Devi embraced her. 'You are here, Jennie.' Her eyes lit up with much pleasure. 'It is so very good to see you. I was wondering . . .'

'I told them, Devi, I couldn't let you down. Such a sweet note too with the card. I knew, I just had to come. It's the old knees, you know how it is, playing up again, I said so this morning, didn't I Patricia?'

'Yes, Mum.'

'I told my knees they would just have to understand, that I was on my way to a grand wedding of my family.'

Her two daughters Patricia and Marjorie and the four grandchildren were waving to raised hands in the tent, happy to see so many they knew.

'It looks like you have managed to fit the entire village under this grand tent, Devi. But I know, there is nothing you can't do. Now don't you disagree with me.'

Turning to Pushpa, Devi said, 'Jennie blessed Vasti when she was yet unborn, and massaged me with those healing hands of hers.'

'And I knew it was going to be a girl. And I said, "I will be at her wedding," didn't I?'

'You did, Jennie.'

'Thank you. A woman of my word I am.'

'Always Jennie, always.'

Two young bright teenagers came forward to assist the guests to their seats, another was helping to take young children to the bathroom.

Gifts were carried upstairs in the house and handed to two substantial-looking women whose businesslike air showed they were on duty. They looked at the gift card and if it was not clear who it was from, or the name on it would not help, they printed an explanation to assist Devi. For instance, under 'Mr Gopaul', they added, 'Boy Boy, lives at the end of Tamarind Road.' The gifts were silent under their wrappings except for a few figures in a box. A hand-painted elephant lifted its trunk high, a rotund Chinese vase sang as blue dragons, starfish and leaves danced around its fullness. There was a magnificent piece of glass: it looked like a splash of water, magnified, frozen in mid air. The card read, *From Dr Mistry to beautiful Vasti, wishing her the joys of life.*

Shami went to the drummers, to tell them that the bridegroom and his party were now five minutes away. The men rose, the leader looked at the others; no word was spoken. He closed his eyes and on opening them, his head lifted and fell like a tumbling wave.

The drums began to dance, the drummers restraining the beat. The energy a pulsating spring – a dancing star. The drumbeat carried all. Now the drummers could hold back no more for everyone's feet were tapping. Dancers were rising.

The village dancers removed their chapals in haste; they had drunk the beat and their soles must caress the warm earth, the drums demanded this. The tempo had risen. The women rose to the challenge, the men closed their eyes as the primeval spirits of the drums were freed. The beat was an intoxication. The dancers' limbs moved into throbbing elation. Their feet and warm thighs responded to the eroticism of sound, carrying the essence of life, the kernel of being. The earth quaked, the waves picked up the force and tsunamis were born.

An exhilaration spread outwards – the bridegroom was here, at the gates! The drums exploded into a copulation of rhythm and energy, the drummers absorbed into the explosion of suns and births of planets.

The dancers whirled in unison with the first rotation, on and on they danced, led by the drums, taken too far, far away from their former selves.

But now, the heightened rhythm must close or the dancers would collapse. The drummers imperceptibly descended from the zenith, their pulsating energy closely bridled, until the dancers' feet were led back to cooler spheres.

Now, it was their turn: the sitar strings struck the air. The bridegroom was welcomed with songs and garlands of sweet marigold. The circling arms of women took the aarti warmth of camphor light to him, his face absorbed its colourful glow.

Uncle Kash guided him to the altar prepared and decorated with a healthy growing banana shoot, abstract

342

designs in coloured rice, clay dias alight, scented garlands, sacred texts and bronze images of divinity. Karan was invited to sit at the altar by the officiating priests who looked at the hands of the clock. The moment was auspicious. A bronze bell was rung. The gathering was called.

He looked around him and, seeing an opportunity to inform the young, conscious that they were fast losing those aspects of their culture that would help to give their lives meaning, he said: 'Today we are all here to celebrate a Vivaha, which is the Sanskrit word for marriage. This ceremony you are about to witness is one of the more important Samskaras of a Hindu, whose entire life, is served by sixteen Samskaras. These are purificatory, ceremonial rites, performed to sanctify the body, mind and intellect of the individual in preparation for his or her next role in life.'

He cleared his throat, adjusted himself. The ceremony commenced.

The pundit's clear voice channelled the sacred Sanskrit chants to herald the invisible, the life-giving; he invited the gods, the elements of our planet and the forefathers of both sides of this union, to witness and bless this bonding. All were silent. From time to time the pundit left the Sanskrit and Hindi texts to explain the ceremony in English so that all present might follow the significance of this ancient rite. He knew that the old language of arrival, its carriage and contents, were fading from memories.

Devi guided Vasti to the altar. All knew it was she, though her face was covered by a thin veil. Her sparkling slippers stayed behind with Karan's shoes as she too entered the ritual ground.

343

As the ceremony continued, tension mounted in the kitchen. The rice was boiling. Timing was crucial for no one enjoys cold rice. The chef in charge was keeping an eye on the clock. He knew when the ceremony would be finished; his timing was perfect – until he was told that seven promises and the requests of the Bride's father would be replaced by a single promise which both would take. On hearing this, his assistants did not panic, their chef's long experience had taught them how to prepare for the unpredictable. They had started twenty minutes earlier, for he had wind of it.

Helpers were busy laying out the plates and glasses on fourteen tables; others were filling paper bags with ludoo, para, gulabjamun and jalebi. These would be handed to the guests on their parting. There were no meat dishes for this was a Hindu wedding where the taking of life, the shedding of another's blood were incompatible with a ceremony celebrating the continuity, the sanctity of the birth of new lives to come.

The chef looked about him, pleased with the feast. Devi had chosen the vegetables with care and he had taken his time. This combination had resulted in superb dishes of cauliflower, aubergine, okras, kerhi, kachouries and sahiena. He would serve the pundit and his assistants his special kachouries soaked in a rich yoghurt. They would also have a fine brass bowl of rasmaila topped with pistachio nuts. The soft paratha roties made with ghee were neatly packed, kept warm, covered with leaves from the forest.

The warm face of the chef looked out and he could hear the chanting of the priest. The bride and bridegroom were circling the sacred fire, offering grains to Agni.

Again he stirred the boiling rice – not long now. He would need to stand by; it should be ready in minutes. While the chef was at his station, the ceremony continued. The pundit explained to the gathering the couple's choice of sharing the one promise. Then, he read it and asked the bride and bridegroom to repeat it after him. When it was done, the pundit considered that he should lighten the uneasiness that might be felt by the orthodox amongst them. He straightened his shoulders and lifted his head: 'The bride was thinking of all the hungry children and the blessings she would receive from them by bringing the delicacies closer to them.' The mothers smiled. 'Yet, the essence of Dharmic Principles are all here knotted tightly as I have done into the weave that joins them as they walked around paying homage to Agni. Nothing has been lost.'

A little girl removed her wet finger from her mouth and pointed. 'Look, Mummy, they are hiding.'

'Sh sh sh,' an old woman cautioned, the sadhus looked round and scowled. The child was about to cry, but a bright, red lollipop, hastily drawn from a handbag, contained her.

The gleaming white cotton sheet – store-new, its former folds still holding – covered the bridal couple. The pundit passed the sindhoor to the bridegroom, to perform Sindhoor Daan. This was the climax of the marriage. This symbolic, yet intimate touching of the bride by the bridegroom signified that the couple were now husband and wife.

Karan stretched his hand to receive the pundit's ornate box. Conscious of its significance, aware that the moment had reached her, Vasti momentarily closed her eyes. On opening them she saw the ring. Karan came forward. Instinctively, she leaned backwards. The eagle's wings were outstretched; gliding, its eyes were fixed, beak and claws steadily swooping towards its prey, descending upon *her*. She heard the flutter of its wings. Suddenly the heat of a midday sun barred by sugared stems was upon her. Her body trembled. '*O God! No. No!*' She was about to raise both her hands to restrain him when her mother's concerned voice came through.

'Vasti? Are you all right?'

She steadied herself, closed her eyes. 'Better now, Ma,' she gasped. 'Felt faint . . . must be the cover.'

With his middle finger dipped in sindoor, Karan caressed the path of her hair and tried to keep to the parting. His hand stretched, her scent was upon him. Her hair path that had opened for him was now red.

He waited for her to look up at him to hold his eyes, but she sat and stared at her feet. This simple sindhoor act witnessed only by the gods who see through covers was completed and the pundit asked that the sheet be removed so that all present might witness the sindhoor mark that bound these two lives as one.

Not understanding the cause of her emotion, this sudden withdrawal, Karan attributed it to her being overcome by his closeness and the confined space under the sheets. She may be claustrophobic, he thought.

Sensing something contrary, the pundit turned to the large anxiously awaiting gathering and smiled mischievously. 'The ardour of this bridegroom was escaping,' he said, smiling yet more broadly. 'He wants to embrace his bride, but she knows it is not the time. It is the way of young men today. In my youth,' he paused, 'such an idea would not have come even to the bravest amongst us, and we were not backward.'

The laughter of relief held the tent. Those who did not hear asked and when they were told, they too smiled with embarrassment. A village elder reflected that the bridegroom's father ought to have told him how to behave at this samskara. A well-dressed woman said, 'Who listens to fathers these days?'

Shami came over to enquire if anything was wrong. Pushpa indicated: 'Listen to the pundit.' He was annoyed that her response to his concern was so inappropriate, but he masked his feelings. Her regret was instant. 'I'll explain later,' she said, soothing. 'Sorry.'

Shami returned to Sukesh Walli and whispered, 'The cover and the altar fire close by made her a bit dizzy. She is better now, as you see. Nothing to worry about.' He smiled.

Living Within a Frame

SHE SPRAYS A mist of delicious scent all over her limbs and thighs; her neck and bosom. Her loose hair too is perfumed.

As she moves across the bedroom to her mirror, her anklets tremble with emotion. The transparency of her nightgown reveals fine shoulders and an elegant neck lifting a shapely form. Her boyish stance has fled, Vasti has blossomed into a bud that will, with the first rains, open into a glorious fullness. There is still, however, an unspoken modesty. Her dressing gown of ruby red satin, slips from the bed and lies on the floor.

A thought rests upon her, addressing the sudden terrors she experienced beneath the ceremonial cover: *You cannot now move outside the given frame. Will you crack the glass, rent the whole, and bring immeasurable pain, to those you hold dear? Stay calm, and you can assist the next generation. Change is best absorbed when it evolves. Then heads do not meet the guillotine nor hearts cease their rhythms.*

The mirror's face disappears momentarily behind the perfumed spray, then re-emerges with a pair of binoculars penetrating a forest of sucrose stems; a young girl's cry fills her ears. Her heart beats faster. The vision has gone. The three Queens materialise. They are staring at the flowing ocean beneath their ship. Each by her stance is offering a thought to Vasti's predicament – how to embrace her wedding night?

Queen Meena suggests an approach of quiet duty. But as Queen Dayita turns away from the ocean, she offers a dancer's imaginative ingenuity – the art of seduction that leaves the seducer and seduced enriched. Vasti hears her, yet still she waits, knowing there is more to come. Queen Dayita speaks: '*Youth is transitory. Life offers only a potent moment, use it to the full. Gain from this encounter. Will you so use your youth or will you harbour past ugliness and whither within. Free yourself from past memories.*

Vasti watches all three. She waits.

The scholar, dark Queen Renu, comes, holding out her hands; her mouth shapes words that Vasti cannot hear, for just at that moment her husband enters. Karan did not knock or await permission to enter. To her dismay, the Queens are lost and the mirror reflects only Karan.

He leads her and she moves with him to the couch covered in white brocade; its pattern of multicoloured freesias delights the eye.

She offers him the finest desert dates, while he pours an aged ruby drink containing the vibrancy of ripened juices. It has set the two crystal glasses aflame. He brings this delicious intoxication to her lips and she drinks. On his offering it a second time, she stays his hand and her soft fingers touch the chiselled beak of the eagle.

Would her limbs readily embrace him? Were they formed for this – responding to a primeval call that echoes back to the beginning of things which collided to give birth to life, to movement, to thought, to desire?

She smiles, slowly caresses his fingers, removing the ring. He allows her to have her way. Again he offers her the rich, distilled wine, its aroma entrancing the room.

The aged cognac is warming her spirit. A feeling of haziness, a lightness of being, comes over her. It is as if all life is a dream, an illusion. Reality has drifted away to the Kingdom of Jyotika. He offers her the warm crystal glass. Again she sips its spirit.

Outside, a part of the ruptured earth called the moon is looking in. Vasti has become as pliant as the water rushes with their naked slender stems bending to their flowing shadows. Then a stream of dark clouds obstructs its face and the two on the couch become indistinct, become one.

Pushpa cannot sleep. The marriage promises put together had helped her to understand Vasti's position; after the ceremony, she noted a withdrawing, a trembling of her sister's lips. It was evidence of the iron will of self-denial – a determination to climb upon the pyre.

She has become anxious and wonders how her sister will cope with this night. Pushpa walks out to the verandah, the cold night breeze making her shiver. Thoughts press upon her: Have we chosen to be who we are? Or are we made to prefer a hidden message, one that Shami calls subliminal? Do we consciously place ourselves onto a path that will lead to a worthwhile destination? Or do we in truth take a route simply to survive, becoming another on the way? Yet, there are those who willingly sacrifice themselves and join the stars. It is their preference. Is Vasti among them?

Who are we?

'We are who we are,' the cold wind whispers, travelling across from another time, bringing the songs of boatmen in the night and the sound of splashing nets.

Devi Nadir walks the length of her spacious bedroom, her footsteps are silent. She sits in her husband's chair, closes her eyes to meditate, to engage with him to guide her. She slows her breathing and is at rest. Nothing stirs. When she awakens, the clock face astounds her. It says two thirty. The dawn will be long in coming.

Devi returns to her bed and finds that she is thinking, *Vasti will prepare her daughters for a change larger than she has experienced.* Her grandchildren will be offered far, far more than she, Devi, can possibly envisage. It is the way of the world. How different it is from the small fishing village, the seashore of her youth where she learned the songs of fishermen and listened to falling rain.

And for Vasti, on the couch with Karan, will the three Queens come to hold her hands, to guide her? She needs their wisdom to cope with her own time. Will it come, and if it does, will Vasti recognise it?

The End

Myths of old India and realities of the contemporary Caribbean, seamlessly interwoven into a tableau of the ordinary lives of Indo-Caribbean girls and women. A fast-moving narrative that both informs and delights. Lakshmi Persaud deploys formidable narrative skill and a penchant for moral conflict between men and women.

Professor Frank Birbalsingh
York University, Canada

Lakshmi Persaud was born in Tunapuna, Trinidad. She has a BA and PhD from Queen's University, Belfast. She has taught at Harrison College in Barbados, St Augustine Girls' High School in Trinidad and Queen's College in Guyana. Having written articles on Socio-Economic concerns for newspapers and magazines for many years, she read and recorded text books in Philosophy and Economics for post-graduate and undergraduates at the Royal National Institute of the Blind. Her short story *See Saw Margery Daw* was broadcast by the BBC World Service. She has written three other well received novels, *Sastra*, *Butterfly in the Wind* and *For the Love of My Name*. Lakshmi Persaud lives in London with her husband, and is the mother of three children.

OTHER BLACKAMBER TITLES

From Kitchen Sink to Boardroom Table
Richard Scase and Joan Blaney

The Demented Dance
Mounsi

The Cardamon Club
Jon Stock

Something Black in the Lentil Soup
Reshma S. Ruia

Typhoon
The Holy Woman
Qaisra Shahraz

Ma
All that Blue
Gaston-Paul Effa

Paddy Indian
The Uncoupling
Cauvery Madhavan

Foreday Morning
Paul Dash

Ancestors
Paul Crooks

Nothing but the Truth
Mark Wray

Hidden Lights – Ordinary Women Extraordinary Lives
Joan Blaney

What Goes Around
Sylvester Young

Brixton Rock
Alex Wheatle

One Bright Child
Patricia Cumper

All BlackAmber Books are available from your local bookshop.

For a regular update on BlackAmber's latest release, with extracts, reviews and events, visit:

www.blackamber.com